BIBLICAL

ABOUT THE AUTHOR

Christopher Galt does not, in any real sense of the word, exist. It is a pseudonym for an award-winning writer already translated into 24 languages.

CHRISTOPHER GALT

BIBLICAL

A NOVEL

PEGASUS BOOKS
NEW YORK LONDON

BIBLICAL

Pegasus Books LLC
80 Broad Street, 5th Floor
New York, NY 10004

First Pegasus Books cloth edition 2014

Copyright © 2014 by Craig Russell (writing as Christopher Galt)

ISBN: 978-1-60598-657-9

10 9 8 7 8 6 5 4 3 2 1

Printed in the United States of America
Distributed by W. W. Norton & Company, Inc.

For E.W.R.

WHETHER it was in the name of God or Science that you devoted yourself to seeking out the Truth, the danger always was that you would find it.

I am so very, very sorry. You have just found it. That which waited to be known.

From *Phantoms of Our Own Making* by John Astor

"What if I'm just in your head?" She looked at him earnestly, for the first time something breaking through into her expression. "Haven't you ever wondered that? Haven't you ever considered that all this – everything and everybody around you – is all just in your head? How do you know I was here before you walked into the room?"

PROLOGUE

The air in the Mainframe Hall felt artificial: cleanroom-filtered, its temperature constant within the smallest fraction of a degree; seemingly immobile, breezeless. Everyone gathered in front of the Project Director gazed up at the virtual displays.

"What you are seeing is a representation of neural activity. It is identical to that of a normal human brain. Your brain, my brain. Except this, for the first time, is a complete computer-generated simulation. Capable of thoughts, maybe even dreams, exactly like any of us experience."

"But it has no body to feel," said one of the journalists. "Eyes to see. Won't it go mad without sensory input?"

The Project Director smiled. "We have restricted neural activity to specific clusters. Nothing here is a complete mind. But, if it were, there has been a lot of research into the psychotomimetic effects of sensory deprivation—"

"Psychotomimetic?"

"Mimicking psychoses . . . causing hallucinations," explained the Project Director. "This research suggests that in such cases where subjects are deprived of genuine sensory stimuli, they hallucinate false ones. See people and environments that aren't there."

"So if there isn't a world around us, we invent one?" asked another of the journalists.

"Effectively, yes. But this won't happen with these simulations – they're restricted to specific functions and neural

1

clusters, allowing us to simulate specific psychiatric disorders and see, for the very first time, exactly how they tick. It will have a massive benefit for mankind."

"And beyond that . . . how far could a synthetic mind – an artificial intelligence like this – go?"

"Theoretically, it would allow us to understand the human condition like never before. It could even be turned onto answering questions about the universe and give us insights into the true nature of reality."

"Aren't there dangers?" asked another journalist.

"What kind of dangers?" Still no impatience in the Project Director's tone.

"People talk about the Singularity – about artificial intelligences overwhelming our own."

"Trust me," said the Project Director, "we are a long way from that. There is no whole mind here. No danger."

PRELUDES

PRELUDES

1

Marie Thoulouze felt the air cool suddenly, a seasonal change seeming to take place in the space of a second, but something more than the sudden drop in temperature caused her skin to prickle into gooseflesh. The sun was still bright, perhaps now even brighter, but the air had changed: not just temperature but pressure, humidity, consistency. She had an oddly intense feeling of déjà vu, that she had been here before and that she had felt exactly the same then, and countless times before that. Maybe it was the occasion: maybe you are aware of history being made.

Marie stood at the back of the crowd that had gathered in the Vieux-Marché and the smell of so much humanity crowded together for such an inhuman purpose filled her nostrils. Pungent. Sour. Rank. The mob gathered in front of her jostled for a better view as a cart trundled over the dried mud of the square. Cheers and chants in a French that Marie found difficult to understand, a French very different from her own. She cast an eye across at the ranks of English and Burgundian soldiers, their glaives and halberds gleaming in the cold sun, who seemed to tense, to prepare, as the cart entered the square.

Marie edged round the crowd, keeping back from the increasingly dense, increasingly agitated throng. There was another, more intense explosion of jeers and catcalls from the Rouennais mob, loyal to the Duke of Burgundy, as a slender, pale girl – clothed in a simple dress of rough cloth, her hair bible-black and unevenly cut to expose a slender white neck, her hands bound behind her – was lifted down from the cart by two English soldiers.

Marie gasped. Her heart pounded. She knew what was about to happen and she muttered a prayer for the girl, her hand reaching up and grasping the crucifix at her neck.

Like a path scythed through wind-writhed corn, the way to the stone pillar at the center of the square was cleared through the crowd by two parallel ranks of breastplated and helmeted soldiers. An old bent-backed woman lunged forward between two of the restraining guards and thrust a wooden cross into the bound girl's dress, lodging it in the neckline before being pushed roughly back into the rabble. The girl's eyes were wild, confused, and she seemed not to have noticed the old woman's act of pity and piety.

A circle had been cleared around the stone pillar, against which a wooden scaffold had been erected and heaped with tar-dipped faggots, logs and barrels of pitch. The only part left exposed of the scaffold was the rough-hewn timber steps that led to the platform at the top. Marie found her way to the cleared path and followed the sad procession to the empty space around the pyre, amazed that none of the English soldiers tried to stop her and afraid that she might be seized at any moment. The mob seemed too hysterical and frenzied even to notice her presence. She watched as the girl was brought to the clearing and made to stand before a seated group of silk-clad clerics. There was an exchange of words, the girl saying something and the clerics replying, nodding. Marie could not catch what was being said, but she knew. She knew exactly.

She watched as the girl was guided up to the platform by the hooded man Marie knew to be Geoffroy Therage. As a chain was fastened around the girl's waist and further rope bonds fixed her to the pillar, two of the clergy stepped forward and raised a cross on a long pole so that it came up to the girl's eye level and she locked her gaze upon it. They held it there while the executioner stabbed repeatedly into the pyre with a lit torch, while the kindling caught into crackling life and the flames began to spit and surge with an intensity that seemed to increase in parallel to the hysteria of the crowd.

Marie heard high-pitched screaming from the fire and thought for a moment it was the desperate sounds of the girl's agony, but there was a chorus of other screeches and percussive snaps and pops, and she realized they were the sounds of combustion: the fire now a single, writhing, surging entity consuming everything in the execution pyre. But then Marie heard other screaming, and realized it was her own voice as she sank to her knees, the heat of the blaze almost unbearable even at this distance.

A Burgundian soldier stepped forward and Marie saw something dark writhing furiously in his gauntleted fist. He swung it with full force and she saw the black cat follow a twisting arc through the air and into the flames.

"She is not a witch!" Marie screamed, pleadingly, at the soldier who did not even turn in her direction. "She is NOT a witch!"

Marie sobbed. Great, wracking sobs as she gazed up at the burning girl. Marie, whose faith had always been deep and pure and complete, could not believe she was witnessing the death of her heroine. How had she come to be here, Rouen, on the thirtieth day of May, 1431, to witness this horror unfold? How could anyone ever believe she had seen this great evil with her own eyes? She needed proof. Positive proof.

Still sobbing, she reached into her pocket for something and held it at shaking arm's length, pointing it at the girl who now burned like a torch atop the pyre.

Marie used her thumb to select the camera function of the cellphone she had taken from her jeans and pressed the button, in an attempt to capture the image that seared into her brain, the image that filled her universe.

The image of Jeanne d'Arc as she passed from one world to the next.

7

2

The thing about the remarkable and the extraordinary is that, if they are part of your everyday life, they become by definition unremarkable and ordinary. That which awakens awe and wonder in others ceases to be noticed. For Walter Ramirez, the extraordinary that had become ordinary, the remarkable made unremarkable by daily exposure, was the Bridge.

The Bridge was known by millions. All around the world people could call the Bridge to mind, even if they had only ever seen its image. The Bridge was an icon, it was a symbol, it was a means of transit. For many, it was a destination.

But sometimes, when you have become accustomed to the uncustomary, there still comes the moment in which you see it as others see it. Ramirez experienced two such moments that Wednesday.

The first was when he drove his marked Explorer out of the Waldo Tunnel. Ramirez was on the early shift and the sun was just about to come up as he drove his prowler out into the infant day. Despite having seen it so many times, the scene that opened out at the tunnel mouth was one to send a small electric current running across the skin and raise the hairs on the nape of Ramirez's neck. There were still lights on in the city, a cluster of bright white and yellow pinpricks in the purple velvet of the immediately pre-dawn sky, shimmering in reflection on the Bay; to his left was *the* Bay Bridge. But ahead was *the* Bridge. Ramirez's beat.

The Golden Gate.

Walt Ramirez had been an officer of the California Highway Patrol for fifteen years, all with the San Francisco Bay Area Command, ten of which had been in the Golden Gate Division, seven of those working out of Marin County station on San Clemente, twelve minutes from the Bridge. The chevrons on his sleeve had been there for three years.

Walt Ramirez looked like a thug in a uniform: a big, broad-shouldered and hard-faced man of forty with huge hands that appeared out of proportion with even his massive build. It was a physical presence that had served him well. In fifteen years as a CHP officer and outside of the Patrol's firing range, Ramirez had unholstered his firearm twelve times in total and had fired it only once, and that had been a warning shot. Generally, when Sergeant Walter Ramirez told someone to do something in his disconcertingly quiet, calm way, they tended to do it.

Although Walt Ramirez might have looked like a thug in uniform, he was anything but. Popular with everyone who got to know the modest, friendly man behind the intimidating presence, Ramirez's senior, brother and junior officers all liked and respected him. He was one of those cops who were in the job for all the right reasons: he cared about people – perhaps even a little too much given the suffering he had had to encounter over the years – and he had become a policeman to help others, not through some need to exert authority over them. With the public he was consistently courteous and respectful, but firm whenever the need arose. His fellow officers knew that he was someone they could rely on in a tight spot, someone who would always have your back. In fact, Walt Ramirez was exactly the guy you wanted to have your back.

And Ramirez's beat was a small but iconic one. Ramirez's beat was the Bridge.

As well as being the shift supervisor on all patrols that covered the Bridge and its approaches on both sides, Ramirez

9

provided liaison with the Golden Gate Bridge Highway and Administration District, which had its own security force, Marin County Sheriff's Department, the SFPD and the US Coast Guard station at Fort Baker, Sausalito, one thousand feet from the Bridge's north tower.

The west side walkway was permanently closed to pedestrians and Ramirez made the Bridge just after 5.30 a.m., when the automatic barrier on the east sidewalk opened. He noticed a group of about thirty people had just cleared the gates, and he guessed they had been waiting for them to open. Slowing down, he examined them across the safety barrier. They were all young people, no one much over thirty, and they were chatting to each other in a relaxed manner. That was something Ramirez, like all the cops who worked the Bridge, had learned a long time ago: to read body language. And to do the mental math of despair: where there were many, as now, there was no risk; where there was the individual, the solitary soul wrapped up in his or her own thoughts, you watched them. The Bridge authority watched them too, on CCTV. And counted lamp poles.

Ramirez called in on his radio and asked Vallejo to patch him through to Bridge security.

"What's the deal with the early birds?" he asked.

"They've been waiting for about fifteen minutes for the gates to open," the Bridge dispatcher explained. "Guess they're just out for an early morning run."

"They don't look like joggers," said Ramirez. "I'll wheel round and take another look."

Ramirez drove the length of the Golden Gate and then back, watching the group from across the carriageway. With the exception of a couple of semi-trailers up ahead, he had the Bridge to himself, so looped a U to come back alongside the group. By this time they were already past the first tower. They were walking together, not running nor stepping out with a particular sense of purpose, and again he noticed that they were all in good spirits, as if enjoying each other's company as the sun came up over the Bay. But something still jarred. He pulled up, switching on his roof bar to alert other drivers. Some of the walkers spotted him and stopped, waiting for him to come over to the barrier.

"Morning . . ." Ramirez said cheerily and the walkers returned his smile.

"Morning officer," an attractive woman in her mid-twenties, dark hair gathered up on her head, answered. "Beautiful morning, isn't it?"

"It is that, ma'am. You all together? A group?"

"Yes . . . yes we are." She frowned insincere concern. "Are we in breach of a city ordinance?"

"No, you're fine. Are you some kind of club?"

"We all work together. I'm the CEO . . . we decided yesterday to take this walk together and watch the sun come up. Is that okay?"

"Sure . . . I didn't mean to disturb you." Ramirez examined her more closely: as a company CEO, the woman looked too young, too wrong. Wrong clothes, wrong type. "What is it your company does?" he asked, still smiling, still keeping his tone conversational.

"Gaming."

"Gaming?"

"Computer games. We design them. These guys are my best teams."

"Shoot-em-up games, that kind of thing?" Ramirez asked. The phrase sat clumsily in his mouth; it was something he'd heard his eldest say.

The woman laughed and shook her head. "No, nothing like that. Alternate reality games, mostly . . . We do stuff like this to remind ourselves that there's a real world out there."

"Like teambuilding, that kind of thing?" he asked.

"Something like. I didn't think we needed to ask permission."

The young woman looked right to Ramirez now. Dot-com-social-network-type right. A world he didn't have much time for and which had sneaked a generation gap in between him and his kids.

"You don't," he said. "Well, you enjoy sunup. Have a good day, ma'am."

"And you, officer." She smiled at him again.

Climbing back into the Explorer, Ramirez watched the group walk on. They all had a careless glow about them – of youth or of the sunrise or both – and he felt a pang of envy. Yet he counted lamp poles. Counting lamp poles was something you learned to do if you were a cop attached to the Bridge, but these were not the type you needed to count lamp poles for.

Shaking the thought from his head, Ramirez switched off the bar lights and started up the engine. As he drove past, the young woman who probably made in a month what he made in a year waved at him.

What was it? What was wrong?

The thought nagged him to another halt and he watched them in his side mirror. The clump of walkers had become a string that stretched along the sidewalk. They stopped. And lamp pole sixty-nine was at the middle. She was in the middle. She was standing at lamp pole sixty-nine. Sixty-nine.

The pole you counted most.

The Golden Gate Bridge was an icon. People from across the country, from around the world, were drawn to its strange beauty; and most of all they were drawn to the view from pole sixty-nine.

He got out of the Explorer and started back.

"Excuse me, ma'am . . ." he called and waved to the young woman. She waved back as, in unison, she and her colleagues climbed over the safety railing and down onto the three-feet-wide girder that Ramirez knew was just over the barrier, about two feet below walkway level.

12

Jesus . . . Ramirez broke into a sprint. Jesus Christ . . . there must be thirty of them. As he ran he could see the flashing lights of other vehicles, alerted by the Bridge authority, racing towards them. Too far. Too late.

Pole sixty-nine.

The Golden Gate Bridge demanded a special kind of cop, because the Golden Gate Bridge was the world's number one location for suicide. Every year, scores of people came to the bridge to cross over something more than San Francisco Bay. They came from all over the country, some from abroad, to walk out onto the Bridge's span where death was always just a four-and-a-half-feet climb over the sidewalk safety barrier and a four-second, seventy-five-mile-an-hour drop. At that speed, impact on water felt like impact on concrete. Hardly anyone drowned: ninety per cent plus died of massive internal injuries, their bones and organs smashed. On average, the Bridge had one known jumper every week-and-a-half with more than thirty known deaths a year; and, of course, there were those who managed to jump without being spotted, their dust-covered cars found abandoned in the car parks.

Of the Bridge's one hundred and twenty-eight lamp poles, it was pole sixty-nine that had felt the last touches of most.

He vaulted over the traffic barrier and onto the walkway. Trained in a whole range of strategies for talking to potential suicides, Ramirez also knew a dozen practiced maneuvers for grabbing and securing an indecisive jumper. But there were too many of them.

"Don't!" he shouted. "For God's sake don't!"

He was near the railing, close to where the young woman stood looking down at the water. He could see them now, all standing on the girder, holding hands.

The young woman turned her head to look at him over her shoulder.

"It's all right," she said, smiling again, this time sincerely, kindly. "It's not your fault, there was nothing you could do. It's all right . . . we are becoming."

As if by a wordless command, without hesitation, they all stepped off in unison.

Ramirez made it to the barrier just in time to see them hit the water. Everything seemed unreal, as if what he had just witnessed could not possibly have happened and he must have imagined the young people on the Bridge just seconds before. He heard his own voice as if it belonged to someone else as he radioed it in, calling for the Fort Baker Coastguard rescue boat. The Bridge security vehicle and the SFPD cruiser pulled up beside him, and the urgent, questioning voices of the other officers came to Ramirez like radio messages from a distant planet.

He turned away from the safety railing and looked at the Bridge, at the graceful sweep and arch of its back, at the red of its soaring towers made redder by the rising sun. For the second time that day he saw the Bridge for what it was, what it symbolized, saw all of its beauty.

And he hated it.

part one

IN THE BEGINNING

By faith we understand that the universe was formed at God's command, so that what is seen was not made out of what was visible.

Hebrews 11:3

The senses deceive from time to time, and it is prudent never to trust wholly those who have deceived us even once.

René Descartes

Anyone not shocked by quantum mechanics has not yet understood it.

Niels Bohr

1

THE BEGINNING

It all began with the staring.

But there were many other things before the staring, before it began. Strange accounts from distant places:

A man in New York died of malnutrition in a luxurious Central Park apartment empty of food but filled with vitamin pills. There was an inexplicable epidemic of suicides: twenty-seven young people jumping in unison from the Golden Gate Bridge; fifty Japanese students camping out deep in the huge Aokigahara forest – the Sea of Trees at the foot of Mount Fuji – sharing food and singing songs around campfires before wandering separately into the dark of the forest to open their arteries; four notable suicides in Berlin on the same day – three scientists and a writer. A Russian physicist turned neo-pagan mystic purported to be the Son of God. A French teenager claimed to have had a vision of Joan of Arc being burned at the stake. A middle-aged woman calmly sat down in the middle of the road at the entrance of the CERN complex in Switzerland, then just as calmly doused her clothing in kerosene and set fire to herself. A Hollywood effects studio was firebombed. A fundamentalist Christian sect kidnapped and murdered a geneticist.

Then there was the graffito *WE ARE BECOMING* appearing in fifty languages, in every major city around the world. On government buildings, on bridges, sprayed over advertising hoardings.

And people started to talk about John Astor.

No one knew for sure if he really existed or not, but there were rumors that the FBI was after him. And, of course, there was the spreading urban myth about the manuscript of Astor's book, *Phantoms of Our Own Making*, that drove mad anyone who found and read it.

All of these things happened before it began.

But it really began with the staring.

2

JOHN MACBETH. BOSTON

Psychiatrists deal in the weird. In the odd. The very nature of their work means they encounter the aberrant and the abnormal on a daily basis. They are in the business of confronting skewed perceptions of reality.

So the fact that the entire world was changing – that everything he'd held up to that point to be true about the nature of things was about to be turned on its head – had pretty much passed Dr John Macbeth by.

But the world did change. And it began with the staring.

Like with the news stories, it was only in the weeks and months that followed that Macbeth began to piece together the clues that had been there all the time. But there had been other clues that he had missed, that had not registered on the scope of his professional radar. But afterwards he remembered just how many people he had seen, without really noticing them: in the streets, on the subway, in the park.

Staring.

There had been only a few in those first days: people gazing into empty space, faces blank or creased in frowned confusion or flashed with unease. They had the same effect on others that cats have when they stare past you, over your shoulder, at something you turn around to see but cannot. Unsettling.

Of course, at the beginning, at the beginning of the staring, no one had come up with a name for it, medical or otherwise. The starers were yet to be called Dreamers.

It was only afterwards that Macbeth remembered the first one he had encountered, an attractive, expensively dressed woman in her mid-thirties. It had happened on his first day back in Boston: he had been walking behind her in the downtown street on that sunny but cold late spring morning. She had walked with city-sidewalk purposefulness, just as he had, but then she had suddenly, unaccountably, come to an abrupt halt. Macbeth almost walked smack into her and had to dance-step a dodge around her. The woman simply stood there, at the edge of the sidewalk, feet planted, gazing at something that wasn't there across the street. Then, as she pointed a vague finger towards the nothing that had caught her attention, she stepped off the curb and into the traffic. Macbeth grabbed her elbow and hauled her back and out of the way of a truck that flashed past with an angry horn blast.

"I thought . . ." she had said, the words dying on her lips and her eyes now searching for something lost in the distance.

Macbeth had asked the woman if she was okay, admonished her to pay more attention to traffic and walked on.

It was hardly an incident: just a distracted woman making an error in roadside judgment. Something you saw almost every day in any city around the world.

It was only later, after the other events, that significance began to attach and he started to wonder what it had been that the woman had seen in the street; that had almost pulled her into the path of the truck.

It was a good room. Not great, but better than okay. The architecture that surrounded him was always unusually important to John Macbeth: its proportions, materials, decor, amount of light.

Macbeth had woken up that morning and the room had frightened him with its unfamiliarity. He had awoken not knowing who he was, what he did for a living, where he was and why he was there. For a full minute and a half, he had experienced complete existential panic: the bright burning star at the heart of his amnesiac darkness being the knowledge that he should know who he was, where he was and what he was doing there.

His memory, his identity had fallen back into place: not all at once, but in ill-fitting segments he had to piece together. It had happened before, he began to remember – many times before, especially when he was in a strange place. Terrifying moments of depersonalized isolation before he remembered he was Dr John Macbeth, that he was a psychiatrist and cognitive neuroscientist trying to make sense of his own psychology by seeking to understand others. He worked, he now remembered, on Project One in Copenhagen, Denmark, and that he was in Boston on Project business. And he had suffered derealization and depersonalization episodes all his life; he remembered that too.

Eventually, he had made sense of the room and the room had made sense of him. That was why environments were so important to him. But, for those ninety terrifying seconds, he could have been as equally convinced by his surroundings that he was someone, somewhere and sometime else.

The room was on the third floor of the hotel that had looked just right on the website but hadn't looked quite as right in up-close reality. It was large, and a tall traditional sash-type window looked out over the street. Macbeth had opened the window, creating at the bottom a breezeless four-inch gap.

Now, sitting in the armchair by the window in the quiet room, his identity and purpose restored to him, Macbeth listened to the sounds beyond. It was something he often did and, like so many aspects of his personality, others would probably have considered him odd because of it. Where most people in hotel rooms would switch on the TV or radio, filling the space around them with expected sounds, or closing in even tighter the borders of their awareness with an MP3 player and earphones, John Macbeth would sit, still and silent, listening outward. With everything quiet in his room, he attended the sounds beyond: from neighboring rooms, from the street beyond the window, from the city beyond the street. Sounds off, they called them in the theater: the pretense of some reality beyond, some action unseen.

Like everyone else, Macbeth had a cellphone and a laptop computer, but used them only when compelled to. Technology was a central part of his work, an unavoidable part of everyday life, but he did not interact well with it. Computer and video games, which he could in any case never understand adults playing, gave him motion sickness, and any sustained inter-action with electronics seemed to make him restless and irritated. The problem he was having with his computer was a good example: a folder he could not remember creating and which refused to open for him, no matter what he did – including hitting the keyboard harder with an angry fingertip, as if a virtual object would yield to real-world physics. The folder had been there for over a month, sitting on his comput-er's desktop, taunting his technological incompetence.

My brother Casey will sort you out, he had threatened it – out loud – on more than one occasion.

Ironically, Macbeth's work brought him into contact with the world's most sophisticated computer technology: he was on an interdisciplinary team of some of the finest brains on the planet, yet more than half their thinking was done for them by machines. And the whole aim of Project One was, indeed, to create a machine that could simulate the neural activity of the human brain, perhaps even think for itself. Outside his work, however, Macbeth eschewed technology as much as was practicable in modern life. His avoidance wasn't founded on some philosophical or moral objection: it was just that technology seemed to make his *problem* worse; loosen his grasp on who and where he was in the world.

24

So John Macbeth chose to connect with the real universe rather than the virtual, listening to sounds outside the room to reassure himself that he really was in the room; that he was there, his mind reaching out into the world and not turned in on itself. It was a meditation he had done since boyhood: before-dark Cape Cod summer bedtimes listening to the sounds of birds or waves or distant trains beyond curtains that glowed amber and red with the low sun. He remembered so little from his childhood, but he remembered those curtains glowing with bold colors and strong patterns.

For the duration of his stay in Boston, Macbeth had booked into a hotel that matched his style but overstretched the budget allocated by the university. It wasn't that he went for conspic-uously ritzy places full of gilt-edged reminders that they were well beyond the reach of the ordinary working stiff; he preferred quality designer hotels and boutique B&Bs – places with char-acter, history, or ideally both. Macbeth's surroundings had to be right. Always. The colors, smells, textures and tastes that surrounded him, even his clothes, were enormously important. A refined materialism that probably seemed superficial. But there was nothing superficial about it: Macbeth had a real need to be in an environment that soothed him, offered some kind of harmony; reconciled his internal and external worlds. It was at the same time meditative and a reassurance of identity. And it had a lot to do, he knew, with his memories. Or lack of them.

Whatever motivated it, he needed it the same way the obser-vant Catholic needed rosary beads.

Boston was Macbeth's hometown. He'd been sent there to repre-sent Project One by the University of Copenhagen. Despite the protests of Poulsen, the Project's director and Macbeth's boss, the university had been keen to use him as a poster boy, seeming to think that Macbeth had a look and manner that most people would not associate with a research scientist, or psychiatrist,

25

and – as an American – he was perfectly suited for liaison with the Project's Boston partner, the Schilder Neuroscience Research Institute.

Macbeth didn't see himself as an ideal ambassador. He knew he could be sociable and witty, but for as long as he could remember he'd been aware of his detachment from others, his emotional and intellectual self-containment. As a psychiatrist, he had studied and understood the 'problem of other minds'; he'd understood it, but had never fully resolved it for himself.

"You okay, Karen?" A rich, authoritative male voice drifted up from the street. "I need you to be okay for the Halverson presentation."

"I'm fine." A woman's voice. Young, refined, educated, defiant. "I told you before. I'm fine . . ."

The voices faded and were replaced by others. Macbeth sat and speculated what the Halverson presentation could be about, what problem the woman had that compelled the man to seek reassurance. From an incomplete and incoherent fragment of reality, he extrapolated a complete and coherent fiction.

Maybe I should become a writer, he told himself. Macbeth the psychiatrist knew that storytelling and mental disorder grew from the same seed: writers scored highly as non-pathological schizotypes. The higher the score, the more disposed they were to magical thinking, the more creative the writing.

He checked his watch: he himself had an appointment to keep.

Phoning down to the front desk, he asked them to call a cab, telling them he'd be right down. Out in the hallway, the heavy door clunked shut behind him and he slipped the plastic card-key into his pocket. The hotel was an old building and the doors looked original. Macbeth imagined the craftsmen who had carved and carpentered them, who had forged and fitted the brass door furniture. He thought how impossible it would have been for these four generations-dead artisans to imagine that one day their doors would lock and unlock with a contactless microchip sweep. It was another form of elaborating a whole from a fragment. Most people got lost in thought, Macbeth told himself often; the difference was sometimes he couldn't find his way back.

He made his way towards the elevator at the far end of the corridor. A pillar midway down the hall blocked the view of the doors, but as he headed towards it, Macbeth saw a tall man standing at the end of the hall, clearly waiting for the elevator car to arrive. A dark man: dark hair unfashionably long, dark beard unfashionably full, dark suit unfashionably cut.

Something about the man, the corridor, the light, provoked a feeling of déjà vu in Macbeth. He shook it off and called to him.

"Hey . . . could you hold that for me?"

The dark man didn't turn or acknowledge Macbeth's request. Instead, he remained blank-faced toward the elevator before stepping forward and out of view behind the pillar.

"Thanks a lot, friend," muttered Macbeth and he hurried along the hall. But when he reached the doors, he found them closed and the electronic display above them indicated that the elevator was on the ground floor. And unmoving. Macbeth stared at the doors, at the LED display and back along the hall to where he had been when he had called out to the dark man, as if there was a calculation to be done; an equation to make sense of the experience.

He shook the puzzle from his head and stabbed the button to summon the car.

3

JOHN MACBETH. BOSTON

Macbeth told the driver where he wanted to go.

"The Scotch place on Beacon Street?" The cabbie Boston-brogued his terminal consonants out of existence. Macbeth always found odd how much he noticed the accent whenever he came back from Europe.

"That's the place," he said.

"Sure thing . . ." The driver executed one of those rear-view mirror assessments of his passenger that Boston cabbies always seemed to do. He frowned in concentration and Macbeth sighed, knowing that the driver was trying to work out where he had seen him before. People were always trying to work out where they had seen him before, but they never could because they never had. Like all the others, the cabbie and the psychiatrist would never really have crossed paths, but Macbeth knew the questioning would start. Sooner or later.

Macbeth sat in the back of the cab in silence, watching the familiar-unfamiliar Boston cityscape slide by, troubled by his lack of connection to an environment he should have felt connected to. Jamais vu, the opposite of déjà vu.

He remembered treating a woman whose brain lesion had left her with permanent derealization and jamais vu: every-thing she had known, had grown up with, had lived with, suddenly ceased to be recognizable. There had been no amnesia: her memories were left intact, but the wiring that connected what she saw with what she remembered had been burned out. The result was that every time she stepped into the apartment she had lived in for five years – and despite knowing her address and that it was indeed her apartment – she would gaze at the furniture, the décor, the pictures on the wall as if she were viewing a home to rent for the first time; nothing seeming in the least familiar.

That was how Macbeth felt driving through Boston: he should have had a sense of being at home, but he did not. His patient, whose disconnection from the world was pathological and total, had learned not just to accept her condition, but to embrace it, to see it as a gift. For her, the world and every day in it was a discovery and she could see her life with an objectivity all others lacked. Macbeth, on the other hand, just felt lost.

After a few blocks, the taxi came to a halt in traffic suddenly thick and unmoving.

"Terrible, this thing in San Francisco. You hear about that?" the driver asked his rearview mirror. The world over, it seemed to Macbeth, the silver lining on any cloud of human suffering was that tragedy always gave cabbies a conversation opener.

"I heard something about it. It's a terrible thing, all right."

"Now what would make a bunch of young people like that want to throw themselves off the Golden Gate?"

As a psychiatrist, Macbeth had half a dozen hypotheses he could have put forward; instead he said: "Beats me."

"I just don't get why people pick one place specially to do themselves in," continued the cabbie, eagerly disconsolate. "I mean, why the Golden Gate? And why that forest in Japan? That's the number two spot for suicide in the world, you know, after the Golden Gate . . . I just don't get it."

"Me neither."

"An awful shame, whatever they did it for." The driver shook his head, then, with a dissonantly cheerful change of tone, asked: "You an out-of-towner?"

"Yeah. Well, no . . . From Boston but I've lived abroad for a few years."

"Back seeing folks?"

"More business, but I do have a brother here. You any idea what the hold-up is?"

"Can't see. Just got to sit it out. It doesn't usually last long. Listen, don't I know you from somewhere?"

"Don't think so," said Macbeth. Here it came: the conversation he had had so many times was starting again. It troubled him that his face seemed familiar to so many people; combined with his poor autobiographical memory it meant he was never entirely sure if he really had met them before or not.

"Sure . . ." said the cab driver to his rearview. "Sure I do. As soon as you got in the cab I recognized you, but I can't think where from."

"Maybe I've been in your cab before," Macbeth said.

"No . . ." The cabbie frowned in frustrated concentration as his recall failed him. Macbeth decided to ride it out, like he always did. "No . . . it wasn't in the cab. Shit, I can't place you but I know you."

"I get that a lot," said Macbeth. "I guess I've just got one of those faces."

"It's not just your face . . ." The taxi driver was now even more emphatic. "Before you spoke I knew what your voice was going to sound like. Like I really know you from somewhere."

"I get that a lot too. There's just something about me that people think they recognize. Maybe I'm some kind of Jungian archetype." He laughed.

"Huh?"

"Never mind." Macbeth leaned forward and peered through the Perspex divider between him and the cabbie and the windshield between them both and the world outside. "No sign of what the hold-up is?"

"Maybe it's a full moon. You know if it's a full moon tonight?"

"No idea. What's the moon got to do with traffic?"

"Everything. Ask any cop," said the cabbie. "Or delivery driver. Traffic goes all to hell. Not just traffic . . . any ER nurse or kindergarten teacher'll tell you that. People act different when there's a full moon. Not so much crazy as just different. They make bad choices, take wrong turnings. I'm telling you, when there's a full moon there are more accidents, more jams. Maybe that's what's causing the hold-up. Maybe it's going to be a full moon tonight."

"Like I said, I wouldn't know," said Macbeth.

"Sure it is. I had a guy in the cab, two fares before you. Wanted me to take him to the Christian Science Church – why he'd want to go there this time of night beats me – anyway, he's the quiet type and doesn't say much. Then, all of a sudden, he starts screaming at me that there's a kid in front of the cab. So I leave half my tread on the blacktop and nearly get rear-ended by a bus. Now I'm telling you, there was no kid. But I can see he really believed he saw one. Funny thing is he's all shook up for a moment then goes all calm again, like he understood why he was mistaken. Full moon. Must be."

The traffic started moving again and Macbeth and the driver fell back into silence.

By the time the taxi pulled up outside the green-canopied bar, the sun had sunk lower in the sky and dressed downtown Boston in red gilt edging and velvet shadow. It was the type of light that awoke something in Macbeth: something deep buried and long forgotten. He felt a kind of melancholy as he looked down along Beacon Street to where the evening light softened the Georgian geometry of King's Chapel.

"You sure I don't know you from somewhere?" asked the cabbie as he took the fare and tip from Macbeth.

"I'm sure."

*

Macbeth couldn't remember exactly where and when he had first met Pete Corbin, but it must have been when they had been at Harvard med school together. As he recalled it, they hadn't been friends then: Corbin had been part of a different set and they hadn't encountered each other that often. But years afterwards, after a joint internship at Beth-Israel Deaconess and when both Corbin and Macbeth had settled into their shared specialty of psychiatry and had worked together at McLean, they had become friends. Or maybe just acquaintances. Macbeth was never very sure where the defining line between the two lay. Pete Corbin was one of those people you gave a call when you were in town and shared a few drinks or a meal with. You talked medicine, you talked hospital politics and you talked mutual acquaintances and shook hands heartily at the end of the night but you did not really, at the heart of it all, know each other. It was the similitude of friendship: just one of the threads spun through society's web and you clung on to it.

So, when Macbeth knew he was going to be back in Boston, he'd given Corbin a call and they had arranged to meet for a meal.

The Gathering Stone was supposed to be Scottish-themed, but with its facing of Portland brownstone and ornate blue-green ironwork curlicuing around the huge windows, its name emblazoned in gold Celtic-style lettering, and its sidewalk A-frame blackboards with names and prices of beers and whiskeys chalked on them, The Gathering Stone did not do much to distinguish itself from the default Boston mock-Irish. Inside, it was all exposed brick, knotty pine and posters of Edinburgh Castle and sword-waving red-headed men in plaid, instead of the usual bicycles outside rural Irish pubs. It was the kind of place that was an undisguised feigning of something else: an honest simulation that wasn't intended to be anything other, or for you to expect anything more, than a simulation. Theme-park ethnicity.

When they had first gotten to know each other, Pete Corbin had commented that Macbeth's surname clearly hinted at some Scottish ancestry. Based on this tenuous logic, it had become the accepted thing that they meet at The Gathering Stone.

Macbeth found Corbin nursing a single malt in a booth beneath a framed print of a vaguely desolate-looking mountain and loch scene. A tall, lanky type with a web of thinning blond hair stretched over a high-domed head, Corbin was wearing a tweed jacket, pale chinos and a blue button-down open at the collar. He had mastered, with deliberate and studied intent, that casual look of the academic. It was a look Macbeth had never tried to emulate: his European tailoring, like so many other things, marking him as an outsider here, in his home city.

"Hi, John . . ." Corbin stood up a little sluggishly and shook Macbeth's hand. "Great to see you again. You're looking as well-groomed as ever."

"You okay?" Macbeth asked as he slid into the booth opposite his former colleague. He'd noticed something weary wearing at the edges of Corbin's broad grin of welcome.

"Me? I'm fine. Just a little overworked. You know . . . same ol' same ol'." Corbin smiled. "You? How's Europe?"

"Far away. Other. But good. It's nice to be home for a while though. It gives me a chance to catch up with Casey," Macbeth referred to his younger brother, who still lived in Boston. "I hear you're doing well for yourself, Pete. A teaching post at McLean . . ."

"Two years now." Corbin gave another fatigued smile.

"I'm impressed," said Macbeth. A teaching post at McLean Hospital in Belmont was pretty much the top end of the psychiatry game. Macbeth's own time at McLean, some years before, had been his last involvement with patient care before his move into research. McLean was something he knew looked good on a résumé. A door-opener. It had opened doors in Copenhagen for him.

Corbin beckoned to a pretty waitress with thick auburn hair who came over and took Macbeth's order for a glass of Pinot Grigio. As she did so she smiled at Macbeth in the way a lot of women smiled at him; since he turned fifteen girls had smiled at him that way. He'd never worked out why: he didn't have movie-star looks, wasn't the most confident of men or have the smartest way with words, but there was something about him that seemed to attract women. Or maybe they just thought that they'd seen him somewhere before.

"Sure you're okay, Pete?" he asked Corbin after the waitress brought his wine.

"I'm fine. Joanna and I have just moved into a townhouse in Beacon Hill . . ."

"You *are* doing well for yourself." Macbeth raised his glass in a toast.

"I guess. Joanna's folks helped us out. To be honest, they're loaded and we couldn't have bought in Beacon Hill without them. Anyway, it's an old historic house and needs a lot of work. It's been more hassle than we thought. An interesting place though. Loaded with dark Boston history."

"Oh?"

"It used to be the home of Marjorie Glaiston. You heard of her?"

"Can't say I have."

"Really? The Glaiston scandal was almost as notorious as the Albert Tirrell case."

Macbeth shrugged.

"Anyway," continued Corbin, undeterred, "the Glaistons owned half of Boston back in the late eighteen hundreds. Marjorie was a famed beauty and socialite. Until she got herself murdered. On our staircase no less . . ."

"She was killed in your house?"

"Yeah. It's funny . . ." Corbin laughed joylessly. "If it had been a house anywhere other than Beacon Hill, and the murder had happened a year ago instead of a century ago, then no one would have been able to sell it. Seems homicide becomes romantic and marketable with the passing of time. Adds to the value. Or at least it sure seemed to when we were trying to buy the house. Truth is, fixing it up's been a real hassle . . ."

"And that's why you're so tired?"

"Not just that. Like I said, work's been crazy the last couple of months."

"I thought that's what our work was supposed to be . . . crazy."

"Not crazy like this." Corbin shook the thought off. "Anyway, let's not talk shop. Or at least, if we're going to talk shop, then it should be your shop we talk. This Copenhagen thing sounds amazing."

"It's cool, I can say that for it."

"But do you think it really can be done?" asked Corbin. "Deconstructing human intelligence?"

"I don't know if that's what we're doing," said Macbeth. "Trying to understand human intelligence, yes."

"But I read in *Nature* that the whole aim of the Copenhagen Project was to reverse-engineer human cognition to help technologists develop artificial intelligences on the same model. Basically simulating a human mind."

"That's only part of it, Pete. My area is pretty focused."

"Focused on what?"

"Like you said, Project One is a computer simulation of the human brain – limbic system, neocortex, the lot – built neuron by neuron and cell by cell. Or really virtual neuron by virtual neuron. My side of it's about programming in disorders and watching the changes in neural activity."

"Isn't there a danger that it'll, well, start to *think*?"

"That's an aim, not a danger. Or at least some level of self-awareness. It's probably inevitable, anyway – if we recreate the architecture of a real brain, consciousness will automatically self-generate. Think about it, Pete . . . we'll be able to simulate psychiatric conditions and map the neural activity specific to them. For the first time ever we'll be able to watch a mind working. It'll revolutionize psychiatry."

Corbin frowned. "I don't know, John . . . what you're creating will be indistinguishable from a human mind, and you're talking about infecting that mind with neuroses and psychoses."

"We've thought through the moral implications and the project protocols clearly define what constitutes personhood. Anyway, we'll be working with parts of consciousness, not the whole. But if Project One does simply 'wake up', we have strict guidelines on how to proceed."

Corbin made a face that again indicated doubt. "But we're all wired to our bodies – connected to lymphatic, digestive and endocrine systems. Our state of mind has as much to do with hormone levels, whether we've had a good night's sleep or what we had for lunch, as with our brains. Your synthetic consciousness is connected to nothing."

"We've taken that into account," said Macbeth. "The program simulates circadian rhythms and endocrine balances and replicates the effects of environment, diet and physiology. It will be connected to a *virtual* body."

"But not to the world . . . surely if your synthesized brain becomes self-aware, it's going to wake up into a world of sensory deprivation. You've read Josh Hoberman on the psychotomimetic effects of sensory deprivation and the research done by University College in London. Subjects placed in light-sealed, anechoic chambers started to hallucinate after as little as fifteen minutes – seeing an environment and people that weren't there. Seems if there isn't a real world around us, we invent one – I see your project brain doing the same thing. I don't think you'll have to worry about introducing psychiatric conditions – your baby's going to be born with them."

"Of course we've thought of that. If Project One self-initiates full awareness, we have programs to simulate sensory input."

Corbin shook his head disbelievingly. "You're kidding . . . You're really going to feed it a fake reality? You should christen your synthetic brain René."

"René?"

"As in Descartes. He said he could never prove that he wasn't a brain in a vat, being deceived by some malevolent demon. Turns out you're the demon." Corbin shrugged. "I'm sorry John, I get cynical when I'm tired. I think this project is the opportunity of a lifetime. I guess I'm more than a little jealous."

"I wouldn't be too jealous. The Project Director, Poulsen, is a real Captain Bligh."

"Well, send me a postcard from Sweden when you're picking up your Nobel . . ." Corbin raised his glass in toast.

Macbeth laughed and shook his head. "Trust me, if there's going to be a Nobelist in the family, it'll be Casey."

"Well, I do envy you, John." Corbin grinned. "Talking about envy, how's your love life?"

"My love life?"

"Humor me," said Corbin. "I need to live vicariously. You no closer to settling down? Whatever happened to . . . Melissa, wasn't it?"

"Melissa moved out West with her job." Macbeth forced a smile. "California. We've lost touch."

"That's a shame." Corbin shook his head. "That's the kind of touch you don't want to lose. She really was something else, John . . ."

"I know. But these things happen. At least they seem to happen to me. I'm not the easiest guy to live with."

"A real shame . . ." Corbin's faraway expression suggested he was simulating Melissa in his mind.

"Why don't you tell me about your work problems?" Macbeth changed the subject.

"Like I said, no shop . . ." Corbin clearly was as reluctant to talk about his work as Macbeth was about his private life and they each retreated into superficialities.

They spent the next hour eating and chatting, the conversation skimming over the surface of each other's lives. Macbeth found he did most of the talking, telling Corbin about his work for the university and his life in Copenhagen; about the similarities to and differences from life in the States and how you changed your personality and expectations to suit your environment. Corbin smiled. Nodded. Commented. But it was very clear that his mind was still elsewhere and his spirit even more sapped by tiredness. Macbeth decided to cut the evening as short as possible. The pretty waitress with the auburn hair came back and, skipping dessert, Macbeth ordered a coffee.

"Sorry," said Corbin. "I've been lousy company."

"Not at all." Macbeth smiled. "It's been great to catch up. But I can see you're under a lot of stress. I do wish you'd tell me what's been going on with your work . . ."

Corbin was about to say something when his cellphone rang.

4

JOSH HOBERMAN. VIRGINIA

Josh Hoberman's heart was pounding.

His wakefulness nauseatingly sudden and total, he felt the burn of acid reflux in his gullet. He woke sitting bolt upright in his bed, unmoving, holding his breath, trying to work out what it had been that had ripped him out of sleep. There was silence. Or near-silence. He heard the sound of a police or ambulance siren somewhere far away on North Shore Drive. A dog barking, again distant.

Nothing in the house. Or near.

He let his breath go and sighed, lifting his watch from the nightstand. Midnight-thirty. Maybe it had just been a bad dream that had chased him out of sleep, or a raccoon knocking over a trash can, or too much coffee drunk too late in the day. Whatever it had been, Hoberman knew he would not get back to sleep for another hour or so. He walked through to the bathroom, urinated and flushed, then washed his hands, looking at himself in the mirror. Someone had stolen his reflection and replaced it with that of his father: same face, same doleful eyes, same shape. He was getting old. He had just turned fifty but the tired bags under his eyes added half a decade to his age. But his hair was still thick and dark. At least he had that. He'd have to do something about his weight though. He was too heavy for his height and it was all around his waist. A heart-attack roll. A heart attack had killed his father. At fifty-four.

Hoberman decided to go back down to his study and do an hour or so's work. The trick was to do something necessary but tedious, something that would tire rather than stimulate.

The house was old. Somewhere around one hundred and fifty years old and set way out on its own, a mile or so back from the road and embraced by a muffle of thick Virginia forest. It had offered the isolation Hoberman wanted; but with the isolation came a degree of uncertainty, of risk.

Hoberman didn't bother with a robe when he walked out onto the landing, switching on the light. One of the benefits of living off the beaten track was that there were no neighbors or passers-by to spy on you. It was as he stood there on the landing, naked but for his shorts, that he heard it. Something or someone outside, moving around the house. He rushed down the wooden staircase and went straight into his office. Opening his desk drawer, he took out the Jericho 941 semi-automatic he kept there. He stared at the gun for a moment, amazed at how alien it looked in his hand and trying to work out what the hell he was proposing to do with it. It had been Benjamin, Hoberman's younger brother, who had given him the Israeli-made pistol, even arranging the license for him, insisting it was essential for Josh, living so remotely, to have protection. A gun like this wouldn't look odd in Benny's hands. Benny knew how to handle weapons, handle situations, handle women. Benny differed from his brother in every possible way.

There was another sound outside, and Josh found himself wishing that Benny had been there. He would know what to do.

He slipped the magazine into the handgrip, switched the safety off and snapped back the carriage, all the way, just like Benny had shown him. Walking back out into the hall, Josh killed the lights and moved across to the front door. He paused, straining to hear any sound from outside, holding his head close to the heavy oak of the door.

The sound of knocking was so loud that Josh almost dropped

the automatic. The kind of knocking that the police do in the middle of the night. The kind of knocking the police had done in Cologne the night they had come for Josh's grandparents and twelve-year-old father.

"Professor Josh Hoberman?" The voice was all business. All authority.

"Professor Hoberman?" it repeated when Josh did not respond.

Josh took a deep breath. "Who is it?"

"This is Special Agent Roesler, sir. FBI. I'm here with Special Agent Forbes. May we speak with you, Professor Hoberman?"

"Hold on . . ." Josh looked around himself: at the hall and staircase behind him, at the study to his left, at his pot belly above the elasticated band of his shorts, at the gun in his hand. What were the FBI doing here? If it *was* the FBI. He switched on the porch light, slid the security chain into place and opened the door a crack, keeping the gun raised but out of sight behind the door. Two crew-cuts in suits looked back at him. There was a black Crown Victoria parked on the drive behind them with a third figure at the wheel.

"Let me see some identification . . ." Josh tried to invest as much authority into the demand as possible.

"Certainly, Professor Hoberman." The young man at the door did not, as Josh had expected, simply hold up his ID, instead handing the black leather wallet to him through the gap in the door. Josh studied it carefully, looking from the photograph on the ID to the face at the door and back again, as if he would really have had any idea how to tell a fake FBI identity card from a real one.

"What do you want? Do you know what time it is?" Josh handed the wallet back.

"Yes, I'm sorry to disturb you so late, Professor Hoberman," Special Agent Roesler said without a hint of apology. "But your help is needed with something very important, sir."

"Needed with what?"

"I've been instructed to give you this . . ." Roesler handed a sealed envelope to Josh, who opened it and read it.

"Do you know what is in this?" he asked the young FBI agent, when he had finished reading the note. "Do you know who sent it?"

"No sir. We're just here to transport you to where you need to be."

Josh stared at the two FBI men for a moment, trying to grasp if what was happening really was happening. "Give me ten minutes to get dressed," he said eventually. "I'll be right out."

He closed the door and, before turning and heading back up the stairs, looked again at the note.

The note headed with the seal of the President of the United States.

5

JOHN MACBETH. BOSTON

Confined by windows he could not wind down, doors he could not open and the heavy gauge mesh between him and the uniformed driver, Macbeth felt an incipient panic as he sat in the back of the police prowl car. This was not, by any means, an environment that offered him harmony.

He tried to focus on the city that slid by outside.

Clear-sky evening had turned to clouded night while he had sat in the bar with Corbin and the streets were now sleek with rain. The cop didn't use the siren or the lights except at intersections, where an abbreviated whoop-whoop served both to clear the way and startle Macbeth. They cut through the Common on Charles, the silhouettes of the trees looking to Macbeth oddly two-dimensional, like stage scenery, before turning towards the towering sparkle of the Prudential Center. As they headed along Huntington, Macbeth could see more blue and white police cruisers blocking access to Christian Science Plaza.

"You the shrink?" the cop with the sergeant's chevrons and the big Irish face asked Corbin as he got out of the patrol car.

"I'm Dr Corbin, the duty psychiatrist, if that's what you mean. This is a colleague, Dr Macbeth . . ." said Corbin as Macbeth slid out of the police car after him. The cop didn't acknowledge Macbeth's presence.

"Yeah, well, we got a religious nut, looks like. Butt-naked on the Christian Science Church roof. He's the angel Gabriel, apparently."

"Anybody talking to him at the moment?" asked Corbin.

"Father Mullachy. From St Francis just over there . . ." The cop had the same thick Boston accent that the cabbie had had. *Ovah they-ah* . . . "I've got one of our guys with him. You never know when a crazy is going to try to take someone with them. Like that thing in San Francisco."

"You've got a Catholic priest talking to him?" Macbeth grinned. "I would have thought that the Christian Scientists would have a demarcation issue."

The sergeant looked Macbeth up and down wordlessly, before leading the way across the plaza. Ahead was a huge domed building that looked to Macbeth like a conglomeration of every style of religious architecture: part church, part cathedral, part basilica, part mosque. He had always thought of The Mother Church of the Church of Christ, Scientist, here in the heart of Boston, as something that should have been built in a theme-park for the godly. Or Las Vegas.

He had visited as a child – Macbeth, Casey and their father tourists in their own town – and remembered being awed by the scale of the interiors. Religious architecture had always fascinated him; particularly the way the dimensions were intended to overwhelm, to intimidate – to remind how big was God and how small man. His favorite part of the visit had been the 'Mapparium' in the Mary Baker Eddy Library: a vast, three-stories-high, inside-out, glass-globe encapsulation of the world as it had been in 1935.

The BPD sergeant led Corbin and Macbeth past the Reflection Pool, a long rectangle of water, dark and sparkling in the Boston night.

"There he is . . ." The sergeant pointed up to a flat-roofed area around the dome with a parapet-walled edge. It was on the original part of the structure and halfway up. A naked figure stood poised on one of the wall's merlons.

Staring.

His focus seemed fixed on something far out over the city. Something in the sky. Macbeth looked in the direction of his gaze, but could see nothing. Even at this distance, Macbeth saw that there was no urgency, no distress in the way the naked man stood, arms at his side. The sight of him stirred an uneasy memory of a patient at McLean. Macbeth's last patient before he went into pure research.

"Maybe he's not serious," Corbin said to the police sergeant. "It's not high enough to ensure death if he jumps."

"Maybe so . . ." said the cop assessing the drop. "But it's still gonna smart." *Smaaht.* He led the two psychiatrists to a side door, through a storeroom and up an internal service stairwell. When they came out onto the roof section by the dome, everything looked different, the height and the shifted perspective making Macbeth feel unsteady.

Here, at close quarters, he saw again that the fair-haired man on the edge of the parapet was poised. Calm. Almost serene. Not the usual jumper. In his late twenties or early thirties, Macbeth estimated. Seen from behind and a little to the side, stripped of his clothes, he looked pale and thin, except for a thickening of the waistline above the hips: a roll of soft fat hinting at a future weight problem. Again it appeared to Macbeth that the naked man was looking at something far away, out in the dark above or beyond the city.

The priest was about the same age as the man on the parapet and crouched, one knee on the floor, resting his elbow on the other, almost in a posture of genuflection. He had positioned himself to the side of the naked man, about six feet off, and Macbeth could hear he was lecturing him, in a soft, patronizing tone, about the sin of self-murder.

"That's all we need," Corbin muttered to Macbeth. "Someone to compound his religious mania. Two delusionals for the price of one . . ."

"Father Mullachy is doing just fine," said the younger cop defensively, his face filled with hostility and ten generations of dumb believing. He could have been the sergeant's son.

"You do realize that if your priest out there validates his delusion, he might just talk him into jumping?" Corbin shook his head and turned to Macbeth. "You'd better hang back, John, seeing you're unofficial here."

"I'll watch and learn . . ." Macbeth smiled and moved over to where the younger cop and the sergeant with the big Irish face stood. From this vantage point, Macbeth could now see something of the naked man's profile.

"You say this guy claims he's the angel Gabriel?" Corbin asked the sergeant.

"Something like that. Or maybe his name really is Gabriel, but you know what these types are like, they run off at the mouth and none of it makes sense. He kept on going on about knowing the truth, having a message, all the usual crap. Funny thing is he's calmer than most."

Corbin nodded and moved closer to the priest and the man on the parapet.

"Hi. My name's Peter . . . I'd like to talk to you. Can I come closer?"

"Not too close." The standing man spoke quietly and calmly but the young priest turned in Corbin's direction and held up a halting hand, his expression impatient. Corbin ignored him and crossed the roof.

"That'll do fine," said the naked man, over his shoulder.

"Hello . . ." Corbin repeated. "I'm Peter. What do I call you?"

"His name is Gabriel," said the priest.

"Is that your name?" Corbin asked the naked man, then turned to the priest, keeping his voice low and even. "Move away, Father. You could do more harm than good."

"I am here to tend to a soul in distress. I have a place here."

"At least move back." Corbin shot a steel thread of warning

46

through his tone. The priest didn't move. Corbin turned his attention back to the naked man.

"Is that really your name? Are you Gabriel?"

The naked man made no hint of having heard Corbin, continuing to stare out over the city.

"You can call me Gabriel," he said eventually and absently, as if talking to Corbin was a distraction. "Call me whatever you want. Anything can be given a name, but that doesn't mean that thing is what you call it. You can give something a name, but it doesn't mean that it is. Tell me, Peter, are you a psychiatrist?"

"I'm here to help you, Gabriel," said Corbin. "That's the most important thing, but yes, I'm a psychiatrist."

"I see. You're here to observe me . . ." Gabriel said, still distracted by something only he could see, far out over and above the city. "To observe me and evaluate my state. Those two things are contradictory, if you don't mind me saying . . . the Observer Effect in quantum physics proves the act of observation itself changes the state of the observed. Did you know that?"

"I'm not here just to observe, Gabriel, I'm here to help."

"To stop me jumping."

"To help you," repeated Corbin. "Help you find a way out of this."

"Like I said: to stop me jumping. We live in a superpositional universe of infinite possibilities, so you'll get the outcome you want: I won't jump. And I will jump. I'll jump and survive. I'll jump and be killed. It's not a choice. All of these things will happen. And none of them will."

"Why are you on the roof, Gabriel? Why are you here?"

"I'm not here. I don't exist."

"That's a strange thing to say. Of course you're here."

"Strange? Not really. I know I'm not here."

"Have you taken drugs tonight, Gabriel?"

47

"The K-hole?" Gabriel laughed quietly. "No, Peter, I haven't taken Ketamine or anything else. I'm not suffering from drug-induced depersonalization. I'm just really not here."

"I see you, Gabriel. That means you're here."

"Does it?" Gabriel said, then gasped suddenly, swaying forward slightly. Everyone looked to see what had startled him. There was nothing. For a moment the young naked man stood frozen, then the tension eased from his pose.

"Does it?" he repeated, still as if Corbin was distracting him from watching some event unfold on some vast TV screen visible only to him. "I'm here because you see me here, is that it? Does that mean if you look away, I won't be?"

"You were here before I came up onto the roof, Gabriel. You were here fifteen minutes ago when the police called me. You were here fifteen minutes before that when the security guard called the police. I couldn't see you then, but you were here, weren't you?"

And before that, thought Macbeth, remembering the taxi driver's account of the distracted passenger he'd taken to Christian Science Plaza.

The young man frowned. "I remember *being* here fifteen minutes ago. I remember *being* before you looked at me. But I am remembering that now. That memory of existence has been generated in this moment. Maybe it's the present memory that's real, not the past existence. Because I *remember* being here fifteen minutes ago doesn't mean I really was here fifteen minutes ago."

"Do you know something, Gabriel?" said Corbin. "I don't like heights. I mean, I *really* don't like heights. Never have. Why don't you step back from the edge? Just a little bit . . ." Corbin glanced meaningfully over to the cops standing beside Macbeth. "No one is going to come close. It's just so that we can talk. You know, without me being all scared about the height."

"Height is a dimension, a measure. It isn't the measure you're scared of, you're afraid of the force the measure exerts on your mass. Gravity. And gravity is nothing to be afraid of."

"I don't know about that, Gabriel," said Corbin, "I've seen gravity make a real mess of people falling from a height lower than this."

"Of the four fundamental forces of the universe, gravity is the weakest. By far the weakest. The other three forces push it around. Bend it and twist it and fuck it up. If you want to be afraid of a force, Doc, be afraid of electromagnetism, or the strong nuclear force. Be afraid of the forces you can't see or feel but hold you together and can tear you apart. Not gravity." Gabriel sighed. "If you don't like heights, you can step farther back. I like it here. Is Father Mullachy still here?"

"I am still here, my son." The priest stood up, casting a nervous eye over the building's edge.

"What's your name, Father? I mean your first name."

"Paul," said the priest. "My name is Paul."

The naked man laughed. "Peter, Paul and Gabriel . . . two saints and an angel. Do you believe in angels, Father?"

"I believe God is manifest in many ways, Gabriel. Many ways to many people."

"I didn't ask if you believed in God. I didn't ask a vague question for you to give me a vague answer. I asked you specifically if you believed in angels . . . you know, anthropomorphic beings with giant wings growing out of their backs."

"That's not what an angel is, my son," said the priest. "An angel is a messenger of God, or even the message itself. More a being of spirit than—"

"Do you believe in angels, Gabriel?" Corbin cut the priest off.

Gabriel laughed bitterly. "Believe? I believe in nothing. But the funny thing is that the nothing I believe in is a nothing where absolutely everything is possible. All things, all ideas, all possibilities. Even angels. If you're a psychiatrist, Peter, then

49

you'll know that angels are real. Not to everybody, but to some. I bet you've had patients who believe totally, completely, that they've seen angels. The fact that the angels exist only in their minds and no one else's doesn't mean they're not real. Angels, demons, ghosts . . ." He paused, his tone becoming troubled. "And monsters. I bet you've seen them all, treated them, cured them. Am I right? Have you cured people of their belief in angels?"

"I've helped patients with delusional disorders, if that's what you mean."

There was a pause. Gabriel's gaze remained fixed on the far-in-the-distance something invisible to everyone else. "You've been very busy recently, haven't you, Peter?" he said eventually. "You've had to chase away a lot more angels and ghosts of late. Many, many more than usual . . . Am I right?"

There was another pause, this time Corbin standing quiet. Something in that silence troubled Macbeth.

"Why do you say that?" said Corbin.

"I'm right, aren't I? There are more people than usual seeking a cure for their visions. What do you tell them? Do you tell them they're mad? Or has it begun with you too? Maybe just the odd thing out of the corner of your eye? Those are the worst. Those are the ones that drive you crazy . . . they're never still there when you turn. Has that been happening to you, Peter? Are you already a seer of visions yourself? Do you now tell your patients that they were right all along? Do you tell them the angels are coming?"

Again Macbeth noticed that Corbin paused before answering. In the silence he could hear the city sounds of traffic in the dark; distant shouting and laughter. Noises off.

"Do you see angels?" asked Corbin. "Is that what you're seeing now, in the sky?"

Gabriel laughed. "Stop reflecting. Deflecting. I want to know if you ever wondered about the reality your patients describe . . .

Have you ever lain in bed at night, in the dark, and questioned whether their reality is the valid one and yours the false? I mean, you must encounter as many people with their own version of reality as those who share the standard version."

"We all know what true reality is, Gabriel."

The naked man laughed. "You mean consensual reality? Reality is reality if enough people believe in it? What if everybody . . . and I mean everybody . . . started to have visions? Everybody except you? Would that mean that you were delusional? Let's put it this way: Father Mullachy here has devoted his life to serve a supernatural entity. But that's acceptable because there's a history to his fantasy and there's still some consensus behind it. But if he devoted himself in exactly the same way to exactly the same set of beliefs, but said it was a giant mouse who lives hidden in the clouds that commanded his presence here, because the giant mouse is worried about my spiritual wellbeing, that wouldn't be acceptable. You would say he was delusional. Big question, isn't it?"

"The only question I'm interested in at the moment is why you are here, Gabriel."

There was another elastic silence before Gabriel spoke. "Have you ever seen a Golden Dart Frog? They're beautiful: bright, beautiful colors, not just gold. And so tiny – less than half an inch long. Do you know what I can't understand about the Golden Dart Frog? Why such a tiny, beautiful creature is the most deadly poisonous animal on the planet. One frog – one half-inch-long frog – could kill five African elephants stone dead inside of a minute. Or twenty to thirty humans. If you put your bare hand on a branch where one has been sitting an hour before, its skin secretions could still kill you. I just don't get it . . . Hey, Father, you got an answer to that? Why God made something so beautiful then made it so toxic?"

"There is room in God's creation for all kinds of thing, Gabriel," said the priest. "There are wonders we may never understand. His reasons may forever be beyond our grasp."

Gabriel laughed and as he did so, his naked body swayed again. Macbeth saw Corbin tense.

"That's good . . . I like that . . . 'wonders we may never understand'. The Pope's get-out-of-jail-free card," said Gabriel. "But we really try to understand, don't we? I mean, of the eight or nine million species on this planet, we are the only one trying to make sense of it all. You see, the Golden Dart Frog makes no sense to me because it carries a thousand times more poison than it would ever need to kill any of its natural predators. And you know something? We're exactly the same. We don't make sense, either. I mean, why are we so smart? We don't need all of this intelligence."

"I don't get you," said Corbin.

"Just like the Golden Dart Frog's been overloaded with poison, we're overloaded with all this brainpower. Brainpower we don't really need to hang on to our place at the top of the pile. Look at all of this . . ." He swept an arm to indicate Boston glittering in the night. "All of this created by an ape. Art, science, music . . . none of it makes any sense. It's absurd. Everything is absurd. What do you think, Peter? You gauge and measure and probe the human mind . . . What's your take on it?"

"Human intelligence?" As he answered, Corbin took a clumsily casual step closer. He was now halfway between Macbeth and the naked man. "Like you said, we're top of the evolutionary tree; it's our intelligence that's put us there."

"Now that's just not true, Peter, and you know it," said Gabriel. "What about dinosaurs? One hundred and thirty million years at the top of the tree. Infinitely more successful than us. They didn't need technology or civilization or culture. Our intelligence is actually an evolutionary threat, not an advantage – it has brought us close to extinction at our own hands within what? Two hundred thousand years of modern humans? Fifty thousand years of behavioral modernity? I mean, that's not even a blink of the evolutionary eye. But in that tiny space of time we have pretty much succeeded in fucking up the planet we depend on and have developed the weapons we need to wipe ourselves out several times over. Yep, Pete . . . dinosaurs have us beat, all right." Again he waved an arm to indicate the city spread out below. "They had all this beat."

"I can answer your question, Gabriel." The priest moved closer, uncertainly, again casting a nervous eye over the parapet's edge. "Our wisdom, our inquiry, is God-given. He gave it to us so that we may *seek* to understand Him. And come to know our sins – the nature of sin. So that we can strive to know God."

"What if I told you," Gabriel said to the priest, "that I know God? That I know God in a way that you could never, ever understand? That I completely, totally understand the true nature of God?"

"No you don't, my son," said the priest.

"But I do," said Gabriel, for the first time with feeling in his voice. Almost pain. "You're the one who's deluded. I've seen the answer, the truth, Father. And it's a big, big truth. A truth so big and so beyond the imaginings of your tiny superstition that you're incapable of understanding it." He paused, and seemed to survey the lights of the city again. "So big I can't bear it . . ."

An upcurrent from the Plaza below lifted and ruffled the fringe of fair hair. Gabriel leaned forward slightly and looked down. Macbeth held his breath and sensed the two cops next to him do the same. Pete Corbin moved forward then checked himself.

Then, unexpectedly, Gabriel stepped back: off the parapet and away from the edge. Father Mullachy looked across to Corbin with an expression of undisguised triumph.

"Better get a blanket," the sergeant told the younger cop and started to cross the roof. In the meantime, the young priest had taken a step towards Gabriel and placed his hand reassuringly on his naked shoulder.

"Everything's going to be fine, my son," said Father Mullachy.

"You don't understand, Paul," said Gabriel and his voice was suddenly clearer, more determined. "We are becoming. We are becoming."

"We are becoming what?" the priest frowned.

Macbeth realized he had seen it first. Everyone else was involved in his allocated role while Macbeth was simply an observer. And he observed. He observed the sudden shift in Gabriel's demeanor; he observed the sudden animation in the until then emotionless face and gestureless body.

"You see, Father Paul," said Gabriel, "all your life you've been asking the wrong question. You've been asking *who* God is. There is no who. There is no who or what or where. The truth is knowing *when* God is. I know when God is. We are becoming . . . We are becoming . . ." Gabriel, smiling, stepped forward and embraced the young priest in a bear hug. "Come and see . . ."

By now, Corbin was running towards them, the two cops and Macbeth behind him. They all froze as Gabriel, his arms still locked around Mullachy, hurled himself and the priest sideways.

The low crenellated parapet that edged the roof caught both men mid-calf and they toppled sideways over the edge and out of sight: Gabriel silent, Mullachy screaming in primal terror.

6

JOSH HOBERMAN. VIRGINIA

Josh Hoberman sat in the back of the black car and felt sick.

As they cruised along the long track to the road, he watched the dark velvet of the trees swallow up his home and douse the porch light he had forgotten to switch off. The track to the main road was unpaved and Hoberman had bought an SUV to make the daily trip from his home to the rail station where he made the thrice-weekly commute to his clinic in DC. The rest of the week he worked at home, in isolation. The Crown Vic's suspension evened out the bumps and ruts in the road into gentler lunges and lurches, and the turbulence was mirrored in Hoberman's gut.

"Where are we going?" he asked Roesler, who sat in the rear with him, the other two agents suited, silent ciphers in the front. Why had they sent three agents?

"I guess you're going to DC, sir, but I wouldn't know for sure," said Roesler with the same perfunctory politeness. Hoberman realized that to Roesler he was a package for delivery, nothing more. "We're only taking you as far as Culpeper airbase. You're being picked up by helicopter there."

"To go to Washington? It's only an hour and a half by car . . ."

"I really don't know where your final destination is, Professor Hoberman. I guess they'll be able to better inform you at Culpeper."

They were on the main highway now and Hoberman sat back in the leather and reflected on the nature of inherited memory and cultural memes. Hoberman was a Jew collected in the middle of the night by armed government officials who wouldn't tell him where his final destination lay; the grandson of a long-dead Jew collected in the middle of the night by armed government officials who wouldn't tell him where his final destination lay.

The rest of the half-hour journey was silent other than when the suit in the front seat made a call to say they were 'nearing rendezvous'. Hoberman was only mildly surprised to see that Culpeper Regional Airport was closed at that time of night, but the security man gave a small salute and let the car pass through the gates.

Gleaming under the airfield lights like some giant beetle, a large black helicopter sat on the runway, rotors already slugging into motion as the car pulled up. Roesler and one of the other agents guided Hoberman with irresistible courtesy beneath the swish of blades to where steps led up to the door. The man standing framed in the doorway was casually dressed in a black short-sleeve polo shirt, light-colored cargo pants and an overdone smile.

"Professor Hoberman?" He extended his hand and his smile. "Thanks for coming at such an ungodly hour. I'm Agent Bundy. Let's get you comfortable."

"Bundy?"

"No relation . . ." the secret serviceman said automatically, still smiling amiably, and stood back to allow Hoberman access to a small space between the pilot's cabin and an opposing door, which Bundy slid open. Hoberman noticed that he was tanned and muscular: the professional muscles of someone whose job required brawn as well as brain. He also noticed that Bundy had the most striking eyes. Dual-colored: the irises banded bright blue on the outside and pale hazel-brown around the pupils.

"This way, Professor Hoberman," said Bundy.

The passenger cabin of the helicopter took Hoberman by surprise. It was bright and luxurious, with cream leather armchairs unlike anything he had seen in any airliner, whatever the class of seating. There was another man in the cabin whom Bundy introduced as Bob Ryerson. Ryerson was wearing a dark, expensive-looking suit and was indecently well-groomed and fresh for the time of night. His physique came out of the same box as Bundy's.

"Is this *Marine One*?" Hoberman asked. Bundy laughed.

"No sir, the main helicopter used as *Marine One* is a bigger craft than this. But *Marine One* is any helicopter that has the President on board, and *only* if the President is on board. But you're right to think that this is an HMX-1 craft: Marine Helicopter Squadron One . . . Presidential executive transport. Please, take a seat and buckle up for takeoff, Professor Hoberman."

"So you and *Bob* here," said Hoberman without taking his seat. "What are you? CIA? NSA? FBI? DHS? Or have I missed something in our fine nation's clandestine alphabet soup?"

"You could say all of the above," said Bundy, smile still in place. "I am officially an FBI Special Agent, but my job description has become . . . *flexible*. Everything's become a little more integrated post-nine-eleven. But Bob and I are both tasked with Presidential security and protection, if that's what you mean. Please, Professor Hoberman, sit down and buckle up and we'll get under way."

"Under way where?" Hoberman remained standing as resolutely as he could manage. "And why? I have a right to know where the hell you're taking me and for what reason."

Bundy smiled indulgently. "I believe you received a note . . ."

"That only told me the *who*, not the *where* and *why*."

"I can answer your first question, Doctor," Ryerson answered. Hoberman noticed his demeanor was less convivial than Bundy's car-salesman cheeriness. "We're flying to Camp David

57

in Maryland. As for your second question, neither of us know why you've been summoned, but we were told to give you this." He removed a dossier from a black leather attaché case and handed it to Hoberman.

The dossier was fastened shut by an unbroken Presidential seal. Hoberman stared at it the same way he'd stared at the gun in his hand. Alien, out of place. Hoberman, standing in the luxury of a Presidential fleet helicopter with its immaculate cream leather seats, cherrywood drinks table and green curtains, felt alien and out of place himself.

"Now, Professor Hoberman . . ." said Bundy, extending his hand towards one of the seats. "If you don't mind . . ."

7

JOHN MACBETH. BOSTON

When it came to the naked man, pronouncing life extinct didn't stretch Macbeth's medical training.

Gabriel had hit the flagstones head first and a gray-flecked halo of blood bloomed around his shattered skull; viscous clots oozed from each nostril and one eye remained wide open, gazing up at the night sky, while the other was half closed, the lid like a carelessly pulled down window blind.

He must have held the young priest in his unrelenting embrace all the way to the ground, because the two men now lay entangled. Corbin and Macbeth turned their attention to Father Mullachy, who lay partly across Gabriel's chest. The priest also stared up at the dark sky, but his chest pulsed rapidly in short, shallow heaves.

"Can you hear me?" asked Corbin. "Father Mullachy? Can you hear me Father Mullachy?"

The priest said nothing, his gaze remaining fixed on the stars above, his breathing still fast and shallow. Corbin pressed an ear to the injured man's chest, first one side, then the other.

"Get an ambulance!" Corbin called over his shoulder to the policemen, then turned back to Macbeth. "How's your emergency medicine?"

"Rusty . . ." Macbeth lied. Emergency procedures were exactly the kind of thing that he remembered. Perfectly. How to do things, processes, facts and methods he had learned; taxonomies, systems, structured knowledge – these were the memories that were catalogued, indexed and filed, dusted and maintained in the warehouse in his brain labeled Procedural Memory and could be brought back into his recall shining bright and working like new. In contrast, when it came to his Autobiographical Memory, Macbeth found himself in an ill-lit storeroom of cluttered shelves that he could never quite find his way around. Real-life remembrances had to be dusted off before he could examine their faded images. Even then he was never sure what truly belonged to his life and what had been borrowed from others.

Corbin was clearly aware of Macbeth's recall of procedure, because he made a 'help yourself' gesture towards the injured man. Macbeth ran his hands over the priest's body, like a cop frisking a suspect. Old skills came back in an instant and as he felt each fracture beneath his fingertips, he announced it to Corbin. When Macbeth examined his ribs, Mullachy made a short moaning sound, the only protest he could manage between breaths; then again, louder, when Macbeth felt around the hips. Shattered pelvis. The good thing was that Mullachy could feel the pain in his lower body, meaning his spinal cord was intact. Macbeth checked the distal pulses then worked his way back to the chest. Carefully removing the priest's dog collar, he inspected his neck: no deformations or serious swelling. Mullachy must have landed in a way that prevented serious injury to his head and spine, the most common cause of death in falls. As Macbeth examined the priest's throat, he saw a rash of small, raised bumps on the skin, like an extreme form of gooseflesh. Whenever he touched a bump, it moved or popped beneath his fingers, the skin flattening but other bumps appearing elsewhere.

"Rice Krispies?" asked Corbin over Macbeth's shoulder.

Macbeth nodded. "Snap, crackle and pop all right . . . Sub-Q air. If the ambulance doesn't arrive soon, we're going to have to improvise a chest tube."

There was now an urgent wheezing to the priest's breathing. He spoke urgently between shallow breaths.

"Unction . . ." he gasped. "Last . . . rites . . ."

"Don't talk, Father," said Macbeth. "Save your breath. You're going to be fine." He turned to Corbin. "Go see if one of the cops has got a pocket knife and a ballpoint pen."

"You're going to tube him here?"

"Not if I can avoid it. The last thing I want to do is attempt some kind of Boy Scout thoracostomy." Macbeth sighed. He looked past Corbin to the lights of the surrounding high buildings; the glass globes of the streetlamps that lined the Plaza. They seemed to sparkle brighter, look sharper, harder-edged. Crystalline. There were patterns in things, in everything, and Macbeth was beginning to see them again.

Not now, he told himself. *Not now. Focus.*

"I just want to be ready if the ambulance takes too long. His thorax is pretty rigid already. He's bleeding out into his pleural cavity. See if the cops have anything I can use . . ."

Corbin nodded and ran over to where the sergeant was herding back, with impatient sweeps of his arms, a small group of onlookers.

"I'm ready . . ." the priest said between breaths. "I'm ready."

"Ready for what, Paul?" Macbeth leaned in close. Even in the streetlight he could see the blue tinge to Mullachy's pallor, his lips darker now. "Save your breath. We're going to get you sorted out."

Something gargled in the priest's throat. Macbeth felt a tap on his shoulder and turned to see the older cop.

"Any news on the ambulance?" Macbeth asked the BPD sergeant.

"On its way," the sergeant said. "There's been some kind of incident on the Common and the traffic's snarled up. What do you need the pen and knife for?"

"Father Mullachy is showing signs that at least one lung has

61

been ruptured and his pleural cavity is filling with air and blood. I reckon there's bleeding lower down as well. There are air bubbles under the skin of his neck and throat. If he doesn't get a chest tube in soon, the pressure's going to squeeze his heart into cardiac arrest."

"And you're going to fix it with a fuckin' ballpoint?" The cop frowned disbelievingly.

"Unless you've got something better."

"There's a responder kit in the cruiser . . . first aid."

"Get me that. But hurry – we don't have much time. And chase up that ambulance."

The cop turned and trotted towards the cruiser, barking into his radio as he ran. Macbeth knelt back down beside the two tangled bodies. Between them, Corbin and Macbeth managed to unravel the naked man's legs from Mullachy's. The dead man now served as a pillow beneath the injured priest and the two doctors had better access to his injuries. Corbin eased open the front of Mullachy's black shirt.

"I'm going to have to go in anteriorly," said Macbeth. "We can't risk turning him over or sitting him up without getting a neck brace on him."

"I'm ready . . . I'm ready . . ." Mullachy repeated it like a rosary, but Macbeth knew the priest wasn't talking about his preparedness for his improvised surgery.

"Just stay focused and stay awake, Father." Macbeth brought his face down so they could make eye contact. "I know it's distressing to have to fight for breath, but that will ease soon. Listen to me: you're going to make it. You're going to be all right."

Mullachy shook his head in tiny, careful movements.

"You . . . don't . . . believe . . . do you?" he asked between pained gasps. "You . . . think . . . it's . . . all . . . a lie . . ."

"Let's leave the theological discussions until we've got you breathing more comfortably, Father," said Macbeth. "Hush now and save your breath."

The sergeant came back with a large blue holdall. Corbin scrabbled through it and handed a pack of latex gloves and four antiseptic wound wipes to Macbeth, who snapped on the gloves and spread one of the wound wipes on the ground, using another to wipe down the skin on the priest's bloated abdomen.

"Better than a penknife . . ." said Corbin as he handed Macbeth the disposable sterile scalpel he had found in the kit.

"Any tubing?" asked Macbeth as he unwrapped the scalpel, watching his hands move as if they belonged to someone else.

Corbin scrambled through the bag again. "Nope."

Another tap on the shoulder. This time when Macbeth turned, the sergeant held out a ballpoint pen in his huge hand.

"I hope you know what you're doing Doc."

Macbeth took the pen and stripped out the ballpoint and refill, leaving the empty sleeve. Corbin handed him a plastic bottle of sterile water and he sluiced out the pen sleeve, wiping it down with a fresh antiseptic wipe before laying it on the one he had spread out on the ground. As he did so, Macbeth felt as if something indefinable had changed in his environment; a subtle shift in lighting, or air pressure, or a vague scent suddenly carried in the air. *Not now.*

The priest was now wheezing loudly, urgently, his eyes filled with tears.

"Is . . . it . . . true? Is . . . it . . . true?"

"Easy, Father," said Corbin, laying his hand on the injured man's forehead. "We'll have you breathing easy in a moment."

Macbeth felt it coming. He always felt it coming, as if his mind had to prepare itself. The feeling he had – that something had shifted in the spectrum of his surroundings – was always the prelude to an episode. He knew it was the stress of the situation that was bringing it on. Stress he no longer felt directly as the episode started to form. He looked across at Corbin's anxious face, then back down to the patient who would die if he didn't act decisively. Immediately.

Everything around Macbeth was now harder and brighter and even more sharp-edged, as if his eyes had been refocused beyond the physically possible. He looked out across the Plaza towards the Reflection Pool. Everything sparkled on its black water, the mirrored lights of the Prudential Center, One-Eleven Huntington and the other surrounding buildings becoming dancing diamonds on its surface. He knew that none of it was real. These weren't real people. The architecture around him didn't really exist.

He heard Corbin talk to him, his voice sharp and clear, but the words, the syllables, meaningless as language became an absurdly abstract concept.

Macbeth didn't exist.

He had arrived at the heart of the event; to the place it always took him. To the same absolute, incontrovertible conclusion: he did not exist. Like Corbin, like everyone else, he was a fiction.

He realized in that moment, as he had realized in all of the moments like it before, that there was a reason why he had such a bad memory for biographical events. His were the patchy remembrances of an invented, sketched-out life.

He looked down at hands so totally disconnected from him that he was surprised when they started moving. One hand held the skin of the priest's chest, exactly at the fifth intercostal space, and pulled it taut between thumb and forefinger while the other made an inch-and-a-half-long incision, cutting deep through the subcutaneous layers. The priest moaned as the hands slid the pen-sleeve tube into the cut.

There was a wet, hissing sound as air and blood syphoned from Mullachy's chest. Corbin jumped back as the blood splashed onto the flagstones.

"Jesus!" shouted the sergeant. "What the fuck you done? He's bleeding to death!"

"It's already spent blood," Corbin told the cop, and Macbeth realized he could understand language again. "He's bled it into his chest cavity already. He could have lost as much as half of his blood supply and you wouldn't have seen a drop."

Macbeth heard the priest take a deep, pained breath, then utter a moan, before beginning to breathe more normally.

Mullachy looked up, locking his eyes with Macbeth's. He grabbed Macbeth's suit collar and pulled him close. The breathing had eased, but his eyes were no less wild, no less desperate.

"I saw it . . ." the priest hissed into Macbeth's face.

"Saw it? Saw what?"

"I saw it," said Mullachy earnestly. "When he jumped . . . when he took me with him . . . he said he would show me. He showed me. I saw it . . ."

"I don't—" There was the sound of sirens and Macbeth became aware of the presence of two men in Boston EMS outfits easing in beside him. One of them was black and with the strange detached observance of detail that came with one of his episodes, Macbeth noticed that the service number on his ID shield started with a one, instead of a four, five or six, denoting that he was a fully trained paramedic rather than an EMT.

"What we got?" asked the black guy. Macbeth stared at him blankly, noticing he had a beard of black stubble strips, separated by shaved bands, giving the impression of a tilled field. Cornrows. Why did he do that? thought Macbeth. Why do people do that? Whenever he was in this state of detachment, Macbeth found the tiny orthodoxies of everyday life bizarre; inexplicable.

"What we got?" repeated the paramedic from under a frown. "You are a doctor, aren't you?"

Macbeth nodded. The world started to make sense again, to settle into its accepted groove, and he knew the episode was ending. Still, his own voice sounded alien to him as, with the emotional content of a weather report, he ran through the facts.

"One fatality on impact: the jumper. He took the priest with him. Father Mullachy doesn't seem to have significant head or neck injuries but he's suffered a major high-energy thoracic trauma with multiple costal fractures and costochondral separation. I heard crepitus during palpation. Reduced breath sounds on the right and significant tension hemopneumothorax, causing tachypnea and subcutaneous emphysema around the neck, which I've eased with an improvised chest tube. Suspected additional subpulmonic pleural effusion. Other significant injuries include an ilium wing fracture and probably other pelvic damage."

"Okay, we got it from here,' said the paramedic. The EMS men put a cervical collar on the priest and placed an oxygen mask over his nose and mouth. Holding him as rigidly as they could, the paramedics eased him off of the other man's body and rolled him onto his side, slipping the long spine board beneath him and strapping him to it.

As Macbeth viewed it all, he still felt detached from everything that was happening, the lack of feeling from his episode lingering. He watched as the EMS crew ratcheted up the gurney. The young priest looked at Macbeth, his earnest, pleading eyes now glossed with tears.

"What kept you?" the younger cop asked the paramedics.

"The traffic was crazy. Backed up all the way here. Couldn't get moving, even with the sirens and lights. Don't ask me why the traffic got snarled up this time of night."

Macbeth looked up at the night sky.

"It's a full moon . . ." he said. "That's why . . ."

66

8

JOSH HOBERMAN. MARYLAND

Hoberman knew little about military ranks, but he knew enough to recognize that the eagle on the officer's epaulette marked him as a full-bird colonel, just as the Asclepian Staff at the center of his Air Force wings identified him as a doctor.

"Hi, Professor Hoberman. Thanks for coming at such short notice and at such an ungodly hour. I'm Jack Ward, Director of the White House Medical Office and Personal Physician to the President."

Hoberman nodded, a little lost for words. He stood with the Air Force doctor in front of a rustic chimney breast of rough-hewn rock that formed the centerpiece of what was, basically, a sprawling wooden cabin. Their surroundings were purposefully bucolic and homey, and had the feel of some upscale but out-of-date summer camp. The name Naval Support Facility Thurmont certainly did not fit with them, which was why they were unofficially but much better known as Camp David.

Bundy and Ryerson had shown Hoberman from the helipad to the Aspen Lodge, the President's quarters, and Ward dismissed them with a "Thanks guys."

Once they were alone, Ward shook Hoberman's hand with what the psychiatrist imagined was military firmness. Maybe, he thought, they had drills in handshaking at West Point or Maxwell or Colorado Springs or wherever the hell these people learned to do things like use the right fork or kill people with a paperclip. Ward was annoyingly, predictably, stereotypically handsome, lean and athletic-looking. It also felt to Hoberman that the President's doctor was a foot taller than he was. On the strength of this evidence, Hoberman decided not to equivo-cate and hate the guy from the outset.

"I guess you know why you're here." Ward nodded to the black-bound dossier in Hoberman's hand. "Please, Professor Hoberman . . . take a seat."

He sat in a club chair that swallowed him up and Ward sat opposite, his expression suddenly serious.

"I take it I don't need to explain the sensitivity of the mat-erial you have just read."

"No, you sure don't," said Hoberman. "Who else knows about this?"

"The President approached me directly and I compiled the dossier myself. So the answer is, at this time, only three people: you, me and the President."

"Why me?"

"I've read several of your papers, particularly on stimulant psychosis and therapeutic psychotomimetics – and I was very impressed with your book on sensory deprivation-induced delu-sions. Given what you've read in the dossier, I'm sure you can see why you were the obvious choice."

Hoberman shrugged. "There are others equally qualified . . ."

Ward shook his head. "No there's not. This is highly sensitive and could not be more important to national security and we need the best brains on it. There were only two choices as far as I was concerned: yourself and John Macbeth, but Dr Macbeth is currently involved in research work in Copenhagen, Denmark."

Hoberman nodded, dismissing the thought that Ward's confidence in him didn't extend to him working out that the Copenhagen to which he referred was the capital of Denmark and not the one in Idaho.

"I can see why you thought of John too." He paused, con-sidering what he had read in the dossier as the government helicopter had swept over the dark Maryland landscape. "What's your take on it, Colonel Ward?"

"I have been the President's personal physician for three years. You get to know a person pretty well in that period. Physically, President Yates is in tip-top condition for a woman of her age; and psychologically, she possesses a very down-to-earth, practical and calm personality. I can also state that there has been absolutely no record of mental illness or instability. I've gone through her entire family history: no indicators of any genetic predisposition to psychiatric conditions."

"Mmm . . ." Hoberman paused, framing his next question carefully. "President Yates has a reputation for – how can I put it? – for *profound* religious belief. Some may say worryingly profound."

"I don't see . . ."

"One man's godly zeal is another man's religiomania."

"President Yates has her faith, yes, Professor Hoberman. But, as I said, she is also a very *grounded* person. Her God is not one who manifests himself, or others, through visions. She is deeply concerned about what she has experienced. But there's more . . ."

Ward crossed the room to a sideboard and lifted a black attaché case identical to the one Bundy had had in the helicopter. While Ward fetched the case, Hoberman looked out through the large sliding glass doors. Dawn was beginning to push gray fingers through the Camp David trees and he could see the outline of a kidney-shaped swimming pool, a diving board at the far end. He reflected for a moment on all of those who had sat where he was sitting, looking out at the pool as dawn broke, discussing in measured but urgent tones landing men on the moon, missiles on their way to Cuba, convention center break-ins, a wall coming down in Germany, towers crashing to the ground in downtown New York . . .

"This is a report by the White House Security Office . . ."

Ward handed Hoberman a document from the case. "It relates to video surveillance of some of the main corridors and hall-ways in the White House. On more than one occasion, the President's behavior has caused security alerts. Basically, President Yates has behaved as if something or someone out of sight has caused her concern or alarm."

"And when the security people arrive, there's no one there?"

"Exactly. I have to tell you that the President has not always been alone during these episodes. Four members of staff have been present when Mrs Yates has been distressed by something only she would appear to have been able to see. Because no one other than you and I has been privy to the nature of these episodes, I'm concerned that rumors may begin to circulate and questions be asked about the President's state of mind. About her fitness for office."

"I have to say, Colonel Ward, that if President Yates has been subject to the delusional episodes described in the dossier you sent, then my professional opinion would tend to come down on the side of at least a hiatus while she's fully psych-assessed. I'm sure there are mechanisms for the Vice President tempor-arily taking over the reins without any kind of *official* transfer."

"I would agree," said Ward, reaching for a second document in the case, "if we were dealing with the President and the President alone."

"I don't—"

"These *episodes*," Ward interrupted, "to which the President has been subject . . . well, to be frank, they're not isolated. This is a confidential report on the airliner crash in Michigan last month. There are transcripts of the conversations between the pilot and co-pilot and between the cabin and air traffic control. You'll see some of the concerns raised by the investigating officer. The FBI and the Department of Homeland Security are running the investigation."

"This is relevant?" asked Hoberman, flicking through the pages.

"Read it at your leisure and judge for yourself. It's one of several instances of people seeing things that weren't there. More than you would normally expect, and the people involved otherwise not prone to delusional disorders."

"So what is it you expect from me?" asked Hoberman. "I mean specifically?"

"To begin with a professional opinion, obviously. But I'd like you to consider staying on here for a few days. If, as I suspect, we are dealing with something broader than the President's experiences, I would appreciate you heading a task force to get to the bottom of it."

Hoberman laughed. "Only if you call it something other than a task force. And what do you mean, 'something broader'?"

"I mean if there is some kind of connection with other incidents, like the airplane crash. I had to ask you to come here because we need to assess and if necessary treat the President on the move, as it were. This is a critical point in her Presidency. You know, of course, about the Deeper Integration Act that's going through the European Parliament, and the Quartet Peace Accord brokered with Israel?"

"Of course I do. I watch the news."

"For the first time since the formation of the State of Israel, we may be about to see a lasting, even permanent peace and possible accession to the EU of Israel, the Palestinian State and Lebanon. I don't need to tell you that such events are changing the political map of the world in a way we haven't seen since the fall of the Berlin Wall. US interests could be compromised if there's not a steady hand at the tiller. When you read the Michigan crash report, you'll see that there's a concern that some kind of neurological agent may have been used. We have to consider the possibility of some agency seeking to destabilize the US leadership."

"You believe the President may have been exposed to some kind of hallucinogen?" Hoberman asked.

"It's unlikely – there's been nothing in toxicology to indicate the presence of an agent – but it's entirely possible. I've no idea *what* could be causing a stable mind like the President's to manifest hallucinations. That's what I'd like you to help me find out."

Hoberman sighed and again looked out the window. There was now a golden tinge to the light as dawn took a less vague shape.

"In that case," he said, "I guess I'd better see the patient . . ."

9

JOHN MACBETH. BOSTON

It was two-thirty in the morning by the time they were through with the police. Macbeth and Corbin sat in the canteen of the Downtown District A1 station on Sudbury, drinking something that could only have been tangentially described as coffee.

"Don't say I can't organize a memorable night out," Corbin said wearily as he pushed the paper cup around the brushed aluminum of the table top, avoiding drinking its contents. If Corbin had seemed worn out in the bar, he now looked barely alive.

Macbeth smiled and nodded, too drained to frame a witty response.

"What happened out there?" Corbin asked without looking up from his cup.

"What do you mean?"

"You know what I mean. You had some kind of absence or altered state. The way you worked on the priest: very efficient, but very detached. What is it, John? Simple Partial Seizure epilepsy?"

Macbeth shook his head.

"Then what?"

"It's like SPS in some ways . . . I get derealization episodes. Depersonalization. I've had them all my life. Or as long as I can remember." Macbeth caught Corbin's expression and laughed tiredly. "Don't look at me like that."

"Like what?"

"Like you're assessing a patient."

"Have you sought help with this? Apart from self-diagnosis, I mean?"

"Of course I have. God knows how many scans and neuro-imaging. But unless an episode is actually taking place during imaging, it's almost impossible to isolate the cause. Temporal lobe epilepsy's been ruled out, they're not migraines, I don't have any lesions or tumors or edemas . . . Stress seems to bring it on, mostly. Like tonight. The weird thing is that it doesn't affect function. In fact, sometimes it even enhances it. If you're detached from a crisis you tend to respond calmly."

"No other symptoms? Other than the derealization, I mean."

"Nope." Macbeth made a face. "Well, I do tend to have lucid dreams more than most. Vivid and lucid."

"Not to the extent of confusing them with reality, I take it?" asked Corbin.

Macbeth laughed. "Going to write me a script for Thorazine, Doctor? No, like I said, my dreams tend to be lucid: when I'm dreaming I know I'm dreaming. Which I suppose, in itself, is quite unusual. But the nature of the dreams is odd too."

"In what way odd?"

"I don't dream about me. About my life. Most people's dreams can be traced back to experiences, worries or other stuff that's current in their minds. My dreams are about things I've read, things I've learned, instead of what's actually going on in my life – like I'm borrowing data to dream, instead of using my own emotions and memories. And I'm never *me* in the dreams. I'm always someone else who's somehow closer to the events I dream about." Macbeth laughed. "I actually dream in third person."

"You do realize that your dreaming style could be linked to your waking derealization episodes?"

"You think?" Macbeth made a sarcastic face.

"You know, John, if there's no underlying physical cause,

it may have a psychological basis. Maybe some kind of trauma . . ."

Macbeth laughed and shook his head. "Like what? I'm not bipolar or suffering from any form of anxiety disorder; I'm generally content with my lot, I had a happy childhood . . . Well, my mom died when I was really small, but I grew up accustomed to it and other than that, I've had a pretty stable and trauma-free life. Dull, almost."

"That you can remember," said Corbin, looking even more awkward. "Your memory . . . well, it's not the most reliable and that, in itself, could be indicative of you trying to distance yourself from something. Some kind of trauma you've buried."

Again Macbeth shook his head. "I think it's more to do with cognitive function. My recall is actually excellent, almost eidetic, when it comes to semantic memory. But my autobiographical memory is crap. It's real life I struggle with . . . It's something I work around. My brother Casey's the same. Not as bad, but his head is never in the here and now, either."

"Well," said Corbin. "If you ever need—"

"Thanks, Pete, I'll bear it in mind. But now that I've shown you mine, you show me yours."

"What do you mean?" asked Corbin.

Macbeth took a sip of his coffee and grimaced. "My God, do they use this stuff to get confessions?" He put the cup down. "I'm talking about you being so strung out and tired; about whatever it is that's going on with your work and that you spent half the evening avoiding talking about. And before he jumped, all of that stuff Gabriel was feeding you about angels and visions. I could have sworn he hit a nerve."

Corbin gazed into his coffee cup for a moment. "You've done some work with psychiatric epidemiology, right?" he asked. "I mean before you got into the brain-mapping thing?"

"Some, yeah. Why?"

"Well . . . I've never before come across case clustering like this. There's been this weird sudden upswing in presentations of a particular set of symptoms. Like some kind of outbreak. If I were a virologist or even an oncologist, I'd look for environmental factors to explain it, but that's just not something you come across that much as a psychiatrist."

"What's been presenting?" Macbeth asked.

"Delusions. More hallucinations than delusions, I suppose . . . and in people with no history of psychological or psychiatric problems."

"And the delusions are similar in nature?"

"Yeah. Completely different in content, but similar in nature. Visions. Ghosts."

"Ghosts?" Macbeth pushed a laugh through the curtain of his tiredness.

"Not just ghosts. All the presentations involve the subject seeing events, items or people from the past. The descriptions of the episodes all begin with a feeling like déjà vu, but instead of it remaining a sensation or a state of mind, they experience what can only be a hallucination, but is completely indistinguishable from reality."

"How many are we talking about?"

"Over five hundred in the last two months within Boston city limits."

"What? That's an average of eight or nine a day . . ." said Macbeth. "And the patients presenting . . . there's no obvious connection between them?"

"Nope. Different ages, ethnicities, classes, professions. The cases are spread out pretty evenly across Boston and there's no developmental timeline. No epidemiological evidence of a source. No Patient Zero."

"And you say the delusions are different in content?"

"One case was an elderly man. He's lived in the same house for the past forty years and his wife died five years ago. Retired Boston beat cop, not the neurotic type or given to emotion and a person of very regular routines: up at six-thirty every morning, breakfast at seven. Except he comes down one morning and finds his wife alive and well in the kitchen, preparing breakfast. But not his wife as she was before she died, but the way she had been when they first married and moved into the house. Like I said, this guy is not the emotional type, but seeing his long-lost bride nearly cracked him up."

"Yeah, well, Pete, you know only too well that seeing a recently deceased loved one, or hearing their voice, is by far the most common form of hallucination. And not a sign of any kind of mental health issue."

"But I told you – his wife's been dead for five years. She's not recently deceased, so why would he start to hallucinate her presence now? And bereavement hallucinations tend to be fleeting. This was sustained and vivid. And it wasn't just his young bride he saw . . . he swears the kitchen had changed back to the way it was when they first got married."

"Did he speak with his wife?" asked Macbeth. "Interact with her?"

"A common element of these hallucinations is that there's little or no interaction between the patient and the people or events visualized."

They both turned as a couple of uniformed cops came in noisily, making their way to the coffee machine.

"So the hallucination is purely visual?' Macbeth asked after they had gone.

"No . . . there's usually an auditory element. In fact, most describe the hallucination as a full sensory experience. The retired cop said he could smell the ham she was frying."

"But there's never any interaction?"

"No direct interaction, but occasionally a sense that the observed in the phenomenon is aware of the observer. Even that is very rare. Generally, the experience is described as like watching a scene being played out, like with the widower watching his wife prepare breakfast. But I did have this one case where the patient claims to have seen herself – but herself as she was over a decade earlier. She also claims that she actually recalls the event from the other point of view . . . the observed rather than the observer. She says she remembers nearly bumping into an older version of herself at exactly the same spot fifteen years before." Corbin broke off, reading something troubled in Macbeth's expression. "What is it?"

"Mmm? Nothing . . . it's just it reminds me of something. But it wasn't the same . . ." Macbeth shook the thought off. "It sounds to me like subjective Capgras Delusion."

"But it's not, John." Corbin shook his head in frustration. "This woman doesn't believe she saw a subjective double . . . that this other self is leading an independent life contemporaneous to hers. What she does believe is that the person she saw is wholly, completely *her*. An integrated identity, not a divided one. She believes that she saw herself from the past."

Macbeth examined his coffee cup. Corbin's description of the case troubled him; and it had reminded him of something: not a patient; something much closer to home. Eventually he said: "Maybe it's just that your patient has had this experience all those years ago, where she's seen someone who looked like an older version of herself, and the idea has lodged in her unconscious. Then, for whatever reason, it has manifested itself in this déjà vu type experience. I'm guessing you've ruled out schizophrenia?"

"No schizophrenia, no epilepsy, no psychotic depression, no neurological abnormalities . . . and, as far as I can see, no underlying medical conditions."

"It could simply be that she is a high-functioning, monothematic delusional, Pete. You know it happens – patients with perfectly normal everyday lives except for a single, very particular, very persistent obsession or delusion."

"But don't you see?" There was frustration in Corbin's tone.

"She's not delusional because she *knows* the event can't have happened. Anyway, it's not just her. A half-dozen cases are referred to me every week. It's always the same: the patient's upset because they've had a single, temporary delusional episode that they recognize as a hallucination – then life goes on as normal without any repetition of the event."

"So what are you saying? There's some kind of delusional bug going around?" Macbeth laughed. "Twenty-four-hour hallucinogenic flu?"

"Why not? It's like an epidemic. Maybe the cause does lie in a virus of some kind."

"Any reports from anywhere else? I mean outside Boston?"

"I've put out a Commonwealth-wide enquiry and been in touch with the federal statistical office, but haven't got anything back yet. You see, some of these cases are so . . ." he struggled for the word, " . . . so *subtle*, that they very nearly weren't reported. God knows how many more have just been dismissed or not even noticed. I mean, if you see a dog chasing a Frisbee in the park, you don't ask yourself if the dog or the Frisbee are really there or not."

"Know something?" said Macbeth. "I think I heard of another case. Just before we met up tonight, my taxi driver told me about a fare who yelled at him to stop because he thought he'd seen a kid in the middle of the road. But there was no kid. The fare was on his way to the Christian Science Church."

"Gabriel?"

Macbeth shrugged.

Corbin remained silent for a moment, bony shoulders hunched in his tweed jacket, elbows resting on the canteen table. "There's something else, John. Something much nearer to home. Literally."

"Okay . . ." said Macbeth. "Let's have it."

"It's not just the increased workload that's been running me ragged. I've not been sleeping much. Nor has Joanna. It's the house . . ."

"The one you're fixing up in Beacon Hill?"

"Yeah. And I don't mean the work or stress of fixing it up. I mean things that go bump in the night." He paused, looking at Macbeth almost as if judging whether he could trust him. "You remember the story I told you about the house? Marjorie Glaiston?"

"The society beauty's murder on your stairs? Yeah, I remember . . ."

Corbin leaned further forward, holding Macbeth in a steady gaze. "I know this sounds crazy, but I've heard her singing, at night. And laughing."

"What?"

"And there's more. I've seen her, John. Marjorie Glaiston."

"You're kidding me . . .' Macbeth laughed disbelievingly. "You're seriously telling me your new house is haunted? That you've seen a ghost?"

"No. Not a ghost. Ghosts don't exist. We both know that. What I experienced was a hallucination. I saw Marjorie Glaiston walk down the stairs. No dramatic scene, just her moving from the bedroom, down the stairs and into the living room, as she must have done countless times while she lived there. One of the most beautiful women I've ever seen. Except I could not possibly have seen her."

"God, Pete . . . it could be something and nothing, you know that. A combination of stress, lack of sleep and stuff you've read about the case and forgotten you read."

"Except for one thing: Joanna was standing beside me when I saw Marjorie Glaiston on our stairs. She saw her too, John. If this was a delusion, it was one I shared with my wife." Corbin held Macbeth with a gaze that was as earnest as his exhaustion would allow. "Whatever it is that's caused this epidemic of delusional episodes that I've been treating patients for over the last few months, Gabriel was right . . . I've got it too."

10

JOSH HOBERMAN. MARYLAND

The introduction was more than superfluous; it was ridiculous.

Of course Hoberman recognized the woman the instant she walked into the lounge room of the lodge. He had never met her before, never seen her in the flesh, but hers was one of the most famous faces in the world. Nevertheless, Jack Ward introduced her to Hoberman as Elizabeth Yates. President of the United States of America.

President Yates was taller than Hoberman had expected. And as she crossed the room to shake hands with him, she projected that amplified presence that the truly powerful seemed naturally to possess. She was fifty-six with hair dyed a shade that was obviously an attempt to match the strawberry blonde of her youth. She had clearly been a striking-looking woman, but her beauty had matured into an almost masculine handsomeness. The most impressive thing about her was her eyes: bright, crystalline blue; eyes that made even the most casual glance deeply penetrating and added yet more power to her presence.

She was dressed in a dark blue suit, as she habitually was. On one jacket lapel was a presidential pin, on the other an enameled stars and stripes. Suspended from the chain at her neck was the symbol that had caused most controversy. The cross that Hoberman knew the President now only wore in private.

For the third time, Hoberman was thanked for coming at such short notice at such an hour.

"I'm afraid I'm working to an even more challenging schedule than usual," she said, her voice deep and, despite the pre-campaign coaching, still tinged with her native Louisiana, as she lowered herself gracefully, purposefully, onto the sofa. "You can imagine that developments in Europe and the Middle East are making exceptional demands on my time."

"I'm sure they are, Madame President."

"You've read the information?"

"Yes, Ma'am, I have." Hoberman wondered if 'Ma'am' was the right form of address. He hadn't used it since eighth grade.

"So what is your professional opinion, Professor Hoberman? Do you think I'm a fruit-loop?"

"Fruit-loop? No, Madame President," said Hoberman. "Delusional, yes, to be frank, I think that is a possibility."

Hoberman looked to Ward for the expected retort. There was none. Nor from the President.

"If I am delusional," asked Yates, "does that mean I am, in your opinion, unstable? I mean, is this the precursor to something worse?"

"I can't answer that, at the moment," said Hoberman. "But we have to get this into perspective. Everyone has delusional episodes or hallucinations to some degree or another and of one type or another at some point in their life. You said yourself that you have a punishing schedule at the moment . . . Stress is the number-one trigger for episodes like this. Or you may simply have some kind of bug."

"As I told you in our briefing," said Ward, "the President has been in excellent health and certainly hasn't registered a high temperature. I think we need to look beyond the obvious, Professor Hoberman. We would not have gone to the trouble of bringing you here if we had not eliminated the usual suspects."

"I know you've ruled out a viral cause. I'm just making the point that very vivid and convincing hallucinations can be brought on by something as simple as the flu." Hoberman flicked through the dossier. "The first episode, two months ago . . . could you run through that again for me? I know it's all documented here, but I'd like to hear it in your own words."

"I was working late in the Oval Office – I actually spend less time in there than you would think, but that's where I hold all major meetings. I'd been discussing the European Union situation with the Secretary of State. When he left, I took a few minutes for prayer."

"This is part of your routine?"

"I pray four times a day, Professor Hoberman. I've been charged with the greatest responsibility, the most important office in the world. It's a charge for which I need a great deal of guidance."

"And you experienced this delusion shortly after completing your time of prayer?"

"I left the Oval Office and let my staff know I was going upstairs to the executive quarters. I was in the main hallway when I saw him."

"President Hoover."

"Yes."

"And you've seen other Presidents?"

"No . . . I mean, I'm not sure." Yates frowned. "Maybe. I was looking out through a window one day, down onto the lawn. I saw a portly man with a bushy mustache. He was in shirt-sleeves and with a small dog. When I asked security how he had been allowed access to the lawn they could find no trace of anyone. But the man I saw was dressed in an old-fashioned way. Collarless shirt, Paisley-pattern suspenders, that kind of thing. You know that already . . ." She nodded towards the dossier in Hoberman's hands.

"And you believe this man was Taft?"

"That's who he looked like. Yes, that's who I thought he was." Elizabeth Yates sighed. "It sounds bad, I know. But it's not like this happens every day. The thing is, I think I've seen other people as well . . . less important people who could not possibly have been there."

"How do you know they couldn't have been there?"

"I don't know . . . Their dress. Their demeanor. I can't explain it, but I can tell they're not from this time."

"President Taft famously kept a cow on the White House lawn. You didn't see that?"

"Are you trying to be funny, Professor Hoberman?"

"Not at all, Madame President. It helps determine the nature of the delusion . . . if you were seeing the expected – the stereotypical image, as it were – that would suggest it's generated entirely in your mind, rather than a misinterpretation of something that is actually there."

"No, Professor Hoberman," said Yates wearily. "No cows. And I haven't seen Ben Franklin flying a kite in a storm either."

Hoberman paused for a moment, fingers drumming on the dossier on his lap. "Do you see anyone other than Republicans, President Yates?"

"Now hold on . . ." Ward leaned forward in his seat. "This really is no joking matter."

"Again, Colonel Ward, it was not, in any way, meant as a joke," said Hoberman, nonplussed. "President Yates has expressed the desire for guidance in this weighty office. If the figures she has seen are of the same political persuasion, then it could simply be a transference of that desire for guidance. I take it you would never consider taking advice from a Democrat, Madame President?"

"You'd be right." She leaned back in the sofa, resting her elbows on the back and holding Hoberman in a steady, ice-blue stare. There was something practiced about the pose, about the confidence. "Am I mad, Professor Hoberman?"

"There's no such thing as mad. No psychiatric professional deals in absolutes like that. The human mind is an enormously varied and variable entity. I need to study the information Colonel Ward has given me on the incidents reported elsewhere. The question is whether you're suffering from a disorder or whether these episodes have been induced by some kind of hallucinogenic agent. But if you are suffering from a disorder, we need to establish what that disorder is, whether it's temporary or sustained, and how we can treat it." Hoberman squeezed out his most reassuring smile. "We'll get to the bottom of this, Ma'am."

"I shall pray that the Lord gives you the strength and the wisdom to do just that." Again she locked Hoberman in her ice-blue gaze. "I shall pray for you, Professor Hoberman."

11

MARY. VERMONT

The silver frame with the gilt edging.

Mary knew that the silver frame with the gilt edging always went to the far right of the dresser. It gleamed in the sunlight that cut a bright angle across the dining room, warming the polished wood of the floor, intensifying the reds and yellows of the spring flowers held by a sparkle of crystal on the windowsill. Like the corner piece of a jigsaw – the one that oriented the others and began the process of reassembling a fragmented picture – the silver frame with the gilt edging anchored the assembly of other pictures, allowing each to slot back into place once she had dusted it.

It wasn't just the silver frame with its gilt edging that fitted that particular picture for prominence: it was Mary and Joe's main wedding photograph, taken only two and a half years ago – Mary smiling with joy at having become Mrs Dechaud, still-uniformed Joe beaming with pride that he had come home from the Army to find Mary, the most beautiful girl in New England, dutifully and faithfully waiting to become his bride.

The far right of the dresser was where the photograph in the silver frame with the gilt edging always went. The place it belonged. Just so. Mary liked everything just so.

Most of the pictures were of Mary and Joe: the wedding, the honeymoon, one of Joe in uniform, trying but failing to look militarily stern. There were others of relatives: aunts, uncles, Mary's brother and his young family, a couple from Joe's side.

There was one picture, a color one of a smartly dressed but sad-faced old woman whom Mary could not place. It was no surprise that she'd lost track of who everyone was, as Joe's family was of biblical proportions: four sisters, two brothers, countless aunts, uncles, cousins . . . At the wedding, they had spilled over onto her side of the church, bolstering what now seemed to be her underrepresented lineage. Of course, growing up in the same small New England town, Joe and Mary had known each other's families, but the sheer scale of the Dechaud clan meant that there was kin, scattered across Rutland County and beyond, whom Mary had never encountered. Like the sad old lady in the photograph. Something about her resolved Mary to ask Joe exactly which of his relations she was.

Mary finished dusting the photographs and was about to go through to the kitchen to make some coffee when she noticed a speck on the silver candlestick that sat on the dining-room table. Joe's Aunt May had given them it as a wedding present and everyone had been amazed at her unaccustomed display of generosity. Joe's Aunt May was certainly not the sad old lady in the photograph on the dresser; she was a notoriously difficult woman, tall and lean with cold, pale green eyes that glittered argumentatively beneath what seemed a perpetual frown. Aunt May, with her sharp tongue and embittered views, was the focus of discord that every family seemed to have – seemed to need, almost. The navigation of uncharted familial waters was the one thing that Mary found difficult about being a new bride: finding herself adrift on the turbulent sea of generations-long established relationships, rifts, allegiances and history for which she had no compass. No, that wasn't true: Joe was her compass. Her lighthouse.

Joe, with his thick, auburn hair, large soft-brown eyes that were more boy than man, his deep, quiet voice and calming, gentle smile. When Joe smiled that way, Mary forgot all about the stresses of newly wedded life. Now, as she absent-mindedly rubbed at the candlestick to remove the tarnish, she was aware of the bright sparkle of their lives together, of the thousand promises their future held.

Theirs had been a truly traditional, even old-fashioned love story. Joe and Mary, whose birthdays fell within a week of each other, had known each other since elementary school, had been sweethearts since fifteen, had married at twenty, as soon as Joe had come back from overseas. It had been one of those things that everyone had expected to happen, the most natural thing in the world. As far as everyone in town was concerned, there was no Joe, no Mary . . . it was always Joe-and-Mary and it always would be. Together they were singular, not plural.

After the formality of a honeymoon in a Burlington hotel looking out over Lake Champlain, they had returned to what they really both wanted: to start their married lives together in the home they'd bought from Joe's uncle. Out of the Army, Joe had started work as a shift super at the marble quarry and Mary had set about making their new house their lasting home.

Mary frowned at the candlestick: she would have to use a silver cloth on it. Maybe it wasn't new as Aunt May had claimed, but second-hand. New or old, Mary didn't much care for the piece, but it was odd that the tarnished spot looked established and was so difficult to shift.

Shrugging, she replaced the candlestick, turning it so the tarnish faced away from the window's daylight. Before heading into the kitchen, she called through to Joe – it being a weekend morning, he would be in his study, hunched over the newspaper – and told him she was going to make coffee. As Mary filled the pot from the faucet, she looked out through the window above the sink. The house was elevated on a hill and from this window she could see out over the gentle humps of forest and field with nothing to shade the house from the spring sun. It was her favorite place to stand and contemplate her contentment. As she was happy to admit, Mary was a young woman of modest ambition and had here everything she could ever want. She knew that Joe felt the same.

She watched the car approaching. She had spotted it after she had put on the coffee and turned back to the window. With only a handful of houses scattered along this stretch of back road, an approaching car more often than not signaled an impending visit. Mary watched the car as it came up North Road then took a turn onto the long driveway up to the house.

"Joe . . ." she called out over her shoulder. "We've got company . . ."

Mary took off her apron and hung it on the kitchen hook before making her way to the front door, again calling for Joe as she did so. She stopped at the hallway mirror to check her hair before stepping out onto the porch.

The grief hit her instantly, totally, devastatingly. As it always did.

Twenty-three-year-old newly-wed Mary Dechaud looked into the mirror and an eighty-four-year-old reflection looked back at her. For the shortest sliver of time, she didn't recognize her reflection in the same way she hadn't recognized herself as the sad, lonely looking old woman in the photograph on the dresser. Mary clasped her hand over her mouth to stifle her cry and the old woman in the mirror did the same. She remembered. In that instant, it all came back to her, as it always did in these painful, searing moments of recall. She turned in the direction of the study to call again for Joe, but stopped herself. Joe was not there.

Mary took a moment to look at the newspaper, neatly folded and masthead upwards on the hall stand beneath the clock, smoothed flat her skirt with hands on which she now saw the marks of age, the thickened knuckles, the blue veins beneath parchment skin, and opened the door and stepped out into the sunlight to meet her two sons, who she now remembered had arranged to come and visit. She grasped the porch rail and leaned on it, simultaneously steadying posture and composure, quietly absorbing the impact of more than half a century suddenly remembered.

"No one is forcing you to leave," said George. "It's just that, well, the way your memory has been of late, both Jim and I think you'd be better off with someone to help you if you need help." George, as usual, did all of the talking while James leaned back in the couch, quiet. It was odd, she thought as she poured them both coffee, how inheritances could be split like that. George looked so very much like his father – the same auburn hair and large, soft eyes – but that was where the similarity ended. James, who outwardly looked nothing like Joe, was his twin internally: gentle, caring, kind. George, in contrast, had collected traits from somewhere else in his genetic background; traits that made him pushy, aggressive, domineering. Throughout his life, George's pleasant looks had been protection and disguise for his inner meanness. Mary knew that the expensive European car parked outside would be his – he had made his way in life by pushing others around or out of his way. He had started with his brother.

Mary thought again about Joe's Aunt May – maybe that's where George got his character, or at least part of it. She felt a rising panic when she remembered how she had puzzled over the tarnish on Aunt May's newly gifted candlestick when it had really sat on the same table, in the same place, for sixty years.

"What do you think, James?" she asked her older son.

"I worry about you here too, Mom. There's no one around for quarter of a mile. If you fell, or got confused . . ." James stumbled over the last part. Mary's memory – the increasingly long periods where the distant and the long-ago became the immediate and present – was the reason for her sons' visit.

"But this is our house . . . your dad's and mine." Mary checked herself when she started to look in the direction of Joe's study.

They were looking for signs, she knew that; small indications of her losing her marbles.

"Dad's been gone fifteen years, Mom." James leaned forward, placing his hand on hers. "You're all on your own here and we worry about you."

"I'm just fine." She smiled. He was a good boy. She tried to recall whom it was he had married and who his children – her grandchildren – were, but couldn't remember. "I know I've problems with my memory, but that's just getting older, that's all."

"What day is it, Mom?" asked George in that nasty, insistent tone he used. "Or month? What year is it, Mom?"

She answered him, giving the exact day and date. In the same way she had a notebook with the names of the current and last three presidents, Mary had a newspaper delivered every day and left it beneath the clock, masthead up, on the hall stand next to the door. Should someone come, she could tell them the time, the day and the date. All she had to do was remember for as long as it took them to ask. Her sons, and sometimes George's wife, a hard-faced, pushy woman whose name escaped her, had called regularly of late, and Mary had the feeling of constantly being tested. She had developed strategies to disguise her memory's increasing flaws.

"We'll leave you these to look at." George laid three brochures, all gloss, dark Florida tans and bright denture grins, on the coffee table. "Will you at least think it over?"

Mary told them she would. Something sat leaden and dull in her chest: despite all of her strategies, all her protests, she knew that her memory was getting worse. A lot worse than either of her sons imagined. No one knew about the long periods she spent living in her past, unaware it was not her present.

"I'll think it over," she said, taking the brochures and coffee cups and setting them in the kitchen.

*

She stood at the kitchen window and watched George's expensive car glide down the drive, out onto North Road and back towards town. Her heart remained heavy as she watched the sun sink lower in the sky, repainting the canvas of forest-covered hills with a warmer palette. She couldn't go on like this. She knew she'd have to leave her home of sixty years and would never again stand at this window, looking out over the hills and fields.

She'd phone James in the morning. Not George, James.

The strangest sensation came over her in the space of a heartbeat. Suddenly dizzy, Mary had to steady herself by gripping the sink's edge. An indistinct, motiveless panic stirred as she was seized by the most powerful feeling of déjà vu she had ever experienced. Her heart picked up pace as she was gripped by a fear that she was having some kind of attack. A stroke. Closing her eyes, she took deep breaths, forcing herself to be calm.

She opened them again.

The sunset was now midday sun. So bright it hurt her eyes. Spring was now summer. She straightened up from the sink and looked out over her favorite view. It was still her favorite view, but it was changed.

It was changed back.

There were more trees and fewer fields: thirty years back, a large part of the forest fringing the road had been cleared to extend the Fisher farm and planted with alfalfa. The forest had restored itself, full and dark and complete, reconquering lost ground.

"Oh dear, no . . ." Mary said to the empty kitchen. She knew she was back in the past. Her condition must be getting worse and she had sunk back into distant memories as her mind slowly and inexorably folded in on itself.

But that wasn't it. She remembered everything.

Mary remembered that James and George had just been here,

that George had driven up in his fancy European car, that they had left the brochures for her to look at, and that she had decided to leave her home of sixty years so that her body could be looked after while her consciousness, her awareness of the world, slowly evaporated.

She reached over to where she'd laid down the brochures, but they were gone. The coffee pot she had bought ten years ago was gone too, and had been replaced with the old one she had used all her married life until the pale blue enamel had all but flaked to nothing. Except someone had re-enameled it and it shone like new. She looked around the kitchen. Everything had been changed: decades of replacement undone, originals returned to their place and the kitchen gleamed with new-old stuff.

This was no trick of her mind. She wasn't wrapped up in her own memories and recreating the past. This *was* the past.

Mary crossed through the dining room on her way to the front door, stopping to check the ugly candlestick Aunt May had given her and Joe sixty years ago. The tarnished fleck on the neck of the candlestick was gone and the silver gleamed flawlessly. What was happening? She could understand her earlier confusion: her mind turning back time while the things around her remaining objective proofs of her true chronology; but this time it was her mind that remained anchored in reality while everything around her had changed.

This wasn't her. This was the world. Something was happening that had nothing to do with her memory problems. Something was really happening to the world around her . . .

Mary heard a voice calling her name. A voice that had lived only in her head for the last fifteen years. She ran through to the hallway and made to open the door but suddenly froze, her hand on the unturned handle. The mirror was to her right.

She turned to it.

Mary Dechaud, the eighty-four-year-old woman, looked into

the mirror and a twenty-three-year-old girl, slim-waisted and lithe, with thick dark-blonde hair framing a pretty, girlish face, looked back at her. Mary lifted her hand in front of her face and examined it, first the palm, then the back. Clear, unblemished, unwrinkled skin; long, slender fingers.

The voice outside called again and she threw open the door, running out onto the porch and waving to the young man with auburn hair and an easy expression as he made his way up from the road end where Dave Gundersson always dropped him off after his shift at the quarry.

It was Joe.

It was Joe smiling and waving as he came home.

When it was over, when the déjà vu subsided, the sky darkened and the world – and her reflection in the mirror – restored itself to the present, Mary sat in the living room and thought about what had happened. She didn't try to make sense of it, just thought about the experience itself. The wonder of it.

After an hour or so, Mary Dechaud picked up the phone and called James. She told him gently and calmly that she had decided she was, after all, going to stay in her own home. She would remain there until the day she died; the day she would be with their father again.

Once she had hung up the phone, Mary tried to remember why it was she was in the dining room. It must have been because she meant to dust the photographs on the dresser, because she couldn't remember the last time she had dusted them.

She started with the silver frame with the gilt edging.

12

JOHN MACBETH. BOSTON

Corbin phoned Macbeth the next day, relaying the information the police and the hospital had given him. After further extensive surgery, the priest was back in ICU — it was by no means certain that he would pull through and his survival thus far had been attributed to Macbeth's actions at the scene.

"By the way," said Corbin, "the jumper . . . his name really was Gabriel. Gabriel Rees. He seems to have been some kind of academic high-flyer. Shit . . ." Corbin cursed his clumsiness. "I didn't mean it like that. Poor bastard."

"I know you didn't. High-flyer in what?"

"Particle physics. Doctoral postgrad at MIT. Isn't that your brother Casey's field?"

"Yeah," said Macbeth. "Maybe Casey knew him. I'll ask when I see him later today. Did the police tell you anything else?"

"Just that he'd no history of mental illness or drug abuse. Not on record, anyway. Exceptionally bright, though. Super-high IQ; but there again, that's pretty much par for the course in that field."

"I guess," said Macbeth, thinking about how his brother shared his IQ, but had been gifted with an infinitely more elegant, more graceful mind.

There was a pause then Corbin said tentatively, "Listen John, what I told you last night . . . about the house . . . do you think I'm crazy?"

"No, of course not. What you experienced sounds like the

same thing patients have been presenting, just like you said. Maybe it really is viral in origin."

They chatted for a while before Macbeth rang off with a promise to keep in touch. He hung the 'Do not disturb' sign on his hotel-room door and lay on his bed for most of the afternoon, staring up at the ceiling, trying not to listen to sounds from beyond the room or think much about anything, and least of all about the events of the previous night.

Eventually his tiredness overcame him and Macbeth fell asleep.

"This is a dream," a voice he recognized told him, even though he couldn't see who had spoken.

"I know that," he replied, unconcerned. "I know I am dreaming. I always know when I am dreaming."

Macbeth found himself standing outside a house and he knew he was in Beacon Hill. It was one of those grand five-story Colonial terraced townhouses with the bay fronts and white stucco around the doors and windows. Louisburg Square . . . he was standing in the street at Louisburg Square. Behind him, he knew without turning, was the little manicured private park with the small statues of Christopher Columbus and Aristides the Just.

He dreamed he stood outside the house on a cobbled street empty of cars. There was a surreal calm to the day and the unmoving air around him felt more indoors than outdoors. Walking up the steps to a front door that swung open at the slightest touch of his fingertips, he entered the main hallway. The house was still a single dwelling, not divided into condos the way many had been over the years. Macbeth knew where he was: the house that Corbin had bought. He also knew *when* he was: a different time, long before Corbin had bought the house.

Stopping at the bottom of the stairs, he rested his hand on the mahogany pommel on the handrail post, the wood feeling warm, as if alive beneath his touch, the hall bright around him.

Macbeth smiled as she came into view at the top of the stairs. Marjorie Glaiston.

She was, without doubt, the most beautiful woman he had ever seen, just as Corbin had said: slender and elegant and her gathered-up hair was a rich gold color. She wore a pale cream ankle-length dress detailed in lace and with a peacock's-eye brooch at her throat. The swirl of emerald and turquoise in the brooch complemented the dazzling blue-green of her large, beautiful eyes. She smiled at Macbeth as if she had been expecting him, her cheeks dimpling, and started to make her way down the stairs.

A man appeared on the landing behind her. Large, broad-shouldered, with massive, ugly hands, his complexion ruddy and his auburn hair and beard framing his face with dark red fire. There was a cruel, hard handsomeness to his features and something terribly dark and violent lurked in his expression. Just as he had known the woman was Marjorie Glaiston, Macbeth knew that the man he was looking at was Geoffrey Morgan.

He wanted to call out – to warn Marjorie as Morgan started to take slow, purposeful steps down the stairs towards her, carrying his dark fury with him – but he found he could not. Unlike his experience at Christian Science Plaza, where he had worked on the injured priest and had felt himself completely detached from the experience, Macbeth felt totally involved with this reality he knew wasn't true reality. Yet he stood frozen, his hand glued to the handrail post, his voice lost to him, as Morgan closed the distance between himself and Marjorie, his huge hands lifting from his sides and reaching towards her.

"You know what's coming, don't you?" The voice he had heard before spoke again into Macbeth's ear and he turned to see standing behind him the naked, broken-crooked body of Gabriel Rees, the man who had jumped to his death. Gabriel smiled and Macbeth noticed that one eyelid was still half closed. "Just like you knew what was going to happen on the roof – the only one other than me who knew – you know exactly what is going to happen here, don't you?"

Macbeth nodded and turned back to see Morgan seize Marjorie. He screamed a scream that made no sound, that failed to part his tight-sealed lips, as Morgan's heavy fingers closed on Marjorie's slender neck. It was as if she hadn't noticed: she still held Macbeth in her unwavering gaze as subconjunctival hemorrhages turned the whites of her beautiful eyes blood-red; her smile for him remained, the dimples still there in the fair cheeks while petechial spots bloomed purple-red as capillaries ruptured under the skin.

Morgan let go an inhuman scream as he crushed and twisted the life from his unfaithful lover: a long, roaring, animal cry of fury and pain and despair. When he let her go, Marjorie tumbled like a rag doll, lifeless and loose, down the stairs and came to rest at Macbeth's feet.

"How real does this seem to you?" asked Gabriel, conversationally. "You're dreaming, but it seems more real than when you're awake, doesn't it? Do I seem more real to you than I did on the roof?"

Macbeth still had no voice to answer Gabriel; instead he raised his silent, accusing gaze back to Morgan, who stood where he had killed Marjorie, his brow dappled with sweat, his eyes still burning, the huge murderous hands hanging at his sides. Then, moving slowly, Morgan reached into the pocket of his tweed waistcoat and pulled out a small derringer pistol. Taking each slow, deliberate step as if his feet were made of lead, he came down the stairs, holding the palm gun at full arm's stretch until he stood in front of Macbeth, towering over him. Morgan pushed the cold, hard steel of the short barrel against Macbeth's forehead.

And pulled the trigger.

Macbeth found himself again looking up at the ceiling of his hotel room. His awakening had been swift but not sudden and something of the dream lingered, as if Morgan's brooding malevolence loitered in some corner of Macbeth's waking world, for a few moments. But he was not afraid. No sweats, no shaking. Despite its horrors, the dream had left him strangely calm.

Corbin sounded surprised to hear Macbeth on the phone so soon after their last conversation.

"The house in Beacon Hill you're doing up . . ." asked Macbeth. "Is it in Louisburg Square?"

Corbin laughed. "Louisburg Square? How much do you think they're paying me at Belmont? I know I told you Joanna's folks were rich, but they're not the Rothschilds. Our place is on Garden Street. Why are you asking?"

"I thought I'd look into the Marjorie Glaiston story," lied Macbeth, not wanting to tell Corbin about his dream.

"I see," said Corbin. "You'll find stuff about Marjorie Glaiston on the Internet; that's where I found the story."

"And you're sure you didn't see a picture of Marjorie before the episode?"

"Do you mean before I saw her on the stairs?" said Corbin. "No, like I told you, it was after. The pictures I found were a match for the person I saw . . . imagined I saw . . . on the stairs. But what you said last night made sense: I couldn't have seen an accurate image of her in a hallucination before having seen what she looked like in real life. I must've seen her picture somewhere before without remembering it."

"It's the obvious explanation," said Macbeth, not wanting to share that he had put a face to Marjorie Glaiston in his own dream. "Anyway, I'll check it out. Let me know if you hear anything more from the cops about Gabriel or how the priest is doing."

Macbeth was annoyed that he was relieved.

Not the Marjorie Glaiston he had dreamt about. He looked at the face on the screen of his laptop and knew it was not the face he had seen in his dream. The real Marjorie Glaiston had had raven-black hair, not blonde, and although her outstanding beauty was equal to that of the woman in his dream, it was of a different kind: dark, arch, smoldering; vaguely wicked. The image he had found had been a portrait painted by her murderer, Geoffrey Morgan. Another picture – a grainy, primly posed black-and-white society photograph – confirmed the accuracy of Morgan's canvas capturing of lover and muse. Macbeth could see that this Marjorie Glaiston had been the kind of woman to drive men out of their senses with lust and envy.

What the hell had he expected to find when searching the Internet for an image of Marjorie Glaiston? Proof that he had developed some kind of psychic link with the long-dead? Even if the face had been the same, it would simply be, just like with Corbin, a case of cryptomnesia – a forgotten memory uncon-sciously remembered. He was a psychiatrist, after all, and knew that there were few mysteries that could not be answered by looking at the one-hundred-billion-neuron-packed, three-pound-weight human brain: each individual brain a complete universe of inexplicable complexity.

But the picture Macbeth found of Geoffrey Morgan did shake him. It wasn't quite the face of the murderer his sleeping brain had invented, but there were distinct similarities: a broad, pale brow above darkly brooding eyes and framed with thick hair and beard. And although his hair looked black in the photo-graph, the description in the text told him that Morgan had, indeed, possessed a head of dark red hair. But, Macbeth told himself, it was not a stretch to imagine a violent, brooding Irish painter with some kind of accuracy.

After he showered and dressed, Macbeth sent an SMS to Casey to confirm their meeting at seven and got an almost instant reply.

During his stay in Boston he had spent as much time with

his brother as possible; Casey had, of course, made the offer that Macbeth could stay with him for as long as he was in Boston, but they had both known that Macbeth would say no: his environment had to be of his choosing.

Macbeth felt good that he was seeing his brother that evening: he was still tired and emotionally drained by everything that had happened in the previous eighteen hours, but Casey always managed to brighten his moods. Looking through the hotel-room window, Macbeth could see that a warm, bright day had taken shape beyond the glass and he decided to take a walk to shake off his lethargy.

The cab dropped him at the Tremont Street entrance to the Common. Macbeth knew he had come here for more than a stroll in the park: Louisburg Square was less than a three-minute walk away on the other side of the Common. Again he became angry at his own folly, knowing he would end up standing in the spot he had stood in his dream, convincing himself . . . convincing himself of what?

Getting out of the taxi, Macbeth felt the effects of stress and lack of sleep take the form of a vague but pervasive déjà vu. It was a feeling he had experienced a lot, throughout his life, and he hated it, mainly because it often preceded one of his episodes. He shook it off and headed into the Common.

A small, rectangular box of a building stood at the Common's entry, looking like some Art Deco mausoleum. It was actually the exit from Boylston T Station and housed the head of the stairwell that led up from the subway. As he passed, Macbeth saw workers in Transit Authority uniforms using brushes and a spray tank of cleaning solution to scrub off a graffito that had been sprayed onto the side wall of the usually pristine station building. The words, in a deep red impervious to the workers' chemicals and scouring, were still legible on the building's flank.

We are becoming . . .

Ellipsis included. He'd seen the line all over Copenhagen, in both English and Danish, as well as here in Boston. It was probably just a line from some pop song, but Macbeth found it strangely profound and laughed to himself at the thought of gangs of philosophers prowling the streets of Boston in corduroys and backwards hip-hop hats.

Nodding hello to one of the workers who in turn ignored him, Macbeth walked on, along the main path through the Common. He mused his way through the park, sinking deep into his thoughts and only half-aware of his surroundings. Despite the sunshine and the sounds of play and laughter drifting from various corners of the park, Macbeth found himself haunted by the dark of the night before.

He didn't know how far he had walked when the nearer-at-hand noise of barking and laughing snapped him from his thoughts and drew his attention to a group of pre-teen girls throwing a Frisbee to each other above the head of a leaping, overexcited dog. The girls were running about and moving with that early-adolescent carelessness that would all too soon be gone, making such innocent activities uncool and childish. The scene sparked a melancholic feeling that seemed to intensify his déjà vu, and in that moment, he resented their innocence and carefreeness. But Macbeth the psychiatrist knew that childhood was often anything but innocent and carefree, and he walked on.

It was pleasant and warm and the sun through the trees danced and dappled the path, but he still could not place himself in the moment and the vague feeling of déjà vu followed him through the Common. Again his thoughts forced him back to the dark roof of the Christian Science Church. What had chilled him most was the calm – the certainty – in Gabriel's expression as he threw himself and Father Mullachy over the parapet edge.

As he and the others had run to the roof edge, Macbeth had

half-expected Gabriel and the priest to have disappeared, as if it made as much sense for them to have vanished into thin air as it did for them to lie smashed on the ground below. Like Schrödinger's Cat, maybe Gabriel hadn't been definitely, definitively dead until Macbeth saw his body.

Macbeth didn't know how far he had walked. He was, as always, deep in thought and only half-aware of his surroundings as he made his way along the path through the Common. The nearer-at-hand noise of barking and laughing drew his attention to a group of pre-teen girls throwing a Frisbee to each other above the head of a leaping, overexcited dog. The scene sparked a melancholic feeling that seemed to intensify his déjà vu and, in that moment, he resented their innocence and freedom from care. The girls were running about and moving with that early-adolescent carefreeness that would all too soon be gone, making such innocent activities uncool and—

Macbeth stopped dead in the path.

This had all just happened. He had seen all this, had had exactly the same thoughts, only minutes before.

He stared at the playing girls, at the park, at the trees and the sun coming through them, at the overexcited dog. Macbeth had learned to live with his bizarre memory, his dissonant sense of time and his habit of detaching himself completely from the moment and becoming lost somewhere outside time and place. Countless appointments had been missed, countless destinations arrived at with no sense of transit from his point of departure.

But this was different.

He had been here, exactly this same spot in the Common, minutes before. He had walked – moved on – but somehow now found himself back. It was absurd, but it was more than a spatial absurdity: not only was he back in the same place, he was back in the same moment. In the same thoughts. The same dull envy of the girls' innocent, careless youth; the same feeling of déjà vu.

Seeing him standing there, the girls stopped playing and stared back suspiciously. They could see him, meaning this was no delusion. He wasn't observing a past event, and he couldn't have witnessed a future event minutes ago. So what the hell just happened?

Déjà vu. That's all it was, he told himself. Déjà vu made particularly acute because of the stressful events of the last twenty-four hours. That must be it. Or some other short-circuit between his prefrontal cortex and medial temporal lobe, creating the illusion of having remembered something. Again he thought back to the Christian Science roof and Gabriel questioning his own memory of having been on the roof fifteen minutes before.

Avoiding the suspicious gaze of the now huddled-together girls, Macbeth walked on, sinking deep back into his mind again, but trying not to think about what had just happened.

As he knew he would, Macbeth found himself on the corner of Mount Vernon and Louisburg. He made his way along the Square to where the house he had dreamed about stood. His pace was slower now; an itchy small trickle of tepid sweat in the nape of his neck telling him he must have walked quickly from the Common, as he tended to do whenever his mind was occupied, which was most of the time.

Unlike in his dream, the building had been subdivided into luxury condos. But there were other differences: significant, structural differences from the house in his dream. As he stood before it, he tried to work out both why he had dreamed about this particular house and why he seemed to have a need to validate his dream in some way. After all, this wasn't the house Corbin had bought, the house in which Marjorie Glaiston really had been murdered. Perhaps it was simply that Louisburg Square represented the stereotype of historical properties in Beacon Hill. Yet this house seemed so familiar. Maybe he had

104

seen it before, in childhood even, the memory idealized then lost, only to be stimulated years later by Corbin's talk of his new home.

Macbeth's dream and Corbin's hallucination were both fictions – simulations generated by the brain grown from some seed in reality. But they were very different processes and came from completely different places. He couldn't really understand why he had come across town to find some connection between them. Like his relief at seeing the 'real' Marjorie Glaiston, it annoyed him that he had wasted time proving what he had known rationally all along.

Macbeth retraced his earlier route through the Common. No déjà vu, no inexplicable reprises. Reaching the Tremont exit, he was about to cross the street when something drew him back into the Common. He was vaguely aware that he was attracting suspicious glances from passers-by as he stood close to the Boylston T station building, scrutinizing its smooth wall.

No graffito. No red legend of *We are becoming* . . . No trace of any spray paint or of the chemicals used to clean stone that was now cool and dry to the touch.

Maybe, he thought, in the forty or so minutes that had passed since he had first entered the park, the Transit Authority team had managed to clean the spray paint off without leaving the slightest trace and had then used some kind of blower to dry out the wall.

But it wasn't like that. More as if the graffito had never been there.

13

GEORG POULSEN. COPENHAGEN

As was his Saturday afternoon custom, Georg Poulsen sat and read to his wife.

It was the way they spent every Saturday afternoon; the way they spent most evenings when he was free from work. Margarethe Poulsen had always loved books, had always described them as her 'other world': an alternate universe into which she could escape when the stresses of the real world got too much. Georg Poulsen was only too happy to abet her escape by reading from her favorite books. Georg Poulsen loved his wife very much.

In particular, Margarethe had a passion for surreal fiction – not science fiction or fantasy-type pulp, but literary magical realism.

"I don't understand why people need to read about other worlds to discover magic," she had once told her husband, "when it is all around us. Reality is the greatest magic of all when you have the eyes to see."

It had surprised Poulsen, but had also filled him with admiration, to discover that his wife – who as an engineer was so grounded in the classical physics of the everyday world – could still see in the universe boundless potential for limitless interpretation.

Margarethe had an especial love of Kafka, Gogol, Zamyatin and the French author Raymond Roussel. Poulsen couldn't understand why Margarethe enjoyed Roussel so much, but she had explained that a writer who committed suicide not out of despair but simply to find out 'what death was like' was someone whose perceptions of reality she would like to read.

And that was what he read to her now: Roussel's fantastical *Locus Solus*. As he read, Poulsen felt an enormous pressure to invest as much into his delivery as possible, to make the characters live for his wife. It was not something that came to him naturally, but he had read to her so often that he'd become skilled at adding drama to the lines he delivered. This was more difficult with *Locus Solus* because there was no Danish translation and Poulsen had to read from an English edition. But as he made his way through the surreal world of the novel – the eponymous country estate of Martial Canterel, filled like a fairground with bizarre and unworldly attractions – Poulsen felt a growing understanding of his wife's attraction to Roussel.

The author was certainly skilled at placing impossible yet indelible images in the mind of the reader. One such image was that of the talking, moving but disembodied head of the long-dead Danton, suspended in the mysterious, sparkling medium of *aqua micans*, in which also swam a completely hairless Siamese cat that operated the controls to agitate Danton's head to life. But what really captured Poulsen's attention was the description of Canterel leading his guests into the mysterious glass diamond at the heart of his estate. There, under the glass, was a sequence of eight tableaux vivants. In each tableau, performers acted out a set scene before a small audience for whom the performance clearly had some emotional significance. Canterel then revealed to his guests that the actors in each tableau were the corpses of the recently dead, and that he had discovered two mysterious substances, *resurrectine* and *vitalium*, to bring them back to life. However, the effect of the injected fluids was that the reanimated corpses were condemned to play out the most important event of their lives, and nothing else, over and over again, for ever.

Ridiculous as the scenario was, Poulsen found himself

wondering as he read if the perpetually repetitious and amnesiac consciousness of Roussel's reanimated dead represented a lesser form of existence, or whether it was no different from moving from one moment to the next in real life. He also wondered if they would experience a feeling of déjà vu as they acted out a scene they had performed once in real life and countless forgotten times in their post-mortem tableau.

Georg Poulsen was a man of measure: in his work, in his life, in his approach to other people, he dealt in discrete, mensurable proportions. So, when he had completed the fourth of the chapters, Poulsen put the book down on the side table. He sat and chatted with his wife about his day, most importantly about the progress that was being made with the Project. The hope it offered. As usual, he talked, she listened.

Margarethe Poulsen had always been a fine-looking woman. He was reminded of that fact every time he took in her aristocratic profile. The very first time he had seen Margarethe, he had taken her for the spoiled daughter of some old-family landowner. Denmark was a culture with a rigorously egalitarian ethic and Poulsen guessed that the pretty young undergraduate's haughtiness would have won her few friends among her fellow students. Yet he remained drawn to her, attracted not just by her beauty, but by the very odd and persistent feeling that he had seen her, known her, from somewhere before.

It had only been after Poulsen had plucked up the courage to speak to her that he discovered Margarethe was really a modest, almost shy young woman. She was studying engineering and, far from being aristocratic, was of humble rural origins. Where Poulsen was a Zealander, from just outside Copenhagen, Margarethe was a country girl from Fyn. Poulsen often thought that the only people Danes mistrusted more than Swedes were each other: Jutlanders viewed Copenhageners as arrogant; Zealanders saw Jutlanders as dour and intellectually pedestrian;

both considered Fyn backwardly bucolic but shared an affection for the island's gentle beauty.

Margarethe's father was an engineer, her mother an elementary school teacher. Typical of *Fynboerne*, Margarethe's parents were open, friendly people and Georg soon realized that they simply wanted the best for their only child; and that they saw him as the best for her.

Georg and Margarethe had soon become inseparable. Theirs had been a touching of minds, of dreams, of mood and belief. Both had become involved in their respective disciplines – he physics and computing sciences, she engineering – with that very Danish impulse to be of service, to do something to improve the human experience.

For the first ten years of their married life, they moved around Europe and from university to university as Poulsen's career had dictated, with one eighteen-month stay in the US, Margarethe finding work lecturing in engineering. The focus had been on Poulsen's career, though: he had become an acknowledged expert on artificial intelligence and most of his research was devoted to finding new and better ways for humans to interact with computers.

When, after a decade of trying, Margarethe told him she was expecting their first child, Poulsen had been beside himself with joy. He remembered that day; how he had stood in the gleam of an imagined future and had felt that the world was just too good, too perfect to be real.

Personal joy was soon matched by professional pride: the University of Copenhagen asked him to head a multidisciplinary team to work on a major new international project. The aim was to replicate the cognitive states and functions of the human brain. The University hoped to have the project started within two years: a similar enterprise had been running in Düsseldorf since 2011, the Blue Brain Project in Switzerland as far back as 2005, and brain mapping was fast becoming the Space Race of cognitive and computing sciences. But the Copenhagen Project was by far the most ambitious: eighty-six billion virtual neurons and a complete, simulated limbic system. An entire human brain, built cell-by-cell in a computer simulation, completely indistinguishable from the real thing. A brain that would think for itself.

It was the computational challenge of the century, and Georg Poulsen had it handed to him.

Professionally, personally, in every way possible, Georg Poulsen had been a happy man.

One evening, two weeks after Margarethe's announcement, they spent the evening with their oldest friends, who had a house near the haven in Skovshoved. It had been a warm, cloudless summer evening and Poulsen had taken the shore road home, turning into Kystvejen and heading back towards the city. Margarethe had sat quietly in the passenger seat, contentedly looking out over the dark waters of the Øresund. It was often so between them: a happy silence in which everything seemed spoken.

Georg Poulsen, a truly happy man, pulled up at the traffic lights at the Charlottenlund Park.

It had taken him nearly a month to wake up. Or at least wake up fully.

Once, during a television debate with a neuroscientist and some kind of woo-woo religious type, Poulsen had argued that not only was the concept of the 'soul' a scientific nonsense, but there was no such single identifiable thing as the mind. He asserted that the root of the human experience was merely consciousness – and that consciousness was tuned into and out of as the physical structures of the brain develop complexity in childhood and adolescence, and unravel in late life or with illness or damage. There was no solid state of mind, he had said, only a flux of cognition and awareness. We were simply, he had argued, more 'here' at some times than at others.

Georg Poulsen's own restoring consciousness had been in flux for a week before he finally broke through and back into the world. There had been temporary, vague resurfacings but, three weeks and four days after he had been waiting for the Charlottenlund Park traffic signal to change, Poulsen rejoined the world.

The news was delivered to him in stages and with deliberate care, the young doctor making sure he understood each piece of information. He was in unit RH4131, she told him, the acute care unit of the Rigshospitalet in Copenhagen. He had been in a traffic accident and had been seriously injured. A truck had run into the back of his car. His skull had been fractured and he had suffered a contrecoup cerebral contusion, which had forced the medical staff to keep him in an induced coma for three weeks. She told him that he had also suffered a minor pulmonary contusion, but that had resolved itself.

Poulsen had listened, tried to wrest meaning from the facts, then had struggled to speak, his mouth dry and furred, his tongue leaden. Eventually he got one word out, the only word on his mind.

"Margarethe?" the doctor had repeated. "Your wife? She has suffered similar injuries to you and is also being treated here."

He had wanted to ask more, to ask about the baby, but he drifted back out of the room, out of the here and now, his consciousness tuning out once more.

They gave him the full news three days later, when he was fully awake and able to sit and had been transferred to a general ward.

"We can take you to see her," the duty doctor explained. "She's in the Neurophysiology Unit."

Poulsen was put in a wheelchair and pushed through the hospital by an orderly and a nurse who could answer none of his questions about his wife. After checking in at the unit's desk, the nurse took him along a corridor of doors and into a room. The window blinds were all but closed and the only lighting was above the bed in which a figure lay, its breathing being done for it by a machine. The room, the figure in the bed, the whole situation suddenly felt completely unreal to Poulsen and for a moment he wondered if he was still in a coma himself, dreaming these horrors. Perhaps it was he who lay on the bed, immobile and his existence sustained by technology, and he was watching himself with some separated splinter of his own mind.

A tall, lean, dark-haired man in his forties, dressed in a surgical coat and professional manner, came into the room and introduced himself as Dr Larssen.

"Is she in a coma?" Poulsen asked.

With gentle authority, the physician guided Poulsen back into the corridor and out of Margarethe's earshot.

"Your wife has experienced a severe closed-head injury," Larssen explained. "There was no skull fracture but she suffered the same kind of coup-contrecoup injury that you are recovering from." Larssen paused. It was the type of professional pause precursory to bad news. Poulsen noticed the dark circles around the physician's eyes, which gave him a perpetually somber appearance. "I'm afraid that in your wife's case, there has been a resultant diffuse axonal injury and a basilar arterial bleed. I'm sorry, but the bleed was into her brainstem. To answer your question, no, your wife is not in a coma, and all indications are that she is conscious, fully conscious . . . but I'm afraid she is suffering from total quadriplegic paralysis."

Another professional pause.

"Dr Poulsen, given your own specialism, I don't have to tell you how complex the human brain is. All our complexity as human beings – our intelligence and our personalities, our volition, how we perceive the world – all of that is in the cerebrum, mainly in the neocortex. All of these are completely intact in Mrs Poulsen. The damage has been done exclusively to the Pons, the bridge between the brain and the brainstem. Do you understand what I am saying?"

Poulsen nodded.

"The Pons is where all of the automatic and basic functions of life are centered – breathing, swallowing, taste, hearing, eye movement, et cetera. These are the functions that are compromised in your wife's case. I'm afraid she is suffering from ventral pontine syndrome, commonly known as locked-in syndrome. At the moment, her paralysis is truly total, including absence of eye movement. Only time will tell how permanent the paralysis is, but I have to be honest with you, based on the data we've obtained through imaging, the prognosis is not good."

"The baby?"

"I'm sorry . . ." Larssen lowered his eyes.

Poulsen wept and the physician remained quiet, allowing him his grief.

"Can she hear me?" Poulsen asked eventually.

"There's no reason to believe she can't," said Larssen. "And any stimulation you can give her is good."

Again there was a pause, Poulsen looking back into the room. Then, with a determined tone, he asked: "Is there a hospital library?"

Now, one year and three months later, and as was his Saturday afternoon custom, Georg Poulsen sat and read to his wife about Roussel's fantastical world where the deceased did not know they were dead, or that the world they inhabited was a staged tableau.

14

JOHN MACBETH. BOSTON

Casey was Macbeth's younger brother by four years. They had been close with each other and with their father, who had always referred to their small family as the 'Three Musketeers'. It had been an expression of sad solidarity; not that Macbeth, and even less Casey, had been fully aware at the time of their father's sadness. Macbeth's mother had been present in their lives only as an absence: Macbeth was six when she died, suddenly and unseen, like a central character in a play inexplicably dying offstage. The older Macbeth discovered that his mother had fallen victim to a Circle of Willis berry aneurysm that had ruptured and flooded the base of her brain with blood. As a child, he had imagined she had simply closed her eyes as if falling asleep; as a physician, he had been able to put together the likely scenario: the intense thunderclap headache, the catastrophic loss of motor control, perhaps a swirl of confusion, vivid hallucination, convulsions and death. A common feature of berry aneurysm was ptosis, where an eyelid would unilaterally half-close over one eye, and he had often imagined her thus – something he had been reminded of when he had seen Gabriel Rees's half-closed eyelid in death and in his dream.

Whatever the details of his mother's death, it had been a sudden, abrupt extinction: Cora Macbeth had been a physical presence in his life that morning and had not that afternoon. His mother had thereafter existed only conceptually, as an idea in a growing mind and, with the unquestioning adaptability

114

of childhood, Macbeth had become accustomed to her absence. Or at least adjusted to it; as he grew up he had concocted detailed fictions about his mother being alive and well in some other place, living some other life, perhaps under a different name, but crying herself to sleep each night as she thought of the sons she'd left behind. He'd even elaborated an alternative in which the truth was being concealed from him and his mother had fallen into a profound and unrousable slumber in which she dreamed another life for herself; perhaps he, his father and brother, their entire world, were simply the imaginings of his dreaming mother.

Whatever the deficit left by a dead mother and a saddened father, it had been compensated by the presence in his life of his brother. Casey was so similar to Macbeth, yet at the same time so very different. As they had grown up, Macbeth had been the trailblazer. Despite the emergent glitches in his psychology, Macbeth had excelled at school. His IQ had been measured at the extreme end of the bell curve, but at that point at which the advantage was possibly a disadvantage, creating the potential for mental stumbles. Then, as Casey had grown older, it became clear that his baby brother was intellectually his match, but there also emerged a grace and symmetry to Casey's intellectual function that marked him for great things.

No glitches.

While Macbeth followed his father into medicine and psychiatry, Casey studied physics, then astrophysics, then quantum mechanics. Despite his youth, Casey was now amongst the most valued brains on the planet and a possible future Nobelist.

It was something that filled Macbeth with both envy and pride. Most of all, he loved his kid brother and any sense of competition had been subsumed by their friendship; the closest Macbeth had. Maybe the only real friendship he had.

*

They met, as agreed, at a bowling alley off Massachusetts Avenue, not far from Casey's second-story apartment in a Back Bay brownstone, in turn a fifteen-minute bike ride over the bridge to MIT.

Casey Macbeth was clearly John Macbeth's brother. He was smaller and slighter, and had a gentler look, but they shared the same green eyes and dark hair and the general architecture of their faces was the same. But where Macbeth was a fastidious and expensive dresser, Casey always looked as if his mind had been on weightier things when he reached into his closet. When he walked into the bowling alley, Macbeth's kid brother was wearing jeans and a dark blue T-shirt that bore the white-lettered caption: *Wanted Dead and/or Alive: Schrödinger's Cat.* Macbeth had once tried to explain to a bemused Casey why not everyone got quantum-physics humor.

The brothers played three games, Macbeth winning easily every time, even when he tried not to. Casey's passion for ten-pin bowling was matched only by his incompetence. Macbeth could never understand how his brother, who could have quan-tified in an elegant equation every force, angle and torque required to make the ball behave in the desired way, so often managed to steer it straight into the gutter.

"I am fulfilled . . ." Casey said with a joyous smile after his third defeat. "Let's go back to my place and get drunk. Sound like a plan?"

"Sounds like a plan," said Macbeth enthusiastically, although he knew neither he nor his brother had ever got completely, recklessly drunk. "After the night I had last night, I could do with a little cutting loose."

"Why? What happened last night?" Casey frowned.

"I'll tell you later," said Macbeth.

Casey's apartment was not what anyone, other than his brother, would have expected from his outward appearance. While his

116

wardrobe suggested mental chaos, Casey's living environment revealed the crystalline order of his mind. Macbeth suspected his brother shared his need for surroundings that delivered some sense of harmony.

"You got everything you need? I mean while you're over here . . . I know it's difficult to pack everything." Casey placed a coaster then a glass of wine on the coffee table in front of Macbeth.

"I'm fine, thanks. The only thing you could maybe help with is my laptop."

"Sure. What's the problem?"

"The weirdest thing – a folder on my desktop I can't open. I can't even remember creating it."

"No problem. Sounds like you've locked it by accident. I'll have a look at it."

"No . . . it's not locked," said Macbeth. "If I click on it, it doesn't ask me for a password or open a message window or anything, it's just like it's a phantom or something."

"A phantom?" Casey laughed. "If you're going to get all meta-physical about computing, then you'd better come over to my side of science. Bring it with you next time you come over."

"Thanks."

"Do you never miss it? Here, I mean?" asked Casey.

"I guess. The Cape more than Boston. But I do enjoy Copen-hagen. I know you'd really like it too."

"We hardly get a chance to see each other," said Casey. "I was thinking that I might come over to see you next month."

"In Copenhagen? That would be great, Casey." Macbeth grinned. "Why don't you stay for a couple of weeks, if you can get the time off. I'll introduce you to some beautiful Danish blondes."

"Sorry . . . It'll be more like a few days. I'm going to be over in England, at Oxford, and I thought I could take a flight across to Copenhagen. I mean, it can only be a couple of hours away."

"Like I say, you're welcome to stay for as long as you want. I'd be delighted just to see you. What's in Oxford?"

Casey took a long sip of his wine and grinned a conspiratorial grin. "The greatest scientific discovery of all time, that's what. Bigger than Higgs, bigger than General Relativity, if you can believe that. You are looking at one of the chosen few . . . the elite, apparently. In fact, you should be treating me with much more deference."

"Okay, let's have it . . ."

"You've heard of Henry Blackwell?" asked Casey.

"Yeah, believe it or not, I am aware of some of what goes on outside the world of psychiatry. What about him?"

"Well, you'll know he's the world's greatest living quantum physicist. He's been working for years on a project that he's been unusually secretive about — or at least as secretive as anyone in the scientific community can be. Actually, there's bits and pieces of the Prometheus Project running all over the world in various research establishments. But Blackwell has kept the core project very close to his chest."

"Prometheus?"

"Yeah, I know," said Casey with a grimace. "But it's big . . . really, really big. The Prometheus Answer is his codename for a Great Unifying Theory. He actually claims he's done it – what Einstein, Bohr, Feynman, Hawking all failed to do. Anyone else and I'd take it with a shovelful of salt . . . Anyway, he's promised it's the greatest revelation in the history of quantum physics. The definitive, elegant solution that solves, once and for all, the way the universe works."

"And you've been invited?"

"He'll be publishing formally in a journal, but he's summoned together a couple of hundred of the top brains in the field from around the world for a special seminar in Oxford. Including yours truly. Basically he's using the symposium as a peer-group launch and I can't begin to tell you what it feels like for Blackwell to have identified me as one of his peers."

"Nothing more than you deserve, Casey. I'm really pleased for you. But why all the secrecy?"

"Things are getting nutty out there. I mean attitudes to science. You've heard of Blind Faith? The fundamentalist Christian group?"

"Yes. A bunch of lunatics."

"They're more than that . . . Blind Faith has gone completely underground since the FBI tagged them as a terrorist organization. We've been issued with a stack of guidelines at MIT and there's going to be all kinds of security at the Oxford symposium – Blackwell's been sent death threats and some kind of half-assed device was intercepted in his mail. I'm telling you, these people are dangerous." Casey shook his head and a lock of black hair fell over his eyes. "We think we live in enlightened times, but there are just as many would-be inquisitors set on persecuting the Copernicuses and Galileos of today's world."

"I don't know what they're all so afraid of."

"Extinction, that's what. Do you know what religion is?" Casey leaned forward, animated. "It's the absence of science. Religion thrived when we didn't understand how the universe worked. With every new discovery, we cancel one more superstitious explanation for a natural phenomenon. Science has been killing religion since the Enlightenment and now it's fighting for its last shred of life. That's why Blind Faith, every Islamic fundamentalist and born-again crackpot has a particular hard-on for Blackwell and his research. I can't blame him for playing his cards close to his chest."

"Well," Macbeth raised his glass in a toast, "I'm really pleased for you, Casey. And it really would be great if you could come over to Denmark for a few days afterwards. Maybe you can explain it all to your dim-witted brother."

"You always put yourself down." Casey frowned. "Truth is, I've always envied your mind."

Macbeth mock-spluttered his wine. "You? Envy *my* mind?"

"You always go on about my focus . . . A friend, Juergen, who's a physicist out at CERN, told me this German word – *Fachidiot* – it means something like 'expert idiot'. Juergen says that's exactly what we are . . . we know a lot about what we do and shit about anything else."

"*An expert is someone who knows more and more about less and less . . .*" Macbeth smiled, raising a knowing glass. "Nicholas Murray Butler."

"There you go . . ." Casey pointed at Macbeth emphatically. "Your head is full of facts and dates and knowledge about stuff other than your work. Me? I'm a one-trick pony."

"I wouldn't complain about the brain you were handed." Macbeth sipped his wine. "And as for my memory for general knowledge – I'd swap it in the bat of an eye for a better re-collection of real life. Give me an autobiographical memory over a semantic one any day."

"We are what we are," said Casey resignedly.

"Ever heard of Cosmos Rossellius?"

Casey shrugged.

"He lived in the sixteenth century. In Florence – formulated all kinds of theories about the memory and its functions – theories way ahead of his time. I should reread him some day . . . try some of his mnemotechnics."

"What?"

"Ways to re-create the real world in your memory. If he visited a place, a church or a castle, say, he had these techniques for rebuilding them perfectly in his memory. God knows I need something like that."

"It's good to hear you're keeping up with the literature . . ." Casey raised an eyebrow. "Sixteenth century, you say?"

"The mind was the mind back then just as it is now. The weird thing is that we've only now discovered that we allocate specific neurons to specific concepts. If you think of a certain person you've known or a place you've been, it'll trigger a set of neurons you've grown specifically for that memory. People really do live in your head. Rossellius was way ahead in his thinking and talked about memory-space as a dimension of existence. He even wrote this description of Paradise and Hell that was as ornate and convoluted as Dante's. The difference was that Rossellius's afterworld was entirely constructed from memories. An eternal memory-space."

"Mmm . . ." Casey poured another glass of wine. "Remember how Dad always talked about the two universes? The Outer and the Inner. Don't you think it's weird the way we've ended up each exploring one?"

"I remember . . ." Macbeth sounded suddenly gloomy. "I still text him, you know. Dad, I mean. Just to tell him small things about my day, that kind of thing."

"John . . ." Casey's tone was balanced between sympathy and warning.

"I know. It's unhealthy and more than a little bit weird. It's just that people exist electronically now. We all have a 'presence' out there in cyberland . . ." Macbeth waved his free hand in the air. "It just helps me to imagine there's still something of him out there. Like I say, nuts."

"I miss him too," said Casey. "We all have different ways of coping, I guess."

The brothers fell into a silence for a moment, each trying to find a way out of the dark corner they'd strayed into.

"Tell me more about Blackwell's huge discovery . . ." Macbeth said at last, with forced cheeriness.

"Basically he's been using simulations to look back in time. Actually to look past time – to whatever there was before that ten-to-the-minus-forty-three seconds after the Big Bang or whatever it was that kick-started the universe and time itself. Everybody is speculating about it but no one knows for sure what he's going to announce." Casey picked up his glass and took a long sip. "Now, tell me what's bothering you. You said something happened last night. What?"

Macbeth sighed, then ran through the events of the night before. He told his brother that the jumper was dead and the priest was still fighting for life. He even told him about his depersonalization episode at the scene while he had been working to save Mullachy's life.

"God, that's awful," said Casey. "You could have called tonight off. I had no idea."

"No, I needed tonight. By the way, this is a long shot, but there's a chance you may know the jumper."

"Oh?"

"Yeah – a guy called Gabriel Rees. He was an MIT . . ." Macbeth let the sentence die when he saw the reaction on Casey's face.

15

KAREN. BOSTON

Sweep. One. Two. Sweep. One, two. Sweep. One, two. Three. Sweep. One, two, three. Right foot first step. Forward. Back. One, two, three. Left foot forward. Back.

She knew there were people looking at her, some laughing, others shuffling in that uneasy way of those confronted with bizarre behavior, as they watched her carry out her small ritual in the store doorway. There were impatient sounds, concerned noises from behind. A man blustered past, muttering something unpleasant and forcing her to one side. Because she had one foot ritually raised, she lost her balance, hopping on the other until the shoulder of her expensive coat came to rest against the sandstone of the store's entry arch. Panicked, she brushed furiously at the material.

That ruined it. She'd have to start at the beginning and go through the whole thing again. Straightening up, she allowed the clot of shoppers in the department store's doorway to uncongeal past her. Eyes lowered, Karen avoided their puzzled or contemptuous looks.

Sweep. She raised her right arm above her head, slicing the air in an arc. One. She swept the arm diagonally down in front of her, left to right. Two. She raised her left arm and performed a mirror reflection of the first sequence of movements. Sweep. She fluttered her hands in front of her, as if winding cotton, starting low to the ground and moving up to eye level. Three. She made flat hand circles before her face, as if cleaning an

123

invisible window. Four. She stepped off the entrance step with her right foot, retracted it. Five. Repeating the action with the left foot, which she planted firmly on the sidewalk, Karen performed two final arcing gestures with her arms: one right, the other left. Six.

She stepped fully out of the doorway and onto the street. With that, Karen Robertson instantly and totally became normal once more, making her way along the sidewalk with the same city-morning purposefulness as the other pedestrians.

Karen Robertson *was* normal. She was perfectly sane. She knew that her behavior in subway cars, under bridge arches, in doorways, was bizarre. She despised the rituals she was forced to perform, and subway cars and bridge arches were places she quite successfully avoided. But doorways – store doorways, taxi and bus doorways, elevator doorways – were impossible to avoid.

People often laughed at her to her face. The odd thing was that she saw how ridiculous her pantomime was; whenever she undertook it, she became totally detached from herself, from the experience, a scornful observer herself.

Karen Robertson had everything. She was a very attractive, successful, thirty-five-year-old lawyer with one of the better-known law firms in Boston, having qualified from Harvard in the top one per cent; she came from a family of New England bluebloods; she bought her clothes in Newbury Street and had the height and figure to carry them off; she drove a Lexus sports convertible; she could have her pick of men; she lived in a sprawling Back Bay apartment. She was clever and ambitious and shone with the gleam of the well-born self-assured.

Karen Robertson had everything, all right. Including a score of twenty-nine on the Yale-Brown Obsessive Compulsive Scale. Severe.

Her psychiatrist, Dr Corbin, had tried to isolate the exact origin of her fear of insects. There had been one event, when

124

Karen had been a teenager: her school had been one of the oldest private girls' schools in Massachusetts; one of those tradition-for-tradition's-sake places where if a pupil skinned a knee she'd bleed blue. Classics, Latin and Ancient History featured pretty high on the curriculum, teaching the patrician classes of today about the patrician classes of antiquity. Karen had hated it. Even then, she had been focused on a business career, and had tired quickly of the school's constant obsession with a distant world that had nothing to do with the reality she lived in.

This particular day, however, the Classics teacher had been bleating on about the aftermath of some battle or other. A young Persian soldier, Mithridates, had been boasting about killing a prince from the opposing army while his own king, Artaxerxes, claimed the kill as his own and sentenced the boastful young soldier to 'death by boats'. The teacher explained that the historian Plutarch had described this form of execution – scaphism – in detail. Mithridates was encased in two boats of exactly matching size, one laid on top of the other and sealed. Mithridates's head, hands and feet were left to project out of the boats, the rest of him inside. His captors force-fed him milk and honey until his belly was full to bursting, then smeared his face, hands and feet with a thick coating of honey, turning his head to the sun. By midday, his face was a single writhing mass of spiders, flies, wasps and bees, biting and stinging. As his wounds infected, other insects ate through his body and found their way inside the boats. Some simply ate his living flesh, others burrowed deep into it to lay their eggs. According to Plutarch, it took Mithridates seventeen days to die, and when they opened the boats, there was a black swarm of thousands of insects—

Karen's scream had ended the teacher's gleeful lecture. It also started Karen's panic attack, emptying her lungs of air, filling her universe with imagined shadows of scurrying things

125

all around her. Eventually, and despite panicked classmates gathering around her, Karen had passed out, sinking into a scuttling, slithering darkness.

After that, Karen had not been able to even think of an insect, to hear a description or see an image of one, without being plunged into a convulsive, suffocating aftershock attack.

While unable to pin down the exact origin of her entomophobia, Dr Corbin had used rationalization and exposure therapy to bring her fear within a range of responses that could be considered remotely normal. But her nightmares were still haunted by monstrous ants with huge sideways jaws, long-legged spiders and scuttling, shiny black beetles.

One aspect of her phobia had endured and had blossomed into her obsessive compulsion: her fear of walking into a spider's web.

This obsession elaborated into the preventative ritual she now undertook every time she passed through a portal or any other situation where an arachnid may have spun a trap for her. In every doorway, she would mechanically perform the same sequence of bizarre sweeping movements to ensure there were no invisible strands of spider silk into which she could walk. Her focus was her face: any other part of her body would cause panic, but the idea of getting a spider web on her face could bring her to the brink of vomiting.

Her rituals were ridiculous, embarrassing, irrational. Like most obsessive-compulsives, Karen knew and acknowledged all of these facts. Dr Corbin had told her that obsessive compulsion was not a psychosis: there were no delusions, no belief by the sufferer that his or her behavior was normal and the rest of the world was out of kilter. Obsessive compulsives knew their behavior was bizarre.

The root of Karen's compulsions lay in rational fears, Dr Corbin had explained, blown up to irrational proportions.

Anxieties could be deferred; unrelated worries and stresses from work or family crises the trigger for panic attacks and obsessive behavior.

Maybe Corbin had been right. The Halverson account was taking up a lot of her time and mental space; for the first time in her corporate law career, Karen felt stressed about a project. And the fear of looking an idiot in front of the client was a big part of it.

And there had been the other thing.

It had happened a week ago, one morning when her doorway rituals had made her late for a meeting with Jack Court to discuss Halverson and she had picked up pace as she strode along the sidewalk.

Karen experienced the strangest feeling of déjà vu. Or something like déjà vu yet subtly different. The city around her had seemed changed, as if suddenly a different time of day. The feeling intensified and she became aware that the sidewalk and the roadway seemed emptier. Over on the other side of the street, where it bordered the park, she saw a small girl dressed in the kind of dress Karen had had when she was ten or eleven. The girl had looked straight at her.

And stepped out onto the roadway.

Karen gave a start, worried that the child would be hit by a car. There was a gap in the traffic and Karen stepped off the curb.

She hadn't been aware of the man who had had to do a quick sidestep to avoid walking into her until she felt his fingers dig into her elbow as he yanked her backwards. Something blasted deafeningly in her ears and a large truck flashed by.

The volume of traffic was suddenly back. The light had returned to a spring morning in Boston. She searched where the girl had stood in the carriageway, the sidewalk behind, scanned the street in both directions. She was gone.

Karen turned to the man who had pulled her out of the path

of the truck and looked at him blankly, dazed. He was an attractive, sophisticated-looking man about her age, with dark hair, a pale complexion and green eyes.

"I thought . . ." Karen pointed vaguely to where the little girl had been, where she could never have been, and let the sentence die.

"Are you okay?"

Karen nodded numbly.

"You should take more care in traffic," he had said. Karen had nodded again and the man turned and headed off down the street, turning at the next corner. She'd stood for a moment composing herself, trying to resolve two nagging questions in her head: how could she possibly have seen what she thought she saw? And the man who had pulled her back . . .

She was sure she'd seen him before.

16

JOHN MACBETH. BOSTON

"You knew him?"

Casey didn't answer for a moment, frowning as he tried to make sense of what his brother had told him. "Gabriel? Not that well, but what I do know of him would make me think he'd be the last person to commit suicide."

"Well, I'm afraid there's no doubt about it being suicide. I saw him jump and take Father Mullachy with him. He was clearly very disturbed."

Casey stared at Macbeth disbelievingly. "Taking his own life is one thing, taking someone else's is quite another. I'm telling you John, Gabriel Rees was as well balanced as I am. Bad example . . . he was much better balanced than me. You say he was spouting religious stuff?"

"It sounded like it could have been religious. And the focus of his attention certainly was on the priest."

"That doesn't sound right on two levels." Casey shook his head and again palmed the lock of hair back from his eyes. Macbeth thought about how often he'd told his kid brother to get a decent haircut. "First, Gabriel was devout all right . . . a devout atheist. Second, although he was certainly no lover of clerics, he wouldn't have hurt a fly. Mind you, I haven't seen him other than in passing for months. In fact the last time I saw him even in passing was a few weeks back. I just can't believe it."

"And you hadn't heard of a member of the MIT community having committed suicide?"

"I haven't been in or spoken to anyone today. And you know I don't do news."

"Yes," said Macbeth, "I know you don't do news." He glanced around his brother's immaculate apartment. No TV. There was a sophisticated and expensive music system that had been sophisticated and expensive in 1979. Casey preferred his music on vinyl and he had spent his spare time repairing and replacing, tinkering and fine-tuning until it looked brand new and sounded, Macbeth had to admit, even better than his own painfully expensive Bang & Olufsen digital system. Macbeth knew Casey's radio was permanently tuned to 99.5, Boston's classical music station. Even his computer, which Macbeth knew was much more powerful than any domestic PC, looked compact and innocuous and was only ever used in connection with his brother's research. Any news Casey happened to give half his attention to came between Shostakovich and Steve Reich, or fractals and wave-function equations.

"The police said that Gabriel was somebody important in particle physics," said Macbeth.

"Not really. I mean Gabriel is bright. Real bright. I mean he was . . . but generally, he was just another doctoral student. The only thing was that he also worked as a researcher for Professor Gillman."

"That's significant?"

"Gillman is one of Professor Blackwell's research partners. The Gillman Modeling Project is part of the Prometheus jigsaw being worked on here, at MIT. I'm not involved directly, but I know that like Blackwell Gillman's pretty secretive about his work."

"What's his field?"

"He's heavily involved in quantum computing and his part of Prometheus is to create simulations of the first moments of the universe. Gillman's a big part of the Oxford symposium." Casey paused. "Did Gabriel say why he wanted to kill himself?"

"He wasn't coherent," said Macbeth. "He kept talking about knowing the truth. That he could see what the rest of us couldn't."

"And did he say anything about what this 'truth' was?"

"Just that it wasn't about who or what God was . . . it was about *when* he was, whatever that was meant to mean."

"Search me," said Casey. "Like I said, Gabriel was solidly atheist. He didn't believe there was a when, who, where or what, when it came to a deity. He was very anti-religion."

"No kidding? I kinda got that idea when he took the priest with him." Macbeth frowned. "There was one odd thing – he kept going on about human intelligence not making sense; that it was crazy that our brains worked the way they did. That it actually put us in danger, rather than gave us an advantage."

"He had a point, poor bastard," said Casey dolefully.

17

FABIAN. FRIESLAND

More skyscape than landscape, this was a part of the world where the sky dominated; pressing down on land and sea and making both merely the ribbon edge of the sky's vast banner. There was the flat blue sea, the flat pale beach rippled by the odd dune, the flat green land beyond wrinkled by the occasional unconvinced hummock; gradations of tone and shade marking the boundaries more than degrees of elevation.

A small-framed boy who was fourteen but would have been taken for twelve walked along a band of beach the color of which matched his hair and the constellation of freckles on cheeks and nose. He wore a faded sweatshirt and jeans and walked barefoot, his sneakers in his hand.

The boy, whose name was Fabian Bartelma, walked slowly, his pace burdened by the thousand anxieties of childhood's end, his gaze sometimes out over the sea, sometimes directed towards his feet and the sand that oozed between his naked toes. It was a Saturday morning. Fabian often spent his Saturdays on the beach or cycling along the dyke. His was a traditional childhood. Traditional but solitary, because no one his age adhered to such traditions any more. Fabian spent most of his time reading or walking or cycling, never displaying any interest in playing computer games, either alone or with friends. Bizarrely, when he did try to play them, Fabian suffered from motion sickness and headaches – despite never once getting sick in the car or on a plane. He had never badgered his parents for a cellphone or mp3 player, nor shown any interest in any of the other paraphernalia of twenty-first-century adolescence. And that had, gradually but ineluctably, disconnected Fabian from his peers.

His parents had bought him a computer for his twelfth birthday and he did use it, but mainly for homework or for looking things up. Even then, he preferred to use reference books. He was, his parents had resigned themselves, a child out of time. Someone out of kilter with the period he had been born into. At home, his bedroom was stacked with books on history: atlases of military campaigns, dictionaries of famous quotations, volumes about the great civilizations of the ancient world, the lives of the Caesars, the evolution of mankind. For Fabian, History was not a subject of study, it was a place: somewhere you could go and explore and discover. A place you could live.

Fabian felt this beach belonged to him. He knew that the shore would have changed over time, the seas pulling and shoving at the coast, eroding and redistributing sand over the centuries, but he liked it here because, apart from the lighthouse which had stood where it was for a century or more, it was an unmarked scene; an untouched landscape. No one else ever seemed to come here and he would walk or sit on the beach for hours, trying to imagine himself into another time. Wouldn't it be good, he thought to himself, if you really could visit the past? If you could travel there for a holiday, like taking a flight to Spain?

The beach arced around the bay like the broad blade of a scythe and Fabian could see where the promontory not so much jutted as faded into the sea, the red and white spindle of the lighthouse the only clear indicator of its end. It was an empty but not desolate landscape, and Fabian could imagine himself as the only person left living on the planet. The world entirely his. He could not quite work out why the idea filled him simultaneously with melancholy and comfort. He kicked some sand before dropping down suddenly to sit facing the sea and scowling against a salt sun, the odd cotton cloud sliding across blue silk. Stretching out his arms, he dug his fingers deep into the sand, as if clinging on to the world. He closed his eyes and listened to the sound of the waves.

An odd feeling.

It was like déjà vu. Something similar, but different, deeper. He was jolted by a sharp push in the ribs and sat up, shielding his eyes as he peered up at the shadow above him. Henkje Maartens, the thick-necked thug who patrolled the school with a gang of Neanderthals. Maartens, with a bully's nose for the different, had singled out Fabian for special attention.

"So this is where you hide, is it?" Maartens sneered.

Fabian stood up, dusting off the sand from his jeans, and cast an eye in the direction he had come. Maartens was alone. That was something at least.

"What do you want?" Fabian asked, moving around Maartens so that he, not Fabian, was looking into the sun.

"I saw you and followed you," said Maartens. "I thought to myself I'll find out what Creepo does in his spare time. What you come down here for? Nice quiet place, is it?" Maartens lolled his tongue out the side of his mouth, went cross-eyed and mimed masturbation.

Fabian knew he couldn't win a fight with the much bigger, heavier-built Maartens. But there was no one here to see the outcome. He would make as much a mess of Maartens's face as he could before taking a beating. It would be a mark, a warning to others that there was a price to be paid.

"Is that it, Creepo? Is that why—"

The impact hurt Fabian's fist. There was an ugly grinding noise from Maartens's teeth and the bully staggered back, shocked and with the sun still in his face. Fabian hit him again, this time in the nose. Maartens's backwards stagger meant that the blow didn't have the force of the first and Fabian hit him again, and again. Maartens stumbled and fell onto his back and Fabian dropped onto his chest, raining blows down on his face. A dark impulse beyond his control drove Fabian on, a thrill rising in him. He was, he realized, enjoying this. Something deep and dark and ancient had stirred within him; something from a history he had not known he had.

Realizing that Maartens, when he recovered his wits, could easily throw the lighter boy off his chest and regain the advantage, Fabian jumped up from him. As Maartens began to rise, Fabian swung a kick into the side of his face. The careful deliberation, the aiming of the kick, shocked Fabian: he had placed it to do as much damage as possible without hurting his foot through his sneakers. He kicked Maartens again, in the mouth. He could see the bigger boy was now seriously dazed, his face smeared with blood; Fabian grabbed him by his hooded top and spun him around so he was face down. Grabbing a handful of hair, he pushed Maartens's face into the sand. He leaned in, whispering into the prone bully's ear.

"If you ever, ever, follow me again, you or any of your buddies, I'll put you in hospital. And in school . . . any smart remarks from any of your posse and I'll wait till I get you alone. You got that?"

Maartens said something in a pleading, sand-muffled voice and Fabian stood up and back from him, ready to strike again if the bigger boy made any move. But he could see not only was there no fight left in Maartens, there never really had been any. Like most bullies, Maartens was a coward. He was crying, his face a paste of sand and tears and blood.

"You got that?" Fabian yelled at him, taking a threatening step forward.

Maartens nodded vigorously before turning tail and running back along the beach. Fabian watched him run, then looked down at his hands: skin reddened and puffed, blood from a split on one knuckle. Shaking.

Where had that come from? Where had that terrible rage been hidden? He sank back onto the sand, sitting with his elbows resting on his knees, his hands loose and fingers still trembling.

He felt vaguely sick and dizzy, his heart pounding in his chest. He remembered the feeling he had had, the feeling just before Maartens had arrived. Like déjà vu, but stronger, deeper.

Fabian closed his eyes and sank back onto the beach, looking up once more at the sky, digging his fingers deep into the sand. He closed his eyes. The pain in his hands faded more quickly than he thought it would, the nausea and the panicky feeling in his chest disappeared with equal suddenness.

It was then that he was jolted by a sharp push in the ribs. He sat up, shielding his eyes as he peered up at the shadow above him.

"So this is where you hide, is it?" Henkje Maartens sneered. His face was unbruised, unbloodied, unmarked.

Fabian stood up, dusting off the sand from his jeans. He looked at his own hands, suddenly healed: no redness, no swelling, no splits. It made no sense at all. But it made perfect sense. In that moment, Fabian knew he was visiting his own history.

He balled his hands into fists and launched himself at Maartens with an inhuman scream.

18

JOSH HOBERMAN. MARYLAND

"The Abrahamic tradition is revelatory," Josh Hoberman said. "All Judeo-Christian religions, Islam included, believe in a God whose presence is parallel to the world of Man and a Truth that will eventually be revealed to the faithful. Interaction between Man and his God – every biblical theophany – takes the form of visions: burning bushes, pillars of smoke . . ."

"And your point?" President Yates walked beside Hoberman, her eyes pathward, her expression serious as she considered the psychiatrist's words. It was for all the world like two friends combining a philosophical debate with a leisurely stroll through the park; except they were not friends and this was no park but Camp David and they were followed, at something short of a discreet distance, by Bundy, the secret-serviceman with the strangely dual-colored eyes.

"Just that you define yourself very much through your faith. It could be that the nature of your faith, your belief in revelation through visions, is making you susceptible to these episodes."

"You think that because God has revealed himself to others I'm deluding myself into believing He's revealing himself to me?" Yates shook her head. "Then why am I not seeing something dramatic or majestic? Visions of President Taft in his shirtsleeves or of a nineteen-seventies White House intern are hardly divine revelations."

"But you *have* expressed to me your belief that the visions are perhaps divine in origin . . ."

"I know that you'll probably hold my beliefs in contempt, but they are my beliefs. More than that, they are the truth and, like you said, that truth will ultimately be revealed. You worry that I maybe think the Lord has a special message for me and this is His way of communicating it. But that's not what I believe. All things that happen in this universe happen at the Lord's command. All of Nature and all in it is of God's creation, these visions included. But I know that they are not a message directly for me, but for everyone. There have been more reports – visions happening all over the world. I'll make sure you're given access to them . . ." She cast a commanding glance over her shoulder at Bundy. "One in particular, a girl in France, has very interesting overtones." She stopped walking and turned to the psychiatrist. "You see, if it's not me . . . if it's everyone who's having these visions, then *that* is what I would take as the hand of God in our affairs. If that's the case, then I know we may be facing a time of final judgment. If that is the case, then I tell you this, Professor Hoberman: I shall not be found wanting."

There it was again: that focus. And that uneasy feeling in Hoberman's gut.

During their discussions over the preceding days, Hoberman had been able to glimpse something of what lay behind Yates's commanding authority and homespun sagacities. And what he had seen had terrified him. To start with, it had been like trespassing on a movie set, peeking behind the building façades to see that there was nothing there other than support beams: Elizabeth Yates was a woman completely, absolutely, astonishingly devoid of personality. Hoberman had sat in on meetings, observed her with others, and seen how her demeanor changed subtly according to whomever she interacted with. He realized that she had mastered the projection of attributes that were not there. She was clearly not a stupid woman, but Hoberman had soon come to realize that her intellectual gifts were modest. It was just that she somehow managed to simulate what was not there and magnify what was, depending on the context and what she wanted to get out of it.

But it hadn't been Yates's lack of intellectual or personal depth that had terrified Hoberman. He had kept their talks informal, general, conversational: but in each discussion he had sneaked in a seemingly innocuous question or observation, each a disguised diagnostic tool. The picture that had emerged was of a woman of singular vision, of unshakeable will, of adamantine faith; all potential virtues in a world leader. They were also potential indicators of something darker.

If there was one thing about the President that was exceptional, it was her focus; and that focus was firmly fixed on a mission founded on the shifting sands of narrow nationalism, superstition and righteous bigotry. In describing her world view, Yates repeatedly used the pronouns 'us' and 'we', 'they' and 'them'. The first person plural extended no farther than the frontiers of the United States, and he got the idea that many within its borders fell into the category 'them' – a subset Hoberman suspected he himself belonged to.

They walked on. Apart from a helipad and a couple of more modern and functional buildings tucked out of view, Camp David was a spread-out collection of timber lodges and cabins set in thick oak and hickory woodland, looped and connected by intersecting forest trails. Not for the first time Hoberman felt strangely claustrophobic in the open air, as if hemmed in by the dense Catoctin forest.

"I take it you have no faith?" Yates asked him after twenty yards of silence.

"I'm a Humanist. I don't share your faith, but that doesn't mean I lack belief."

"But you don't believe in God?"

"No. I think the universe is too wonderful and mysterious to be explained away so simplistically. Glibly, almost. If you don't mind me saying, Madame President."

139

"Everyone is entitled to their opinion, Professor Hoberman."

"Are they?"

Yates looked at him for a moment. "So your beliefs are founded in science, is that right?"

"Yes."

"Science is a tool," said Yates. "A facility given to us by God. Science and technology are means to an end, not an end in themselves, yet so many treat science as a religion. There are high priests, evangelists and bigots in science, just as there are in every religion."

"I don't see science in that way. I believe it is the *only* way of understanding ourselves and our universe. But my belief or lack of it isn't the question. It's yours that's important and whether it's in any way linked to these visions." Hoberman paused for a moment. He watched a Broad-winged Hawk traverse with a single beat of wing the span of blue between the swathes of hickory. "What concerns me most is how you may interpret any future hallucinations. Attribute some meaning that isn't there."

"Are you saying that I'm unfit for office?" Yates stopped again and held him in her professionally honed gaze. "It strikes me that you are commenting on the beliefs and personality that were in place before these episodes began."

"The phenomena and your personality are inextricably linked; it's impossible to evaluate one without considering the other. As for your fitness for office, I can only comment clinically – anything else is for others to decide."

"Indeed it is, Professor Hoberman. It's for the American people to decide, and they have already made their will known. I have been charged with steering this great country, perhaps the only nation that knows the Lord's blessing, through the trials that lie ahead."

Again something sparkled cold and dark in the bright blue of her eyes. She broke the gaze, smiled and continued their walk.

"The weather seems to be smiling on us," she said conversationally, switching mode as he had seen her do so many times in the last few days.

"It does indeed," said Hoberman, looking into the sky above the path, where the Broad-winged Hawk again appeared briefly as it performed a beatless arc, scouring the forest for prey.

19

JOHN MACBETH. BOSTON

The priest died the next day.

Macbeth was browsing in the big bookstore on Harvard Place, wondering – as he passed the huge display of e-readers – how much longer books would be books; things you could touch page by page, when his cellphone rang and Pete Corbin told him the news.

"He wouldn't have lived so long if it hadn't been for you, John. You gave him the best chance of making it."

"Not a good enough chance, obviously," said Macbeth. "By the way, Casey did know Gabriel – not well, but he knew him." Macbeth relayed to Corbin what his brother had told him about the young doctoral student. As physicians, both Macbeth and Corbin had learned to encounter death dispassionately, but there was something about their experience on the roof that was different. Macbeth guessed Corbin was struggling as much as he was to make sense of it.

"How much longer are you staying in Boston?" Corbin asked.

"Till the end of next week. I'm spending Monday and Tuesday at the Schilder Institute – that's my official reason for being here. Why do you ask?"

"There's a patient at Belmont I want you to see. I've done all of the clearances . . . I think you'd be very interested, given your research work. When would suit you?"

"I've got dinner with Casey tonight, but other than that I'm free till Monday."

"Friday morning then. Ten-thirty. That okay?"

"Sure, I'll be there."

"See you then. And John?"

"Yeah?"

"I really am sorry Mullachy didn't make it."

That evening, Macbeth met Casey for dinner in a purposefully jocund, mahogany-paneled, beer-garden-type place close to the Common. As he waited a beer's length for Casey to arrive, Macbeth cast his eyes around the restaurant: waiters, dressed in waistcoats and long white aprons and carrying trays single-handed and shoulder-high, wheeled and weaved between the tables delivering steins of bier and heavily laden plates. Again Macbeth reflected on the comforting absurdity of a simulation of another culture, another country and another time, but somehow the compulsory cheeriness was welcome. Necessary.

Casey arrived at the door and scanned the hall, grinning across the cluster of tables when he spotted Macbeth. The smile was uniquely Casey: boyish, mischievous, bright and ingenuous; a smile that Macbeth knew he had grown up seeing, that had been a constant accompaniment to their play together, but it bothered him to the point of small panic that he could not remember any single incident of that smile; that his memory of it, like his memory of almost everything, was general rather than specific.

"I thought we were having dinner, not planning a putsch," said Casey with a wry smile as he looked around before responding to Macbeth's offered handshake with a hug.

"I felt in need of some *Gemütlichkeit* . . ." Macbeth waved to attract a waiter's attention and ordered a pitcher of beer.

"Tough day?"

Macbeth told Casey about the priest's death and asked if he'd been able to find out any more about Gabriel Rees's recent history.

"There's not much to tell," Casey explained. "Everybody says the same thing: Gabriel was so wrapped up in his work with Professor Gillman that he hadn't done much in the way of socializing, but any that he did, he seemed fine. No hint of him being in any way troubled."

"How well do you know Gillman?"

"Well enough, I suppose, but I haven't seen him for a while. Gillman isn't the most approachable of people. Spiky, is the best way of describing him. That or a bit of an asshole. He's traveling to Oxford with me for the Blackwell symposium."

"Really? If you get a chance ask him about Gabriel, see if he knew anything about him being disturbed."

Casey frowned. "God knows how many patient suicides you must have had to deal with over the years, what is it about this one that's got you so curious?"

"Firstly, thanks for the vote of confidence in my clinical skills – it may surprise you that only one of my patients killed himself. And he was my last patient in clinical practice."

"Shit, I'm sorry, John. That was a crass thing for me to say. I forgot about him."

"That's okay. Truth is, something about Gabriel reminded me of that last patient at McLean. Not that their delusions were in any way similar – my patient was suffering from Dissociative Identity Disorder, or at least that was *my* diagnosis, even if I got my ass in a sling for it. There was no hint of Gabriel believing he was anyone other than himself." Macbeth shrugged. "I don't know, there was just something about Gabriel's calm that reminded me of that case. Maybe that's it. I really don't know."

They sank into silence for a moment.

"Did you bring your laptop?" asked Casey.

Macbeth reached down and lifted the small case that rested at his feet.

"I'll have a look when we get back to my apartment . . . see what I can do."

"I've never really gotten into computers, despite the work I'm doing on the Project."

"Sometimes I think you were born into the wrong decade. The wrong century."

"I'd be weird whatever century I was born in." Macbeth shrugged. "Go back too many centuries and they'd have burned me at the stake."

"I can see this is going to be a fun evening," Casey said over his beer.

"Sorry. It's been a trying couple of days."

Casey nodded, then looked around again at the beer hall. "How did you find this place? It's not your usual speed."

"Melissa brought me years ago. I think she was trying to be ironic. That was before she discovered I didn't do ironic."

"I was sorry when it didn't work out with you and Melissa. She was good for you."

"It doesn't seem to work out with me and anybody." Macbeth took a sip of his beer and looked at his glass contemplatively. "Do you know what Melissa said to me? That she was tired of me not being there, even when I was."

"What was that supposed to mean?"

"Come on, Casey, you know exactly what she meant. We both do. There's something missing with me, some tiny gap that seems to become a chasm when people get to know me. What Melissa meant was she was tired of coming home to an empty room, even when I was in it."

"Jesus . . . you are in a great mood tonight."

"Sorry. Like I said, I—" Macbeth broke off mid-sentence, a strange feeling seizing him: the same powerful feeling of déjà vu he'd felt in the Common. But even more intense this time, and accompanied by a feeling of being off-balance. He gripped the edge of the table, staring at his pressure-whitened fingertips. This was happening too often. This wasn't déjà vu; this wasn't one of his typical episodes. He was having some kind

145

of cerebral incident: a TIA or something similar. He needed medical attention.

And then he saw Casey's face.

Casey was looking directly at Macbeth but wasn't seeing him. He was frowning in concentration, trying to make sense of some experience personal to him. Macbeth realized that whatever was happening to him was happening to Casey too.

It went very quiet.

The restaurant had been bustling and noisy, the sounds of the diners' conversations and laughter, the clinking and ringing of delivered and collected porcelain and glass resonating in the high-ceilinged room. But now the restaurant had fallen silent.

Macbeth looked past Casey. Everyone was still, each in his or her private universe, trying to make sense of what had happened. Slowly, people returned to conversation, their voices low and quiet, concerned, as they shared their experiences.

"You all right?" he asked Casey.

"What the fuck was that?" Casey looked scared and something protective, almost paternal, sparked in Macbeth.

"Did you feel like really strong déjà vu?" asked Macbeth.

Casey nodded vigorously, relieved his experience had been shared. "Exactly like . . ." He looked around. "Shit . . . everybody?"

"Everybody, as far as I can see."

The buzz of conversation picked up in the restaurant. Urgent exchanges; desperate sharings.

"There's something still not right," said Casey.

"Like something's changed? The temperature or the air quality?"

"Have you had this before?"

Macbeth nodded. "There's more, Casey, Pete Corbin told me—"

It started as a tinkling. The glasses and bottles behind the long mahogany bar, as if rattled by a heavy truck or a train

146

passing. Except there were no rail tracks anywhere near, and the streets in this part of Old Boston were too narrow for anything much bigger than a cargo van.

Again the restaurant fell quiet as everyone turned to the bar. A young, fresh-faced barkeeper stared back, white-faced and confused. The rattling ceased and there was an eternal second of stillness, a near-total silence broken only by the ticking of the huge, round Victorian bar clock. Macbeth was struck at how sharp and clear each measured tick was, as if his hearing had suddenly become enhanced.

Screams.

It was as if the whole world shuddered, trying to shrug them off its shoulders. Macbeth reached for Casey but was thrown from his chair, landing heavily on the polished wooden floor. He tried to get up but his balance was impossible to find as the floor shuddered and shifted beneath him. He fell again, this time his cheek and the side of his head slamming even harder onto the floorboards. He lay stunned for a moment, his ear pressed to polished oak, his newly acute vision picking up painfully sharp detail on the sparse flecks of dust and grime on the sedulously swept floor. And through the floor, he could hear the Earth. He heard it bellow and moan, crack asunder deafeningly. He felt every vibration, from the minutest to the most momentous, resonate through his body.

An earthquake. A major earthquake. They had to take shelter.

He began to crawl around the table to Casey. When he found him, his brother was lying on his side, as Macbeth had been, bleeding from a head wound. Macbeth elbow-shuffled across the floor to his brother and checked the wound: it was superficial and Casey was conscious but confused.

"Casey!" Macbeth shouted over the clamor of other shrill voices. "Casey . . . We've got to get under the table!" He grabbed his brother by his jacket and pulled him towards him and into the shelter of the table.

"Shouldn't we get out of here?" Casey yelled back. "If the building comes down, we'll be buried!"

"We're safer here. If we go out into the street we could be hit by falling masonry. We've got to sit tight. Wait it out."

Casey nodded but didn't look convinced. Everything around them shook and shuddered, but there was no sound of anything falling onto the table. The shaking intensified, the vibrations resounding in Macbeth's skull, in every inch of bone.

It stopped. Again the restaurant was filled with desperate, terrified gasps and cries. But the shaking had stopped.

He felt the floor beneath them drop, as if they were in an elevator whose cable had snapped. Macbeth and Casey were thrown upwards and he simultaneously grabbed hold of his brother and the single central column leg of the table. They smashed into the floor as the direction was reversed and the world seemed to lunge viciously back at them. All around them there was renewed screaming.

The movement stopped. There was no more shaking.

His fingers biting protectively into his younger brother's arm, Macbeth lay with his bruised cheek against the floor, trying to catch his breath.

It was over. Not just the earthquake.

Macbeth got to his feet, easing Casey up, righting his chair and sitting him down. His forehead was bleeding freely, but again Macbeth could see it was more abrasion than laceration. He took his pocket handkerchief, folded it, and guided Casey's hand up to hold it in place.

"You okay?"

Casey nodded.

"I've got to go and see if anyone else needs help. Will you be okay here?"

"I'm fine . . . Go."

Macbeth allowed his procedural memory once more to over-whelm every other mental function and he made his way around the room. By the end of his sweep, he had placed two head injuries in a recovery position and had strapped two fractures with ties and belts. Most people were simply in shock and none of the injuries, including the head traumas, were serious; Macbeth was content that he had everyone who needed attention comfortable until EMS arrived.

He noticed the young bartender was still at his station, his face bleached of color and the thousand-yard stare of acute stress reaction. Macbeth placed himself directly in the bartender's line of sight, forcing him to focus.

"Are you all right, son? I'm a doctor . . . There's help on its way."

"Nothing . . ." The young bartender turned away from Macbeth and stared around himself in wonder, shaking his head and his eyes searching the gantries, the shelves of glasses, the rows of bottles. "I don't believe it . . . nothing, not a single glass. How can we have had an earthquake and not a single glass get broken . . . ?"

Macbeth followed the bartender's gaze, then turned and scanned the restaurant, looking beyond the distress of the diners. The bar clock, the large wall mirrors, the Victorian prints on the walls – all sat perfectly square, not a single frame askew. The only broken glass and crockery was where it had been knocked from tables by the diners as they fell to the ground. Apart from that there was no physical evidence of an earthquake having taken place.

As if it had never happened.

20

GEORG POULSEN. COPENHAGEN

Despite a sky the color of damp salt hanging dully over the car park, the grounds and the city beyond the window, Georg Poulsen told his wife it was a lovely day outside: a deceit he often performed. Sometimes he would tell Margarethe that it had been raining, but the garden had needed it and it was brightening up now. Mostly, he painted a bright and cheerful picture of the world that lay outside the small pool of her consciousness. It was as if Poulsen was trying to coax his wife out of the prison of her tube-bound body by simulating a better world and brighter reality.

Project One had been set up in the University's Niels Bohr Institute on Blegdamsvej, literally next door to the Rigshospitalet. It meant Poulsen could visit his wife at lunchtimes and any other moments he could steal from his work. It also meant that he was constantly pulled in two directions: working as much and as long as he could to develop the interface program he believed would ultimately help Margarethe, while compelled to visit her as often as possible. And both were at the expense of any time for himself. A new reality to which Poulsen had committed totally.

Today, he had come straight from the Institute. He sat at Margarethe's bedside and told her that his work was progressing better than expected, far ahead of schedule.

He told her what his work could mean: that another world awaited her. A world where she could walk and dance, where she could sing the way she always had while working in the garden.

A world where they could be together with the baby she didn't know she had lost.

He meant everything he said, knowing that, if he was successful in all of his aims, he would be able to offer Margarethe exactly that kind of world. But, like when he described the weather, he did not tell her that the home, the garden, the holidays she would enjoy – the Georg Poulsen and the baby she would be with – would be ersatz: a neurologically counterfeit existence that would stimulate her brain and deceive her into feeling the sun on her face.

"I know you want to live a full life again, Margarethe," he told her. "I want you to know that when I am not here with you I am working on achieving exactly that for you. I love you and all I want is for you to be happy again."

He stopped speaking for a moment. Another visiting-time deceit was always to seem cheerful; as if the horror of Margarethe being entombed in her own flesh was nothing more than a temporary setback. So, whenever he lost his composure, whenever the grief and misery and anger that tore at him each and every day threatened to show in his voice, as it did now, he fell quiet.

In the normal world, in the all-senses environment that most people lived in, Poulsen knew that an undertone in a voice could go unnoticed; and that, conversely, in the sensorially pared-down universe that Margarethe inhabited, his voice would be magnified, filling all space – meaning any defect, any subtlety would be amplified and detected instantly.

After a moment, he composed himself, opened the book on his lap and started to read. *Avatars: a Futurist Fantasy* had been another of Margarethe's favorite finds; she had always sought out obscure gems in unlikely places, and this novel had been unearthed in an antiquarian bookstore one blustery Saturday afternoon in Larsbjørnsstræde. The author 'Æ', whose real name had been George William Russell, was known more through the writings of others than his own, even appearing as a character in James Joyce's *Ulysses*.

Margarethe had once told Poulsen that she found it wonderfully ironic that the two protagonists in Russell's novel were themselves never shown directly to the reader or spoke their own dialogue, but were represented exclusively through their description by other characters. She'd also told him that Russell, as a young art student, had begun to experience what he described as 'waking dreams of astonishing power and vividness', in which he saw other worlds and realities that he claimed had been placed into his consciousness by a mind other and greater than his own.

Poulsen spent two hours reading to his wife; as always investing as much life into the voices as his reading talents would allow.

He was such a frequent visitor that he had gotten to know all the regular members of the hospital staff and had forged something of an informal relationship with Larssen, the department's chief physician, who was aware of Poulsen's involvement in cognitive sciences and provided an interested audience whenever the scientist felt like discussing his work. However Larssen, like the rest of the hospital staff, got to understand that Georg Poulsen was a man of few words on any subject other than his wife's condition and treatment.

About two months after his own discharge from the hospital, he had been in to see his wife when Larssen had asked him at the end of his visit to step into his office.

Larssen was a lanky arthropod-like man who seemed to be all angles, with dark hair, a sallow complexion and eyes that seemed ringed with grayish circles at all times of day. His office was not particularly small, but he seemed cramped behind his desk, spider-joint elbows resting on the blotter.

"Your wife's condition has stabilized," he told Poulsen. "There's no immediate danger of a further bleed into the Pons, so there's little risk of further neurological damage."

"Meaning?"

"Your wife has made little to no progress over the last three and a half months. Many cases of LIS self-resolve, but these tend to be where the patient has been locked in for a week or less. The best recoveries are from patients who have been quadriplegic and anarthric – incapable of speech – for minutes or hours rather than weeks."

"So you're saying that you've given up hope on Margarethe? Is that it?"

"What I'm saying is that I feel we are looking at a condition of sustained morbidity. Locked-in patients, without complications, can live in that state for decades. If we don't lose them within a month of the trauma, the average survival is over five years."

"What's your point?"

"Simply that we should now be looking at the best quality of life we can give your wife. In time, that life may even be outside this hospital. Perhaps even at home. There are many support services available from the state to help. We're all aware of your commitment to your wife and I know that you would do everything you could to stimulate her. Bear in mind we're a long way from making any firm decisions, but we really should at least start to think about the longer term. But don't feel that it's something you have to do. It's a huge burden to take on . . ."

Poulsen sat quietly for a moment, imagining a new kind of life, a different kind of life. A new reality.

"When can she come home?" he asked, eventually.

21

JOSH HOBERMAN. MARYLAND

Josh Hoberman had daily conversations with Ward, the President's personal physician. Despite his antipathy towards Ward being military – and being Ward – Hoberman felt that at least he was a man of science and the only person with whom he could discuss the President with some degree of frankness. Even with that, Hoberman realized early on that Elizabeth Yates had surrounded herself with people who would amplify her sense of ego and mission.

However, it had been Ward who'd called Hoberman in and who hadn't protested at the psychiatrist's more candid observations. Even with that, Hoberman remained cautious in how he approached some of the more sensitive issues surrounding the President's state of mind.

He hadn't been back in Aspen Lodge, the President's residence, since that first night and most of his meetings with Yates and with Ward had been in Laurel Lodge. His sleeping quarters were in Dogwood Cabin, the walls of which were festooned with photographs of previous, eminently more important guests. Camp David was equipped with the most up-to-date technology, yet still had the feel of a nineteen-fifties upscale summer camp or country club, and as he sat under the gaze of foreign premiers past and present, it was by far the weirdest place he'd ever practiced psychiatry. He guessed it was an environment that reflected the mood and tone of its principal occupant. Under Elizabeth Yates, despite the deliberate bucolicism, that mood was less than cozy.

"Have you read the reports about this thing in Boston?" Ward asked.

"I've read them," said Hoberman. "And the other events."

"And?"

"And it would appear you were right – that we really are dealing with something that is pandemic, rather than focused on the President herself."

"So why do I get the feeling you are not ready to sign this off?" asked Ward. He was in civilian clothes, a sweater over his shoulders, the sleeves tied in a loose knot at his chest, sipping single malt from a chunk of crystal. Hoberman tried to banish the unhelpful thought that the army doctor could make spare change modeling for glossy knitwear advertisements.

"Okay . . ." Hoberman sipped his own whiskey. "This is strictly between us? At the moment, at least?"

"Of course."

"This goes beyond my original brief, but I think it has a bearing. Let's say that these hallucinations the President has had are due to the same cause as the other reported cases. That would suggest that there is nothing *particular* to the President causing her to see what she sees, other than some kind of unidentified infection."

"Go on . . ."

"My concern isn't with the cause of the hallucinations, but with the *effect* they may have on the President's underlying psychology."

"Are you saying there is a pre-existing concern?"

Hoberman handed Ward three stapled-together sheets of printed paper. Putting his whiskey glass down on the side table, Ward read the notes.

"Do you see my concerns?" Hoberman asked after Ward had finished.

"I see them, but I dispute them. I have known President Yates for years. If she was exhibiting this kind of pathology, I would have noticed it."

"Not necessarily. This personality type is very adept at concealing its full nature. And, let's face it, some of the indicators of the condition can be taken as positive attributes in people who need to, well, be in charge . . ."

Ward said nothing, reading through the notes again.

"As you can see, I've isolated most of the key markers. She scores highly on all but the fourth facet – the antisocial facet. It could be that she has learned to conceal this better than the others."

"You cannot be serious," said Ward.

"I am serious. It is my firm opinion that Elizabeth Yates is a psychopath – an *extremely* high-functioning psychopath, but a psychopath none the less. I personally don't think that this is uncommon in politicians, if I'm honest. But in the President's case, her absolute and total belief in her own infallibility, combined with her impulsiveness and religious monomania, could lead her to make disastrous choices. I am seriously concerned that the religious or other interpretation she may put on a future hallucination could be the trigger for exactly that kind of disastrous choice."

Ward again sat silently for a moment. "You've discussed this with no one else?"

"As I said, it's between us for the time being."

"I'd like you to keep it that way. Do you mind if I hang on to this?"

Hoberman thought for a moment. "Sure . . ."

22

JOHN MACBETH. BOSTON

In fifteen years as a psychiatrist, Macbeth had never experienced or heard of anything like it. The media was full of it the next day; not just in Massachusetts but across the States and around the world. The Phantom Boston Earthquake was how it was described in most headlines.

It had taken the EMS an hour and a half to reach the restaurant. Crews had been diverted all across the city and beyond to deal with the injured. There had been casualties across the entire seaboard of Massachusetts from Rockport to Plymouth, and as far inland as Worcester. The earthquake was felt throughout the state, and there were reports from across the border in Nova Scotia and New Brunswick of people feeling the ground shaking.

Most casualties were fall injuries, eight of which had been fatal when people plunged from balconies, fire escapes or other elevated places. The greatest number of fatalities had arisen from automobile accidents where drivers had lost control. In total, thirty people had died, more than a thousand had been injured.

And there hadn't been a single case of structural damage.

The Weston Observatory's seismographs hadn't even flickered. Earth Sciences Departments across New England and beyond confirmed the Weston results, with every billion-dollar resource and backyard amateur seismograph being checked.

No earthquake. The whole city and half the state had simply lost its balance.

In one day, Macbeth spent more time watching television and on the Internet than he probably had in the whole preceding month. Conspiracy theories and bad-taste jokes, both of which Macbeth attributed to the same double-figure IQ bracket, started to emerge in the afternoon. Official statements possessed the same intellectual worth as far as Macbeth was concerned, some hinting at a virus affecting victims' vestibular systems. The truth was that there was no explaining deaths from an earthquake that absolutely did not take place.

The thing that caused the greatest stir was when analysis of the spread of injuries was mapped out: a pattern emerged that was strangely consistent with a genuine earthquake. Despite there being no geophysical evidence, the collation of injury statistics and witness accounts revealed a pattern consistent with an earthquake epicenter out in the Atlantic, about twenty-five or thirty miles east of Cape Ann. From the descriptions gathered from various locations, the experience was deemed compatible with an earthquake magnitude of six on the Richter scale.

It was later that following day that someone put it all together: probably some anonymous researcher in a TV station backroom, doing a simple cross-referencing of the data. And it was ready for transmission by the time Macbeth tuned into the evening news.

The Phantom Boston Earthquake had become the Cape Ann Ghostquake.

It dominated the specially extended edition of the news. Old woodcut prints of crooked and cracked buildings with the date 1775 provided the background to the hairstyles, professional tans and studied gravity of the news anchors. Everyone from seismologists and historians to crackpot psychics and religious-nut doomsayers had their piece to camera; politicians talked a lot and said little, spinning official lines; scientists of all persuasions were interviewed and all were at a loss to explain the phenomenon. The most likely explanation put forward remained that of a virus causing some kind of loss of balance and auditory hallucinations. After all, no one had actually *seen* the earthquake.

But what exercised the media to the point of fever was that the epicenter identified by casualty-mapping coincided exactly with that of the Cape Ann earthquake of 1775. Weston Observatory had, for years, been running computer models of what would happen if the same type of earthquake were to hit the hugely expanded population and settlement of contemporary New England. The casualties caused by the 'ghostquake' matched what the computer had predicted. Exactly.

Most of the Boston injuries had taken place in the Back Bay district, where the city had been expanded in the nineteenth century by building on infill poured into the Bay. Infill, the seismologists had explained, was the least stable and most susceptible to tremor of all ground types and the brownstones and other architecture of Back Bay had always been the most at risk from seismic activity.

Macbeth had his own theory – still vague and slowly coalescing – about what had happened, and it had to do with what Pete Corbin had told him.

Whatever had happened, whatever the cause, Boston had been shaken in every sense: Macbeth saw it on the streets he walked through, in the anxious, confused faces of passers-by.

The question in everyone's mind was: why Boston?

Then the reports from all over the world started to come in.

23

ETHAN BUNDY. MARYLAND

Special Agent Ethan Bundy was shirtless and sockless as he prayed.

He was in the Camp David quarters allocated to him, kneeling at the side of his bed, fingers interlocked tight, forehead pressed against the hard ridge of his knuckles, elbows resting on the bed's edge.

Camp David had been buzzing with activity all day, President Yates gathering information and opinions on the events in Boston. Video conferences had taken place with experts in every field and she had even had a meeting with the Hebrew, Hoberman. Bundy had been privy to it all, at her side or in the background, silent and supportive. None of it made sense to him and he could tell that the so-called experts were no less confused than he. In spite of himself, he had, in a rare quiet moment, asked the question that had been on his mind all day.

"What does it mean, Madame President?"

Elizabeth Yates had turned to him, grasping his elbow and locking her eyes with his. Three words. Three words were all she spoke, yet they had electrified him.

"The Rapture comes!"

Bundy prayed hard. He prayed for salvation, to be among the righteous chosen. He sought forgiveness for the lives he had taken in the past and asked for the strength to take the lives he would be commanded to take in the future. Most of all, he begged the Lord's acceptance of his impurity. He prayed for singularity, for a wholeness he knew he could never possess. President Yates, he knew, possessed that purity; she was a true and singular instrument of God, His chosen representative on Earth. Bundy, on the other hand, was neither pure nor singular.

He was an abomination.

Ethan Bundy knew exactly who he was, what he was. He was both the murderer and the murdered. He was Cain. He was Abel. He was both and he was neither. God had given him the Mark so that he should discover who he was, to taunt him with the knowledge of his own duality, with the awareness that he was damned to wander the Earth as both killer and victim, in an endless, seamless interweaving of two fates, of two souls.

He should have known earlier, recognizing his inner otherness from the outer otherness of the eyes that looked back at him from the mirror every morning: pale irises with a golden-brown inner band around the pupils and an outer band of the lightest blue. Eyes so pale that they hurt in the mildest sunlight. Eyes that drew attention, remark. He should have known from them.

But it had only been later, after he had started working for the Bureau, that Bundy had experienced the epiphany, the discovery of his true nature. He had been on a case in Kentucky, working out of the Louisville field office. It was the usual hillbilly cottage industry: a cannabis farm miles from any road and accessed by a rough, winding track. Skills learned nearly a hundred years before in the time of Prohibition and moonshine-stills were still applied: the track booby-trapped with razors and fishing-hooks strung at eye level on monofilament fishing line, concealed pits filled with snakes or bristling with six-inch nails. At the end of the track was a suntrap hollow waist-high and blue-green with marijuana plants; a large wooden shack, concealed from aerial detection by a lattice of branches and leaves, tucked into its far end. It wasn't the kind of thing the Bureau normally got involved in, the local sheriff's department and the DEA holding the purview, but in this particular den they had found a haul of cash that was suspected to be counterfeit, making it a federal matter.

The forensics team had been examining the cash in situ – wrapped in plastic and exposed through torn-up shack floorboards – when Bundy and his colleagues arrived. The technician had been using a UVA Wood's lamp to inspect banknotes for signs of forgery. Bent over his work, he had not heard Bundy approach and had turned suddenly when the FBI man called to him. As the forensics man turned, the Wood's Lamp had still been switched on and its dim glow had fallen on Bundy's face. He would never forget the crime scene technician's expression. Shock. Fear, almost. Bundy was used to people reacting to his unusual eye color, but this had been something different.

"What is it?" Bundy had asked.

The forensics man switched the lamp off and narrowed his eyes as he examined Bundy, as if searching for something now gone.

"Your face . . . under the UV light. I think you should maybe see a dermatologist."

"What are you talking about?"

"There was something showed up under the light."

"What? What showed up?"

"Marks. I don't know what they were."

"Shine it on me again."

The forensics man had reluctantly done as he was told.

"What do you see?"

"Like I said," the technician frowned, examining Bundy's face but still uneasy, as if looking at something dangerous or frightening. "Marks on your skin. These lamps show up all kinds of stuff. Maybe you got sun damage or something. I'd get it checked out."

He had switched the lamp off and they had discussed the case, but Bundy could see the professional tone was just a curtain the technician had pulled over his unease at whatever it was he had seen under the artificial light.

Bundy had not made an appointment to see his doctor right away. Instead he had ordered a black light lamp over the Internet, the one that now sat in his bedside drawer, the one he took with him almost everywhere. He had stood in front of the mirror and shone the lamp on his face. Then he had seen it. He had seen the Demon and it had taken his breath away. He had seen the Mark of Cain. Not just on his face.

Bundy squeezed his eyelids tighter shut, his hands tighter together, prayed harder. As he did with every prayer, he ended his supplication with another plea for singularity, for the Mark to be gone. For the stain on his soul to be expunged from his body.

Standing up from his amen, he walked through to the small bathroom, first taking the UV lamp from the nightstand. The stark bathroom light emphasized the sculpture of his muscles, the tanned smoothness of his skin. Flawless, unmarked, perfect. However tight his schedule, Bundy always managed an hour of weight work every day, carefully rotating the muscles he worked on so that each set had a rest day, varying the type of exercise on a weekly cycle to circumvent muscle memory. He had become an expert on maintaining his body's bulk, shape and definition. He also used creams, screens and emollients daily on his skin. The tan was fake, applied each day. He knew that the same lack of melanin that had made his eyes so light made his skin susceptible to sun damage and melanoma. The dermatologist who had examined him had told him that – just before he referred Bundy to genetic counseling. But that wasn't why he used sunscreen daily. Ethan Bundy was afraid to get a real tan. He was afraid what a real tan would reveal to the world.

He examined his reflection in the mirror. Even in this unflattering light he could see the perfection of his body, the strength of his jawline, the handsome regularity of his features. Then he saw his eyes. His eyes were always there to remind him of his impurity. He switched off the bathroom light and stood, still looking at his reflection, silhouetted black by the soft light coming in from the bedroom behind him. Now he could not see his eyes.

"Please Lord, please remove the Mark from me. Please forgive me for the murder of my brother. Please take his soul from mine, his body from mine. Please forgive me and make me singular."

He drew a breath, then switched on the black light lamp.

The Demon. Cain. The Marked One.

The lamp glowed dimly purple in the dark bathroom. The fact that it shone at all was an indicator of its inefficiency: UVA light being invisible to the human eye, the purple glow was the escape of shorter-wavelength light through the nickel oxide filter. The bitter irony for Bundy was that this invisible light made visible that which was hidden in normal light. It revealed his true nature.

His prayer had not been answered.

Smooth- and tanned-skinned Ethan Bundy looked into the mirror and the Demon Cain looked back at him. Cain whose skin bore the Mark of his fratricide. The Mark had its own dark beauty: like the stripes of a tiger, bands of darker skin looped and curlicued on his face, arched and twisted around his neck and over his shoulders. A dramatic V, a diamond shape set into it, swept up from his chest. His entire body was covered in swirling, coiling stripes. He shone the light onto the back of one hand, then the other. Each seemed tattooed with a diamond, from the base of which issued other stripes that looped around his wrists and snaked up his forearms.

Bundy felt the same ache he always felt when he observed his true nature.

He switched the lamp off and the bathroom light back on. His humanity was restored to him.

*

The geneticist had explained it to him carefully, slowly, checking that he understood what she was saying. It still made no sense to him. He was twins. Not *a* twin, but both twins.

"It's called tetragametic chimerism," she had explained. "Non-identical twins in the womb, one of which, detecting the presence of a competitor, envelops and absorbs it."

"I killed my brother?"

"You absorbed him," she had explained. "Two complete sets of chromosomes in one fetus. Your brother still lives inside you. You *are* him. You are both twins."

"That's why I bear the marks?" he had asked.

"They're called the Lines of Blaschko. We all have them and they are probably the pathways taken by epidermal cells during the development of the fetus. They become visible in some skin disorders but are generally invisible to the naked eye. For some reason they are more pronounced in chimeras, probably because one twin has darker skin than the other. That would explain the central heterochromia – your dual-colored eyes. One twin has hazel eyes, the other blue."

"I hate them . . ."

"I don't know why," the geneticist had said. "They're very striking. Count yourself lucky – many chimeras have full heterochromia: one eye one color, the other another."

Despite the scientific jargon, Bundy knew the true meaning of the lines. He had been born a killer, having taken his brother's life in the womb, and he bore the Mark of Cain for it. And he had been born plural, with a dyadic nature. Good and evil.

He had despaired at his condition until he had met President Yates, then a senator of uncompromising vision and ambition, possessed of an unshakeable will. She had shown him the way. God's way.

All Nature is duality, President Yates had explained. So much beauty yet so much cruelty. For there to be life and growth there has to be death. For there to be Good, there has to be

Evil. And sometimes, she had explained, we have to do evil things for Good ultimately to triumph.

He had shown her his Mark. She had seen it. Touched it . . . Bundy completed his night-time ritual, brushing and flossing his teeth. He had just climbed into bed when the door opened. President Yates stood silhouetted in the doorframe, carrying a document in one hand.

"Ethan," she said with quiet command, "I'm afraid we're going to have to do something about Professor Hoberman."

part two

A TIME OF VISIONS

Something unknown is doing we don't know what.

Professor Sir Arthur Eddington, astrophysicist

24

FABIAN. FRIESLAND

The bullying stopped before it had really started, but then the looks, the suspicions, the whispers, had begun.

His jaw broken, three teeth dislodged, a rib cracked and suffering from severe concussion, Maartens had been off school for two weeks, the first three days of which had been spent in hospital in Leeuwarden, and when he returned his face had still been badly discolored and distended, his jaw wired shut.

From scrabbled-together scraps of rumor, Fabian worked out that Maartens must have staggered his way back to the edge of town before fainting in the street. An ambulance and the police had been called. Violence was rare in a small coastal community such as this and they could see from Maartens's injuries that they were dealing with multiple assailants. Assuming the assault had taken place where Henkje had been found, they wanted answers but he'd been in no condition to provide them until a good twenty-four hours later. It was then that the police had pressured him for the identity or description of his assailants.

So he gave them exactly that. Henkje described three older boys, about seventeen or eighteen, none of whom he recognized; in such a small community, that meant they must have been outsiders. When Henkje told the police that one of the boys had asked him for money, he had thrown in that his attacker spoke with some kind of foreign accent. When he had told the foreigners that he had no money on him, they had launched into an attack against which he was defenseless, beating him to the ground and kicking him. The attack, he explained, had taken place a few hundred meters from where he had been found.

The police had accepted the story, as had the wider community, eager to believe that such brutality had to have come from outside their small world. Henkje's embellishment of foreign accents had set older heads nodding with sad sagacity: such things were to be expected these days.

While Henkje had been off school, his entourage of lesser bullies had left Fabian alone. Fabian was pretty sure that they knew nothing of what had really happened: they simply lacked the focus Henkje had provided and were too busy dealing with the indignity of their leader's humiliating beating.

The sight of the returning Henkje, his puffed-up face a rainbow of greens, purples and blues, his jaw wired shut, did even more to chasten their strutting. It was on the second day of Henkje's return that Fabian encountered him in the school corridor, between classes and without his friends. Their eyes met and Henkje's fell immediately to the floor; in that moment Fabian knew his troubles were over as far as Maartens and his cronies were concerned. But there was no sense of triumph: whenever Fabian saw Henkje, which was seldom, as the bigger boy clearly made an effort to stay out of his way, he was filled with an urge to apologize, to somehow make amends, to explain about the déjà vu experience on the beach. But none of it made sense.

Henkje's jaw remained wired for a month. But even after the swelling and discoloration had disappeared from his face, he was a changed boy. And it was just about the time that his jaw had been unwired that Fabian also noticed a change in the others. First Henkje's friends, then others in the school began to avoid Fabian. Avert their eyes. Even Robin Hoekstra, who was the closest thing he had to a friend and sat next to him in

History, seemed to be avoiding him. Fabian considered confronting Henkje, but he let it go. In many ways, it suited him that his peers kept their distance; he had always felt that he didn't belong with them, that he was adrift in time, geography and society.

Three months on from the attack, but completely unconnected to it, the Maartens family moved out of the area and inland, to Bakkefean. Fabian no longer had to face his guilt in the school hallways. But the others. The others remained distant, almost fearful of him. He even began to catch the odd strange look from a teacher.

Life went on. Fabian still returned to the beach each week, seeking comfort in the spot he had always gone to, but it was somehow less special now, as if the sand he sat in was still soiled with Henkje's blood.

He sat again on the beach by the rock, the vast sky pressing flat land and sea. Everything was the same as the day he had encountered Henkje and everything was different. The sky was still as big, but today vast billows of gray-white clouds, like the sails of ghostly ships, slid across its shield and the temperature was several degrees cooler.

Once more, Fabian thought back to the fury that had been unleashed. He had become an animal, a thing of base instinct and mindless violence. What troubled him most was that he had enjoyed it, a thirst being slaked. He had never, in his fourteen years, felt more vital, more alive. His world had never felt more real.

He sat with his back to the stone, poking at the sand with a salt- and sun-bleached stick, his thoughts wandering.

It came upon him suddenly and completely: the same feeling. Like déjà vu but not déjà vu. More intense. He sat bolt upright, casting his gaze around him. Everything was the same: the sky, the temperature, the light. Nothing had changed, yet he felt his heart beat faster in his chest, his pulse rushing in his ears.

It terrified him that this could be the prelude to another act of uncontrollable violence, or another episode where time repeated itself.

He scanned the sea's horizon, swept his gaze back to the promontory and to the dunes and the dyke behind him. Everything was the same, unchanged. But something *was* different. It was just that he couldn't see it. Yet. He scanned the horizon again, turning in a slow three-sixty-degree circle: concentrating, narrowing his eyes, seeking out each detail.

The promontory. Something was wrong with the finger of grass and sand that insubstantially prodded the North Sea. His vague panic suddenly became specific, concentrated. The lighthouse. The lighthouse was gone. Fabian staggered back a few steps. How could the lighthouse, which had stood sentinel on the promontory for one hundred and fifty years, suddenly disappear? He closed his eyes tight, but when he opened them again, it was still gone.

Like a sudden surge of nausea, the odd feeling rapidly intensified, reaching deep, deep inside him. This was beyond déjà vu, beyond a feeling of inexplicable resonances: this was a seismic shift in his sense of place and time, the universe around him, within him, reconfiguring itself. He began to shake. Another wave, even stronger.

The ship-sail clouds had disappeared, the sky now clear. The chill in the afternoon air was gone. Fabian knew he was not somewhere else – this was still exactly the same space he had occupied a second ago – this was *sometime* else.

Voices. Distant. Behind him.

He spun around and looked back towards the land. Like the lighthouse on the promontory, the gentle green swelling of the dyke had disappeared. There was now no clear demarcation between beach and land, instead the sand smudged into a mud-brown band, in turn smudging into an ugly tangle of scurvy-grass, sedge and plantain. How had he come to know what these marsh grasses were? Why was this alien landscape not alien to him? Fabian was snapped out of his thoughts by the sounds of voices again. Many voices. He could not see who was talking but reckoned that they were somewhere beyond the band of marsh grass. To his surprise, he realized he was no longer afraid – not in the slightest bit afraid – but he instinctively felt the need to approach the voices with stealth. He stepped forward, heading inland towards the towering grasses, and felt himself sink up to his knees. Looking down, he saw the soft pale sand had been replaced with dull gray mud. Wadden. He ploughed through the mud, a slow, laborious wading that cost him his sneakers and sucked his sports socks from his feet. Again he was surprised by his lack of surprise: nothing made sense, yet everything was somehow just as he expected it to be.

It took Fabian ten sweating, heaving minutes to traverse the Waddenzee mudflats and reach dryer sand and the fringe of tall grasses. Once he was free of the mud's clinging embrace, he looked down at his naked feet and his jeans, sodden and caked with mud. Whatever was happening to him, whatever this was, it looked, sounded, felt and smelled real. If he was going mad, he was going completely mad in every sense. He pushed his way through the grasses, staying hidden in them as he reached their landside edge. Easing them apart like curtains, he peered through cautiously.

A village. Or a camp. Or something in between.

There was a dozen or so unevenly spaced wooden lodges clustered around a square of scraped-bare earth. Each lodge was elevated a foot or so from the ground by stout wooden stanchions; timber-framed and beamed, the walls wattle and daub, the roofs composed of densely woven thatch. Unlike the pristine, sharp-edged geometry of Fabian's brick-built home that proclaimed Man's independence from Nature, these lodges seemed organic, constructed from natural materials gathered from their immediate environment – mud and seagrass straw and rough-hewn timber. They seemed still part of the landscape, fused with it.

Smoke curled up into the clear sky from a fire in the raw earth central square. A group of children ran around, playing tag and laughing and squealing as they evaded or submitted to capture. They looked like any group of children, apart from their odd clothes. A woman came out of one of the lodges, climbing down the hewn-log steps, balancing some kind of wood and hide bucket on her hip. She wore a weary maturity around her like a heavy cloak – she was a woman and not a girl – yet Fabian guessed she could only be a year or two older than him. Her hair was red-blonde and gathered up into a knot behind her head. She was pretty, her features regular and well-defined, but Fabian could see even at a distance that her skin was roughened and reddened on the nose and cheeks, as if weather-beaten. He ducked back as she turned in his direction, her face empty of expression. There was no sign that the young woman had seen Fabian hiding in the rushes, but she headed straight for him. He sank back as much as he dared without creating a telltale ripple in the long stalks of seagrass. He could see her clearly now: she wore a yellow tunic, a long mustard-colored skirt with a slightly longer petticoat beneath. Fabian could tell that he was looking at an outfit that did not belong to his time. For a moment he contemplated the insanity of his situation and wondered if he was looking at some kind of re-enactment – maybe they had set up some kind of living museum: a Dark Ages theme park. But that didn't make sense; it didn't explain the disappearance of the lighthouse or the dyke, or the Waddenzee mudflats having shifted position.

Maybe, he thought, ghosts do exist. Maybe this was a village of the dead.

The woman was now directly in front of him. She tilted the leather bucket and spilled its contents into the seagrass, almost tipping them directly onto Fabian. The water she spilled smelled foul and the odor seemed to seize Fabian by the throat, causing him to cough. He knew he had given away his presence and there was nothing for it but to reveal himself fully. His mind raced as he tried to find the words, form the sentences, to explain the inexplicable.

He stood up.

He was now face to face with her, only a meter or so apart. He could see the detailing on the brocade band that held her hair back and on the fringe of her tunic; he could see the flaky redness across her nose and cheeks, he could smell her scent, the odor of her body, not an unclean nor unpleasant smell.

"I'm sorry . . ." He found some words. "I didn't mean to startle you. I—"

She looked straight through him, as if he wasn't there, staring out into the grasses before turning and heading back whence she came. She hadn't seen him. He had not been there.

This was no phantom village. The woman had been no ghost, Fabian realized. *He* was the ghost.

25

JOHN MACBETH. BOSTON

People, Macbeth knew, liked to scare themselves with spook stories. As a psychiatrist he understood the mechanism: the ghost story reader or horror movie fan thriving on simulations of frightening environments with which to tease and confuse the amygdala, that most ancient and primal of the brain's structures, into believing there is real and immediate danger; the chemical signals sent from amygdala to hypothalamus in turn releasing epinephrine, norepinephrine and cortisol into the system.

Except, of course, everyone in their heart of hearts knows that a ghost story or a horror movie isn't real, so the adrenaline-buzz can be enjoyed at one remove and without real fight or flight, the fear becomes mitigated, vicarious and packaged for entertainment.

Macbeth, with his odd detachment from the world as others saw it, often noticed the way catastrophe and suffering were reported on TV: conveyed with professionally synthetic modulation and intonation, as if natural voices were somehow inappropriate. Macbeth wondered if it was, just as with horror movies, a deliberate repackaging of fear to keep it at one remove. There had been rare times, of course, when the professional demeanor had fallen away, the fear had become immediate and the reporters became real people. Oddly enough, those rare occasions had been when reality had turned on its head and looked more like a Hollywood disaster movie, like the unreal reality of planes being flown into New York towers.

The reporting of the events in Boston was becoming like that. The New England media's handling of the 'ghostquake' was mixed and confused. The event made no sense, yet people had died and almost everyone in Eastern Massachusetts had experienced it. Professional gravity yielded to a more fundamental, more genuine anxiety.

Especially when it emerged that Boston had not been alone.

Phantom earthquakes in France and India, both on the sites of major historical quakes, had left people injured and killed. Just like the Boston episode, the effects of major seismic events had been felt, the tremors and shaking of the earth experienced by those present, but again there had been no physical evidence of real seismic activity of any kind.

It was no longer a spook story. Serious efforts were put into establishing exactly what could be causing the effects. The epidemic proposal continued to be put forward: a virus or other agent was attacking the vestibular system of victims. The remarkable coincidence that everyone seemed to suffer attacks of imbalance and auditory hallucination at *precisely* the same moment seemed not to feature in anyone's thinking.

There were, of course, a hundred crackpot hypotheses generated by the conspiracy theorists, the religious Right and the otherwise deranged. The Illuminati were behind it all, creating the chaos from which to establish their New World Order; aliens were causing it, using mind-control beams to confuse the human population before a full-scale invasion of Earth; God was punishing humankind for turning its back on Him and worshiping the false gods of science; the government had developed a new weapon and it had gone wrong, according to one conspiracy theory, or they had deliberately tested it on Boston, according to another. And there were those who exploited the situation and the gullible: claims were made that the phenomena could be controlled and conjured at will and tickets were sold for live concerts by Elvis, Frank Sinatra and Caruso.

Generally, people went about their normal business, but their faces in the street were anxious and uneasy, as if mistrusting everything they saw.

In the meantime, Macbeth's Boston schedule went ahead as planned. Colleagues in Copenhagen called to ask if he'd experienced the earthquake; he regretted admitting he had, for it resulted in endless questions about what it had been like and what he thought had caused it.

Casey's head injury had been as minor as Macbeth had suspected, but he was clearly troubled: Casey was someone whose logic and intelligence made sense of almost any puzzle, but the experience in the restaurant was beyond even his rationalization. He insisted that Macbeth move into his apartment for the rest of his stay in Boston.

"I know you like to have things just so," Casey said. "But so do I . . . I think we can harmonize our just-sos for a few days. I don't know about you, but after what happened the other night, I think we could do with each other's company."

Comforted by the thought of moving in with Casey, Macbeth's reluctance to cause his brother trouble was largely for show and he agreed to check out of his hotel.

The woman behind the hotel reception desk was young and attractive, with very dark hair swept back from a pretty face and large blue eyes. He'd spoken to her a couple of times before and when he checked out he picked up again on the way she smiled at him. She was very much Macbeth's type and in different circumstances he would have initiated a date, but there was too much happening, too many things taking his mind out of the moment. He apologized for checking out early and said he understood if he had to pay in full for the nights he had booked.

"That's not a problem Dr Macbeth, I'm just sorry you're having to cut short your stay in Boston."

"Oh, I'm not really . . . It's just that my brother has asked me to move into his apartment till I leave. Things . . . I mean people . . ." Macbeth struggled to articulate the thought. "Things are a little different after what happened the other night."

She nodded understandingly. "Well, perhaps we'll see you again . . ."

"I'm sure you will." He smiled.

"You've stayed with us before, haven't you?" she asked, with that familiar frown of concentrated recall.

"No, this is my first stay in the hotel."

"Really? I'm sure we've met before . . ." Her frown remained.

"No, we haven't." He smiled. "Believe me, I would remember."

He was about to turn from the reception desk when, over her shoulder, he saw a framed photograph of the dark-haired and bearded man he had seen in the hall by the elevator. Macbeth was relieved that he had been able to deal with the pretty girl and not the man who hadn't held the car for him.

"The owner?" he asked the young woman, nodding towards the picture.

"My father," she said. "And yes, this was his hotel."

'Was?"

"Dad died when I was very young. My mother has run the hotel since. Twenty-three years now . . ."

The driver of the waiting cab popped the trunk and started over to take Macbeth's luggage when a pair of sunglasses and a dark suit full of shoulders stepped out of the town car parked behind the taxi.

"It's okay," the suit said to the taxi driver. "I'm here to take Dr Macbeth where he needs to go."

The driver shrugged, shut the trunk and got back into his cab.

"Are you from the Schilder Institute?" Macbeth asked. "I wasn't expecting a ride. I'm afraid we'll have to make a detour – I've got to drop my stuff off at my brother's place."

"That's not a problem, sir, and we'll drop you off at the Institute after, but I'm not from there." He reached into his coat pocket and produced a wallet with an official ID. Macbeth saw the blue capitals.

"FBI?"

"Special Agent Bundy. I wonder if you could help us with a couple of things. We won't take you out of your way and you will be on time for your appointment at the Institute."

"Bundy?"

"Yes sir, as in Ted. No relation." The FBI man smiled.

"What's this all about? What on earth can I do for the FBI?"

Agent Bundy held out an arm in the direction of the town car. "Maybe we could talk on the way. I'm conscious of your schedule, doctor."

Macbeth shrugged, allowed Bundy to take his bags and followed him to the car.

Macbeth had the same sense of claustrophobia in the back of the Lincoln that he had felt in the police prowler. The windows were tinted dark, which seemed to remove him further from the city they drove through. The driver didn't turn or acknowledge Macbeth as he got into the rear with Bundy.

"So," said Macbeth when they were under way, "what can I help the FBI with?"

"Have you heard of someone called John Astor?" Bundy removed his sunglasses and Macbeth could see that he had the most striking color of eyes. Almost like targets, each eye had a narrow band of orangey-brown around the iris, surrounded by a wider band of bright green-blue. It made his gaze disconcertingly penetrating.

"Heard of him, yes," said Macbeth. "But that's all. To be honest, I thought he was a bit of an urban myth – him and this mysterious book of his. Why do you ask?"

"But you have no knowledge of John Astor other than these rumors?"

"The name has a significance to me, but it's not at all connected."

"Oh?" Bundy leaned forward.

"I had a patient – years ago, when I was at McLean. He was exhibiting symptoms of what appeared to be Dissociative Identity Disorder."

"And his name was John Astor?"

Macbeth shook his head. "No, that was the name he gave one of his alters."

"Alters?"

"Dissociative Identity Disorder is sometimes called Multiple Personality Disorder. Some trauma, injury or pathology causes the patient to seek refuge in different identities. Alternate identities or alters. One of his alters used the name John Astor."

"What happened to this patient?"

"He's not your man, if that's what you mean," said Macbeth. "I'm afraid he died. Suicide. One I lost."

"I see." Bundy thought for a moment, holding Macbeth with his striking eyes. "Have you heard of a group of people who call themselves the Simulists?"

Macbeth frowned. "No I haven't. Why do you ask?"

"But you have heard of Blind Faith?"

"Yes . . ." Macbeth sighed, making no effort to conceal his impatience. He looked out at a glass-darkened Boston. "I've heard of Blind Faith."

"And, of course, you knew Melissa Collins?"

Macbeth turned from the window. "Melissa? What about Melissa?"

For a moment Bundy seemed to be assessing Macbeth; his reactions. "Don't you know?"

"Know what? What the hell is this all about?"

"I'm sorry, Dr Macbeth, I thought you would know by now. The mass suicide from the Golden Gate Bridge. Melissa Collins was the leader of the group. She was the CEO of the company they all worked for."

Macbeth stared at Bundy. He had heard about the suicides, had known they were young people, but being in Copenhagen he had never read the details, names. Melissa? Melissa had been one of them? While his brain processed what Bundy had told him, he noticed a dark stain camouflaged by the diagonal stripes on the FBI man's tie. Melissa was dead and all Macbeth could think about was what the genetic reason could be for Bundy's unusual eye color and where he had gotten the stain on his tie.

"Melissa . . ." Macbeth heard himself saying again. Bringing himself back, he shook his head vigorously. "I don't believe it. Not Melissa . . . there is no one I know less likely to commit suicide than her. And I'm talking as a professional psychiatrist as well as someone who was involved with her. Whatever happened, I know she didn't throw herself off the Golden Gate."

"I'm afraid there is no doubt about it. No doubt at all. Not only did she jump, she seemed to lead the others to as well. It was witnessed by a police officer and recorded on security cameras. You never suspected her as being potentially suicidal?"

"No, of course not. Melissa was the most well-balanced person I know, and the very last person to take their own life." Macbeth thought about what he had just said and how it echoed almost exactly what Casey had said about Gabriel Rees.

"When was the last time you saw Melissa?"

"About three years ago. Before I went over to Denmark. We . . . well, we went our separate ways. She took up a research post in Los Angeles. I had no idea she had moved to San Francisco or had set up a software company, so when I heard about the Golden Gate thing, I simply didn't put it together." Macbeth shook his head. "I just can't believe it."

"And at that time, the last time you saw her, was she involved with any particular group?"

"What kind of group?" Macbeth found himself blaming Bundy for his own confusion. None of what he was hearing made sense. He was also confused by his own lack of grief, but he knew that would come. Eventually. The world reached John Macbeth in arrears, through the delaying relays of his weird internal wiring.

"I mean, did she have any particularly strong religious affiliations, or involvement with belief groups? Particularly fringe belief groups."

"Melissa involved in a cult? That's crazy. She had no time for religion, mainstream, fringe or otherwise. As far as I'm aware, she was an atheist. No . . . If that's the story behind what happened to her, I don't believe it."

They were on the other side of the Common now, Boston still flat and smoked-glass dark.

"We have evidence that she was involved with a group that meets many of the criteria of a cult," said Bundy. When he spoke, the FBI man seemed empty of expression or emotion. Maybe a lack of affect was trained into you at Quantico.

"What? You think Melissa was involved with Blind Faith?"

"No, not Blind Faith. Did she ever mention John Astor to you?"

"Astor? No, not that I can remember. I don't think either of us had heard about him at that time. It's only over the last few months—"

"Did she ever mention either Samuel Tennant or Jeff Killberg?"

Macbeth thought for a moment then shook his head. "Who are they?"

"One of the people Melissa was working with in San Francisco was called Deborah Canning. Canning is also from Boston – do you know if Melissa knew her before she moved to California?"

"If she did, she never mentioned her to me. Now, could you tell me why you're so interested in Melissa if it's a case of simple suicide?"

"Twenty-seven young people throwing themselves off the Golden Gate Bridge at the same time could never be described as simple suicide," said Bundy. "The California Highway Patrol are still investigating the event. My interest lies in the circumstances behind it."

"So why do I get more than a whiff of the Homeland Act?"

"There are a number of toxic cults out there at the moment; some are potential threats to national security. I'm simply looking into any possible connection between what happened in San Francisco and certain persons or groups of interest. To be honest, there's probably none, but we have to go through the motions."

Macbeth nodded, even though Bundy did not strike him as a through-the-motions type.

"Ah, we're here . . ." Bundy said with a smile that made no effort to reach his strange eyes. Macbeth could see they were outside Casey's apartment building. "We'll wait for you while you drop your stuff off, then take you to the Schilder Institute. It's the least we can do for taking up your time."

"You didn't take up my time and you saved me the fare. But I'll take a cab to the Institute. I've got a few things to do here first."

"If you're sure, Dr Macbeth. In the meantime, thanks for your time and help."

After he got out and the silent driver placed his bags at his feet, Macbeth watched the town car glide down the street and around the corner. As he did so, he reflected on the fact that he now stood exactly outside his brother's apartment, even though he hadn't told either Bundy or his driver where Casey lived.

26

KAREN. BOSTON

It was two weeks and one psych visit after the incident in the street.

Karen still performed her doorway rituals; still led a perfectly normal life outside those abstract moments of ceremony. Dr Corbin expressed no concern about what had happened in the street, explaining that her OCD made her no more prone to delusions or hallucinations than any one else; what she had seen was either a real girl who had simply stepped back onto the sidewalk and out of sight, or it had been a simple case of pareidolia, where the brain adds a visual two-and-two to make five. We all do it, he said.

Nevertheless, the episode troubled her. She had lain in bed recalling the imagined little girl and the real man who pulled Karen to safety – trying to work out where she had seen him before and how she had known what his voice would sound like before she heard it.

And she wasn't alone: others had seen things that weren't there. The whole city had been shaken by an earthquake that hadn't happened. How could she be sure she hadn't experienced a hallucination? Or that she wouldn't have another? But her OCD rituals remained her priority: they had to stop.

Dr Corbin had suggested she take time off to do an intensive period of 'deprogramming', as he called it. He could refer her to a New York clinic that specialized in deconstructing OCD rituals, taking them apart step by step, while also carrying out deep phobia therapies. Karen had resisted, explaining she couldn't just drop everything for some kind of nut-job detox. There was the Halverson meeting coming up. Maybe then – maybe after the Halverson meeting.

Karen's employers were tolerant, if not entirely supportive, when it came to her OCD. And anyway, it didn't make that much of an impact on her work: her firm was housed in a modern, clean-lined building with light decor and most of the offices were open-plan. Karen's own office had wide double doors kept perpetually open. The ritual for leaving or entering her office through such a large portal was simpler and less obvious than the usual: she bowed low, as if passing through a tunnel, keeping as far away from the corners as possible, finishing with a flourish of web-busting hands as she straightened up. She also made an effort to be first in the office each morning and carried in her handbag an extendible duster, which she would run over the jambs and corners of the doorway.

But the Halverson meeting was not taking place in her firm's offices.

The Halverson Building was an ornate mid-nineteenth-century edifice of Portland stone; all history-inundated nooks and crannies on the outside, marble and oak on the inside. As Karen, her boss Jack Court and her two corporate liability co-workers made their way through the foyer, having first patiently waited for Karen to complete her entrance ritual, she eyed the ceiling cornicing, the angles, details and edges of the paneling, the marble statuary mounted on plinths, the corners where the walls met.

A fact is not a dead thing. A fact is alive and can grow; wields huge power. A fact that lived constantly in Karen's head was that the world crawled and seethed and teemed with insects. There were more types of insect – nine or ten million species – than the rest of Nature combined. Ninety per cent of all life, other than bacteria and single-celled organisms, was insect. It was they who ruled the planet. And this old building with its countless hiding places was a haven for them. They were there, in the shadowed places and unseen spaces, waiting.

"Are you okay?" she heard Jack Court ask her. "I need you to be okay, Karen."

She nodded. Then again, more firmly. She was not going to let this win. She was not going to have people ridicule or pity her any more. And she was not – definitely not – going to let it screw up this account.

The Halverson group of companies was a world-spanning empire: behind five hundred household brands, behind the logistics organizations that brought a thousand more to markets around the globe, and – rumor had it – behind the election of half a dozen senators and, at least in part, the current President. The reason Drew Halverson had not stood for Presidential office himself, it was said without much irony, was because it would mean a diminishment of his power and influence.

That Halverson was personally heading the meeting signified its importance. After a decade of rapid growth and merger, there was governmental concern that the Halverson Group was beginning to hold too much sway over the nation's economic destiny, compounded by public unease over Drew Halverson's close relationship with President Yates, whose strong religious beliefs he shared. There were even rumors of prayer sessions in the White House.

In addition to the four members of Karen's team, there was a guy from the DOJ's Anti-Trust Department and a woman from the Federal Trade Commission. The FTC woman was small, dumpy and not making a good job of being middle-aged and eyed Karen with the intense animosity that the homely reserve for the comely. The Feds were there by invitation – part of Halverson's very public commitment to total transparency – and it was up to Karen and her team to convince them that the proposed schedules of expansion, which included making Halverson the biggest national exporter to the soon-to-be-federalized European Union, did not violate Anti-Trust legislation.

She had spent a great deal of time preparing for this presentation and, as Jack Court introduced her, Karen felt calm, composed, ready. Whatever else was going on in her life, Karen was a consummate professional.

She took her place at the podium and started her presentation. In much the same way that she felt detached during her OCD episodes, whenever she was making a presentation she felt separated from herself. She saw herself, heard herself. And she was good. Really good. Five minutes in, she caught Jack Court's expression and knew that he was thinking the same.

She had it nailed. Every possible infraction was revealed as well within the FTC's rules and the Department of Justice's guidelines. Even the frump nodded approvingly as each box was ticked, each corner shown uncut. All the time Drew Halverson sat at the head of the conference table and smiled an approbatory smile.

Halfway through she felt it: the same sensation she had on the street immediately before she had seen the little girl. Like déjà vu.

Focus.

She pressed on with the presentation, but the feeling of unreality, of repetition, of otherness intensified. She stumbled over a couple of lines, causing Jack to frown and Halverson's smile to fade.

The air changed. It became not just different, but alien; like no air she had experienced before. Heavy, dense, moist and rich, clinging to her skin like a warm, damp vestment and oiling her mouth, her nostrils, her lungs.

The sunlight through the window dimmed. Everything was becoming vague. Inconsistent.

Karen gripped the sides of the lectern, the only thing that seemed solid, real to her.

Focus. Concentrate. Work through it.

Something fell onto the angled lectern. A tight black disc, about the size of a dime, that must have come from the ceiling. It had a shiny, ridged appearance, a coil of geometric pattern. She jumped back and brushed it off the lectern with the back of her hand. Karen looked up but could not see where it had come from. She started the last section again, not looking up to see her audience's reactions. Three more black discs fell onto the lectern, two bouncing straight off, the third rolling down her notes before being caught on the page rest at the bottom.

"What the hell . . ." Karen began, this time looking up at the others who now stared at her the same way people stared at her in shop doorways. The fat bitch from the FTC was smiling malevolently. But it was as if they were all looking at her from behind thick, rippling glass, or a screen of viscous film.

Karen's confusion was gone in an instant. The terror that now filled her left no room for anything else. As she watched, the black disc twitched, then uncurled. A pelmet fringe of hair-like black legs rippled nauseatingly from the flanks of the four-inch-long, three-quarter-inch-wide millipede, and Karen heard the scuttling rattle of a thousand sharp feet on the paper of her notes. Something shrill and penetrating filled the room and Karen realized she was screaming. The room, her audience, the building around her were now just layers of glassy, rippling outlines.

There was a sound above her. Karen looked up and barely noticed that the roof of the building had gone and daylight filtered through the fronds of impossibly tall ferns, her attention focused on the granular cloud that tumbled towards her. Hundreds, thousands of curled-up millipedes fell on her: into her hair, onto her clothes, into her screaming mouth. The podium, the floor, everything turned black with them as they uncurled and scuttled across every surface, over each other's bodies. Over Karen. She spat them from her mouth, tore them

191

from her hair, stamped on them in a demented frenzy. She looked to the others for help, but they were gone. The Halverson Building with its wood paneling, marble floors and Portland stone was no longer there. Not even as a glassy outline.

I am mad, she thought through her panic. I have gone insane.

She had been in a room. The room had had a building around it; there had been a city around the building. But the conference room was gone, the Halverson Building was gone, Boston was gone.

She was surrounded by a forest.

The millipedes had stopped falling but still she clawed frenetically at her hair, face, body. She felt her whole body itch. God oh God oh God . . . She realized they were inside her blouse. They were crawling up her legs. She tore her navy jacket off, ripped at the silk of her blouse. She was covered with them. They scurried over her, each one a ripple of pin feet on her skin. Urgent hands beat, clawed and swept them from her. Feet stamped at a seething black carpet of them.

Karen ran, stumbling over roots and tubers, getting up and running on . . . anything to get away from the churning, writhing mass of millipedes, still furiously brushing them from her body as she ran. The ground was mulchy, moist, and her high heels had been sucked from her feet after only a few strides. She ran and ran but there seemed to be no end to the forest.

There was no sense to this. What had happened to her? What had happened to the world? Think, Karen, she told herself. Use your brain. Make sense of this. She stopped running and checked she was clear of the crawling bugs. With a shudder she scrubbed the last of them from her skin.

Something else made no sense: Karen, insensitive to anything except her terror, had lost track of how long she had been running, but she knew it had been a while and over difficult terrain. So why wasn't she out of breath? Her breathing was heavy, but not labored, as if she had trotted up a flight of stairs rather than run for her life through a tangle of subtropical forest.

The forest. The inexplicable forest.

It was dense and dark, but unlike any other she had ever seen. Everything around her was impossibly tall but, for the most part, they weren't trees. Impossibly tall ferns – huge, branchless trunks topped with fronds – soared above her, crisscrossing each other to create a green cathedral of vaulted ceilings. There was no grass beneath her feet, or anywhere to be seen, just a dense, sodden carpet of moss and lichen. Even these seemed supersized: thicker and bigger. And the air: the cloying, rich, thick air.

Standing there, Karen sought desperately to make sense of what was happening. This forest that wasn't a forest, this air that wasn't air, this world that wasn't her world.

Insane.

Maybe *that* was the explanation: she was mad. Whatever Dr Corbin had said to reassure her, Karen knew she had had psychological problems. Was the insanity surrounding her really just insanity within her? Was this all some kind of elaborate delusion or hallucination?

Despite the sticky heat, Karen realized she was shivering, trembling almost convulsively. If this was a hallucination, then it was convincing enough to have put her into shock. A spasm in her gut caused her to double over and she vomited onto a clump of ferns. The spasms continued until there was nothing left in her stomach to expel and her retching became dry and pained her muscles.

Straightening up, she wiped her mouth with the back of her shaking hand and looked down at herself. Her jacket, blouse and shoes were gone; her stockings were ripped and laddered. She was left wearing just her skirt and brassiere. Karen the city lawyer was half-naked and half-demented in the middle of an alien jungle. If this was a delusion, then it was one that invaded every sense. However improbable, this world didn't just look real, it smelled, tasted, felt and sounded real.

Karen needed to find help, but the dense foliage made every

direction look the same. Deciding to press on in the direction her panic had first impelled her, she stumbled through the undergrowth for an hour, her mouth dry, her head aching. After throwing up and in this heat, she knew there was a real danger of dehydration. Driven by the need to find water, Karen pushed on, parting curtains of ferns and clambering over algae and moss-slimed rocks.

She froze. Something was moving. To the right and hidden from view. Karen realized at that moment that there had been something else odd about the forest: no sounds. No bird song or cries. No monkey calls. Absolutely no animal noises. No hint of anything moving around.

Until now.

She stood still, straining to hear above the rushing sound of the pulse in her ears. Another sound. Another scuttling insect, but this time something big. Karen sobbed as she began running again, charging through the undergrowth, blind to hazards, focused only on getting away from whatever had been scurrying towards her, hidden in the foliage.

She was under its surface, the water filling her nose and mouth, before her brain had time to register the river. The forest had opened out so suddenly, staying dense and impenetrable until the very edge of the water, that she hadn't seen the wide expanse of river until she plunged headlong into it. Kicking her way desperately back to the surface, her hand found a low, smooth rock with an edge she could grip and hung on while she coughed, retched and spluttered the water from her body, gasping huge lungfuls of air.

Once more she sobbed disconsolately: was there no end to these torments?

She took a moment to compose herself, her cheek pressed against the sleek, cool surface of the rock. Again she was amazed at how quickly it took her to recover her breath, as if the air in this green hell was somehow richer.

The rock beneath her cheek moved.

Karen jumped to her feet. The hump of smooth black stone moved again, and more of it emerged from the gritty mud. No scream this time: Karen stood mute and watched as it slowly twitched and quivered and wriggled itself free of the soil it had buried itself in. A segmented back arched, black lobster-like legs sprang up and out. And still Karen, struck dumb, watched as the giant millipede, eight feet long and two wide, emerged from the earth. Two long antennae, segmented like the legs, twitched into life, each moving independently, circling and probing as if tasting the air. Like a column of legionnaires sheltering beneath their shields, the millipede's legs rippled as it began to move. Still frozen in fear, Karen remained still even when she felt its legs ripple over her naked foot. Unaware of what had woken it from its slumber, the monstrous arthropod weaved its way back into the forest undergrowth.

She stood, shaking, at the river's shore for an hour, until the sky darkened. With the sunset, the river came to life and she watched as a mist rolled along its waters and a pair of birds swooped and wheeled. Except the birds weren't birds, they were dragonflies with two-foot-long bodies and four-foot wingspans and the mist was billowing clouds of millions of mayflies. One of the dragonflies flew over to where Karen stood and hovered on gossamer wings three feet from her face. She found herself hypnotized by the two huge compound eyes set like a mask on the colorful head; each was a mosaic of tiny hexagons, an almost synthetic geometry so precise it looked like they had been designed by computer and assembled by a master glass-maker. Through her fear, she actually found the dragonfly beautiful.

Now Karen knew why there were no animal cries here. No bird song. This was the empire of insects. Her own private and very personal hell.

So there was no surprise when she turned from the river to

see a scorpion beetling towards her, its tail arched and sting ready, its claws raised as if prepared to attack.

A scorpion the size of a man.

Something happened to Karen in that moment. Something changed. Like when the giant dragonfly had hovered in front of her, she was able to see past her fear. This was not real. None of this was really happening: not a begging, terrified denial, but a rational, logical conclusion. This had nothing to do with her phobias or compulsions, this was about the epidemic of hallucinations.

She drew a deep breath and stood completely still. The scorpion's eyes were directionless globes dotted on the creature's skull plate and there was no way for Karen to tell what it was looking at, what it could see. She understood enough about natural history to know that there were different ways of seeing: some animals perceived heat or motion instead of or as well as light. For all she knew, the monster heading towards her saw in infrared and was looking deep inside her, watching the beating of her heart.

But this wasn't real. The scorpion couldn't see her because it wasn't there. Or, in its world, she wasn't there. Wherever or whenever this place was, life here was on a massive scale, and all of that life was insect. Insect. And Karen, the entomophobe, lost in an unreal world of giant insects, was making observations, was drawing conclusions, was using logic.

She remained still as the scorpion reached her, passing so close that hard, bristling hairs on its segmented leg scraped skin from the thigh exposed through her torn business skirt. Holding her breath, she watched the monster pass. She realized that although this was definitely a scorpion, it was more than its enormous size that made it different from any that Karen knew of. It had giant claws, but everything about it was giant and these claws were smaller in proportion to its body than on normal-sized scorpions. Rows of spikes bristled from the claws, as if intended to sweep victims into the jaws, rather than simply seize them. Another anomaly: the rear set of legs were flattened out into blades, like the oars of a rowboat.

It's aquatic, she realized. A giant, aquatic scorpion and we don't belong in each other's time. It can't see me and it's going to go past me and into the water.

Don't move, she told herself. Don't breathe. Don't scream. This is all unreal.

Karen closed her eyes tight, shutting out this impossible tableau. It's because you have a phobia, she forced the thought into her brain. You have picked up whatever virus it is that is causing people to see things, and you're seeing insects because your mind is picking up on what scares you most. This is all no more real than a dream.

But even with her eyes closed, Karen knew the hallucination persisted. In the dark vault of her skull the scuttling of the scorpion still echoed, the abrasive kiss of arachnid leg on human skin still stinging on her thigh.

She felt strange. Lightheaded. Her legs gave way and she fell onto the mossy green mulch. The feeling of déjà vu overwhelmed her once more.

The air thinned. The light changed. The forest vitrified, became transparent, rippled glassily. She closed her eyes. The ground she lay on suddenly felt hard and unyielding.

When she opened her eyes, Jack Court and the others were leaning over her, their faces troubled. And above them she saw the ceiling of the Halverson Building restored. She heard their voices: anxious, urgent. She wanted to tell them she was okay, but for a moment she lay still, convincing herself that what she was seeing was the real world, and what she had just experienced was not.

27

JOHN MACBETH. BOSTON

The Schilder Neuroscience Research Institute was a tangle of glass and steel angles constructed on what had been, until a couple of years before, a parking lot for the other university-related buildings in the neighboring city blocks. Designed by some Finnish architect whose name was all vowels and umlauts, the Institute looked to Macbeth to be completely out of place with its neighbors, like some over-exuberant tourist visiting from Helsinki.

Even with all Casey had told him about anti-science fanatics, and after his bizarre encounter with an FBI man with a serial killer's name, the level of security at the Institute still surprised Macbeth: airport-type metal detectors at the entrances and uniformed security wearing sidearms. There hadn't been a single door he'd passed through without needing a member of staff to swipe the lock with their IDs.

"We've had all kinds of threats and a couple of improvised devices mailed to us," Steve Edelman explained. Edelman – one of the Institute's directors and Macbeth's main contact – was a small, overweight and enthusiastic man in his fifties. "We have to be on our toes."

Macbeth spent the Monday and Tuesday in the Institute, discussing the prearranged Project One agenda, but he could tell, as the Schilder's chief scientists sat around a conference table listening to his presentation, the hum of the projector's fan emphasizing the silences between bullet points, that they

198

were just going through the motions. Copenhagen Project One had ceased to be the focus of the Institute's attention and he guessed that, as a major psychiatric research unit, much of its effort would be going into resolving the phenomenon that had hit the Institute's native city.

His suspicions were confirmed when the meeting wound up and Edelman steered Macbeth into the hall.

"There's something else we'd really like your opinion on," he said, allowing his habitual smile to fade.

After Edelman security card-swiped the way through several sets of double doors, Macbeth found himself in a part of the Institute he hadn't been in before. Eventually, Edelman swung open a meeting-room door.

The four people at the table stood up as Macbeth entered. The first was what Macbeth would have called the corporate science type: more Lacoste than lab coat; expensive, branded, black polo shirt, smartphone in a belt holster, sand-colored chinos, expensive side-parted Ivy League and smiling with perfect orthodontic confidence. He looked to Macbeth as if he'd stepped straight off his Cape-anchored yacht. Edelman introduced him as Dr Brian Newcombe, a syndromic surveillance specialist from the World Health Organization.

"This is Professor Margaret Freeman, our Delusional Disorder specialist . . ." Edelman introduced a middle-aged woman in a white surgical coat over a kaftan-type, ankle-length dress. "And this is Dr Frank Gebhardt and Dr Sonia Reynolds, from the Centers for Disease Control and Prevention."

Gebhardt and Reynolds were both dressed in the dark suits and had the look of government functionaries rather than physicians. Macbeth guessed that, whatever the show was, they were running it.

"What can I do for you?" he asked.

"The people around this table," explained Gebhardt, "represent the management team of a task force that the World

Health Organization have put together. The focus of this task force is the event that took place last week in Boston, and other similar occurrences around the world. I assume that you experienced the so-called Cape Ann Ghostquake first hand?"

"I did," said Macbeth.

"I take it that as a professional psychiatrist, you would lean towards the event being the result of some kind of mass delusional episode?"

"I don't know what to believe, if I'm frank. But if I were to hazard an opinion, I would say that it was some kind of conversion syndrome or MPI episode, although I've always found Mass Psychogenic Illness a very loose diagnosis."

"We've considered MPI," said Brian Newcombe. "And there are parallels with previous events, like the West Bank Fainting of 1983."

"I'm aware of the other examples of MPI, but they've all been typified by the eruption of common physical symptoms across a large group of people, like in the West Bank case. Some have caused people to have hallucinations, but I have never, ever heard of an instance where people share exactly the same hallucination."

"The closest comparison we can find predates reliable medical records," said Gebhardt, the Disease Control man. "The Dancing Plague in Europe in 1518. People started to dance bizarrely in the streets, hundreds at a time, until they died of exhaustion or heart failure . . . but even that is a clutched-at straw. We simply have no historical analogs."

"But we've got plenty of examples happening right now," said Brian Newcombe. "We've had reports of delusional episodes all over the world: not just earthquakes but all kinds of event, some innocuous and mundane, others terrifying and dramatic. These episodes are hallucinations experienced by individuals, shared between two people or small groups of four or five, or occasionally the type of mass delusional episode that we've seen here in Boston."

Macbeth nodded as he processed this information.

"You don't look surprised," said Sonia Reynolds.

"I'm not. I have a colleague here, Dr Peter Corbin working out of Belmont. He's had a rash of patients who are completely rational and with no history of psychiatric conditions presenting with the type of hallucinations you describe. Dr Corbin thought that it was something confined to Massachusetts, but that's clearly not the case. What exactly is the geographical spread?"

"Global," answered Gebhardt. "Every continent, every culture. The majority of the reports are from the developed world, but that's maybe just because reporting mechanisms are better. We've applied epidemiological analyses, but there is no pattern emerging and absolutely no sense of an outbreak source."

"But you are treating this as some kind of viral outbreak?"

"That's all we can do at the moment," Edelman answered. "The usual diagnostic criteria don't apply and these episodes manifest in all four delusional forms: mood-congruent, mood-neutral, bizarre and non-bizarre. The personality type, the schizotypy, the age, gender, race and cultural background of the subjects are all totally variable. But the sheer spread of these events suggests either some kind of virus or an environmental agent."

"So you don't go with this vestibular system virus crap?"

"Whatever this is," said Gebhardt, "it affects all the senses, either singly or in combination, so no . . . we don't buy into a balance-disturbing agent. Listen, Dr Macbeth, we are assembling a team of experts to monitor and analyze these incidents. We would appreciate it if you joined the team."

"I have my work on the Project . . ."

"We'll explain the situation to your university in Copenhagen. We need someone capable of seeing through systems and patterns – looking beyond the stats. You have a reputation for just that."

"There are better candidates, I have to say. Josh Hoberman, for one."

"We've been trying to reach Professor Hoberman, but have failed so far. Even if we had him in the team, we'd want you on board too." Gebhardt pushed a red file across the table to Macbeth. "The most important information is in there. You'll see that there have been several incidents, going back a couple of months, that were not originally attributed to these phenomena."

Macbeth picked up the file and flicked through it. He found a world map flagged with initialed tags. "What does MDE stand for?"

"Mass Delusional Event. IDE stands for Individual Delusional Episode."

"Shit . . . there's thousands of them . . ."

"And the frequency is increasing, exponentially," Brian Newcombe answered. "The hallucinations are becoming more frequent, more spectacular, involve more people – and they're lasting longer. And they've gone polymodal – engaging all the senses. The subjects now experience the hallucination as if it were real life."

Macbeth looked though the file. A common pattern had been established: the subject's normal routine suddenly interrupted by a sense of unreality and a particularly strong and unpleasant feeling of déjà vu. To start with, they knew something was wrong, that they were having some kind of neurological or psychological episode, but then they began hallucinating so vividly they lost all objective insight. The hallucination would become a delusion as they started to believe in its reality.

"The problem we have is that we believe there are milder forms of these episodes occurring all the time: hallucinations integrated into the real world," Sonia Reynolds added. "Transduction of distal object to percept is mimicked perfectly – the real and the unreal are indistinguishable."

"There's another development we should tell you about," Edelman said gravely.

"Yes?"

"A hallucination is a hallucination, of course. An unreal thing that should have no real physical effect. The fatalities and injuries during the so-called ghostquake here in Boston were all attributable to the victim losing balance. But there is one instance that is causing us great concern: a woman who suffered a broken arm. The fracture was caused by falling masonry from one of the buildings affected by the earthquake – except there was no earthquake and no structural damage. No falling masonry. She suffered a real injury from an unreal object."

Macbeth stared at the surface of the table for a moment. "We all know a delusion or hallucination can result in psychosomatic injury. Delusional religiomaniacs often develop stigmata – sometimes open, bleeding wounds – on their hands and feet where Jesus was supposed to have been nailed to the cross. Formication is common in drug withdrawal and entomophobia, and in some cases, where the patient believes they are being bitten by the insects they hallucinate are crawling over them, they develop bite-like lesions on their skin."

"But a broken arm?"

"We are clearly dealing with extreme forms of hallucination," said Macbeth. "It could be that an unusually severe movement or muscle spasm caused the fracture in a disease-weakened bone. Have you checked for an underlying medical problem? Osteoporosis, Paget's Disease, osteosarcoma?"

"Of course we have," said Newcombe. "The patient is in otherwise excellent health, added to which the fracture was comminuted and impacted, suggesting force trauma. And she had abrasions and a laceration on the skin consistent with having been hit by something large and irregular-shaped."

Macbeth shook his head. "This is all very difficult to believe."

"We all agree, but it's happening," said Gebhardt. "Dr Macbeth, will you join our team?"

"There's something I have to tell you first," said Macbeth. "In addition to feeling the earthquake just like everyone else, I'm pretty sure I've suffered from at least two, maybe three, minor hallucinations where I've seen people or things that weren't really there. If this is a virus, then I'm infected."

"Last night, my husband brought me a cup of coffee in my study," said Margaret Freeman, who had been silent till then. "My husband died three years ago, Dr Macbeth. Everyone in this room has experienced a dubious percept in the last week. If this is a virus, then we're all infected."

28

FABIAN. FRIESLAND

Although he was pretty sure no one could see him, Fabian decided to keep out of sight, edging around the settlement, using the long beach grasses as cover. The feeling of déjà vu had gone, but this place, this time persisted. Everything around him, his experience of the world, had become crazy; but Fabian knew he was not insane. Or maybe that's what it was like to be crazy: to think everything else around you was mad and not you.

Fabian now had a clear view of the settlement and its central square. The woman had returned to the village, the empty leather bucket swinging at the end of her slender arm like a bell on a rope. A group of village men had gathered in the square, all dressed in clothes that Fabian found difficult to date. He guessed they were early medieval, but this was no finery: no silks or fine linens, instead robustly woven fabrics of simple design. The men wore rope-belted, yoke-necked shirts, formless pants gathered at the shins into leggings which were in turn held in place by crisscrossing hide ties. They were outfits that could have belonged to any period from the end of the Stone Age to the Middle Ages. Whatever the era, the villagers' clothes were the practical, resilient wear of the yeomanry. These people were peasants.

One of the men, younger than the others and wearing a mustard-colored shirt, broke off from the group and went over to the woman Fabian had first observed. They stood talking for a few moments and Fabian watched them, detached and involved at the same time. From her hair being tied in a knot behind her head, Fabian knew the woman was married and he could see that she had little time for the youth. It struck Fabian that their entire story was laid out before him to be read. Then a thought struck him – he had known the woman was married from the way she wore her hair – how had he known that? Had he read that somewhere and forgotten he had read it? Why was it that Fabian, a stranger in this time, seemed instinctively to know so much about it? Why did this experience seem so much more real than the fourteen years he had spent in that other reality?

His thoughts were interrupted when a man in his thirties, long-bearded and armed with spear and shield, came into the village. Fabian realized that the older man – and he was the oldest person he had seen so far – had come in from the direction of the promontory. He walked up to the youth who had been dallying with the woman and began to berate him loudly. Fabian found it odd that he was hearing a language he had never heard before, but there were many words scattered through it that sounded like the Frisian he and his family spoke. The younger man offered apologies and bowed his head, the older thrusting shield and spear at him to take and pointing back towards the promontory. The youth in the mustard shirt shuffled off shamefaced, some of the other men jeering at him as he went.

Fabian followed him out and along the promontory, no longer attempting concealment from people to whom he was clearly invisible. There had been something about the dejection of the young man that had inclined Fabian to follow him into his solitude. They were now near the end of the promontory, where the lighthouse should have stood but didn't. The young man stood, spear in hand, gazing out over the sky-flattened silk of the sea. Fabian grasped the significance of the youth's scolding: this was some kind of sentry duty and he had failed to turn up for his allotted watch. But watch for what?

The young man laid shield and lance on the grass and sat

down, cross-legged, resting his forearms on his knees. It was a relaxed pose, but Fabian noticed that he kept scanning the empty horizon. Whatever the threat was, it was real enough to keep the village slacker attentive.

This could not all be in his mind. Fabian had been here, in this world, this time, for thirty-five minutes. No delusion or fantasy or trick of the mind could be sustained for so long. A panic rose in his chest at the thought that he might be trapped here; it wasn't the idea of being imprisoned in this time that troubled him, rather that his confinement would be solitary – invisible and intangible in a half life as a phantom. He stood up suddenly, trying to calm himself. Maybe it was as simple as him dreaming: maybe he had fallen asleep while resting against the stone and had dreamt everything that had happened since. If it was all a dream, then it was like no other he had ever experienced – more vivid, more convincing, more sharply defined than his waking life.

He decided to walk over to the youth and touch him on the shoulder, to shove him and see if he reacted. But before he could, the youth jumped to his feet, leaving spear and shield on the grass. Flat-hand-shielding his eyes against the brightness of the huge sky, he peered out over the waters, his attention locked on some distant, fixed spot. Fabian followed his gaze but could see only the vague shimmer of water and sun, fudging the line between sea and sky. He turned again to the village youth, just in time to see his posture become even more rigid, intense: whatever he thought he had seen before, he clearly knew he was seeing it now. Again Fabian followed his line of sight and again saw nothing. He echoed the youth's posture and shielded his eyes, narrowing them against the glare. Now he saw them: three indistinct, vague smudges on the horizon. Whatever they were, they were heading towards the promontory, avoiding the Waddenzee mudflats.

Boats. But boats without sails, lying low in the water.

The youth on lookout duty turned on his heel and ran back towards the village as if fleeing from the Devil himself. And he yelled. A desperate scream of a single word. It was in a long-dead language yet that single word was one that Fabian understood clearly and unequivocally. A single word unforgotten from a forgotten time; a word that had passed through the generations, more than a millennium of history, and still had the power to terrify.

And to thrill. Now Fabian knew why he was here, what it was he was here to observe. He didn't run after the mustard-shirted youth towards the village; instead he stood on the promontory and watched the three smudges draw nearer, take form, grow more distinct.

The masts, articulated and until then lowered on their pivots to make the ships more difficult to spot from land, were suddenly hoisted, as were the huge square sails, a single one on each ship. Like the legs of huge sea beetles, ranks of oars stretched from each flank and bit into the sea, the three ships picking up pace, cutting mercilessly through the waves towards the promontory.

Standing there, an electric thrill coursing through every fiber, Fabian made out two things at the same time: the giant black raven embroidered on the red pane of the first longship's sail, and the running village lookout shouting again, desperately, his single word warning.

Vikings.

There was no fear. It wasn't that Fabian felt detached from what was happening in the way he had always felt detached from events in his everyday waking reality. He felt excitement. Added to which he had no reason to believe the approaching Vikings were any more likely to be able to see him than the others he had encountered.

Fabian knew that he now stood in a world and at a time where every certainty he had grown up with, every rule of conduct, every constraint, no longer held sway.

The ships were things of great beauty: sleek, elegant slivers of clinker-built oak, each twenty meters or more in length, which seemed to glide towards Fabian as if just touching the water's surface and no more. The black Raven of Odin loomed at him from the billowing sail as the first longship, driven by oars working like synchronized pistons in a time long before the idea of a piston had even been conceived, slid past where he stood on the promontory. He could see the round shields arranged along the rowlocks, the gleaming, spectacle-visored helms of the warriors. Forty, maybe fifty men.

The second longship glided past. As in the first vessel, one man stood at the bow, holding the slender, arching neck of the dragon-headed prow and leaning forward to check the water's depth, guiding his ship into the narrows beside the promontory. Fabian, who had read countless books on these Norse marauders, knew that they would beach the ships, which were double-headed and could be rowed back out to sea without having to be turned. He ran along the promontory, keeping pace with the last of the ships, waving and shouting excitedly to the Vikings who could neither see nor hear him.

Even at a sprint, Fabian only just reached where the first ship beached as the Vikings spilled out. He had expected to hear them yell battle cries, but they disembarked swiftly and silently, obviously unaware that they had been spotted and had lost the element of surprise. Within a couple of minutes, one hundred and fifty men were landed. Sword blades, spear tips and shield bosses glittered and gleamed sharp-edged and bright in the sunlight. Fabian was aware how crisp and clear everything was; much more than it was in normal life, as if his vision – all his senses – had been enhanced, or as if someone had photo-edited reality, turning up the definition, intensifying the colors, refining the contrast and sharpness. He was surprised to see that the Vikings were not the tangle-haired wildmen he had always thought them to have been: they were groomed, beards trimmed and combed, helmets and ringmail burnished to gleaming.

Except for one group.

Twenty or twenty-five Vikings from the first ship stood apart from their comrades and Fabian sensed instantly that there was something strange about these men. Strange and intensely dangerous. To begin with, they were dressed very differently: where the other men wore ringmail or quilted doublets, these heavily muscled men were bare-armed, their torsos covered only by waistcoats of thick, brown-black fur. Some didn't have helmets, instead wearing the cured heads of wolves or bears on their heads, a curtain of pelt over their necks and shoulders. The faces of all were blackened, as if with ash or fire-soot, and the masks of darkened skin emphasized teeth exposed in twisting snarls, tongues that lolled red from gaping mouths, the whites of eyes that were wild and darting. Mad.

Fabian noticed that these men also wore more marks of battle than their comrades. Their naked arms were covered in the ugly welts of ill-healed wounds, some ancient, others still raw and red. Their faces too, beneath the dark staining, were sword-scarred and battle-deformed; one warrior lacked much of the left side of his face, which had a deep cleft, as if ax-struck, running from brow to cheek and only one white eye gazed out battle-tranced from the mask of black soot.

To Fabian, these men looked as if they belonged to another species, unrelated to their shipmates and completely inhuman. Also unlike the others, they were not quiet, but making strange sounds: grunts and moans as if in pain or frustrated by confinement. Animal sounds. Fabian noticed that the other Vikings took care to remain behind and a little distant from these men. With each second, they seemed to become more agitated and restless and Fabian noticed they all had leather pouches that hung from hide straps around their bare necks. Every now and then, one of them would use his fingertips to spoon some kind of green-gray pulp from the pouch, shoving it into his cheek. One of the men fell to the ground, pounding at the earth with his fists and issuing a high-pitched screech through gritted teeth. His frenzy seemed to intensify the dementia of his companions, increase their growling and moaning. Fabian saw another of the men, the one closest to where he now stood, place his knife in his own mouth and bite down on it, blood streaking his ash-blackened beard, his round-eyed stare insane.

Fabian felt the thrill in his chest intensify. He knew who these men were – if you could call them men – what they were. He understood the reason their comrades stood behind them: you held a deadly weapon by the hilt, not the blade. These were furies about to be unleashed. They were the shield-biters, the demon warriors. The rough fur they wore on their naked skin gave them their name: the bearskin shirt that was called a *ber serkr* in their own language.

These were the Berserkers. And they were about to be let loose.

For some reason he could not fathom, Fabian felt the same pain of unbearable impatience, of a great pressure within crying out to be released, and let out a howling yell that echoed the growing cries of the Berserkers. He let it die when he saw the Berserker nearest him, the man who still held his blade between clenched, bloody teeth, turn in his direction. He looked straight at Fabian, his wild, maniacal eyes suddenly locked with his.

He could see him.

Fabian froze. The Berserker's face lost, for a moment, the unfocused, insane stare and tilted slightly sideways, blood-flecked drool tracing its way down the inclined edge of the knife in his mouth, as if he was trying to make sense of what he was seeing. Fabian's euphoria evaporated too and was replaced with a raw, real fear that he was going to die here and now, in a place and time he did not belong.

Suddenly the other Berserkers roared in unison. The Viking broke his gaze from Fabian's and turned towards where the village lay, behind the skirt of seagrasses. Two hundred meters off, the men from the village had assembled, some fifty of them, and had formed a rank of kneeling spearmen, a second rank of archers behind. They did their best to look resolute, but Fabian knew he was looking at fifty dead men; and he guessed they knew it too. He turned back to the Berserker at the same time the Berserker turned back to him. The warrior frowned, peering at the spot where Fabian stood, but this time there was no eye contact. It was clear he could no longer see the boy from another time.

The blackened-faced warrior turned away and fell back into his battle trance, combining with his comrades to form a single seething, writhing mass of violent intent. They roared and bellowed and howled and hissed, beastlike, at the village defenders. Their screams and cries became less and less human, each passing second bringing them closer to the beasts whose pelts they wore. One, then a second Berserker tore at his hose to reveal his erection, waving it at the enemy. The others stamped and twisted, the knot of fur-clad warriors convulsing as a single spasm coursed through them.

One Viking, a handsome blond man of about thirty, his clothing, helmet and arms identifying him as the chief, moved swiftly round to stand in front of the Berserkers, holding his arms wide in a gesture of restraint. Fabian guessed that the chief was probably the only warrior capable of controlling, if only temporarily, the Berserkers' frenzy. The village archers let loose a desperate volley of arrows which fell some distance short of their targets. The Viking chief saw his chance to launch an attack between reloads and, with a bellow of command, pointed his sword in the direction of the villagers.

It was like a great wave of concentrated hate and violence being released. The Berserkers screamed insanely as they surged headlong, some stumbling in their lust for killing and eagerness for death.

Fabian forgot all about his fear and became swept up again in the excitement, the base, animalistic thrill of the moment.

Everything he had thought he hated about that part of himself suddenly made him feel more alive than he had ever felt. Except, he realized, for the day he had brutally beaten Henkje Maartens. But there was no space, no time for the thought and it swept from his mind as the Berserkers rushed onwards with a chorus of low bellows and high-pitched screams.

A second rank of twenty or so Vikings followed the Berserkers; these broad-shouldered men bore no swords or shields, instead each carrying a heavy double-headed ax. Compared to the seething insanity of the attackers ahead of them, these warriors were disciplined and ordered, arranged in evenly spaced rows, axes balanced on shoulders. While the Berserkers ran screaming towards the defenders, these axmen walked at a steady, measured pace, allowing the gap between them and the Berserkers to open up.

Fabian ran as fast as he could, falling in behind the Berserkers. He could smell them, more animal than human, something dark and base suffused in the odor. A second volley of arrows arced into the air and rained down on the attackers, many finding their target, most missing. The wounded Berserkers did not fall or even slow in their attack: some snatched at the arrows and pulled them from their bodies, the arrowhead barbs tearing out flesh; others seemed oblivious to the arrows in their bodies and charged on.

It was not just the most brutal thing Fabian had ever witnessed: it was a thousand times more brutal than anything he could ever have imagined. The Berserkers ran straight into the defenders' ranks, shattering them and sending some running in terror. Those who remained were defenseless against the inhuman onslaught. All the Berserkers seemed possessed, demonic. Sword blades flashed briefly before being blood-dulled; each Berserker rapidly and repeatedly stabbing his opponent in a bloodlust frenzy, continuing to ram his sword or knife into the body over and over again, long after it was clear his victim was dead. Many of the Berserkers were themselves mortally wounded, their bodies rent open or necks spouting blood, but even in their death throes they fell onto their opponents, clawing and raking at them with bare hands, biting into necks or faces and ripping flesh with their teeth. The air fumed with the rich copper smell of blood and Fabian stood entranced by how horrific, how bestial the Berserkers were. How magnificent they were.

Once they had killed enough to break through the ranks of villagers, the Berserkers charged on towards the village itself. The defenders, who had lost more than half of their number, made an effort to regroup but the axmen were now upon them. Fabian watched, hypnotized by the rhythm of the axes. Compared to the Berserkers, there was something mechanistic about the axmen's assault. Again it was not at all how Fabian had imagined a Viking attack: the evenly spaced axmen had taken their axes from their shoulders and had begun to swing them, long before they reached their enemies, in a regular motion like a sideways figure-of-eight. The swing of each axman left no gap with that of his neighbor and when they reached the remainder of the defenders, they scythed through them as if harvesting corn. Again there was no defense: the heavy, double-edged axes sliced though air, flesh and bone with the same callous ease.

The rest of the Vikings who had been following on, armed with sword and shield, ran through, overtaking their ax-wielding comrades and following the Berserkers into the village. Fabian ran on too, something dark burning in his blood. He started to come across bodies: a second line of defense had been set up by the villagers and had met the same fate as the first. A cluster of rent-asunder corpses and several disembodied limbs marked where the line had been swiftly overwhelmed. He spotted one body, its face pulped beyond recognition by spear or sword; Fabian recognized the boy he had watched on lookout only by his blood-blotted mustard shirt.

Nearer the village, the bodies were more scattered, women and children among them, some clearly having tried to run to safety but cut down, their backs hacked to raw flesh and the rear of their skulls caved in.

The young woman he had seen when he had found the village lay close to the lodge from which he had first seen her emerge. She lay on her back, sightless blue eyes staring up at a cloudless blue sky. Her skirts had been hoisted to her waist and her white thighs exposed, as were her pale breasts through the ripped-open tunic with the carefully embroidered brocade collar. A surprisingly bloodless single sword wound beneath her chestbone marked where a Berserker, having finished with her, had ended her life. Fabian looked down at the cruelly pathetic scene of her death and was amazed at how little he cared about her suffering.

When he reached the village, he saw that the Berserkers were more frenzied than ever. They were now killing everyone and everything they found. Children lay slaughtered next to livestock and some Berserkers fell upon women and raped them on the bare earth of the square, bellowing like beasts. When the other Vikings reached the village, the chief at their head, they tried to contain the Berserkers as much as they could, shepherding women and children to one corner of the square. Any thoughts that Fabian might have had that this was inspired by any sense of humanity were dispelled when a boy of about eleven made a break for it. He was caught by one of the Vikings who drew his sword across his throat, cutting deep into the neck and letting him fall lifeless to the ground: an example for others thinking of escape. To Fabian, the cold, calm ease of the murder seemed far worse than the demented frenzies of the Berserkers; he also realized that these women and children were not being saved by the other Vikings because of their humanity, but because of their value: they were booty, slaves to be kept or traded.

It was over.

The Berserkers were gathered in the village square, all still wild-eyed, panting and restless despite the fact that some were mortally wounded, but still so detached from their bodies that they were unaware of their dying.

Fabian had his answer. He knew why he had been brought here to see this; he understood now where the violence he had launched against Henkje Maartens had come from. Whatever flowed in these men's blood flowed in his too.

The feeling came over him again. The world shifted in the universe and the sky changed hue, the air changed texture. Fabian felt disoriented, dizzy, lost in time and place.

Everything was gone. The village, the Vikings, the bodies of the dead, the rich cupric odor of blood in the air. Fabian didn't need to turn to see that the dyke was restored behind him or that the lighthouse once more stood sentinel where a thousand-year-dead youth in a mustard shirt had once scoured the sea for longships.

When he did turn, he saw that the man who had been walking his dog along the shore had reached where Fabian sat, his back against the stone.

He was an old man, in a time when old meant being beyond sixty instead of approaching forty. His white hair ruffled in the sea breeze. His eyes, staring at Fabian, were full of horror.

"Did you see?" he asked Fabian, his voice tremulous, terrified; a frightened child's voice from an old man. "Did you see it too?"

29

JOHN MACBETH. BOSTON

After he got back to Casey's from the Schilder Institute, Macbeth checked his email to find three lengthy messages from Poulsen in Copenhagen, each with specific questions that Macbeth could not answer fully without direct access to his team. That, he guessed, was the point Poulsen was making: he needed Macbeth back in Copenhagen.

The ghost folder on his computer desktop taunted him after he closed his email. It didn't open, as he had known it wouldn't; his repeated clicking on the icon habitual and vaguely compulsive, like someone absently picking at a scab they know they should ignore. It was Melissa who filled his thoughts and he felt something cold and heavy starting to coalesce in his gut: the deferred sense of loss he had known would eventually come.

Casey had given him a key for the apartment and the first thing Macbeth had done after Bundy dropped him off had been to note down the names the FBI agent had mentioned, while they were still fresh in his memory.

Now, as he sat alone in the apartment, Casey at work in MIT, Macbeth opened his web browser and searched for the names. Nowadays people – as he had explained to Casey in weak justification for sending texts to their year-dead father – existed not just physically, but virtually. Melissa would still be out there somewhere, a ghost of scattered electronic data.

He found the website of her company, as well as a dozen references to it and its work, including a business section profile of Melissa from the *Chronicle*. The company website was the thing that troubled him most. On the 'about us' page, Melissa stood front and center in a photograph with her key staff. They all displayed the essential sunrise-industry credentials of youth, informality and cool. Yet they were all dead. No one had suspended the website, because there was no one left alive to suspend it: a *Marie Celeste* adrift on the waters of the Internet.

Scanning the caption for the photo, Macbeth noticed that the company's deputy CEO was called Deborah Canning. He checked again the note he had made after talking to Bundy: Deborah Canning's name was there. Macbeth went through the full list of victims of the Golden Gate mass suicide: she wasn't listed. Not everyone involved with the company had died, after all. Maybe she was who Bundy was looking for.

He checked the name John Astor. Macbeth had heard the rumors about him, of course: everyone seemed to have heard them, yet no one seemed to know who Astor really was. The Internet was surprisingly empty of references to him: Macbeth's search results were dominated by the two John Jacob Astors of the famous family: one the dynasty's founder, the other a descendant namesake who went down with the *Titanic*.

What mentions he could find of the contemporary Astor were on conspiracy sites, one of which claimed the FBI and Homeland Security had red-flagged any site referring to the 'leading Simulist thinker, John Astor'. Macbeth remembered Bundy referring to 'Simulists'. There were the usual paranoid ravings about a global conspiracy and Macbeth decided to stop chasing a ghost and try the other two names dropped by the FBI agent.

He had no problem finding either.

Jeff Killberg had been one of the world's leading movie effects specialists. His company had been behind the CGI effects of some of the biggest-grossing movies over the last five years, and had been the target of the firebombing attack by Blind Faith eighteen months earlier. Macbeth couldn't understand why religious zealots would deem special effects as an offense to God.

Killberg, a mix of creative and technological genius, had played his cards, and his patents, close to his chest, doing most of the key research and development himself. He would, apparently, 'farm out' elements to his employees and outside contractors, but nothing that would give an insight into the central concept or innovation he was working on – exactly how Casey described Professor Blackwell's methodology.

Killberg had recently announced he was about to unveil new visual effects technology that would shake the movie industry to its core and offer moviegoers a completely new, totally immersive experience. The technology was never revealed: Jeff Killberg had been found tortured to death and hideously mutilated in his Pacific Heights home. Someone had worked on him very expertly with some kind of blade. The secure computer suite in the basement of Killberg's house had been stripped, systematically and totally. Despite the previous religiously motivated firebomb attack, suspicion for the murder fell on Killberg's commercial rivals. The computer effects industry had become, it seemed, literally cut-throat.

What troubled Macbeth most was that one of the companies to which Killberg had farmed out work had been Melissa's gaming technology company.

Samuel Tennant.

Again Macbeth's search was easy. There were references to Samuel Tennant across the Internet: photographs, articles, forums. Tennant, it seemed, had everything: looks, brains, money. A lot of money.

Tennant was rich twice over, having inherited family wealth but also amassing a second fortune through the companies he had set up himself. Having studied molecular biology at Caltech, Tennant had combined scientific understanding with business nous and set up a string of related biotech R and D companies, all of which seemed to have won significant government contracts. The most commercially successful part of the Tennant empire was, however, cosmetics research: Tennant had ring-patented several anti-ageing skin agents that beauty-product companies paid through the nose to buy as an ingredient.

Tennant – unlike the retiring, almost reclusive Killberg – had cultivated a playboy image. There were dozens of press pictures of him, mainly being seen where the young, rich and glamorous were expected to be seen.

One photograph took Macbeth off-guard. It was a society shot taken as Tennant was leaving some glitzy Platinum Triangle party. The girl on his arm was slim, with thick, shoulder-length dark hair and large, strikingly blue eyes. And she looked happy; in all the time they had been involved, Macbeth could not remember ever seeing Melissa look as unguardedly, completely happy as she did in that photograph.

He sat and looked at the picture for a long time, the uneasy feeling in his gut taking a more defined form. Melissa had been connected to both dead men, one professionally, one personally. And there was more to the Tennant story. A lot more.

There had been a buzz of press stories, conspiracy theories and half-assed speculations about what had happened to the young billionaire, the most reliable article from the *New York Times*. Eighteen months before, Tennant, the partygoer and bon viveur, had suddenly dropped off the West Coast social radar. Even his colleagues and employees had seen less and less of the young tycoon, and those who had had been alarmed by Tennant's sudden loss of weight. The last press photograph, of a gaunt Tennant failing to fill his expensive tailoring, confirmed something was far wrong. It had been assumed that the young man had fallen victim to illness, probably cancer, and his privacy had been respected.

But there had been no cancer.

The *Times* headline read: AUTOPSY REVEALS BIOTECH ENTRE-PRENEUR DIED OF MALNUTRITION. It had been one of those stories that had registered with Macbeth at the time without him taking much notice of it: a strange story, but at a time of general, and increasing, strangeness.

Tennant had been found dead in his New York penthouse, to which he had retreated presumably to remove himself as far as possible from his colleagues in California. Increasingly reclusive, he had refused even janitorial or cleaning staff access to his apartment, and was scarcely seen outside it.

His reclusion became complete invisibility and total silence.

Eventually, Tennant's concerned family and colleagues had entered the apartment, accompanied by police and the apartment building's management. The scene that had confronted them had been bizarre. Tennant had been found sitting in the middle of his opulent apartment, surrounded by designer furniture, fine art and sculpture valued at two million dollars. The temperature- and humidity-controlled apartment was also found to contain half a million dollars' worth of high-tech electronics. Thirty thousand dollars in cash was found in a desk drawer and his wardrobe contained nothing but the most expensive designer wear.

Yet, in the whole of the apartment there was no food other than three apples in the refrigerator. Kitchen cupboards were empty of food but stacked with vitamins and supplements. Vials of human growth hormone were the only things other than the apples found in the refrigerator.

And in the middle of it all, looking out over Central Park through the apartment's vast picture windows, sat Samuel Tennant. Not only was the thirty-four-year-old entrepreneur dead, he had been dead for three weeks. During that time, the dehumidifying air conditioning he had had installed to keep his computers and electronics in the optimum conditions, coupled with the lack of fatty mass in his body, had begun a process of mummification. Accurate measurement had been difficult, but it was estimated that Tennant had weighed less than seventy pounds at the time of his death.

Macbeth leaned back in his chair, staring at the screen and trying to work out what connection there could be between Tennant's bizarre death, Killberg's horrific murder and Melissa's inexplicable suicide.

He had just gone back to the article on the Golden Gate suicides and noted down the CHP police officer's name when he heard Casey's key in the door.

30

ZHANG. GANSU PROVINCE

Looking at herself in the mirror, she brushed back blonde hair that was between red and gold from her oval face, her forehead wide and pale above bright green eyes, before fastening her hair behind her head with the clasp she had until then held between tight lips.

A foreigner gazed back from the mirror. Or at least parts of a foreigner. Hers was a face that spoke of two worlds, two hemispheres, but belonged to neither; a face whose detail – the high cheekbones, the shape of her eyes, her small, heart-shaped mouth – was Han Chinese, but whose general form and architecture, whose skin tone and hair color, was European. It should have had the effect of making her look like the child of mixed parentage, but it didn't because she wasn't. She looked exactly what she was; she looked like many others from her village but like so few in a nation of one and a third billion.

Growing up in Liqian, Zhang Xushou had not felt foreign or different, because there had been so many others in her village with hair shaded from red and blonde to chestnut and auburn; eye colors from hazel to green to pale blue. It had been an accepted part of her childhood, when her universe had extended only as far as the stumps of the ancient city walls at the edge of the village. It had only been when she went to the senior school in the neighboring village that Zhang Xushou became aware that there was something different, odd, about her village. About her.

It was then she had heard the legend of the legionnaires: the tall blond Roman soldiers, separated from their commanders in the ill-fated expedition of Marcus Licinius Crassus against the Parthians. The legend told that legionnaire survivors of the battle ended up impossibly far east and lost in the Gobi Desert, eventually washing up on its shores and finding refuge in her village, then a frontier city, where they were pressed into service by the Han Dynasty.

At one time, Zhang Xushou and her kind were shunned, mocked. As the borders of her world had expanded, so had her understanding of what it was to be other, different; to be one blonde head in an ocean of China Black. And then, as she grew older, she had begun to stand out from the crowd even more. Literally. The length of bone her ancient genetics had given her made her taller as a thirteen-year-old girl than many of her male teachers at the school. At an age and in an environment where conformity and acceptance was everything, Zhang Xushou had been subjected to hostile stares and name-calling; mainly *wai guo ren*. Foreigner.

Her isolation had not made her resent her individuality but value it, embrace it. She welcomed the nicknames, turning insults into compliments and particularly liking it when others called her *Lijian*, which meant Greek or Roman. Her heritage became a passion, then an obsession. She spent hours reading all she could on the Roman Empire, about the six thousand lost legionnaires, about the people and culture of Europe. She pinned pictures of Western models and pop stars on her wall.

Then, as she grew older, she saw attitudes change around her. Tourists began to visit Liqian to stare at the villagers who paraded proudly and often took money for interviews from the Chinese and foreign press. One day, a day she would never forget, a film crew from an Italian television station came to the village. She had, at first, been disappointed because the Italian men in the crew had not been much taller than the average Han Chinese, and their hair had been as black. But then she saw the reporter, dressed in baggy cargo pants and sweatshirt, her hair tied back into a clasp at the back of her head. Her hair. Her bronze-gold hair, exactly the same shade as Zhang's. Zhang Xushou had thought the Italian journalist the most beautiful woman she had ever seen. Zhang's joy had been immeasurable when the Italian woman had spotted her and, recognizing her as one of the 'Roman' children, had come over and chatted to her as best she could through the medium of a squat, stern government translator.

After the film crew had gone, Zhang had sought out a friend who she knew had a hair clasp similar to the Italian woman's and bought it for much more than the clasp was worth. From that day forth, Zhang Xushou had worn her hair scraped back from her face and clasp-fastened behind her head.

About a year after the Italians had visited, the people from Lanzhou University had come. They had taken photographs of the village, examined the ancient ruins of the old city, had talked to the villagers. Among the university people had been specialists interested exclusively in the thirty families in the village who everyone agreed looked like *wai guo ren*. These rubber-gloved specialists had asked Zhang Xushou to place a cotton bud in her mouth and rub the inside of her cheek, before placing the cotton bud in a sealed tube. Each of us, they had explained, had a secret history within us, coiled up tight in spirals. Their job was to unravel these histories. Zhang had stared at them with her bright green eyes in the frank and defiant way that had gotten her into so much trouble at school and had said: "DNA? I may be a Gansu village girl, but I know what DNA is."

The university people had smiled and explained that they had done tests on the other thirty families and it would prove, one way or another, if she was the distant descendant of a Roman.

And it did. Or at least, when the results had eventually come back, they proved to the excited villagers that what they had always believed was true: they were nearly as much European as they were Chinese. The archaeologists in the team also confirmed that the village was, indeed, the site of the ancient fortress city which had stood guard on the western frontier of the Han Empire. The government, however, maintained that the results proved nothing more than Zhang Xushou and the other Lijian families belonged to some sub-clade of the Han ethnic group.

But Zhang Xushou never stopped believing.

Life had returned more or less to normal after that, other than the Roman-styled gift shops and café that the enterprising locals had set up for the tourists, who came in even greater numbers. Zhang had done her own research and had learned about others in Gansu region and beyond who shared her foreign looks. No hint of legionnaires about them, but of ancient races of Celts, of Tocharians, of the *Wusun* – the Grand-children of the Raven – who, a millennium and a half before, Yan Shigu had described as apes: green-eyed, red-haired savages.

She scoured the Internet, which was easier and more fruitful than visiting the nearest library in Yongchang, reading up about mysterious people: about the three-thousand-year-old bodies found, perfectly preserved, in the Taklamakan Desert; looking at photographs of Cherchen Man and the Beauty of Loulan: tall, blond and red-haired people who had lived in western China nearly three thousand years ago. Zhang knew the chances were the origin of her distinctive look lay with these people and not with some mythical Roman, but she clung on desperately to the romance of being the Legionnaire's Daughter.

Now, as she prepared to leave her village to attend university in Lanzhou, she also prepared for a life as a foreigner in her own country. And her identity became even more important to her. In the evenings, she would walk to the edge of the village and watch the sun set behind the Qilian mountains, gazing out over the desert sands and allowing the dimming light and distant dust clouds to play tricks and conjure imagined outlines of some faraway phalanx.

But then there had been the talk of the Age of Visions.

It had started with reports of strange occurrences in bigger towns far away: third-hand tall tales made taller through the magnifying glass of village gossip. Stories had begun to circulate of people seeing their ancestors, seeing past times; witnessing cataclysmic events or the moon twenty times its size in the daylight sky. People, especially the old, superstitious villagers, began to talk of the old religions and their tales of an Age of Visions that marked the End Times; about the return of *Hundun*, the spirit of chaos from before time began. One old man, Zhia Bao, who was Hui Chinese and supposed to adhere strictly to Islam, announced portentously that what was happening was that the Wall of Heaven had been breached. He explained that it had happened once before in mankind's history, but the creator-goddess Nüwa had stopped the gap with her own body.

"If what you say is true," Zhang had heard one of the villagers ask, "what will become of us if the Wall is breached?"

Zhia Bao had taken a long, contemplative pull on his pipe, playing the village elder of older times. "According to the legends, then the world of heaven and this world will collide and all things will end."

It had all been the excited speculation of distance: the thrill of a threat at one remove. But then there was talk of a panic in the streets of Lanzhou, of people running from monsters that could not be. Then strange happenings in Yongchang. But it was when one of the women in the village itself, a woman deaf for twenty years, had said she had heard the sounds of marching men and clashing metal coming from the desert, that Zhang knew that something momentous was about to happen. It was then that she began to sit for hours at the edge of the village, watching the sands beyond. Waiting.

The legion was coming.

31

JOHN MACBETH. BOSTON

When Casey got home, Macbeth told him about his meeting with Bundy, and what he had found out about the names the FBI man had mentioned; about Melissa's connections to two dead men; and about Bundy's interest in John Astor and the Simulists.

"He seemed to want to know more about them than about Blind Faith, who I'd have thought would be a bigger priority for the FBI," Macbeth explained. "Have you ever heard of the Simulists?"

"Sure," said Casey. "Don't know why the FBI would be interested in them at all. They're an odd subset of the scientific community. A bit weird but definitely harmless."

"And John Astor?"

"Their figurehead. Maybe a real person, maybe not. That goes with their set of beliefs."

"I don't get you."

"Religion and science don't mix. Like I said, the first only exists in the absence of the second. But the Simulists are scientists who believe we need religion – that there's a basic human need for belief, whether that belief's crap or not. So what they did was make science itself their religion. They believe God doesn't exist yet, but will come to exist. Because we will create him. Science will make us God."

"*We are becoming* . . ." said Macbeth. "The graffiti I keep seeing."

"That's them. For the Simulists there is no Judgment Day – just the Singularity, when Man and technology combine and human becomes posthuman. Have you heard of Clarke's Third Law?"

"Yes," said Macbeth. "As a matter of fact I have: *Any sufficiently advanced technology would be indistinguishable from magic.*"

"Why doesn't it surprise me that you know that?" Casey smiled wryly. "Anyway, the Simulists take it one step farther – that any sufficiently advanced form of human intelligence would be indistinguishable from God. They believe it is our destiny to emerge from the coming Singularity as posthuman, then superhuman, then demigodly, then godly."

"And Astor?"

"He's their prophet – supposed to have written this super-encrypted book that's buried in the virtual world and reveals itself only to the chosen. It's all science but all mystic at the same time. Like the supposed trinity of God's nature, Astor's nature is supposed to be a duality – virtual and physical. The Simulist part of it all comes from their belief that, as super-intelligent posthumans, we will create super-simulations of people, worlds and universes, indistinguishable from reality. Simulations where the people living in them don't know they're not real. We become the gods of other realities."

"Sounds like a cult. And crap."

"Less crap than existing religions. I come across some mind-bending stuff in my work, infinite possibilities and impossibilities. Things that look like magic, except they aren't – there's always an equation or a principle to explain them. I think Simulism started out as a joke or a thought experiment – you know, to illustrate the fallacy of religion – but Astor's book is supposed to contain some kind of revelation. A scientific revelation, not a religious one. Whatever it is, it's made some Simulists take their beliefs very seriously."

"You know a lot about it."

"There was a real fad for it at MIT for a while. Big with

quantum physicists. But when it all stopped being lighthearted, it kinda died out."

"Do you know if Gabriel Rees was involved with them?"

Casey shrugged. "Can't say. But I'd doubt it."

Those last days in Boston were a difficult and confusing time for Macbeth.

Like everyone else, he found himself watching the news more than usual. There were more reports of bizarre happenings in locations all over the world, but objective reporting of subjective experiences was all but impossible; added to which no one could be sure which hallucinations had really taken place and which were staged for fifteen Warhol minutes.

But there were other, more tangible threats to be reported. One effect of the visions had been a steep rise in religiomania: fundamentalists of all complexions became more fundamental, radicals more radical, extremists more extreme. Every cleric saw in the happenings a justification for his own brand of superstition and bigotry. Across the US, firebrand preachers announced the beginning of the Rapture while sermonizing xenophobia, intolerance and mistrust; throughout Europe and the Middle East, mullahs and ayatollahs called the faithful to jihad. Closer to home, an unassuming, white, male, divorced car salesman who, as far as anyone was aware, had never set foot outside the continental US, walked into the crowded foyer of a computer software company in downtown DC. Shouting "Allahu Akbar", he detonated the bomb he had hidden in his rucksack, killing himself and eight bystanders. The same day, an unidentified gunman of Arab appearance opened fire on shoppers in an Apple store in Oregon, killing seven before being gunned down himself by police.

In the meantime, Macbeth spent a lot of time dealing with Professor Poulsen by phone and email, assuring him that he wasn't going to accede to Brian Newcombe's request and join the WHO investigative team. Whenever Macbeth discussed the bizarre occurrences around the world with him, Poulsen seemed to regard it as small talk; a trivial distraction.

While Casey and the rest of Boston struggled to come to terms with the inexplicable experience of the 'ghostquake', Macbeth sought his own coming to terms with Melissa's death and the equally inexplicable circumstances surrounding it. It took three calls to the California Highway Patrol before the three-hour time difference, Macbeth's schedule and Ramirez's duty roster came into alignment.

"What can I do for you, Dr Macbeth?" Ramirez's voice was deep and quiet, his tone strangely unlike what Macbeth expected from a police officer.

He told Ramirez who and where he was and why he was there, his former relationship with Melissa Collins and his disbelief that she would commit suicide.

"I'm afraid there's no question of it," said Ramirez. "I saw her and the others jump myself. I'm sorry."

"Melissa was the least suicidal person I knew . . . Is there any chance that it's a case of mistaken identity?"

"There's no way. We've a positive ID and, anyway, I've seen photographs of Miss Collins. It was her all right."

"When she jumped, was she distressed? Or do you think she could have been under the influence of anything?"

"That was what got to me the most . . . she was perfectly calm. Contented almost. As for drugs or alcohol, the autopsy tox screen came up clean. You knew her well?"

"We lived together for a while, before she moved to the West Coast. We hadn't been in touch much since. At all, really."

"And she never showed any signs of any kind of mental instability in the time you knew her?"

"None. None at all."

There was a silence. Macbeth hated telephone conversations because he found silences and pauses difficult to read. He guessed that Ramirez was thinking through what he had told him.

"Do you mind me asking," Ramirez broke the silence, "why it has taken you so long to get in touch? It's been over two months since Miss Collins died."

"I only just found out. I mean, I'd heard about the Golden Gate suicides, and the others in Japan, but didn't know the details. Like I said, I live and work in Denmark. It was only when the FBI – Agent Bundy – spoke to me about it that I found out Melissa had been involved."

"The FBI?" There was something in Ramirez's quiet, even voice. Suspicion, perhaps. "I'm surprised we weren't informed. How long are you staying in Boston, Dr Macbeth?"

"Just till the end of next week. My boss in Copenhagen wants me back even sooner than that."

Another pause.

"Okay," said Ramirez. "I'm supposed to be coming to Boston in a week or so, following a lead on this thing, but I'll try to bring it forward. Would you spare me some time if I can get there before you leave?"

"Sure," said Macbeth. "But I would have thought your investigation into Melissa's death would be over, given that it is such a clear case of suicide."

"It may be clearly suicide, but it's a high-visibility case and there's pressure to establish what drove them all to jump. I'm really coming to Boston to find out what I can from Deborah Canning, the only member of the company who was not there that morning, to see if she can cast further light on it all."

"Deborah Canning? Deborah Canning is in Boston?" Macbeth was genuinely taken aback. Why had Bundy, the FBI man, not mentioned it?

"That's what I've been told. She's suffered some kind of breakdown and I've only just gotten permission to interview her. She's been admitted to McLean Hospital . . ."

*

232

Macbeth was glad he'd moved in with Casey. He often found it a challenge to relate to other people, a dissonance in frequency sometimes making it difficult for them to connect with him. But Casey, though a very different personality, was at least on the same wavelength. He got Macbeth.

That week, they talked a lot, late into the night. Macbeth told Casey all that he had found out about Melissa and the strange connections between her death and those of Killberg and Tennant. He also shared everything about what the WHO team had told him.

"So, are you going to work with them?" asked Casey one night as they sat sag-shouldered with weariness in his kitchen, drinking tea.

"I just can't. I know it's an honor and important and all that, but there are others much better qualified. My work in Copenhagen is just as important, and no one can take my place. I've said I'll offer opinions on data when I can, but that's it."

"I don't know, John, something weird's going on. Like a plague or something. A plague of the mind." Casey made a face and encapsulated the phrase in quote marks finger twitched in the air. "People are scared. I'm scared by it all. Today I jumped back onto the sidewalk because I didn't see a car coming. If he hadn't sounded his car horn he'd have hit me. But after the car was gone I actually found myself questioning whether the car had been there at all. People are going nuts. They don't know what to believe. I'd have thought getting to the bottom of it would be the psychiatric challenge of the century."

"Are you still going to the Blackwell symposium in Oxford?"

"Of course I am."

"Then you ought to understand. The Copenhagen Project is as important to me as Blackwell's Prometheus Project is to you. We are on the brink of understanding the mind completely. And I honestly believe that the answer to whatever is happening around the world isn't going to be found by looking for patterns in epidemiological stats."

"I guess." Casey sighed resignedly and leaned back in the kitchen chair. "By the way, I had a look at your laptop."

"Great . . . Did you get that folder open?"

Casey shook his head. "Couldn't. You can't even click on the icon or get info on the size of the folder or even if it's empty."

Macbeth shrugged. "I'll ignore it then . . ."

"I wouldn't do that. There's something about it I don't like. You've a lot of sensitive stuff on your computer, relating to your work. I've a bad feeling that your laptop's been hacked and the folder has been put there."

"Some kind of Trojan?"

"Trojan viruses are usually hidden deep in your hard drive and more often than not are invisible without anti-virus software. No . . ." Casey frowned. "No, this is something different. I've virus-checked and copied over all of your major files onto a portable hard drive – but none of the software, in case that's infected. I've got a spare laptop that I can loan you."

"You think that's necessary?"

"I've never seen anything like it before." Casey gave a confused laugh. "You know, it's almost a perfect analogy for what's happening around us: that folder of yours is a ghost – a phantom, like you said. I actually began to question whether it really was there on the screen or whether we're hallucinating it."

"You're letting this get to you too much, Casey," said Macbeth. "Things are what they are. These episodes are still isolated and rare. I would have thought you of all people would be immune to media hysteria about it."

"I guess . . ."

They had given it a name: TNHS. Temporary Non-Pathological Hallucinatory Syndrome. The American Psychiatric Association had assigned the syndrome a DSM number, and the World Health Organization adopted the designation for its own ICD.

Macbeth was not at all sure that the name reflected the experience, or that there was enough non-anecdotal data on which to base it – and there was certainly still no established etiology – but he could understand why they had come up with the name. The media, not just in the US but around the world, had begun to call it 'Boston Syndrome' and there was a real need to give the experience an official name, to suggest to the public that the medical community had isolated and defined something. The use of the word 'temporary' had no doubt been included to assure people that, if they had such an experience, it was not a chronic problem.

Despite declining Newcombe's request that he join the investigation team, Macbeth had agreed to work with them at the Schilder until he left for Copenhagen. He recommended again that they try to get in touch with Josh Hoberman.

Hoberman, Macbeth was told, seemed to have disappeared from his home in Virginia, and hadn't been seen at his clinic for over a week. Given the threat level posed to scientists by Blind Faith and others, the police had been informed.

Macbeth also recommended that the team involve Pete Corbin, who, after all, was at hand in Boston and who had first spotted the emergence of the syndrome; a suggestion to which he had gotten a lukewarm response.

Macbeth called Corbin on the Thursday morning.

"You still okay for tomorrow at ten-thirty?" asked Corbin. "I still would like you to see this patient of mine. I can't help thinking this case is connected to everything else that's happening. I'd just like your take on it."

"Actually, Pete, that's why I'm calling. There's another patient I'd much rather talk to, if that's possible. I've been told that she's at McLean for treatment. Her name is Deborah Canning."

Corbin didn't answer immediately. Another difficult to read phone silence; maybe he was annoyed that Macbeth didn't want to see his patient.

"Shit . . ." Corbin said eventually. "Now this is really weird, John. Deborah Canning is my patient. Deborah Canning is exactly the patient I wanted you to see . . ."

32

JOHN MACBETH. BOSTON

The cabby who drove Macbeth out to Belmont lacked the inquisitive chattiness of the one who'd taken him to his first meeting with Corbin, and Macbeth found himself grateful for it. It didn't surprise him: road accidents had increased steeply in the last week as drivers took drastic evasive action to dodge obstacles or people that appeared suddenly from nowhere.

McLean Hospital, just outside Belmont, had always seemed to Macbeth to be a cross between a very upscale country club and an Ivy League university campus. It wasn't a single building, but a spread-out collection. There were a few larger, more modern, more institutional-looking structures, but in the main McLean comprised red-brick and stucco Colonial-Revival or Jacobethan-Revival buildings, simulating architecture that had been past-tense even to the Victorian designers who had conceived them. It was all set against an expansive backdrop of trees and parkland. Affiliated to Harvard, McLean was probably New England's top psychiatric hospital and it was an environment that gave some outer peace to those suffering from inner turmoil. Macbeth had enjoyed his time here. Until his last case.

The taxi dropped him off outside the main administration building.

"Glad you could make it, John," Pete Corbin said as he led Macbeth back out of the building. "My patient's over in one of the residences – we can walk. Did you feel the quake?"

236

"Like everyone else. You?"

"Joanna too. What's happening, John?"

"Some kind of Mass Psychogenic Illness . . . maybe viral in origin, like you thought, maybe not. In the meantime, they've tagged it as Temporary Non-Pathological Hallucinatory Syndrome, meaning it's a sure bet everyone'll stick with Boston Syndrome. You still getting presentations?" asked Macbeth.

"More every day. I've never seen anything like it."

"Did you know Deborah Canning worked with Melissa?"

"No. I knew she was connected to the Golden Gate suicides, but like you I never connected them with Melissa. I can't believe it."

"You and me both," said Macbeth. "So, if you were unaware of the connection, why do you want me to see her?"

"Because she's exhibiting delusions that remind me of Gabriel Rees before he jumped from the Christian Science roof. And I've this gut feeling that it's all connected to what's going on – to Boston Syndrome – in an odd way."

The path they took, dappled by the bright spring sun probing through the trees, eventually opened up to immaculate lawns on either side. The residence was a Colonial-Georgian mansion that looked more like the private home of some New England bluebloods than an institutional facility.

"She's in here?" Macbeth asked, suddenly uneasy.

"Yes." Corbin's expression became grave. "Dammit, she's actually in the same room. Sorry John, I didn't think."

"Forget it." Macbeth forced a smile. "Ancient history."

"You sure?" asked Corbin. "I could bring her down into the main building . . ."

"No need. I'd forgotten myself until I saw the residence."

All physicians lost patients at some time during their career. For psychiatrists, the threat that hung over them was always that a patient, sometimes with a sudden and unpredicted change of mood state, would take their own life. It had happened here, with someone in Macbeth's charge. His last case in clinical medicine had occupied the room now taken by Deborah Canning. There had been accusations of poor judgment and a deeply flawed diagnosis; but Macbeth had been his own biggest critic and his doubts about his own ability to relate to people, to read them, had led him away from patient care and into pure research.

"You sure?" Corbin asked.

"I'm sure."

"Okay." Corbin led the way into the residence. "As you know, Debbie worked in the gaming industry, as Melissa's deputy, designing and programming computer games. She's a hugely intelligent woman and when an intellect of that size turns in on itself, it's a strong enemy to overcome. She's a paying patient here and started off as a self-admission. Her family are here in Boston and about six weeks ago she turned up at their door from San Francisco without warning and in a real state of distress. She had simply walked out of her office, bought an airline ticket with her credit card and had flown across the country without stopping to change her clothes or pack a bag. Four days after Debbie arrived in Boston, Melissa and the entire company committed suicide."

"Does she know?"

"I made a clinical ruling that she shouldn't be informed – and that caused problems with the police, who were desperate to question her – but I'm pretty sure she knows. She has either intuited the fact or maybe she ran away because she knew what was planned."

"So what are you treating her for?"

"Her condition is very difficult to define. Unlike Gabriel Rees, she does have a clinical history: bipolar symptoms for most of her post-adolescent life, and treated for ADHD as a teenager. When she admitted herself she was in the depths of a Psychotic Major Depression. I started her on Asenapine, but have eased

238

her off. I just don't feel the answer to what ails her can be found pharmacologically, so I've been carrying out intense therapy sessions."

"Why did you want me to come and see her?" asked Macbeth. "I mean before you knew the connection with Melissa?"

"Over the past four weeks . . . I guess the best way of putting it is it's like Debbie's started to fade away. She's the most florid yet logical case of derealization and depersonalization I've ever come across. She simply doesn't accept that she exists or has ever existed. I hope you don't mind, but after what happened with Gabriel, and given that you have some personal experience of depersonalization, I thought you could give some extra insight. To be honest, I'm despairing a little with her: she has detached herself so much from any sense of self that I can't seem to reach her, far less bring her back."

"So you're looking for a second opinion from a colleague with a similar screw loose, is that it?" Macbeth said, smiling.

"Let's say from someone who can empathize with at least some of what's going on in her mind. Listen, John, this really is the most extreme case I've come across. It sounds crazy, but sometimes I find myself believing her: that the reason I can't reach her is because she really isn't there . . ."

The corner room, with its double-aspect windows looking out over the lawns and copses of trees, was exactly as Macbeth remembered it. Other than the official fire notice on the back of the spring-hinged safety door, it was as un-institutional as the building that housed it. It was a bright, airy room with pale blue walls and the large abstract painting that hung above the single bed was a bland arrangement of shapes in pastel blues and greens; no strident geometries or colors to agitate here. The furniture was certainly new and functional, but an attempt had been made to fit with the residence's period and style.

Deborah Canning, dressed in jeans, sneakers and a dark blue T-shirt, was sitting in an upholstered armchair by one of the windows. Macbeth recognized her instantly from the photograph on Melissa's company website. She sat erect but not stiffly, her elbow on the small table, her hand resting on a large hard-back art book.

The first thing Macbeth noticed about her was her serenity. The calm in her face and posture was almost infectious and seemed to fill the room with a sense of peace. An attractive woman in her early thirties, Deborah would have been beautiful had her mouth not been a touch too small and her nose a touch too long. Her eyes, though, were striking: large, bright and emerald. She had a pale complexion and her hair was an unremarkable shade of light brown. She turned and smiled a quiet, polite smile when the two physicians entered.

"Hello Debbie," said Corbin. "This is a colleague of mine – the one I told you about – Dr John Macbeth."

"Like the Scottish king?" she asked, turning to examine him.

"Like the Scottish king," said Macbeth.

"But which Macbeth are you like?" she asked.

"I don't understand—"

"There are two Macbeths," she said, her voice calm, the intonation soft. "The historical Macbeth – the 'real' Macbeth, a very successful and much-loved king – and the fictional Macbeth, Shakespeare's ruthless murderer and tyrant. It's the bigger fiction that everyone remembers, not the smaller truth. So which of your namesakes are you more like – the remembered fiction or the forgotten fact?"

"I'm afraid I'm not in the slightest bit regal or made of Shakespearean stuff . . . I'm the Macbeth who struggles to balance his credit card. Do you mind if we sit down?"

She nodded and both psychiatrists pulled chairs across to the window and sat facing her.

"What have you been doing today?" Corbin asked.

"Doing?" she frowned. "There have been sounds from outside. Voices. Birds, mainly. A couple of trucks, faint."

"Do you like to listen to the sounds, Debbie?" asked Macbeth.

"I don't listen, I hear. And I only hear them because other people hear them."

"But you do hear them . . . You are here to listen to them."

"*Cogito?*"

"I beg your pardon?"

"Descartes's Cogito . . . the hammer you're trying to use to crack open my delusion. If I perceive, then I think. If I think, therefore I am. *Cogito ergo sum.*"

"Well, maybe something like that."

"You want to know the joke of it? Descartes got it almost right . . . it should be: I think therefore I *think* I am."

"You're wrong, Debbie," said Macbeth. "You know you exist, but because of the problems you've been having, because of some trauma, you are trying to distance yourself from that reality. It's a defense mechanism, that's all. I know you exist. Dr Corbin knows you exist. We can both see you and hear you."

"I'm afraid that logic doesn't hold. I know something about these things, about cognition and perception. In my work I used tricks and devices to play with people's perception. Because I exist as a percept in your mind, it doesn't mean that I really exist as a distal object in reality . . . Am I using the right words?"

Macbeth smiled and nodded. "Yes, Debbie . . . you're using the right words."

"What if I'm just in your head?" She looked at him earnestly, for the first time something breaking through into her expression. "Haven't you ever wondered that? Haven't you ever considered that all this – everything and everybody around you – is all just in your head? How do you know I was here before you walked into the room? You think I'm delusional, but the truth is there's really only one difference between me and everyone else: I *know* I don't exist, everyone else has suspected it at least once in their lives – questioned the reality of the world around them or of themselves."

"So why do we all accept we exist?"

"Because the deceptions are piled up, layered one on another, from the time we're kids. Deceptions, concepts, social constructs. We build a consensus about what reality is, about our own existence, and anyone who questions it is considered delusional."

"What about philosophers? Quantum physicists? Neuroscientists? Don't they question reality? No one considers them delusional."

"They're considered abstract thinkers. No one questions their take on reality because no one understands it. They dress up what is simple and observable in everyday life in a language that no one else can understand. They cloud the truth instead of illuminating it."

"What is this truth?" asked Macbeth.

"You know about Timothy Leary's eight-circuit model of consciousness?"

"I've heard of it," said Macbeth.

"The eighth circuit is where the truth lies. The Overmind. The quantum mind. Consciousness is the most difficult thing to pin down; why I see the world from my window and you from yours. Have you never wondered if we all share the same, single consciousness and we just experience it one viewpoint at a time? That maybe when you die you will wake up as me, or Gandhi, or Hitler, or the starving African child you saw on the TV? We don't think about it because our thinking is suppressed. This so-called reality is contingent on the suppression of cognitive liberty. We ban mind-altering drugs, we create religions, to confine and channel the thoughts of others and ourselves. How do you know that I am not an invention of your perception?"

"Because I'm not that imaginative, Debbie. I know you exist."

"Like I said, I know a lot about perceptions of reality. I am considered to be the best ARG programmer in the States. One of the top three in the world."

"ARG?"

"Alternate Reality Games. Total immersion in another reality. I learned all the tricks – and invented more than half of them – of how to fool the human mind into believing it is somewhere it's not and experiencing an environment that isn't there." She smiled again and Macbeth noticed the corner of her mouth tremble. "Would you do me a favor? Look behind you. Humor me . . . Please, both of you, look behind you and take a note of what you see."

They both turned and took in the room.

"Now turn back to me and don't look behind you again."

They turned back.

"Tell me what is behind you. Whatever you do, don't look to remind yourself."

"Behind us? Your room, Debbie," said Corbin. "Your bed, the dresser, the robe . . . the painting on the wall, the door into the corridor . . ."

"You see," she said. "You are looking at me now but you are picturing the room you saw. Re-creating it in your mind even though you can no longer see it."

She looked into the space between them, beyond them, behind them. Her face lost its serenity: for a moment there was pain and despair in her expression, then it faded, replaced with cold, empty calm.

"Do you know what I see? Now that you're not looking? Everything you described was there, but only when you looked. It was there *because* you looked. It's gone now. I can't see it because I can't generate it. It does not exist because I do not exist to create it."

"So what *is* there, Debbie?" asked Macbeth.

"Nothing. There is nothing there. Just a void that I cannot describe to you because it has no dimension, no color, no shape."

Her face remained calm, but her eyes glossed and a tear found its way from the corner of her eye, tracing its way down her cheek.

"I am looking past you and there is nothing there. I am looking past you into the most terrible emptiness."

33

ZHANG. GANSU PROVINCE

Zhang Xushou screwed her eyes against the harsh, too-bright sunlight. Like the other pale-eyed Lijian from her village, she was sensitive to the desert light, but today was different. Today, as she sat once more at the village's edge, the sun seemed to have spread across the sheet of sky, intensifying instead of diffusing in it; the horizon indistinct between the sky's brilliance and its sand reflection. She felt as if she stood before a brighter sun of some unremembered past time. The vague feeling became a cogent déjà vu that became a potent sense of unease and unreality. She stood at the edge of the village and closed her eyes tight, taking a moment to calm herself, to collect her thoughts. Maybe she was coming down with something; or maybe it was just the stress of going off to university.

Or perhaps this truly was the Age of Visions and when she opened her eyes, she would see her Roman forefather, along with his cohort, march gleamingly out of the desert. After all, she had waited so long.

When she did open her eyes, the sun was still too bright, but less so than before. And she knew it was no bug, no fever, nothing playing tricks with her mind. What she was experiencing was truly external, truly there.

But it could not be.

Zhang stood on the edge of her village and looked out over the Gobi Desert. Except the Gobi Desert was no longer there. An ocean of sand had been replaced with a true ocean of sun-sparkled blue water. Zhang now stood on the shore of a sea or a lake that stretched as far as she could see and ozone fumed in the air, filling her nostrils. She staggered back. It wasn't just impossible, it was as impossible as it could be. An ocean where a desert had been for thousands of years, a desert that had been expanding by more than three thousand square kilometers a year.

A desert that was now suddenly, inexplicably, gone.

The strange thing was that she knew she was not going mad. What she was witnessing was insane, but she knew that it was an external insanity. What she was seeing was clearly a hallucination, but it was not she who was hallucinating it. The image of the Wall of Heaven crumbling, put in her head by old Zhia Bao, filled her with fear. She felt her heart thudding in her chest and a panic rising from deep within.

And then she heard it. Behind her.

The sound of something monstrous.

Zhang Xushou turned to the sound. Every muscle, every tendon and fiber was frozen solid by a total fear that surged through her nervous system, robbing her of the ability to move or speak or breathe. Something deep and locked in the most primitive part of her brain exploded; she was beyond fight-or-flight impulses. She was completely, totally, at the mercy of her own terror.

That, and the thing she now faced.

It was a monster. Wolf-headed, wolf-shaped, wolf-like, but tiger-striped and five times the size of any wolf, it was a demonic thing from nightmares: a giant yellow-eyed snarl of fur and teeth and jaws. In her terror, Zhang didn't try to make sense of the creature, to understand the nonsensicality of a wolf bigger than a horse, but something registered in her brain that it was more than the monster's size made her think of something other than a wolf. It had a bulky, heavily muscled body, thickly furred, but the monstrous head, and those improbably

246

massive jaws, seemed out of proportion even with the huge body.

The wolf-monster hadn't seen her. It pawed its way malevolently across the sand to the water's edge. And it was then she noticed it didn't have paws or claws: the beast's feet were like nothing she had ever seen before . . . if anything more like the hooves of a goat, but more angular, sharper. She searched her memory for anything she'd seen in a book, heard in a far-fetched tale or fairy story that spoke of a chimera like this.

The Tiangou. The demon dog of Chinese legend who ate the sun to cause eclipses. This thing, this monster before her . . . that's what it must be. The Tiangou existed, she realized – not the way it did in legend, in superstition, but in the here-and-now real world. This was the reality on which the legend must have been based.

But the sea – that didn't explain the sea where the desert had been. And why had she never heard of other sightings of this beast?

The creature still had not seen her, and Zhang's mind screamed mutely to her body to move, not to run, but edge slowly away and back up towards the village. For a moment her reason failed to thaw the ice of her fear that still bound her motionless, but then, painfully slowly, without taking a breath and with her eyes locked on the beast, she began to ease one foot back, then another.

The Tiangou snapped its vast head in her direction, surprising her with the speed it could move such a massive skull. It let out a roar. Not like a lion's, or a wolf's, not like any creature she had ever heard: a long, deep, thunderous bellow that Zhang Xushou felt resonate in her bones. It sunk its improbable head low between bulky shoulders that moved like slow pistons as it walked. Zhang had never seen this monstrous creature before, but she recognized the way it moved: the slow, measured pace of a predator preparing to attack.

247

The Age of Visions.

Zhang thought back to all of the stories she'd heard: about people panicking because of things that were not there, weeping at the sight of loved ones long dead. Visions. Visions cannot hurt you. Visions are not real. But what she faced, no matter how improbable, was as real as anything else she had experienced in her life.

Another bellowing roar from the Tiangou. It slouched forward then paused, yellow eyes dead and cold. Zhang knew the attack was coming. The monster closed the gap between it and her in an instant.

She closed her eyes.

Zhang kept her eyes squeezed tight. She clasped her hands over her ears and commanded the Tiangou, the desert-ocean, the too-bright sun to be gone.

When she opened them again, the sea still sparkled under a brilliant sky, the air still smelled and felt different. But the Tiangou was no longer in front of her. She heard it roar again and she spun around to see it now behind her. And she saw at the same time another impossible beast. The monster's attack had not been launched at her, but at this other creature. It looked to Zhang like a rhinoceros, but again too big and without a horn on its head, instead having two flattened, spoon-like protuberances projecting from the end of its snout. The Tiangou had clearly already attacked the other creature: Zhang could see a hideous gash ripped through a leather armor of thick, folded skin. The beast let out a long plaintive bellow as the Tiangou raised itself up onto its hind legs, twisting its neck and opening the huge jaws wide. It fell upon its prey, its jaws clamping on the back of the creature's neck. Despite its prey being robustly built, the Tiangou's jaws crushed through hide, muscle and crunched through bone. Zhang felt sick at the sound. All strength seemed instantly to drain from the creature

248

and it sank to its knees before keeling over with a reverberating thud. The Tiangou tore mercilessly at its flesh, feeding on it even before the last of its life had gone from it. The air fumed with the stench of blood and raw, torn flesh, adding to Zhang's nausea. She realized that the Tiangou was between her and the village; there was no cover, no place to run. She would have to pass it and its meal to get to safety. Speculating that the wolf-monster was too engrossed in its feeding frenzy to notice her, she moved in a wide arc, always resisting the impulse to run, never taking her eyes from the monster.

She moved steadily, making sure her pace was slow enough not to trigger a predatory reaction from the monster, but quick enough to pass by before it had finished tearing the last of the flesh from its victim.

The beast raised its massive head, the muzzle caked in blood and ripped sinew from its prey, and stared straight at Zhang with cold, dead yellow eyes. She froze, measuring the distance to the first houses in the village. There was no way she could get halfway there before the wolf-monster would be on her, tearing through flesh and crushing bone with its vast jaws.

This was it. This would be how and where she would die and she was not able to put a name to the thing that brought death to her. Then she realized the beast was not looking at her, it was looking through her, in the same way it had before it attacked the strange giant rhinoceros-type creature. To the beast, she didn't exist.

The Age of Visions. What she was experiencing looked, felt and smelled real, but it was a vision, an illusion. It was no more real than something on the television or in a movie.

She was convinced it was a hallucination, but did she have the courage to put that conviction to the test? Zhang took a sideways step: a wide, confident step. The wolf-monster's gaze remained fixed and did not move with her. Another step. The monster roared and again Zhang felt it reverberate in her flesh, resonate in her bones. It was real. She fought back the panic that surged through her and took another sideways step, then another. She was now out of the creature's line of sight, but it still did not turn to follow her. After a moment, the Tiangou lost interest in whatever it had stopped to look at, turned back to the rent cadaver of its freshly dead prey and began once more to tear at its insides.

Zhang broke into a sprint towards the village. She ran as she had never run before and without looking back to see if the monster, hallucination or not, was chasing her.

34

JOHN MACBETH. BOSTON

Macbeth found himself becoming very aware of the room, as if Deborah Canning was drawing him into her ever-tighter circle of perception. A breeze picked up outside and the sunlight in the room dimmed for a few seconds, before brightening again.

"So why don't you see anything behind us, Debbie?" he asked. "And how is it we can see it when you can't?"

"Imagine this," she said. "You're in a hall of mirrors, dozens of them angled to create endlessly recursive reflections. You're surrounded by an infinite number of yourself. How can you be sure you're the real you and not one of the reflections?"

"Because I can think," said Macbeth. "And a reflection can't."

She laughed, quietly and a little bitterly. "That's where you're wrong, Dr Macbeth. The project you're working on – you're holding up a mirror and creating a reflection of the human mind. But that reflection will think. Believe itself to be real."

Macbeth was taken aback for a moment. "How do you know about my work?"

"We discussed it."

"We?"

"Melissa and I. She talked about you, often. But we talked about your work more."

Macbeth was about to ask something else – to ask what Melissa had said about him, then checked himself.

"So you're saying you are a reflection," he said. "But I see you, Dr Corbin sees you. We know you're real."

"No . . . you're just being deceived into believing I'm real. Are you familiar with *trompe l'œil?*" Deborah lifted the heavy art book from the window-side table and handed it to Macbeth. *The Misled Eye: the Art of Deception.* Reaching over, she turned the pages while Macbeth held the book. She stopped when she reached a photograph of a painting hanging in a gallery. It was of two young men climbing a stairway that curled out of sight. The picture was framed conventionally on three sides, giving it the look of a doorway into the wall rather than a painting; at the bottom a real three-dimensional wooden step, the same color and construction as the ones in the painting, projected out and down to the floor. The composition created an optical illusion of depth and dimension.

"Charles Willson Peale's *Staircase Group*," Deborah explained. "The figures in the painting are life-size . . . Peale's sons. You can't really get the full effect from a photograph. The impression was powerful enough to fool George Washington into believing it was real when he saw it for the first time. *Trompe l'œil* has a history that goes back into the classical world: Roman and Greek murals painted to deceive the eye and make interiors look bigger and grander. When the Renaissance master Giotto was still an apprentice to Cimabue, he painted a fly on one of his master's frescoes. The fly was so lifelike that Cimabue tried to brush it off the wall." Taking back the book, she closed it and placed it exactly where she'd picked it up from, each movement precise. "You see, Dr Macbeth, it is the easiest thing in the world to confuse the senses, to deceive the mind into accepting something is real when it's fake."

"So who is being deceived, in your opinion? You for not seeing the room behind us or us for seeing it?"

"We are all being deceived: you into believing I and the room exist; me into doubting my lack of existence. But when I focus on it, when I accept I don't have presence independent of the minds of others . . . that's when I can see the nothing."

"So we exist because we see what you can't?" asked Macbeth.

"No. You don't exist either. We are all reflections. You just *think* you exist and that the room exists. I *know* I don't and it doesn't."

Macbeth lifted a hand and indicated the window. "Just a moment ago, the light in the room faded and the edge of the curtain moved. I don't need to look outside to know that the wind has picked up, or see the cloud that passed across the sun and dimmed it for me to know that the cloud and the sun were there. Not everything needs to be sensed or experienced for us to know that it's there."

"I've read Hegel and Kant too, Dr Macbeth. As for trees and clouds and things-in-themselves . . . you know what I did for a living – I created worlds. Thousands of them. Programs so complex and convincing and environments so real that, for hours on end, people left this reality to live in mine. There were breezes and clouds and trees in my worlds too."

"And it's perhaps exactly that work that's damaged your association with reality," said Macbeth. "Listen Debbie, I know you think this is an experience unique to you, and that something has been revealed to you that no one else can understand, but you've got to believe me that this is a very common disorder. I think you have a form of Delusional Misidentification Syndrome. It's a common disorder but the details vary: Capgras Delusion sufferers believe friends and family have been replaced by identical imposters; Fregoli's Delusion makes you think that everyone in the world is actually the same person in disguise,; Cotard's Delusion convinces you you're dead and Reduplicative Paramnesia makes you believe you have been kidnapped and transported to an exact copy of the world. Can you see the similarity to what you're feeling?"

"These are all delusions and a delusion is a lie. What I know is no lie."

"The thing about a delusion is, by definition, you cannot

recognize it as false," said Macbeth. "It seems real and logical. You're a very intelligent woman, and that means your delusion itself is intelligent. Elaborate and well-informed."

Corbin tapped Macbeth lightly on the arm, then said to Deborah, "You're getting tired. We've leave you to get some rest. Dr Macbeth and I will come back to see you soon, if that's okay with you."

"If you like." She turned to the window, her face emptying of the little animation that had been there. "I won't be here. Still."

35

JACK HUDSON. NEW YORK

Jack Hudson did a mental calculation of the age of the commissioning exec producer sitting opposite him and guessed that he had worked in television longer than Tony Elmes had been alive. The TV industry had become an infantocracy, falling into the careless, inexpert hands of adolescents, their shiny, fresh faces full of blank enthusiasm and their heads full of guff. But, if Hudson was honest with himself, it had always been that way; it had been like that when he himself had been a young man with a shiny, fresh face full of blank enthusiasm and a head full of guff.

Jack Hudson's face wasn't fresh and shiny any more. The middle-aged man who stared back each morning from the shaving mirror told him that, confronting him with a reality Hudson couldn't accept. Dark good looks and even darker vigor had turned saturnine and sullen. How could he be in his late fifties when he'd been twenty-five just the other day?

It wasn't that Elmes was a moron or ill-educated – far from it – it was just that he belonged to that plugged-in, instant-info generation that seemed to have appeared from nowhere. Nor, really, was Elmes an asshole, but at this precise moment it comforted Hudson to think of him as one.

The two men sat in a doorless 'encounter space' on the fourth floor. Hudson remembered when meetings had been in offices or conference rooms – rooms with doors. People didn't have meetings any more, they had 'head-to-heads' in 'encounter spaces' installed to 'deformalize interactions between creatives'. It was all bullshit. When he had started in the business, if you wanted to 'deformalize creative interactions' you took a director and producer to the bar on the corner of Fifth and got drunk. Some of Hudson's best documentary ideas had been pitched through a whiskey glass. Now he sat, his despair oozing into the soft leather of the low club chair, with an exec producer who looked as if a barman would ask him for ID, in a doorless fourth-floor room that was all soft couches, occasional tables, corporate artwork on the walls and an espresso machine in the corner.

"All I want is to make good television, Tony," he repeated.

"That's what we all want to do, Jack. And that is exactly what we do here." Elmes answered with a hint of admonishment.

"I mean good television the way we used to. Quality TV, quality documentaries, quality dramas. Not more reality crap."

"Jack, we don't produce crap. Reality, yes – crap, no. There is a public appetite for reality shows and there is no way to avoid them. What we do here is create reality television that strives to be better than the rest."

"Great . . . competing to be the tallest man in Lilliput. Reality shows and soaps are lowest-common-denominator television – you know it, I know it, everyone does. It's not even reality – it's real people *pretending* to be real people, playing their own lives like movie parts. It's lame, it's cheap, it's feeble-minded."

"That's just elitist crap, Jack. I never took you for an intellectual snob."

"Saying that we shouldn't screen child pornography simply because there would be a market for it isn't elitism or intellectual snobbery, it's simple common sense and decency. The only thing stopping some people in this business catering for needs like that is because it's illegal. Take that away and Christ knows what would happen."

"You don't really believe that, Jack . . ."

"Don't I? Give people enough license and they lose all boundaries. The idea of comedy in the Roman Coliseum was to have contests to the death between gladiators who were blind, crippled or kids. And in the arcades beneath the Coliseum, you could buy anyone for any purpose, including children. That's what people will sink to . . . the only difference between now and then is we have the technology to deliver it faster and better. The Internet is our Coliseum and television is catching up. We need to take some kind of moral stance."

"Moral stance?" asked Elmes incredulously.

"You know what I mean . . . I just want to make television we can be proud of."

"I appreciate that. And there is no one working in this department who is not aware – who is not in awe – of your pedigree and reputation. But the time for the kind of program you're pitching is past. I'm sorry – and I really *am* sorry – but that's the simple fact of the matter."

"You telling me I'm washed up, is that it? No place for my documentaries in this Brave New World of pseudo-celebrities and fake reality?"

"Christ no, Jack. But I *am* saying that the Golden Age of television, as it is imagined, is behind us, much as it pains me to say that. We can no longer justify the budget for what are basically political documentaries. We don't broadcast television, we narrowcast it. I don't know if we can even call it television any more – at least as many people watch our output on PCs, tablets, handhelds, smart phones as do on conventional television sets."

"Doesn't that just mean that we have a bigger than ever audience? People are smart, Tony. They're only dumb if you treat them like they're dumb. I believe there's an audience for this . . ." Hudson stabbed a finger at the two proposals that lay on the table between them.

"I'm sorry, Jack, but we're not the people to make them. This

257

isn't about winning Big Sky or Full Frame awards, it's about winning viewers. About solid Nielsen." Elmes sighed, leaned back in his chair and ran the fingers of both hands through his dark hair. As he pushed his hair back from his brow, Hudson noticed with malicious gratification that Elmes's hairline was receding. I may be getting old, Hudson told himself, but at least I've got a full head of hair.

"I know it's difficult to accept," continued Elmes, "but things have changed. This is all about living reality, not the Ken Burns effect. Like you said, at one time American TV audiences were interested in the world around them, looking outwards and into the lives of others. That's all changed. Television isn't a telescope any more, it's a microscope. It's all about looking inwards, at ourselves, at lives like ours. I'm not saying that's right, but that's the way it is."

"So that's it?"

"That's it. Or at least as far as your pitch ideas are concerned. Sorry." Elmes leaned forward, resting his elbows on the table and closing the distance between him and Hudson. "I want you to know something Jack: I watched your stuff all the time, when I was at school and then college. All your documentaries. I always considered them – and still do – as an essential part of my education. You were a huge influence on me . . . an inspiration. And a big part of why I chose television as a career."

Hudson held his hands open in a *so-what's-your-point?* gesture. It was a small-minded, ungracious act and he knew it.

"Yours is a talent that is still needed," Elmes continued, undeterred. "A talent we can still use to great effect. Your name behind a project still carries a lot of weight. Gravitas. And I think we have something that would be perfect in your hands. Something that would benefit from a producer of your experience. And it is a documentary."

"Okay, let's have it," Hudson sighed.

"Have you ever heard of someone called John Astor?"

36

JOHN MACBETH. BOSTON

Macbeth and Corbin crossed back over the open green space of the Upham Bowl, in front of the main administration building courtyard, passing a maple tree that stood elevated on a small knoll. When he'd been at McLean, Macbeth had spent many afternoons sitting on the grass at the foot of that particular tree, writing up research notes. He had always understood why, for many, McLean had provided an environment for creative effort: it had been here that Sylvia Plath's bell jar of depression had been lifted, albeit temporarily, inspiring the poet to write her only novel.

"So what do you think?" asked Corbin as they sat eating lunch in the de Marneffe Cafeteria.

"About the Carbonara or about Deborah Canning?" Macbeth stirred his pasta with his fork. "I'm beginning to get an unpleasant feeling that you *didn't* forget about my last patient here. The one I treated in that very same room."

"Debbie is exhibiting the same classic Dissociative Identity Disorder traits your patient did: depersonalization, derealization, amnesia and personality-trait loss."

"Yeah, I get that." Macbeth frowned. "But my patient displayed the key symptom: multiple personalities. Debbie doesn't have multiple personalities; she's struggling to hang on to the one she's got."

Corbin leaned forward. "What if there are alters – personalities she retreats into but doesn't show us? These absences

259

she has – the long periods she believes she doesn't exist because there's no one there to validate her existence – she could be escaping into other identities. It's just that her alters play out internally, in her head, and we don't get to see them."

"Listen Pete, any Dissociative Identity diagnosis is controversial. There have been *no* diagnoses outside the US and even here there's a large body who think it's hooey. I stuck my neck out with my DID diagnosis of my last patient here and it ended up with him dead and me before a committee. It's the reason I went into research. You want my opinion on Debbie? Cotard's Delusion. It's the most elaborate and coherently structured case I've seen, but that's what I'd go for."

"But she doesn't believe that she's dead," said Corbin.

"Believing she's non-existent is the same thing and more consistent with her internal logic – plus her work has added a very specific twist. Patients with Cotard's Delusion of Death often believe they inhabit the world as disembodied spirits. It's just a belief in ghosts is not part of Debbie's premorbid intellectual architecture."

Corbin finished a mouthful of food. "I know DID is controversial and that you had your fingers burned – but I went through your case notes and I think you were right. Your patient's suicide was unforeseeable, given his progress, and had nothing to do with your diagnosis. I think that Debbie is displaying many of the same symptoms."

"God, Pete, that's a stretch." Macbeth thought for a moment. "Okay, let me talk to her again. There's a cop coming in from California – Ramirez. He wants to talk to her if you're okay with it. I'd like to be there too."

"Okay," said Corbin cautiously. "But I want you to remember that I called you into this as a colleague and a professional, not because of your previous involvement with Melissa. I want Debbie to remain the priority."

Macbeth nodded. "Of course." He gave Corbin Ramirez's contact details.

"I'll see what can be arranged." said Corbin. "By the way, I meant to show you this . . ."

They had reached the main administration building. Corbin struggled with the file he was carrying, eventually taking out a foolscap sheet of lined paper and handing it to Macbeth. It was filled from top to bottom with neat, very small and very careful handwriting.

"When she was first admitted, Debbie spent entire days writing that same line, over and over again. I have thirty pages exactly the same as that one."

Macbeth read the line.

WE ARE BECOMING.

37

JACK HUDSON. NEW YORK

"John Astor the founder of the Astor dynasty," asked Hudson, "or John Astor the Internet spook everyone's talking about?"

"The latter," said Elmes. "And he's more than an Internet spook. Much, much more. The FBI have a strangely serious interest in him and he's rumored to be connected to some kind of cult."

"One of these fanatical religious groups?" asked Hudson.

"This is where it gets confusing. Some reports link him to Blind Faith, the fundo-Christian group, others with a group calling themselves the Simulists, some kind of science-based Doomsday cult. They're behind the *we are becoming* 'graffiti' you see all over the place. Remember how they found the billionaire Samuel Tennant starved to death in his Park Lane penthouse?"

"I remember . . ."

"Tennant was connected to the Simulists. There's a rumor that, just before he did his Howard Hughes act, he claimed to have gotten his hands on a copy of Astor's book, *Phantoms of Our Own Making*."

"This is all beginning to sound like some New World Order, Illuminati conspiracy crap," said Hudson.

"Hear me out, Jack. I put a researcher onto Astor's history. Turns out there is one. It doesn't make much sense, but it's there."

"In what way doesn't make sense?"

"For a start, the chronology of it means Astor should either be dead or impossibly old. He was important in twentieth-century philosophy, but more as a shadow than a figure. He's claimed to be the author of several incredibly influential philosophical works, none submitted for publication and most in the form of private correspondence with other philosophers, particularly philosophers of science."

Hudson leaned forward. "Go on . . ."

"Well, despite his correspondents being meticulous preservers of such writings, none of these letters or essays have survived his death."

"But he's supposed to be still alive . . ."

Elmes shrugged. "We don't know when, where, how or even if he died. Nor do we know where and when he was born. You see, John Astor's existence only comes to us through these writings. Almost as if he exists only in reflection by others. I'm telling you, it's a mystery. And one I think you are the best person to clear up . . . and to make one hell of a documentary about it."

Jack leaned back into his chair again, his expression wary. "And exactly how is a piece about a mysterious twentieth-century philosopher, who may or may not have existed, sexier than the European Integration piece I've just pitched?"

"Okay . . . For starters, we know that philosophers from Henri Poincaré to Karl Popper and a whole lot of others were aware of or had contact with Astor and many were greatly influenced by him."

"So?"

"Just taking those two examples, Poincaré died when Popper was ten years old. How could Astor have had peer-level friendships with them both? For that matter, how could he possibly still be alive today? Yet there are mentions of him – of clearly the same character – in the writings of half a dozen philosophers of science right through the twentieth century, up until today. And this is the doozy – there's an urban legend that if you manage to track down the manuscript for Astor's book, reading it drives you mad. That's what's supposed to have happened to Tennant."

"Okay . . . here we go," Hudson sighed. "For a moment I thought we were discussing something credible and worthwhile."

"You want to do something quality, Jack? That's what I'm giving you. Have you heard the rumor about the book or not?"

"I've heard it. Pure crap."

"Maybe so, but the fact is that fragments of the manuscript have been found – buried deep in the Internet. They're supposed to be from Astor's book, the book Tennant got hold of before he starved himself to death. But the really big thing is what this manuscript is all about. The earthquake that never was in Boston, and all of the other stuff that's going on all around the world – people having visions, seeing ghosts – in his book, Astor is supposed to have predicted them happening."

"Come on, Tony – you know all kinds of conspiracy nut are all over the Boston thing. Everything from aliens to the CIA to the Illuminati to secret Nazi mind-weapons hidden deep beneath the Antarctic ice. In fact, there's one website that claims it's all of the above working together." Hudson shook his head. "Sometimes the intellectual power of our great nation leaves me humbled."

"Well, while all of these conspiracy theories are the usual . . ." Elmes struggled for the right word.

"Apophenia," Hudson helped him out. "The tendency to see patterns and connections between things where there are none. Joining up dots that aren't there."

"Apophenia," Elmes repeated. "Is that a word? Anyway, all of that crap is going on and it's confusing the real issue, which is that we're not getting the whole story. These hallucinations are happening all over the world and they're getting bigger and worse. The story is that this Astor manuscript not only predicted exactly what is happening, but explains it. And it's that explanation that's supposed to be so momentous and terrifying that it drives you mad."

"You said yourself that the fragments that have been found have been on the Web . . . how do you know it's not just some geek making it up as he goes along? Post-rationalizing events after they happen?"

"This isn't the first time Astor's authored a mysterious work with a restricted circulation. In the nineteen-sixties there were rumors of another book called *The Last Mortals*. It's supposed to be linked to the latest manuscript *and* there was a rash of suicides connected to it, just like with this one."

"You believe all this crap?"

Elmes sighed. "I believe there's enough in it to warrant an investigation, at least. Are you interested or not?"

"In my time, I have exposed political scandals, humanitarian tragedies, war crimes . . . do you really think that I'm going to take on some half-assed conspiracy theory bullshit like this?"

"I take it that's a no?"

"That's a no."

"I really don't think you can afford to say no to any project at the moment, if I'm frank, Jack." Elmes pushed the red file across the table to Hudson. "Do me a favor . . . at least read through the information first, then give me an answer."

Hudson regarded Elmes for a moment. Despite what he wanted to believe about the younger man, he was sincere. A good kid. A good kid who shouldn't be his boss, but was. Hudson stood up, picking up the file from the table.

"I've already given you my answer," he said. "But I'll take a look."

Jodie Silverman was waiting for them in the hallway with a tablet PC tucked under her arm. Or more correctly, she was waiting for Elmes and largely ignored Jack Hudson's presence. Silverman was dark-haired, attractive without being exceptional, with a good figure smartly dressed. She was the kind of studio pussy that Hudson had bagged by the dozen, back in the day. But things had changed: attitudes, mores, even regulations about workplace behavior. And Hudson wasn't the man he had been. Silverman was one of those edgy, flinty, chip-on-the-shoulder career bitches, but that didn't stop Hudson speculating that Elmes was maybe fucking her.

"Hello Jodie," said Hudson. "You're looking lovely today."

He laughed out loud when she ignored him.

"We've got a production schedule meeting at eleven," she told Elmes. "I've brought your notes." She tapped with a varnished nail the tablet PC she held. "You okay?"

Elmes had stopped his progress along the hallway, a strange expression on his face, his posture almost unsteady. "Whoa . . . I just had the most weird feeling of déjà vu . . ."

"Not again . . ." Hudson laughed at his own witticism. Silverman didn't and he thought about how she really, really needed to get laid.

"You okay, Tony?" she asked again.

"I'm fine," Elmes said. "But that was weird." He shook his head and gave a small laugh. "I'll let you know if I start having visions."

"Visions?" asked Hudson.

"Boston Syndrome – that's the way it's always supposed to start, with déjà vu. Or so they say."

"Well, try to hallucinate a project for me that's worth doing."

"That's what I've just given you, Jack," said Elmes in a tone that warned Hudson he was pushing his luck a little too far. Elmes stopped again. "Do you smell something?" he asked.

"Other than corporate bullshit, no . . ." Hudson said.

"I'm being serious . . . Do you smell burning?"

"Burning?" Silverman became suddenly alert and sniffed at the air. "No . . . I don't smell burning."

"Me neither," said Hudson.

Elmes remained silent for a moment then again shook his head. "I was sure I could smell burning. It's gone now." They started along the corridor again and reached the elevator hall, a wide, bright space about twenty feet square. The two side walls were floor-to-ceiling glass, looking out over Midtown Manhattan. "I've got to go to this scheduling meeting, Jack. Promise me you'll give that –" he tapped the red file Hudson held "– the consideration it deserves. We're going to be doing something on it, one way or another, and I'd really rather that it was you at the helm."

"I said I would look at it and I will. But I think—"

"Don't say you can't smell that?" Elmes cut him off, looking around the elevator hall anxiously.

"I don't smell anything," said Hudson.

"Me neither . . ." Silverman looked anxiously at Hudson, then back to Elmes.

"You're kidding . . ." Elmes sniffed urgently at the air and began pacing the hall, scanning the corridors leading to it, examining the elevator doors. "How could you not smell that? It's getting stronger. Shit . . . something's burning somewhere."

"I don't smell a thing . . ." said Silverman, her groomed corporate composure gone.

"Do you smell it? Tell me you smell that . . ." Elmes turned to Hudson, waving a hand to indicate the air around them.

"Take it easy, Tony . . ." Hudson stepped forwards and placed his hand on Elmes's shoulder; the younger man shrugged it away, looking at Hudson as if he were mad.

"Christ . . . Christ . . . something's on fire . . ."

"Calm down . . . There's nothing. Take it easy . . ."

Suddenly, Elmes backed away, shrinking back and pressing himself against the wall opposite the elevators. "Look! For fuck's sake, look!"

"Look at what?" said Hudson, who then turned to Silverman. "Get someone! Get a doctor."

"The smoke!" Elmes began coughing. Scrabbling his way along the wall as if trying to escape something the others could not see. "What the fuck is wrong with you? We've got to get out of here . . . We've got to get out of here now!"

"Jesus . . . look at his eyes!" Silverman said. Hudson could see the producer's eyes all right: red, inflamed, streaming with tears. Elmes started to cough uncontrollably, to splutter, saliva sleeking his lips and dangling in viscous threads from his mouth, his face red. He tore desperately at his unbuttoned shirt collar, as if it was strangling him.

"I told you to go and get a fucking doctor!" Hudson yelled at Silverman, who backed away, her gaze fixed on the gasping Elmes. "Go!"

She turned and ran.

Hudson stepped forward and grabbed Elmes by the shoulders. "Listen, Tony . . . you're having some kind of attack. You're seeing things. Jodie's gone to get help . . . in the meantime, try to stay calm."

"You're mad! You're crazy! We've got to get out of here! Look!"

"Look at what?"

"The flames, for Christ's sake! The fire! Jesus! Jesus!"

"Tony, there's no fire . . ."

Elmes shoved his colleague away violently, causing him to fall backwards. When Hudson got up, he saw Elmes extend his arms like a blind man, his wide-open, streaming eyes unseeing. His coughing was now constant, wracking, and he seemed to fight for every breath.

Silverman came sprinting back up the corridor with an overweight, shaven-headed man in a white short-sleeved shirt and black pants.

"There's an ambulance on its way . . ." The security man stared unbelievingly at Elmes. "What's wrong with him?"

"I don't know, but stay back . . . he's violent with it."

Still Elmes stumbled around, patting his way along the wall towards his colleagues who watched, ready to grab him should he fall.

"God . . ." said Silverman. "It's like he's gone blind . . ."

"Help me!" Elmes yelled desperately. "For God's sake help me!" He began stamping his feet, performing a bizarre dance as if trying to shake something loose from his legs. His eyes were wild, watching something terrifying, something monstrous, that only he could see.

He screamed. A scream like no other that Hudson had ever heard: a high-pitched, inhuman whine that was no longer about fear, but about pain. Falling to the floor, Elmes began writhing, clawing, convulsing – all the time to the terrible music of that inhuman scream. He flailed and tore wildly at his clothes, kicking and twisting on the polished floor.

It was then that Hudson and the others saw it happen.

Elmes's skin – on his face, on his hands, on the chest laid bare by his frantic tearing at his shirt – turned crimson. It bubbled and peeled, then began to blacken.

"Jesus!" said Hudson. "He's burning . . . He really is burning." But there were still no flames, no smoke, no signs of combustion outside Elmes's tortured body. The scream became something else: a thick, treacle gargle. Now they could smell the overpowering, sickly sweet stench of Elmes's roasted flesh.

Hudson turned to the security man. "For Christ's sake get a bucket of water."

"But there's no fire . . ."

"To throw on *him*, you idiot." Without the slightest idea what he could do to help him, Hudson dropped the red file he'd been carrying and rushed forward to kneel beside where Elmes lay on the floor. He was no longer convulsing: his movements were small and tight. His skin was gone, the exposed flesh a mix of red raw and black crust. The thick hair on his head fizzed and crackled to sparse patches of blackened wire. Hudson could see gray-white subcutaneous fat bubble and boil. Eyelids gone, Elmes's eyes were shrunken, desiccated. No more movement. Hudson tried to check for a pulse but drew his hand back as if stung, the blackened flesh hot and burning his fingertips.

He straightened up and watched as the now dead Elmes curled up into a blackened gargoyle, the contraction of dried-out tendons drawing up his legs, twisting tight his arms and making claws of what was left of his fingers.

Hudson heard Silverman retching and the security man's voice: sounds that seemed to come from a million miles away. He was also aware of distressed, alarmed voices as others from the building gathered behind him.

"What happened to him?" the security man asked again.

"I don't know . . ." said Hudson. "I have no idea. I thought he was having one of those hallucinations, but this was no hallucination. Spontaneous combustion, maybe . . . but I thought that was a myth. No one has ever actually documented it . . ."

"That was no fucking myth . . ." said the security man. "That was real . . ."

Hudson realized the security man was right. It was the only thing that made sense. Hudson was confused, in shock, disbelieving. And what added to his disbelief and disgust was the way a single thought penetrated all of those feelings. A thought that was unworthy of him, unworthy of anyone.

No one has ever actually documented it. If only I'd had a camera crew with me.

38

JOHN MACBETH. BOSTON

When Corbin called Walt Ramirez from his office, the CHP officer apologized for the short notice but explained he was planning to fly in the next day, and asked if he could interview Deborah when he got in, perhaps seeing Macbeth after that.

"You're in luck," said Corbin. "I'm at McLean now with Dr Macbeth. I'll put him on." He handed the phone to Macbeth, who made arrangements with Ramirez.

"You okay with me sitting in?" he asked Corbin when he handed back the phone.

"Sure. Like I said, I'd value your insight and I don't think we're there yet with a diagnosis. Anyway, this connection with Melissa means you have a personal interest and I have to admit I don't like cops interviewing patients during treatment."

"Ramirez sounds okay," said Macbeth. "Has the FBI been in touch?"

"The FBI?"

"Yeah. I was approached by a Special Agent Bundy—"

"An FBI man called Bundy? You're kidding me . . ."

"We had a cozy tête-à-tête in the back of his car the other day. And it's not just his name that you would remember – he has very striking eyes: the most defined case of central heterochromia I've seen."

"I can honestly say I'd remember any visit from the FBI, far less one from someone with dual-colored eyes and a serial-killer surname. What's his interest?"

"Cults. Fringe groups. John Astor."

"There's a connection?"

"It would seem Bundy believes there is, but I told him he was way off base with any idea that Melissa would be involved with a cult."

"The Melissa you knew, John. The Melissa Debbie knew seems to have been a very different person."

Macbeth nodded glumly as the press snapshot of a relaxed and happy Melissa with Samuel Tennant flashed in his recall.

"What about the WHO team?" Corbin changed the subject. "You going to collaborate with them?"

"As much as I can. The Copenhagen Project demands all of my time. And my boss, Georg Poulsen, sure as hell raised a lot of objections to me coming to Boston in the first place, even though I'm here on Project business. He's made it very clear he wants me back on Project One as of yesterday. I'm telling you, he's got to be the most driven man I've ever worked with, almost like he's got some personal as well as a professional stake in the Project."

"What kind of personal stake?"

Macbeth shrugged. "He's one of the most aggressively private men I've ever known. I learned quickly not to ask about anything outside Project business."

"Surely he understands how important it is to get to the bottom of these events?"

"He's convinced the Project supersedes everything else. But I have to admit I'd like to help pin down what the hell is going on." Macbeth paused, as if unsure whether to commit his next thought to words. "You see, Pete, I have a personal interest in finding out what's behind this phenomenon."

"Oh?"

"Right at the start of all of this, you told me about a female patient who had come to you having suffered one of these hallucinations. You said that she 'met' a younger version of herself, and that she could remember having the experience as a young woman, from the other perspective. Remember?"

"Of course."

"Do you remember the day you decided to become a psychiatrist, Pete? I mean the exact moment?"

"Not really . . . I kind of drifted into it, following my interests once I qualified. I guess I always had a leaning towards neuroscience."

"Me, I wanted to be a psychiatrist since I was a kid," said Macbeth. "I remember the exact day, when I asked my dad what he did for a living. I was about eleven or twelve. He did a lot of his work from home, out on the Cape, and I used to go into his study a lot . . . When I think back, I must have really distracted him from his work, but he never complained. I'd come in with my books and encyclopedias and a dozen questions about planets and countries and dinosaurs . . . He always smiled and told me to sit and answered them.

"Anyway, this day I asked him what it was he did. I mean, I knew he was a psychiatrist, but I didn't really know what that meant."

"And what did he say?"

Macbeth smiled at the recollection. "He told me that every living person had a mind, and every mind is like a universe, filled with billions of thoughts like stars. He said each person is at the center of his or her own unique universe shaped out of all of their unique experiences and knowledge, everything they have ever seen or heard or felt, even read or learned. He told me that sometimes that universe can be a lonely and frightening place. Sometimes people get confused about what is real and what isn't, what they remember and what they imagine. He said that being a psychiatrist was like being an astronaut: exploring each mind and finding new places and new wonders, and letting each patient know that they're not alone."

"Pretty good description, if you ask me," said Corbin. "And that convinced you to become a psychiatrist?"

"No. There was something else. While he told me all that, there was someone else in the room. I hadn't seen him when I came in but then I saw him: a man sitting in the corner, watching and listening."

"A patient?"

"My father never treated patients at home. Then I realized that Dad couldn't see the man in the corner. Only I could see him. And the man in the corner could see me. Listen, Pete . . . I've never told anyone this, only Casey."

Corbin nodded. "Go on . . ."

"I thought the man in the corner was a ghost. I told my dad about him and he asked me where the man was and what he was doing. I explained that he was just sitting, listening to us. Dad told me there were no such things as ghosts, but that sometimes the mind could invent things. He stayed very calm, but I know now that he must have been running through a dozen diagnoses in his head. He told me that I was a very bright boy and that I read a lot of things, a lot of facts, and that sometimes the brain could become overloaded. He came over to me and put his hands on my shoulders and made me look him straight in the eye, telling me not to look over at the man until he told me to. He explained to me that I was tired and had been out in the sun too much and that when a brain gets tired it gets confused and puts things you see together in the wrong order. He told me there was no man in the corner, that it was just a trick of my mind. He said that when I looked again the man would be gone. I did look and the man was gone.

"That was what convinced me to become a psychiatrist. I had experienced for myself the way the brain can deceive, how it can make the unreal seem real; and how a psychiatrist can show the way back to reality."

"Wow . . ." Corbin shook his head slowly. "You know how easily these things – isolated delusions or hallucinations – can happen in childhood and adolescence. I'm assuming it was isolated . . . Did you see the man again?"

"You asked me why I was so interested in your patient. That's why . . . because I have seen him again. Exactly the same man I saw that day sitting in the corner of my father's study. For the last five years I've seen him every day: every morning when I look in the mirror to shave. It was me, Pete. Me as I am now."

39

MARKUS. GERMANY

There were twenty of them, not including the driver: sixteen school students and four teachers. Markus Schwab, who normally never approached anything with eagerness or haste, made sure he was first on the bus. His alacrity had not been inspired by the idea of the school trip, and certainly not by any enthusiasm for its destination, simply that he wanted to get to the back of the coach so that he was assured the rearmost seat by the window.

It wasn't that Markus hated his schoolmates; in fact, for a seventeen-year-old, he was markedly lacking in the venom of adolescence: he did not hate his life, he did not hate his parents, his teachers or his schoolmates. It was simply that they bored him: their enthusiasms, their crazes, the way they jabbered on about things that meant so much to them but really didn't mean anything at all, their obsession with inconsequence – that was what would have angered Markus if he could have summoned up the energy to care.

So Markus made sure he got the seat at the back of the coach, next to the window. That way, he could turn to the glass and watch the world slide by, the earphones of his MP3 player filling his skull with music.

This trip, it had been explained to the students, was particularly important given everything that was happening with Europe. History was becoming shared. The context for every nineteenth- and twentieth-century event was now seen as that of the prolonged birth pangs of a new nation. Europe was no longer just a geographical term, it was an identity.

"You young people," Herr Hartz, who taught history, had explained before they set out for the coach, "are living at a time of massive significance. When I was your age, Germany had just reunited and what it meant to be German, and Germany's place in the world, changed overnight. You young people will be the first generation for whom being European and Europe's new place in the world will be more important than a sense of being German. What we will see today underlines why such progress is important. Why narrow nationalism is the greatest evil in political thought."

Blah, blah, blah . . .

Markus had listened to Hartz's pre-trip speech with the same dull indifference with which he listened to all of his lessons. School was a redundant social construct and the man was a bore. Markus didn't resent him for his dullness: he was a school-teacher and ipso facto his intellect was blunted and scopeless.

Ipso facto.

Despite his best efforts, languages, dead and alive, interested Markus and he had excelled at them. The truth was that he had excelled at most subjects and it annoyed him that he was not convinced enough in his own ennui to fail academically. But that was where the paradox lay for Markus: to fail would take effort, to succeed was easy. At least that was the excuse he allowed himself to avoid the inner shame of taking some kind of bourgeois pride in the achievement of socially expected goals.

But for today, he achieved both of his goals: the seat at the back and the isolation it afforded. There were more seats in the coach than passengers and everyone else had clumped together at the front of the bus, leaving Markus to his little empire of bench and window.

The journey, Hartz monotoned, would take two and a quarter hours, and they would stop for lunch en route. As soon as the teacher took his seat, Markus plugged in his earphones and turned his attention to the world outside. Two and a quarter hours. One hundred and thirty-five minutes of isolation. Despite himself, he felt a small contentment warm his chest.

Once they were under way, Markus pressed the play button on his MP3 player and watched the suburbs of Stuttgart pass through his window of attention. A house would appear, sometimes a figure in a doorway, coming out of a driveway car or working in a garden, the hint of a life before and after its brief flicker across the shield of the bus's automotive glass. Markus didn't find his detachment from the passing world strange or concerning; to him, it was as natural as any state of being could be.

One of the secrets he kept from the world was the music he listened to. His peers seemed united in their love for industrial metal: comically dark lyrics to harsh, dissonant grinding; the perfect accompaniment, he supposed, to adolescence. Markus, in contrast, listened to a wide variety of musical forms but mainly, as he did now, Bach. The irony was not wasted on Markus, who had no interest in the past and for whom history was the dullest subject on a dull curriculum, that he listened to music written over two and a half centuries before. He reconciled this paradox by telling himself that the music belonged to his time, not Bach's. As far as he was concerned and like all knowledge and all arts, it simply came into existence at the time he, Markus Schwab, first discovered it.

Beyond the window, the houses thinned out and the trees thickened to the accompaniment of the Brandenburg Concertos. The road took the bus along the bank of the Neckar: the river to the right, the side Markus sat on, and steeply rising vineyards to the left. It was an agreeable day, the sun making the water sparkle, the sky pleasantly flecked with wisps of cloud. Everything looked satisfyingly manicured and clean: Nature in Man's dominion.

They stopped in Ulm for lunch. It was a cafeteria-type affair and Markus was forced to share a table with Imke Paulig and two of her idiotic friends. The trio sat and exchanged hand-shielded laughs and whispers, their faces empty and stupid. Occasionally, Imke would throw what was clearly meant to be a meaningful look in Markus's direction. He ignored her, which seemed only to encourage her.

Their hushed whispers became more urgent and serious at one point and Markus could not help eavesdropping as he pretended to look out the window. The girls were talking about the news from Boston, in the United States, where there was some kind of strange virus making people have vivid daydreams – seeing things that weren't there, such as hundreds of people experiencing an earthquake that did not really take place. But it wasn't just happening in Boston.

"You know what I think?" said Stefanie, Imke's dark-haired friend. "I think it's all the drugs the Americans take. It's maybe all caused by some new drug that's gone wrong."

Markus could not contain himself. He turned to the girls. "Yeah . . . I heard that too. And there's another new drug . . . here in Germany. This one is even more dangerous."

"Really?" asked Stefanie, leaning forward.

"Yeah . . ." said Markus. "It has these terrible side effects . . . apparently it affects both your brain and your anus. All of your shit goes into your brain and you start thinking with your asshole."

Stefanie got up and left the table. The others followed her, Imke last of all.

"You know something, Markus," she said as she left, "if anyone's the asshole it's you."

Markus shrugged a give-a-shit shrug and watched Imke's back as she crossed the cafeteria; but he knew, despite himself, that he did give a shit about what Imke thought of him.

He noticed that Herr Hartz had intercepted the girls, clearly having seen that there had been some kind of incident. The history teacher started to head in Markus's direction, a casual idling walk cast as clumsy disguise over his mission. He sat down next to Markus.

"You know something," Hartz said, watching Markus with small, dark eyes like a shark's set in a human skull, "you are very lucky to have been given the intellectual gifts you have. If you want to go about feeling superior to everyone else, that's your business . . . but when you set out actively to make others feel inferior, then it becomes mine."

"I don't have a problem with the inferiority of others, Herr Hartz," said Markus. "But I do have a problem with stupidity."

"People can't help their intellectual capability or lack of it."

"That's not what I'm talking about," Markus said, exasperated. "Like you say, people can't help their mediocrity. What I despise is their celebration of it. Stupidity isn't something to be pitied, it's something to be feared. Stupidity is what will kill us all, eventually. I could be wrong, but I get the feeling that's the point of this little excursion."

"I take it you have no enthusiasm for this trip."

Markus shrugged. "I don't see the point. Well, no, I do see the point, but I don't feel that point applies to me. I get it. I've always got it. I don't have to have it shoved in my face."

"Well, one point you could take from it is how dangerous it is to consider oneself superior. A lesson you could take much from." Hartz paused, squaloid eyes scanning the cafeteria for a moment. "Listen, Markus," he said when he turned back, "you've excelled in every history test I set because you know the expected answers. You have a huge capacity for remembering facts and dates . . ."

"Then I don't understand what the problem is," Markus said, although he understood perfectly.

"You're playing the game, the system. It's my job to recognize and develop young minds, particularly a mind as full of potential as yours is. And that means going beyond just what is expected of you. You have a particularly fine mind, Markus. A fine mind that needs developing."

"I develop my own mind. And if you mean developing an interest in history, then I can't. I'm sorry, Herr Hartz, I know you mean well and I appreciate everything you've said, but I give as much as I can give to a subject that I don't feel has anything to do with me."

"How can you say that?" Hartz seemed genuinely shocked. "History has everything to do with every one of us. History is what makes us, what has shaped the world we experience."

"The world is what the world is. I deal with that. We cannot live in the past. We can only live in the present."

Hartz laughed. "Where does that leave me? I'm a historian. That's not just my profession, it's what I am. I am connected to the past."

'No you're not . . .'" Markus adjusted his tone and his expression. "Sorry, Herr Hartz, but with the greatest respect, you're not. The past is a matter of record, not a place you can visit. It no longer exists. All that exists is the here and now. I read this book, not that long ago; the author was exploring reminiscence . . . the nature of remembrance. The main character in this book was in late middle age and has succeeded in life. He is happy and content. He meets a friend from his youth and it starts him thinking about the past. Before he knows it, he buys a song, downloads this track he hasn't listened to since he was about my age. He puts on his headphones, closes his eyes and plays the song; then like Proust biting into a madeleine, he's taken right back to that time in his life. For a moment he believes it is possible to travel back in time with your thoughts, to re-create the past in your head and relive it. So he listens to the song again, and again. Then he realizes that the track is now in the present, not the past. It's not some scratchy vinyl record he plays on a turntable but a digital download on an MP3 player. He's listened to it so much that it no longer conjures up his teenage bedroom but the luxury apartment he lives in." Markus shook his head. "When we go on a field trip like this, we look at old buildings and you describe them as sixteenth-century this or fifteenth-century that – they're nothing of the sort, they're twenty-first-century objects. They exist here and now, no matter when they were assembled. In a hundred years' time they'll be twenty-second-century objects. The past is the past, the dead are buried. There are no lessons to be learned from the long-ago, only the here and now."

Hartz sat silently. There was no anger or animosity in his expression, just a faint sadness, as if lamenting some defect, some disability, in his pupil.

"All I can say," he said at last, "is that I honestly believe you're wrong. We have to remember the past. Learn from it. That's what today is all about. What you say doesn't just make me sad – it terrifies me."

It took less than an hour and a half to get there from Ulm. Despite everything he had said to Hartz, despite everything he had promised himself, he did feel something like a chill when he first saw it.

What disturbed him was exactly what he had said to Hartz did not happen: something that should have been left in the past existed in the present. As the bus headed along Alte Römer-strasse, just before it turned into the road leading to the visitor center and car park, he saw it: something that he had only seen before in black-and-white representation, in an imperfect record of a past reality, but there it was in full living color, in solidity and presence. The wall that stretched along the side of the modern road was topped with barbed wire and broken by square-based, robust towers, each tower topped by wrap-around windows under an overlapping pyramid hip roof.

They got off the bus in the car park in front of the visitor center. Hartz disappeared into the center and returned with an attractive, dark-haired woman who introduced herself to everybody as Anna and informed them that she would be their guide. Once she checked everybody was ready, she led them through the metal-gated arch of the Jourhaus and into the main compound.

In spite of his determination to remain untouched by the experience and his knowledge that the three words wrought in iron and set in the center of the gates were a 1960s replica of the original, Markus could not keep out the chill as he read them.

ARBEIT MACHT FREI

Markus, along with the others, maintained an appropriately dignified silence, listening to the young, pretty woman recite old, ugly facts.

They were guided around the only two barrack blocks standing. Except they weren't the real barrack blocks at all, but exact replicas built in 1965. What, he thought, was the point of that? What happened here was so monstrous it should not be represented in simulation.

What Markus had found fascinating had been watching the others. The whole group had an earnestness about them that, he knew, was not always the case with school visits. Some of his classmates were genuinely interested, but in the same way they would be in an art gallery or museum. But others were clearly affected by what they saw and heard; he noticed that Imke Paulig had been quiet throughout the tour and her face had grown very pale when they had been shown the crematoria. Some people, he knew, claimed that they could still smell a hint of burning flesh and ash when standing near the ovens. Markus smelled nothing and thought how easily some people allowed themselves to be deceived by their own imaginations.

For Markus, this was simply a place where something very bad, unforgivably bad, had happened a long, long time ago. Something that was nothing to do with him. Whatever *Erbschuld* debt was owing, it had been paid by or was still owed by the generations before him, not him. Despite his seeming disdain for others, Markus was sensitive enough to care about wrongs, about inhumanity. The crimes that had been committed here had been terrible and abhorrent, and he felt bad about them, but in the same way he felt bad about crimes committed in Stalinist Russia, in Serbia, in Rwanda or in a dozen different places and times.

After the guided tour, the school party was told they could walk around the grounds themselves, to take time for personal reflection.

Markus chose, as always, to be alone, watching the others from a bench beneath a willow tree. Part of him wanted to be moved, to feel something resonate within him, but it didn't.

This place belonged to the here and now. The events that had taken place here had been tragic; the place itself was not. All it was to Markus was a not unpleasant, if somewhat municipal environment. If anything, it was calming, peaceful.

Maybe it was the weather that was making him feel like that: it was difficult to equate a blue early summer sky and the sun on your face with a place of such suffering and death. But, he realized, the sun must have shone back then too.

Markus thought about plugging in to his MP3 player, but worrying that it might seem disrespectful, he simply leaned back and stretched his arms along the back of the bench, closing his eyes and tilting his face up to the sun.

Markus Schwab sat on the bench in the sun and suddenly experienced an odd sensation.

The best way he could describe it was a feeling like déjà vu.

40

JOHN MACBETH. BOSTON

Casey handed him a pearlescent sliver of titanium. Much slimmer and lighter than the laptop he'd been using, it looked to Macbeth like something too advanced for his time. He was just old enough to remember the world before the information technology revolution and just occasionally, like now, he felt he was living in the future.

"Your new toy – four times the memory and more than twice the speed of your old one. I've loaded all your essential stuff onto it."

"No phantom folder?" asked Macbeth.

"No phantom folder. If you don't mind, I'll hang on to your old laptop for a while, see if I can debug whatever it is that's causing the folder to appear. I'll bring it over to Copenhagen when I come."

"Sounds good. Thanks."

"You're welcome. More coffee?"

Macbeth shook his head. They were in the kitchen, having spent the evening in Casey's apartment, making arrangements for Macbeth's departure and for their reunion in Copenhagen in a couple of weeks. After his lunch at McLean, Macbeth hadn't felt very hungry and instead of going out for a meal, the two brothers sat at the table eating sandwiches and drinking coffee.

Macbeth was glad he'd moved in with Casey. On the streets, on the subway and in public spaces, there were more and more people to be seen trancelike, lost to this world, inhabiting another visible only to them. Reports were coming in from around the world of visions, mass events. His brother's apartment was a pleasant, calming refuge. During his time in Denmark, Macbeth had learned a word: *hygge*. *Hygge* was one of those foreign words that was a complete concept, a feeling: a single word that could not be translated into a single word. *Hygge* was the feeling you got, or the atmosphere you created, when you made your home cozy and relaxed in chosen company, loved ones or oldest friends. Staying with Casey was *hyggelig*.

In many ways, Macbeth and Casey were more like twins than brothers separated by four years. It was a strange thing that Macbeth sometimes felt jealous of his brother, of his success, of the clarity of his intellectual function; strange because it wasn't envy of another person, it was envy of a better version of himself.

"If I can't fix it myself, do you mind if I have a friend at MIT take a look at your laptop?" asked Casey. "He's an expert."

"Not at all."

Casey pushed his coffee cup around the melamine for a second, something clearly on his mind.

"You okay?" asked Macbeth.

Casey shrugged. "I'm beginning to get a bad feeling about this Oxford symposium."

"You are?" asked Macbeth, genuinely surprised. "What kind of bad feeling?"

"I don't know. Something's been bugging me – you know, the kind of gut feeling you can't put your finger on – ever since whatever the hell that was that happened when we were in the restaurant."

"I think everyone's had that kind of feeling since then, to be honest, Casey."

"I guess . . . but this is different, like I know something but I don't know I know it yet." Casey made a face. "Just sounds dumb."

"No, it doesn't," said Macbeth. "Sometimes your unconscious puts things together but isn't ready to let your conscious in on it. It'll come to you. But it's not surprising you're uneasy with all this crap going on at the moment: Blind Faith, Islamic terrorists and every other kind of religious nut seem to be coming out of the woodwork to attack science."

Casey thought about what his brother had said, then shook his head. "It's more than that – maybe not even one thing but a lot of small things I just can't connect."

"Like?"

"Like when I asked around if Gabriel was involved with the Simulists, no one could say for sure. But they did say Professor Gillman is involved with them, apparently. Heavily involved. And there's the Prometheus Project itself."

"What about it?"

"I don't know." Casey shook his head frustratedly. "I don't even know for sure what it is. But I *do* know it'll be a huge leap forward. Maybe a leap we're not ready to take."

"I don't get you," said Macbeth.

"Do you never think how odd it is that we're alive right now? In our lifetimes we've seen the greatest technological advances in human history. Out of all the two hundred thousand years of human history, all our achievements have been squeezed into one century, and most of them into a couple of decades. And it's speeding up."

"Is that necessarily a bad thing?"

"It depends. It's taking us to the brink of the Singularity, when technology and artificial intelligence will surpass human intelligence. Some say that'll be the end of us, others that it'll be the beginning – that human evolution will cease to be a natural process and become a planned one. Planned by us. We're about to change who and what we are as a species. Every technology is accelerating and it's impossible to predict what our lives will be like in only twenty or thirty years. And with all of this going on we suddenly get an upswing of religious fundamentalism and obscurantism. It's almost as if, without really understanding why, the religious fundamentalists and the anti-science crackpots are trying to save us from the Singularity. Maybe it's an instinct in us as a species."

"And that's what's been bothering you?"

"Maybe. Partly. Like I said, it's a lot of other things. These hallucinations too."

"That's understandable."

"I don't just mean the events in themselves, I mean their nature. A hallucination is personally subjective and by definition false, something perceived to be real but which isn't, right?"

"Right."

"But you and I – and everyone else – *shared* the same hallucination. And the earthquake we experienced matched a historical event perfectly. Shouldn't a hallucination be personal and subjective – and divorced from *all* realities, even a past one? Who ever heard of thousands of people sharing exactly the same hallucination at exactly the same time?"

"What's your point?" asked Macbeth.

"What I do for a living – what Gabriel did – is to look into a universe so tiny that it defies understanding and where all the laws of ordinary physics are turned on their head. What we express through the abstract language of equations either sounds incomprehensible or delusional as soon as you try to express it in ordinary language or outside the scientific community. Physics began as a study of natural forces and now it's about the nature of reality itself. And there is something wrong with reality right now."

"You're saying you think these hallucinations aren't psychological, but something to do with external physics?"

"I'm saying they could be. It's almost like windows in time opening up. I don't know. I couldn't even begin to formulate a theory on why that should happen. All I know is that the Prometheus Project is the biggest leap we've made in a generation and it coincides with all of this weirdness."

"You can't seriously believe there's a link?" asked Macbeth.

"Listen, without getting all technical, we don't know what spin an electron has, what form it has, until we look at it. The thing is, the electron doesn't take that form *until* we look at it. A photon only decides to be a wave or a particle when someone observes it. We are coming to the conclusion that the entire universe is without definite form until *we* look at it. It's a super-simplification, but the fact is that everything is in every possible state and none of them at all until we look. What if Blackwell's work has looked into a new and unknown part of reality? Maybe the simple act of looking has caused something to change, to take a definite form." Casey paused. "Do you know what my definition of reality is? Each of us is wandering around in the pitch dark, each shining his or her own little flashlight, lighting up one small piece of the universe. All objective reality is, is when enough of us point our flashlights at the same spot. The people you treat, the delusionals and the schizoid . . . all that's happening is that they're illuminating some alternative reality."

"And that is almost exactly what Gabriel said . . ." Macbeth nodded thoughtfully. "But I still don't see—"

"Maybe we're shining our torches on more than one reality. And maybe that's got something to do with—" Casey was cut off by the ringing of the phone. When he answered it, Macbeth could tell instantly from his face that it was bad news.

Very bad news.

There was no television in the apartment, so they used the laptop Casey had given Macbeth to get the TV news as a live Internet feed. It was the usual jumble of a breaking story: the camera darting instead of panning, pulled in one direction then another, magnetized by shouts and sirens or the sudden tumescence of a fireball. The light and the colors were polarized on the screen: bright yellow and orange bursts and flickers against the dark blues and turquoises of the evening sky; silhouetted figures appearing and disappearing against the brightness of the flames as firefighters and cops rushed back and forth.

"Fuck . . ." said Casey. "Holy fuck."

The image cut to an on-the-spot reporter, her perfect makeup illuminated imperfectly in the spot of a camera light, chaos in shadow and amber glow behind her.

"At this time, Boston PD are reluctant to point a finger at any particular terrorist group, and have not yet even confirmed that the blasts and resultant fire here at the Massachusetts Institute of Technology were caused by terrorist devices, but it seems clear that this has been a coordinated series of attacks on MIT. Furthermore, unofficial sources have suggested that responsibility for the explosions has been claimed by Blind Faith, the fundamentalist Christian group. The group has already been blamed for an escalating series of attacks on research institutions and individual scientists over the last year. It is too early to confirm if Blind Faith is in fact behind this tragedy that has caused so much damage and so many deaths. I'm afraid we still don't know exactly how many fatalities we are dealing with."

"Do we know where the explosions took place, Kathy?" asked the baritone of an invisible male news anchor.

"All indications are that there was a sequence of six large blasts, three of which each took place in a different building within the MIT campus. The first blast took place in –" she referred to her clipboard notes "– in the Dreyfoos Tower of the Sata Center, where the Computer Science and Artificial Intelligence Laboratory is located. The second blast took place directly across Vassar Street, in the Brain and Cognitive Sciences Building. The third took place in the Fairchild Building, in the

Haptic Technology laboratory, which I am told specializes in touch-based interfaces between humans and technology. But it was the Gillman Quantum Modeling Project, located in the Pierce Laboratory on Massachusetts Avenue, which seems to have been the main target, with three bombs – and I think it's safe to assume that these were indeed planted and remotely detonated devices – exploding in the space of one minute. Professor Steven Gillman is said to have been present in the building at the time of the explosions and is, as yet, unaccounted for, along with fifteen fellow scientists. Firefighters have so far been unable to get to the seat of the fire where temperatures are said to be excessively high even for a blaze of this nature."

"Shit . . ." Casey turned away from the screen and began pacing the kitchen, shaking his head. "I can't believe it. That's exactly the unit Gabriel Rees worked in, the team he was on . . ."

41

MARKUS. GERMANY

Markus opened his eyes and quickly sat upright.

Out of nowhere, the sky had darkened: mid-afternoon had become late evening in a matter of a second. But it was more than the time of day that had changed: Markus felt chilled bullets of rain on his face and the air had suddenly become cold and infused with a strong smell. A disgusting smell that seemed like the odors of urine, feces, sweat and unwashed linen all combined and magnified.

The neat rectangles of pale gray gravel were gone. The open space was gone. In its place were rows of barrack sheds, like the ones the guide had shown them, leaving only a small court-yard between them and the administration building, with the Jourhaus to one side. Markus stood up suddenly from the bench, as if stung, but when he looked back the bench was gone. The willow was gone. The smell. That clinging, sickening stench that seemed to swell and eddy in the air as the cold breeze changed direction.

None of this made sense. What had happened to the other students in his party? Where had all of these other barracks come from? He could no longer simply walk across the square so he took the path that had erupted from nowhere and headed back to the Jourhaus. It was a path of bare earth, but earth that had been pressed flat and brushed. This was insane.

A shrill, sharp sound made him jump: the blast of several whistles. He looked in the direction the sound had come from.

Four men trotted out of the main administration building and into the courtyard square, urgently blowing their whistles. The four trotting men were in uniform. Black uniform.

This cannot be happening. The thought burned in Markus's mind. This simply cannot be happening.

The smell that had been eddying in the breeze became a sickening tidal wave as the doors of the barrack huts opened and figures tumbled out. They were people but it was like they were a different species of people: half ghosts already, tangles of impossibly thin limbs beneath striped prison uniforms; skull faces beneath formless, peakless caps.

The smell came from them. Markus knew it was more than being unwashed: it was the smell of disease and death. The guide had explained that in the last months of the camp, and stretching into the months after liberation, the death rate at Dachau had soared because of typhus.

What was he thinking? Why was he rationalizing this experience by equating it to a past reality? These people were not real. What he was seeing was not real. It simply could not be real.

The prisoners shuffled hurriedly onto the courtyard Appell-platz, forming rows. Markus noticed how their shambling became geometric precision. Everybody stood still and at some kind of attention. Shoulders sagged, heads hung. Coughs resonated. He was looking at an assembly of the dead. The long dead. The half dead even in their own time.

The four SS men, three with forage caps, the fourth with a peaked officer's cap, ceased whistling and stood in the posture of authority: all with feet planted wide, the officer with his hands on his hips, the NCOs holding thick, short staves in front of them. Between the SS men was a low wooden trestle of some kind, the purpose of which Markus could not work out. The officer took a step forward.

"This is a punishment assembly," he called out. He had a

thin, ugly voice and spoke with a Saxon accent. "To demonstrate the penalty for stealing from the prisoner shop."

Markus knew from the tour that there had indeed been a prisoner shop, where inmates could pay – if they could afford it and in the tokens they had been given on arrival in exchange for their cash – hugely inflated prices for meager additions to the starvation diet they were fed. He felt sick with foreboding: he also knew that all profits from the shop had gone directly to the SS. If someone had stolen from the shop, then the punishment would be severe.

Why am I thinking like this? He cursed his folly. These are not prisoners, these are not real SS. What I am experiencing is a delusion, a hallucination. Think it through, Markus, think it through. He had read the reports of people all over the world imagining that they were seeing things – people and events that were not really there. A bug, they thought. Some kind of virus. I must have caught it too, he thought to himself.

But still the foreboding remained.

A fifth SS man, another forage-capped NCO, came out of the Jourhaus. He was holding a shackled prisoner by the elbow and walking so quickly that the prisoner had to perform a rapid shuffle with his leg-ironed feet. The prisoner was, like the others, emaciated and stooped, but even with that was a full head taller than his escort. Even from a distance, Markus could see that the manacled man was terrified, pleading to the oblivious guard in a quiet but high-pitched voice, like a beseeching child. Markus could also see the marks of a beating on the man: blood smeared across his nose and chin, one eye swollen and closed.

Stop. Markus's command did not make it past a thought and remained unvoiced. I should shout. I should tell them to stop. Maybe they'll hear me. Maybe I can make them stop.

But he didn't shout or call out. He didn't move nearer. There's no point, they can't hear me, Markus lied to himself. He knew the reason he did not shout out was because he was afraid of exactly that: that they would hear him.

The urgent, high-pitched chatter became a whimpering as the prisoner was forced to his knees in front of the low trestle. Unfastening his manacles, they stretched his arms out wide and re-fettered them on the trestle, forcing him down onto the wooden structure, his head turned and his cheek pressed against the wood.

Dear God no, thought Markus. Yet he remained motionless, stayed silent.

"This," proclaimed the Saxon officer, "is the justice you may expect for stealing the property of the Reich." He turned to the NCOs. "Carry out sentence."

It was the ease, the relaxed nature of their preparation, that sickened Markus most. The four NCOs stood two on each side of the man; each hunched then relaxed his shoulders, shook the arm holding the heavy club. It reminded Markus of golfers preparing for a swing.

"Proszę!" the fettered man pleaded, his voice wet and muffled. "Proszę! Wybacz mi! Proszę, nie rób mi krzywdy!"

The NCOs ignored him and were clearly establishing the order in which they should carry out their work. Nodding.

"Proszę!" Then in a desperate, pleading, Polish-accented German, "Please! Please sirs! Beg to forgive! Beg to forgive! Do not please to do that!"

The Saxon officer laughed, then nodded to his subordinates. The first NCO, a short, squat block of a man, swung his club up into the air and brought it down onto the prisoner's extended right arm at the elbow-joint. A sickening crack sounded in the damp, cold air and then another sound, like the whistle of a boiling kettle, that Markus did not immediately recognize as a human scream.

Like roadworkers driving in a bridge pile, the four black-uniformed NCOs swung in rapid, coordinated rhythm, blows raining down on the prisoner. On his arms, on his back, on his shoulders, but never on his head, clearly for fear that unconsciousness would rob him of his pain. The sound of each blow sickening, the inhuman screams of the prisoner cutting through the air, through Markus's skull.

Sinking to his knees, Markus sobbed. He looked across at the assembled prisoners. They stood mutely, their faces blank of expression and empty of emotion, most looking down at the ground.

Do something! Markus wanted to scream at them. There are more of you than them. Do something! But again Markus's voice failed him.

The rain of blows continued. Occasionally, an SS man would step back, the others carrying on the rhythm while he took a break, then he would rejoin the battery to allow a colleague to take a turn resting. After a while, the officer waved a hand to halt the beating.

The prisoner no longer screamed. Instead his wet, rheumy wheezing echoed in the otherwise quiet of the square.

Another casual gesture from the officer and the SS men walked off the parade ground, without dismissing the assembled prisoners who remained standing to emotionless attention, eyes downcast.

No one moved. No one moved for ten minutes. For twenty. For an hour. And all the time, the parade square echoed with the squelchy wheezing of the dying man. Eventually, Markus began to walk slowly, nervously casting his eyes up at the guard towers, making his way to where the punished prisoner remained shackled to the trestle.

The prisoners arranged in rows did not seem to acknowledge Markus, to see him, but they had given him the impression that even if he had been visible to them, they would not have seen him, blind as they were to anything other than their own immediate and visceral struggle to survive.

He knelt down beside the beaten man. Markus could see that he was now far from the shore of life, drifting farther with each passing second. His body had not had time to contuse, or perhaps was too anemic to bruise, and Markus could see that his arms and torso were severely deformed where the blows had fractured arm and collar bones, forced ribs into shattered concaves. Eyes closed, his breathing was now a wet wheeze, viscous bubbles of blood ballooned from his nostrils, his lips encrimsoned.

"I'm sorry," sobbed Markus. "I'm so sorry."

The dying man opened his eyes and looked directly at Markus.

"Dlaczego?" he said in a moist almost-whisper between ruckling breaths. "Dlaczego nie możesz mi pomóc?"

"I don't understand," said Markus, overcoming his shock that he was really there, visible and real, to the man. He reached out a hand to touch him, to comfort him, but stopped short, afraid that his touch would simply add to his agony. Or perhaps simply because he did not want to confirm another dimension to this insanity, this hallucination.

"Why did you not help me?" the prisoner asked wetly in German before his eyes glazed.

42

JOHN MACBETH. BOSTON

This is a dream, he told himself. Not a hallucination.

Macbeth had slept fitfully and what sleep he had managed was laced through with dreams in which he was aware of his own dreaming. In this dream he was a young boy again, standing at the door of his father's study; except the study was impossibly huge, the ceilings gravity-defyingly high and the too-big walls with their overfull bookshelves stretching orthogonally to an impossibly distant vanishing point.

His father was not sitting in his chair, instead standing with another man and a woman in front of his desk. The sight of the other man, whose face he could not see even when it was turned in his direction, terrified Macbeth. The woman was the most beautiful he had ever seen: Marjorie Glaiston, or at least Marjorie Glaiston as she'd appeared to Macbeth in his previous dream. The three adults didn't notice the young Macbeth as he entered and made his way over to them, nervously clutching his encyclopedia to his chest. They were all too interested in what they were looking at to pay heed to him; something vast sparkled and flashed and glowed, suspended in the air of the study in front of and above them. It was a thing of light and no substance, a massive ball of color and luminescence that formed patterns out of nothing: amazingly complex patterns that took shape and changed and elaborated before disappearing, only to be replaced by other even more complex patterns. Macbeth, in his dream a boy in mind as well as body, stood mesmerized by it. He now pressed close to his father and slipped his hand into his, making a huge effort not to look at the other man.

"What is it?" he asked his father.

"We've built a mind," his father said, without taking his eyes off the substanceless universe sparkling and floating in the study's air. "We are becoming gods because we've built a mind."

The other man turned to the boy. Macbeth expected him to be the grown-up version of himself, but he wasn't. He was someone else and something else: something dark and bad and gigantic compressed down into the shape of a man. Macbeth looked up into his face and as he did so, felt a warm trickle run down his leg. The man looked back at him but had no eyes, eyelids opening and closing as if there had been eyes where there were none. There was nothing in the eye sockets, Macbeth could see that: not that they were empty, but that they were filled with nothing: a gray-black void that stretched for ever.

"You want to know who I am, boy?" asked the man. His voice was a deep and cultured baritone, his accent difficult to place. Maybe New England, maybe British or Irish. His tone was at once neutral and hostile, as if he had no real interest in Macbeth yet wanted to do him great harm.

Macbeth didn't answer; didn't nod or shake his head, just stood in a pool of his own fear and urine.

"You know who I am. You know my name. You know what I am. What is my name?"

Macbeth said nothing, lost in the dark of the eye-socket voids.

"WHAT IS MY NAME?" the man bellowed, causing Macbeth to jump and drop his encyclopedia.

"You are John Astor," said Macbeth, his voice shaking, leaning tight against his father's body, squeezing his hand.

"It is a complete mind for us to explore," said Macbeth's father, oblivious to his son and the man. "Complete."

"It's the most wondrous thing," said Marjorie Glaiston with

299

a Boston Brahmin drawl. "Most wondrous." Macbeth noticed she was dressed formally and of the period she had lived in.

The Eyeless Man leaned over towards Macbeth, conspiratorially. He tilted his upper body and head, twisting the mouth he shielded with the flat blade of his hand, silent-movie-conspirator-style.

"Do you want to know something, young John?" he asked.

Macbeth nodded, scared to anger the man again.

"This mind. This thing we've made from nothing . . . it thinks it's real. It's the funniest thing, but it really believes in its own existence . . . that it lives in a real world." Astor laughed, then whispered, "But I made it all up. It is a fiction that believes itself to be fact and I am its author."

Macbeth started to cry. He looked down to where the encyclopedia lay, one corner of the glossy book jacket breaking the meniscus edge of the urine splash on the teak floorboards. "I want to stop," he pleaded. "Please Mr Astor, I want to stop dreaming."

The Eyeless Man leaned forward, levering his face down and into the terrified boy's. Macbeth looked into Astor's hollow eye sockets, a void so big yet so empty that it made his own eyes hurt.

"Everybody dreams," Astor said in a maliciously quiet voice. "Everything is made of dreams. You love your books, don't you? You hide away in them, finding answers to questions you haven't asked yet, so you can fill your head with knowledge and truth, except that knowledge is deceit and truth is lies." He paused, grabbed Macbeth by the shoulders, his bony fingers sinking painfully into young flesh, then screamed into the small boy's face: "WAKE UP!"

Macbeth woke up. His heart pounding in his chest, he did an inventory of his surroundings. It was still dark, but he knew he was in Casey's spare room, and he could see everything in shades of shadow. He felt a moment of stark panic when he saw someone sitting in the corner, quietly watching him, then realized that it was just his jacket hanging on the back of the chair, with his suit pants neatly folded on the chair cushion.

He gave a small laugh at his own stupidity. A grown man, a psychiatrist and research scientist, a rationalist to the core, yet he was afraid of shadows. Despite acknowledging all of these truths, and despite wanting to will himself back to sleep, he reached over and switched on the bedside lamp, responding to the need to fill every corner with light.

He blinked in the brightness.

Astor stood hunched by the bed, looking down at Macbeth. Unlike in the dream, Astor was no longer compressed down into the size of a normal man; he was huge, perhaps fifteen feet tall, crammed into the room, his long legs bent, his shoulders hunched and pressed up against the ceiling. His head, twisted round on a crooked neck, was directly above the bed, looking down at Macbeth with his still hollow eyes filled with a dark gray void. Through his terror, Macbeth realized he knew what the void was, what it meant.

Macbeth tried to scream, but nothing came from his mouth. He tried to get out of the bed, but was completely paralyzed. I can't move, he thought.

"You can't move," said Astor.

I can't breathe, thought Macbeth.

"You can't breathe," said Astor, who smiled a too-wide smile, a one-hundred-tooth smile, and bent his head down towards the helpless, paralyzed, silently screaming Macbeth.

He woke up. The room was bright, filled with natural, not electric light. It was morning.

Macbeth gathered his thoughts. A hallucination. A hypnopompic hallucination, created in that place, that state of consciousness, between sleep and wakefulness. False awakenings, vivid hallucination, sleep paralysis – all were common features of the hypnopompic state; and hypnopompic states almost always followed lucid dreams, where the dreamer was aware of dreaming.

Nothing more than a hiccup in the reticular activating system, he told himself: the connection between brainstem and cortex that regulates states of wakefulness.

He knew all of that; had learned it in his psychiatric training.

Yet he still took a moment to check the bedroom for shadow people in the corners.

Casey was up and preparing breakfast for them both.

Macbeth had gotten up early, mainly to separate himself from the environment of the dream, but also because he was keen to find out what had happened overnight. He and Casey had stayed up until just after 2 a.m., watching the news and discussing its consequences. Casey had made frantic calls and sent SMS messages to all of his colleagues; similarly, whenever he put his cellphone down it would ring, with one or other of his fellow MIT physicists checking he was all right. By the end of the night, six co-workers were unaccounted for.

"Any more news?" Macbeth asked as he walked into the kitchen.

"Not much," Casey said over his shoulder while pouring a coffee for Macbeth. "What there is is bad enough. The death toll could be as high as a couple of hundred. They still haven't located Gillman. I just can't believe this, John."

"I really wish you'd reconsider Oxford," said Macbeth as he sat at the kitchen table. "That's got to be a prime target for these lunatics." Before retiring to bed, Macbeth had beseeched his brother not to make the trip to Oxford, but Casey insisted he had to go. Another reason for Macbeth's early rise was to try again to dissuade his brother from the trip.

"The Prometheus symposium is just too important," Casey

said. "Too important for my career, and I'm not going to let a bunch of anti-science crazies scare me off. And I still think it may cast light on everything that's been happening."

"You still think there's a connection between the hallucination phenomenon and Blackwell's work? I really can't see how there could be any credible scientific link."

"Like I said, when you work in quantum physics you see things differently . . . Michio Kaku once said that we're like radio or TV sets, tuned in permanently to one channel. But as well as the reality we're tuned into, there are countless other realities occupying the same space and time – other stations broadcasting in the same location but on different wavelengths."

"And you think maybe something's messing with the remote, is that it?" said Macbeth.

Casey shrugged. "All I know is that we've got these mass hallucinatory episodes taking place for no reason and now, on top of that, religious nuts targeting facilities devoted to neuroscience and physics – the two fields that could hold the answer. Speaking of targets, I take it you're not going into the Schilder Institute again?"

"The place is already like Fort Knox," said Macbeth. "But no . . . I won't be back there before I leave. I am going into McLean this morning though, to see a patient of Pete Corbin's. By the way, I'm off early tomorrow morning . . . no need for me to disturb you. But I'll see you tonight."

The phone on the kitchen wall rang and Casey answered it.

"Sure. He's here . . ." He held the receiver out to Macbeth.

"Hi, Dr Macbeth? It's Brian Newcombe here. Terrible thing that happened last night."

"It certainly was," said Macbeth. "We were just saying that it is a good thing that the Schilder has such tight security."

"Sure, sure. Listen, there have been other developments . . . I really need to talk to you before you go back to Denmark. I'm sorry to press you, but this is very important."

303

"I'm afraid I really don't have much time . . ." Macbeth felt annoyed at the intrusion: he was going to spend his last evening in Boston with Casey, not talking shop with Newcombe. "I'm going out to McLean this morning – any chance we could meet there later, maybe after lunch? I can't give you a specific time, but—"

"Belmont's fine," Newcombe cut him off. "I can combine a visit I need to make at the Neuroimaging Center. I'll give you my cell number and you can ring me when you're through."

"Okay, I'll see you there."

43

JOHN MACBETH. BOSTON

The Starers began to be called Dreamers.

Like everybody else, Macbeth was getting used to the sight of people standing stock-still, focused on something not there. Mostly, it would be an individual in the middle of a busy street or in a park, but increasingly it would be a group of connected or unconnected people: sometimes a handful, sometimes a hundred, all locked out of the time and space they had occupied until just a second before and into a new reality. The worst was when it happened to someone behind the wheel of a vehicle. The morning after the MIT bombings, there was more bad news on the radio: a truck driver had ploughed his eighteen-wheeler through commuter traffic on the Adamski Memorial Highway, crushing everything in his path. Fifteen dead.

The official advice was that no one was to drive alone, and all speed limits were temporarily reduced. That unique human ability to adapt – to adjust to a differing reality and to normalize the abnormal – was already taking hold.

And on the streets there were more Dreamers.

The Massachusetts Department of Public Health had set up THS Response Teams – THS standing for Temporary Hallucinatory Syndrome. Teams of two EMS technicians, or a technician and a BPD cop, would move the affected person out of harm's way. If it was a brief seizure they would stay with the patient; prolonged cases were taken to one of the hundred shelters that had been set up citywide.

As well as the THS Response Teams, there were more cops on the street. The neurogenic immobility that accompanied the hallucinations was a godsend to criminals. Pickpockets and perverts accosted the temporarily insensible; apartments and homes were ransacked while the occupier was physically at home but mentally occupying some other, distant place.

Macbeth took a taxi out to Belmont. The driver behind the wheel explained the fare would be double the usual. Macbeth found the city-authorized increase reasonable, given that, for safety, there were now two drivers sitting in front of him through the Plexiglas.

There was no chat this trip. No one said to Macbeth anymore that they thought they'd seen him before. Feelings of inexplicable reminiscence were something you no longer acknowledged, in case they brought on a feeling of déjà vu.

As he sat in the back of the cab, Macbeth slipped from his briefcase the titanium sliver of technology that Casey had lent him, unfolded it and checked his email. Four from Georg Poulsen. There had been at least two emails from his boss every day he had been in Boston, and usually a couple more from members of Macbeth's research team, obviously under pressure from Poulsen in Macbeth's absence.

It was getting that Macbeth couldn't stand the man.

The Project hadn't been long started before everyone on the hand-picked team became aware that Dr Georg Poulsen, the short, unassuming-looking Dane heading the Project, was a very driven man.

With funding of two billion euros, double the European Union grant to the Düsseldorf project, the Copenhagen team's aim was to build a fully functioning analog of a human brain, allowing the scientists involved to short-cut the testing times for neurological drug treatments and to take exponential leaps in understanding human cognitive function. But breakthroughs in brain–computer interfaces were also sought and Poulsen had taken personal charge of the Interface Team. He seemed obsessed with the quest to find better ways for humans to interact with computer technology and it hadn't taken long for the Interface Team members to protest about Poulsen's unreasonable expectations, others complaining about the disproportionate emphasis placed on interface research.

Suspecting some personal motive, Macbeth had made an effort to get to know his Danish boss. The descriptions given by Poulsen's former colleagues – of a typically relaxed and easygoing Dane with a good sense of humor who enjoyed the social aspects of academic life as much as its intellectual challenges – jarred with his own experience of the man. Macbeth found his boss remote and businesslike to the point of hostility. No one knew what went on in Poulsen's private life, and no one asked.

Macbeth read through the emails: the usual demands for immediate answers to questions that could easily wait until he got back to Copenhagen. Macbeth decided that was exactly what they would do and he quit out of his email.

He was just about to close over the lid of the laptop when he noticed something sitting on the screen's desktop.

"Son of a bitch . . ." he muttered, as he clicked on the folder that had appeared out of nowhere. Just as it had on his old computer, the icon refused to yield to his clicking. Macbeth frowned: Casey knew his stuff when it came to computers, and it worried him that whatever was causing this ghost folder was smarter than his brother. Closing the laptop, he slipped it back into his case, sat back in the taxi's seat and watched Massachusetts slide by.

It can be the smallest of things that bring the seriousness of a situation home to you, thought Macbeth, as they pulled up at traffic lights in Belmont. The lights changed to green but the queue of traffic didn't move. The usual blasting of horns was less emphatic than usual and the queue of cars, in a quiet and orderly fashion, pulled out and passed the station wagon that sat immobile, three cars' lengths from the lights. As the taxi passed, Macbeth saw the woman driver in profile as she sat perfectly still, hands on the wheel, mouth slightly agape and her gaze through the windshield unfixed.

Macbeth leaned forward and asked through the small window in the Plexiglas: "Shouldn't we stop and help?"

The second driver turned. "Sorry, pal . . . there's so many of them these days. We see two, maybe three each fare. If we stopped for every one we'd never get anywhere."

Macbeth didn't protest but sat back again in the taxi. Despite his efforts to put them out of his mind, the emails from Poulsen nagged at him. He took out his cellphone and called the airline. The female Customer Services voice answered his question with a public-affairs prepared script.

"As you know, sir, there are always two pilots on every flight, as well as a flight engineer. But, to ensure your complete safety and peace of mind, all of our transatlantic flights will have a complete backup crew and a medical officer on board until such times as public concern has abated."

Macbeth thanked her and hung up. He didn't ask what happened if everyone on the plane had the same hallucination at the same time; how multiplicity could possibly be a precaution against a syndrome that was known to affect hundreds of people simultaneously.

He keyed a second number: an international call. After a while he was put through to the person he had asked for in Danish.

"I'm glad you'll be back tomorrow," said Georg Poulsen. "All teams, except yours, are ahead of milestone delivery targets. You have a lot of catching up to do."

"Professor Poulsen, I'm forced to remind you once more that I am not here on vacation, but representing the Project. On your behalf. And you may be aware that there has been a lot happening over here since I arrived."

"I heard," Poulsen said without emotion or expansion. "Can you attend a meeting in the Project briefing room tomorrow at, say, three-fifteen p.m.?"

"No, I can't. I don't get into Copenhagen until the small hours and, not even allowing for jetlag, I wouldn't be ready for a meeting in the afternoon. And anyway, I'm not sure that I should be flying back at all. There have been major transportation accidents caused by this outbreak or whatever it is."

"I'm aware of that. As, I imagine, are the airlines. I'm sure they have taken all appropriate safety measures." There was a pause. When Poulsen spoke again, the imperiousness was gone from his tone. "John, I'm sorry that I push so much. It's just that we are so, so close to a breakthrough. I need you here . . . Can you try to make it?"

Macbeth sighed. "I'll be there. If the pilot doesn't hallucinate that he's captaining a submarine."

He hung up just as the taxi reached the main entrance to the hospital, but was stopped at a roadblock improvised with two police cruisers. It was only after Macbeth's ID was checked, and the young female cop had called the hospital to confirm his appointment, that the taxi was allowed through.

Unlike the last visit, the skies over the parkland grounds of McLean Hospital were leaden. After the taxi dropped him off outside the main administration building, it turned and headed back down the drive. He watched it go and felt strangely abandoned. A man in his thirties, dressed in a hooded sweatshirt and jeans, stood at the foot of the steps and slightly to one side, watching him. Macbeth's attention was drawn to him because of the strange intensity of the man's gaze. Disinhibited frankness, Macbeth had learned over the years, was something that came with a whole range of mental disorders. The man was clearly a patient and not a visitor or staff.

Macbeth smiled as he walked past him but was halted by his grip on Macbeth's arm.

"Is *this* the substrate?" The man leaned into Macbeth and whispered conspiratorially.

"What?"

"Is *this* the substrate reality? I've gotten confused." Looking into the distance, he frowned. He turned back to Macbeth with the smile. "I didn't think you'd ever come back. I didn't think you'd risk it . . ."

"Well, I'm back now . . ." Macbeth smiled at the man. It was such a forgettable face that he could have been a patient during Macbeth's time at McLean, but it was more likely that he was just spieling his delusion.

"I didn't know what to do . . ." The patient, anxious again, furrowed his brow. Macbeth looked around for an orderly. "It has started. It has started. It has started. It has started and I don't know what to do because you haven't told me what to do. You went away and didn't tell me what I'd to do when it started like you said it would. We all need you to tell us what we have to do; what you need us to do. We've been waiting for you."

"It's all right," Macbeth said soothingly, easing the man's grip from his arm. "I think you're confusing me with someone else."

"No, I know who you are. I know exactly who you are. You have to tell me what to do, Mr Astor . . ."

An orderly appeared from nowhere and gently but firmly guided the patient away before Macbeth could answer. As he was led away, the patient called out urgently over his shoulder.

"Don't forget, Mr Astor. Don't forget about Clarke's Third Law."

Corbin was in the main reception area when Macbeth came in. An unusual quiet and restraint hung over the McLean psychiatrist the same way the clouds hung over the hospital.

"Brian Newcombe asked me to remind you that he's here to talk with you whenever you're free," Corbin said as he led Macbeth into the meeting room.

"Sure . . . Everyone wants a piece of me today."

As they entered the room, Macbeth was taken aback by the physical presence of the tall, dark-haired and brutal-looking man waiting for them.

"This is Sergeant Walt Ramirez, of the Californian Highway Patrol," Corbin explained.

Macbeth shook hands with Ramirez.

"We spoke on the phone." Macbeth recognized the quiet baritone. Ramirez was wearing a dark suit with the unconvinced discomfort of someone who spent most of his time in uniform. "Thanks for making time to meet me."

"Anything I can do to get to the bottom of what happened to Melissa, although you do understand that you'll have to stop the interview if Dr Corbin says so. Deborah's treatment and rights as a patient override all other considerations."

"I understand that Dr Corbin's already gone through the ground rules. Are you sitting in on this?"

"If you don't mind . . ."

"Fine by me." Ramirez shrugged huge shoulders. "Dr Corbin tells me you're something of an expert in this field."

"So he keeps telling me."

"How's Casey?" said Corbin. "I take it he's all right?"

Macbeth nodded. "But he's shaken up by the whole thing." He turned and explained to Ramirez, "My brother is a physicist at MIT."

"I see . . ." said Ramirez. "That was a terrible thing. That and the thing at Caltech."

"Caltech?"

"Haven't you heard?" Corbin frowned. "During the night three bombs exploded in the Annenberg Center. The target was a research project."

"What kind of research project?"

"Computing. Information technology," the Californian cop answered. "Something to do with artificial intelligence research.

And those people who threw themselves off the bridge worked with that kind of stuff. I know it was gaming, but it was pretty far-out-there stuff, as far as I can see."

"You think there's a link between the mass suicide of gaming researchers and these attacks on science establishments? I can't see the connection."

"There's a lot of things that don't seem to be connected, but are. After I'm through here I'm flying to New York. Did you read, a couple of months or so back, about a guy who starved himself to death at home in a swanky New York apartment building? Until recently Tennant was involved with Melissa Collins."

"I only just found that out," said Macbeth. "You're investigating this in the belief that Melissa somehow persuaded Tennant to commit suicide too, by starving himself to death?"

"No, no . . . Not at all. They had gone their separate ways some while before. And Tennant was doing anything but committing suicide, at least deliberately. Melissa Collins and Samuel Tennant were both Transhumanists. I guess you know what that means?"

Macbeth nodded distractedly. Something was beginning to form a picture, but it was still too far out of focus for him to make sense of it.

"The NYPD are still investigating his death," said Ramirez. "Not that they think it was murder or even suicide, as such, but just before his death, Tennant electronically transferred half a million dollars to an offshore account, apparently in payment for some rare manuscript or other. There's no trace of the money or of the manuscript. It may not even have been in physical form."

"That's an expensive download," said Corbin.

"As for his death – from what the NYPD found out, Tennant was obsessed with calories. He didn't eat proper food, but this supplement crap all the time. He thought it would make him live longer. He got that wrong, that's for sure."

"Calorific intake," said Macbeth. "There's evidence that if you exist on an extremely restricted calorific content, you can extend your life by as much as a quarter. But if you overdo it . . ."

"Exactly," said Ramirez. "He was obsessed with something called the Singularity, which he thought would happen sometime in the next ten to fifty years. I don't understand that much about it, but he had some wild idea that he could achieve immortality if he managed to live until the Singularity. As for the group, that's why I'm going to New York. But I came here to talk to Deborah. To see if she can cast any light on the whole thing."

"This group," said Macbeth. "Did they call themselves the Simulists?"

Ramirez looked at Macbeth. For the first time it was a cop's look: assessing, weighing him up.

"How did you know that?"

"Bundy told me."

"The FBI man you said spoke to you?"

"Yes. He said Tennant was involved with the Simulists but didn't say anything about Melissa being connected."

"I haven't been able to locate Agent Bundy to ask him," said Ramirez. "In fact, the FBI were less than cooperative and said they don't have an Agent Bundy. I was hoping Deborah Canning could help."

"Then I suggest we ask her," said Corbin, extending his hand to indicate the door. "Shall we?"

"Just one thing," Macbeth said, halting Ramirez as they made for the door. "This manuscript he paid five hundred thousand for . . . do you know what it was?"

Ramirez nodded. "*Phantoms of Our Own Making*, by someone called John Astor."

44

ARI. ISRAEL

Ari Livnat had the strangest feeling: as if someone, somewhere at the extreme edge of his hearing, was drawing fingernails across a blackboard.

He was hot and tired and bored, which was normal for this type of detail, but underlying the tedium was a nerve-jangled itchiness. Even this close to the sea, the air was desert air: skin- and lip-crackingly hot and dry. But Ari had the feeling that there was something odd, something extra in the air.

Ari stood beside Benny Kagan and the others of his platoon, hunch-shouldered in combat olive, scuffing the sand with his boot, rifle hanging muzzle-downwards in his grasp, watching the protestors. It struck him that these young men, all of whom were pretty much the same age as Ari, were going through the motions with the same lack of enthusiasm that he was. Maybe some of them had been coerced to be there too. Conscripted into compulsory protesting. Or maybe just because history demanded it.

History was something Ari despised; mainly because, having been born where and when he was, he'd had too much of it foisted upon him at birth. History had been the music he had grown up with and he was sick of the sound of it ringing in his ears. History defined him, more than if he had been born Italian or Finnish or Greek or American. And, at that moment, Ari would have given anything to have been born with any of those historically unencumbered nationalities. For as long as he could remember, he had been compelled to wear his perceived history – Masada, blood libels, anti-Semitic canards, pogroms, the Holocaust, the Wars of Independence and Attrition – like a yellow star. And he wanted no part of it.

Ari was a most reluctant soldier – a conscript. He had thought of refusing to serve, but he had no religious or political justifications for refusal, he wasn't a swimsuit model or other celebrity with a legal dodge to pay for, and then there was Ari's father to think about. There were many things in life that Ari was cynical about, but his father was not one of them. Ari's father had fought in both the Six Day and Yom Kippur Wars, having been taken prisoner in the latter and thrown into the hell of al-Mazzeh prison. Joe Livnat was a gentle, quiet man, to whom his son was devoted. His father had never discussed his treatment at the hands of the Syrians, but Ari had learned from other sources about the filth and disease, the torture and beatings that almost all captured IDF prisoners had endured. The thing that had upset Ari most was the way his father always withdrew into silence whenever questioned about those times – a quietness, Ari suspected, that had something to do with the shame of the surrendered.

And that was what Ari hated most about history: no matter how hard you tried, some of it was simply inescapable. He knew his father would have understood, perhaps even supported him, had he decided to dodge his draft, but Ari had felt the need to go through the motions for his father's sake, as if refusing service would have confirmed a family trait, somehow, and compounded his father's quiet shame.

So now Ari stood in IDF olive drab under a desert sun. And now that the worst of the conflict between Jew and Arab seemed to have passed, he could hope that the only thing the State of Israel would expect him to kill was time.

He took a drink of water from his canteen. At least this was no dusty border crossing or middle-of-the-Negev road checkpoint. But he would much rather have been relaxing on the beach with a chilled beer. At the moment the beach was empty, the parasols closed and the beach loungers unoccupied. As Ari looked out over the azure waters of the sea, he could see the Shayetet 13 patrol boats positioned in an arc, shielding the shore from terrorist and tourist alike, and the faint, fuzzy smudge of a distant SeaCobra helicopter patrolling the hazy horizon between sea and sky. More history was being made here in Eilat today: behind him in the air-conditioned luxury of the five-star hotel he and the others were guarding. More history that Ari didn't give a shit about, other than that one result of the conference now taking place might be that he would qualify for an EU passport.

The sky brightened suddenly, then dulled.

Ari had had too much to drink the night before and having to stand around in the desert sun was making him feel odd. He felt faintly dizzy and an unsettling, unpleasant surge of something like déjà vu seemed to sweep over him. His head hurt; his sinuses throbbed and the pressure in the hot air was palpable. A storm coming. The unconvinced breeze that had loitered all morning suddenly strengthened into a resolute wind that caused the sand to swirl and eddy at his feet.

He looked over at the hulking form of Gershon Shalev. Shalev was someone who didn't feel history was a burden; he wore it as if it were a badge of his own fashioning. The tall, heavy-shouldered Haredi had been transferred from the Netzah Yehuda Battalion for reasons that Ari and the rest of the platoon had been left to guess about. There had been rumors, of course: someone knew someone who said that Shalev had a reputation; that he had been active in a Price Tag gang back in the days of the illegal West Bank settlements. Whatever his history, Ari hated Shalev and everything he stood for. He hated all über-Jews who tried to tell him who and what he was and what he was part of. There had been as little contact as possible between the two soldiers: Shalev having little or nothing to do with Ari, probably having identified him right away as an apostate, a *min*. But in truth Shalev had said or done nothing to inspire Ari's ire. His simply being there had been provocation enough: his payot sidelocks, his religious observances, his soldierly discipline.

Now, standing there feeling odd, and that the air was changing around him, with his nerves itchy and raw for a reason he couldn't pin down, Ari stared at Shalev and felt his hatred swell and blossom.

"Look at him . . ." Ari turned to Benny Kagan, the short, skinny, good-looking corporal who stood next to him, and jutted his chin in the direction of Shalev. "The guardian of Israel . . . just itching for a sign from God telling him to squeeze a clip or two into those Palis." Ari nodded to the knot of lacklustre protestors who had bussed into the coastal tourist town to protest against the accord being signed. There were fifty, sixty maybe. Others had been turned away, but this token protest had been allowed, just for show.

"You don't know that, Ari." Benny shrugged bony shoulders somewhere in his too-big uniform shirt. "Gershon's all right. You're too tough on him."

"Look at him." Ari nudged Benny. "I bet he's pissed with everything that's happening here. The Quartet Peace Proposal has screwed up his chances of being the warrior protector of Eretz Yisrael. He's the type who thinks political policy should be shaped by burning bushes, rather than people making decisions for themselves. I mean, what do we really know about him? He must've fucked up real bad to get kicked into this unit. Fuck!" Ari cursed as the wind swirled around him and cast a cloud of Negev sand into his face. "Fuck!" he cursed again, removing his sunglasses and wiping his right eye with the back of his hand. It took him a moment to get the grains out of his eye, his back turned and hunched against the wind. He replaced

317

his sunglasses with his army-issue eye shields and noticed that Benny and the others had done the same.

"Where the hell has that wind come from?" he said. "There was nothing forecast . . ." He looked over at the protestors, who seemed unfazed by the sudden change in weather.

The day had turned a dull yellow-gray as a fog of swirling sand clouded the air. Ari pulled his kerchief over his mouth and nose.

"Great . . ." shouted Benny. "This is all we need. A sandstorm. It must've blown in from the Negev . . ."

Ari looked at the sky, the air now visible, granular. "No . . . it's coming from the wrong—"

The sound cut him off.

A sound that shook the earth beneath his feet, that seemed to resonate and shudder in his bones.

45

JOHN MACBETH. BOSTON

Deborah Canning was sitting in exactly the same place, in exactly the same pose. Even the glossy-covered *trompe l'œil* art book was arranged at the same angle on the window-side table. The only differences from Macbeth's last visit were that she wore other clothes and the window was closed. It was like, he thought, looking at the same painting for the second time, seeing the same elements but also picking up on new ones.

Seeing her again, Macbeth could very easily have been convinced that Deborah Canning really did only come into existence when others were present. Or maybe only when he was present.

It wasn't just the consistency of Deborah's context that disturbed him. Macbeth was haunted by a more distant memory of the unchanging room, as if the faded image of another time superimposed itself. He remembered sitting in this room, talking to his patient – his last at McLean – whom Macbeth had diagnosed as exhibiting multiple personalities.

Pete Corbin introduced Walt Ramirez to Deborah. The colossal, tanned policeman with his huge hands and broad-beam shoulders seemed to fill the room and it reminded Macbeth unpleasantly of the false awakening from his dream. Deborah seemed unfazed by Ramirez's massive presence. Instead she nodded quietly and smiled without meaning.

Corbin chatted idly for a moment, asking Deborah about her day, to which he got near-automatic, empty responses.

"You seem troubled, Detective Ramirez," Deborah said.

"Sergeant Ramirez," he corrected. "I'm a Patrol Sergeant. In what way troubled?"

"Like you have more questions than you know to ask."

"I do have questions about Melissa. You know what happened?"

"Yes I do. I see, you're trying to understand it."

"That's right. It's important to me that I understand it. Not just as a policeman, but for me."

Deborah nodded. "I understand now – you were there?"

"Yes. That's why I need to understand. Do you know why Melissa and the others did what they did?"

"They were becoming."

"What does that mean? Becoming what?"

"You wouldn't understand. You're not programmed to understand."

"I'd like to try."

"Melissa, the others, me . . . we saw the truth. It was time to become."

"What truth?" Ramirez strained to remain patient.

"That our future has already happened."

Ramirez sighed.

"I told you you wouldn't understand." She smiled gently.

"I don't understand either," said Macbeth. "How can our future have already happened?"

"It means what you think is now, what you think is the present, is simply the past. Except we're not the real people who lived then. We're not even their ghosts. We're just living out a tableau. Puppets."

"That doesn't make any—"

Macbeth halted Ramirez with a hand on his elbow. "Debbie is here for psychiatric help," he said quietly. "You cannot expect everything she says to make sense to you. To get to the truth you have to work around her syndrome."

Deborah Canning laughed as if faintly amused.

320

"Was there some event, something that happened to make them do what they did?" Ramirez rephrased his question.

"Just that we saw the truth. We were developing a new game. Our biggest project ever – completely intuitive, completely involving – and it had applications way beyond gaming. Jane McGonigal once said there should be a Nobel Prize for Gaming. Our baby would have won the first."

"What was so special about it?" asked Ramirez.

"Its size, the sheer complexity of the programming, its mechanics . . . but most of all the environment it created. Melissa forged a partnership between our company and Jeff Killberg. This was a new generation, a paradigm shift in gaming; we called it Reality Pervasive Envirogeering."

"Could you explain that to me, Debbie?" asked Ramirez. "Simply, so I can understand."

"You know how realistic computer games have become. Well, we took it to a completely new level – we created a virtual gaming environment more complex and convincing than any other ever developed. Everyone complains that virtual and alternate reality games remove people from the real world . . . but this game was a perfect simulation of *this* world. City streets, landmarks – everything was exactly as it is in real life. The difference was that the gamer could bend time and reality – like having superpowers in the real world. But the really big thing was the pervasiveness of the game . . . It merged virtual reality, augmented reality and *real* reality." For the first time, Macbeth saw real animation in Deborah's expression. "Effectively superimposing a gaming world on the real world. We realized that we could totally erase the line between game life and real life."

"It sounds more like cause for a celebration," said Ramirez, "not a suicide pact."

"You don't understand." It was Deborah's turn to be frustrated. "What you saw wasn't an act of desperation or sadness. It was a becoming."

"Tell us more about the program," said Macbeth.

"You've heard of Pervasive Game Syndrome, sometimes called the Tetris Effect?" she asked. Macbeth nodded. It was a psychological phenomenon, where the shapes of falling Tetris blocks, or images from any game, persisted in the gamers' minds long after they had finished playing.

"Well, the environment in our new game was the ultimate in that. That's why we called it Reality Pervasive. This potential of the game to enhance people's lives was limitless – people suffering from paralysis, locked-in syndrome, all kinds of debilitating problems, could live a real life free of their disabilities. They could live a full life in a generated reality."

"Like in the movie *Avatar*?" asked Ramirez.

"No, not like some CGI cartoon – like *this* . . ." Holding out her hands, she indicated the room around them.

"So what was it you discovered while developing this program?" asked Macbeth. "What was this truth you uncovered?"

"The program began to self-elaborate, building complexity in itself, by itself. Then we realized it was connecting wirelessly with other programs that we hadn't built. Not just with Killberg's TIME program, but others. One in particular."

"Which program was that?" asked Corbin.

"We couldn't track it. The program had become autonomous and was making its own decisions. Connections. Like neural connections . . . a brain. But whatever this program was, it was massive. I mean government-run massive, or maybe some major research project, and we were afraid we'd be accused of hacking into high-security systems. But we weren't doing it, the program was."

"None of this explains why Melissa killed herself," said Macbeth. "Or the others."

Deborah turned to the window and looked out through glass now flecked with raindrops. She remained silent for a moment.

"It was a joke," she said at last. "A bit of fun. You see, it really was a computer-generated world just like this, but with the ability to overlay itself on this one."

"What was a joke, Debbie?" asked Ramirez.

"Do you know what happens if you type 'recursion' into Google Search, Sergeant?"

"What's 'recursion'?"

"In programming, recursion is when the result of an operation is the operation repeating itself and its results, over and over again. In art and other uses it's where an image repeats itself within itself, infinitely. Anyway, type 'recursion' into Google Search and it'll ask, 'did you mean recursion?' Programmer humor. We did something similar, for a gag."

"What?"

"We programmed ourselves into it. Alternate versions of ourselves. Just avatars really, but when the program began to self-elaborate . . ."

"What happened?"

"We saw it . . ." There was a great sadness in Deborah's face, in her voice. "We saw through all the levels of the game. We saw all levels of ourselves. All the overlapping realities, none of which were real."

Ramirez turned to Macbeth and shrugged helplessly.

"Debbie," said Macbeth, "what does that mean?"

"It means they were both right."

"Who were right?"

"I know Dr Corbin suspects I suffer from multiple personalities. He's right, I do. We all do. Remember I said about our reflections?"

"Who else was right?" asked Ramirez.

"John Astor. The future really has already happened. And we really are phantoms of our own making."

46

ARI. ISRAEL

It stopped. The sound, the shuddering of the earth beneath their feet, the swirl of windswept dust all ended as suddenly as they had begun. There was a moment of stunned silence.

"What the fuck was that?" shouted Benny, who stood, like the others, with his legs wide and braced, arms out from his body, as if trying to balance on solid ground.

"Earthquake . . ." Ari stood the same way, motionless, as if expecting something more.

They looked at each other, around themselves, checking the world was still there. Ari noticed the protestors watching them, as if puzzled more by the soldiers' actions than by the shock that had coursed through the bedrock beneath their feet.

"Maybe it's not real . . ." said Benny. "You know, like that thing in Boston."

Ari shook his head. "That was real. They get tremors here . . . Eilat had a quake back in '95. To do with being on the edge of two plates or something. Chill . . . it's over."

Eventually some of the tension eased from the soldiers' posture. Ari shook his head and laughed.

Again.

This time stronger.

The ground heaved and pulsed. Again a wind came from nowhere, the air granular, laden with desert sand. The movement in the earth brought Benny to his knees and Ari struggled

to stay on his feet. His eyes locked with Shalev's, who was supporting himself with one hand braced against the armored personnel carrier.

Another deafening noise. But this time unlike the first two sounds; unlike any sound Ari had ever heard. A massive shudder coursed through the ground beneath their feet, as if something deep within the earth had cracked open. And with the tremor the wind seemed to pick up in severity. Benny and the others were shouting, but their voices were drowned out in the storm. Ari could no longer see the elaborate frontages of the resort hotels. Everything was becoming lost in a swirl of sand and debris, but he was sure he should still have been able to see the hotel. Dismissing the thought, he moved over to help Benny get to his feet, but a sudden gust lifted the small corporal from the ground and into the vortex of sand and palm fragments.

"Benny!" Ari screamed, running towards his friend. The wind hit him like a tidal wave, forcing the air from his lungs and, now stronger than gravity, ripped the ground away from beneath his feet. A primeval panic rose in him as he realized he was helpless against the force of Nature. Ari felt a strong grip close on his arm and he turned to see Shalev, who started to drag him towards the flank of the personnel carrier.

"We need cover!" the Haredi shouted in Ari's ear.

"Benny! What about Benny?"

"I'll go back for him. I'm heavier than you." Shalev placed his broad hand flat against Ari's chest and pushed him hard against the side of the carrier, then down so he was sitting, his back propped against it. "Stay here!"

Ari watched as Shalev pushed back into the storm, his outline fading.

The storm ceased.

It happened within a space of seconds. The wind was gone. The dust and sand hung in the air for what seemed an age, then settled slowly. The sand-caked shapes of the rest of the platoon became clear again, most prone on the ground, easing themselves to their feet, like clay men rising from the earth. He saw Shalev haul Benny to his feet. They looked at each other through the now faint curtain of suspended desert sand.

Ari moved away from the personnel carrier and towards the group of soldiers. He still could not see the outline of the hotels behind them, but the sun now probed the dust with bright fingers. It looked like the end of the world.

Ari had his back to it.

He realized in that sliver of a second that he had his back to it. Whatever it was, it was right behind him, right now. He knew that by the faces of the others as they stared past him towards the sea; by the shock, the awe and the terror in their expressions. But a terror greater than could have been caused by the storm. He saw Shalev sink to his knees slowly, his mouth agape. Benny Kagan stood frozen.

It was behind him. He could hear it thunder and growl. He could feel it cause the earth beneath his feet to shiver and shudder. Whatever it was that was behind him, he did not want to turn. Whatever sight had made statues of his comrades, he didn't want to see it. He must not turn.

He turned.

As he did he felt the ground shake again, as if the whole world beneath his feet had dropped ten meters before crashing to a sudden stop.

The storm that had passed over them was now a whirlwind, but a whirlwind like no other Ari had seen. The funnel was fifty meters across and arched and twisted a kilometer up into a vast, fuming, black cloud. And beneath it . . . beneath it . . . Beneath it Ari saw something he could not believe. That he had never believed, that he had refused to believe, all of his life.

"Oh God . . ." Ari muttered. "Oh God, oh God, oh God . . ."

It had happened. It had happened and it had happened here. Where they were . . . this had been Yam Suph. This had been the Sea of Reeds.

This was where Moses had stood.

With a certainty he had never experienced before in his life, Ari knew he was witnessing God's covenant. The sign of God's protection of His people.

Ari Livnat stood on the beach at Eilat and stared out at the impossible. He gazed at the two titanic walls of water that rose up like gigantic mounds of heaped, rippling glass, a channel cleared between them. Lightning fizzed and crackled and sparked across the impossibly vertical surfaces of the water. Ari knew what he was seeing and refused to believe he was seeing it. But he was seeing it.

Ari Livnat was watching the Red Sea part.

He did not know how long he had stood there, gazing at it, seeing it, believing it. Eventually he turned back from it and walked past Shalev who, still on his knees, was rocking back and forth, repeating a prayer over and over. Ari told Benny and the others to follow him as he walked over to where the protestors still stood, staring at the soldiers, confused, mute, unmoving. Disbelieving.

He knew in that instant that they had not seen what he had seen. What the others had seen. A sign that was not for them. A message from a God that was not theirs.

A colossal, irresistible certainty settled on Ari and unslung his carbine from his shoulder.

"Kill them," he said to the others in a dull, cold voice. "Kill them all . . ."

There was a sound like more thunder. But this time not from the sky.

47

JOHN MACBETH. BOSTON

The lead had lightened from the sky and Brian Newcombe, waiting for Macbeth on the steps of the Administration Building, suggested they take a walk around the hospital grounds.

Macbeth agreed, but he was still haunted by Deborah's delusion: it was an occupational hazard of psychiatry that sometimes the alternate reality of a patient's delusion would loiter in the corners of your mind, like a book you'd just finished reading.

Newcombe cut straight to the chase. "I've been asked to persuade you not to return to Denmark."

Macbeth laughed. "That's impossible. I'm flying out tonight . . ."

"We'll take care of all of that. We need you here much more than the Copenhagen Project needs you in Denmark."

"Well, that's all very flattering, but as I told you, if you can track him down, Josh Hoberman is much—"

Newcombe cut Macbeth off. "Josh Hoberman was fished out of the Potomac this morning, his neck broken."

Macbeth stopped. "Murdered?"

Newcombe nodded, his expression serious beneath the Cape yachtsman tan. "More than likely by Blind Faith. There've been more killings. And more bomb attacks – Washington, London, Haifa. Islamicists *and* Blind Faith are both involved. And some anti-secular, anti-technology, ultra-orthodox Jewish extremist

group has claimed responsibility for the Haifa bombing. And there's news breaking about something else happening in Israel. A massacre. I'm telling you, John, we're looking at a world stripped of reason – a new Dark Age with competing superstitions ripping each other apart in holy war."

"And they're using the hallucination epidemic as justification . . ." said Macbeth.

"All this anti-progress, religiomanic crap is feeding on the phenomena. They don't accept they're hallucinations, they believe they're God-given 'visions'. Every mullah, evangelist, every shade of cult crackpot in between – is pointing to these events as the sign of an approaching Rapture or Second Coming or whatever the hell it is that's promised in the particular brand of eschatology they peddle. We've got to get to the bottom of it and stop it in its tracks before the whole world loses its reason."

"I see your point, Brian, but I just can't let Poulsen down. The best thing I can do is continue with my work, which is exactly the kind of thing these lunatics want to bring to an end. Anyway, I'm not an epidemiologist," Macbeth said as they passed the knoll beneath the maple tree.

"We're not dealing with an epidemic, and you know that. There's no pattern, no statistical focus, no patient zero." He sighed, taking a moment to collect himself. Macbeth could see the stress was beginning to unravel Newcombe's professional cool. "We're dealing with something unprecedented. These events are beginning to have physiological consequences. People are being hurt – really, physically injured – by things that aren't there. A TV executive in New York hallucinated that he was burning to death. No one else around him experienced the hallucination, but they saw his skin flake and his flesh blacken. The autopsy confirmed death by thermal injury, despite there being no fire, and his lungs were damaged in a way consistent with smoke inhalation, but there wasn't a single smoke particle to be found in his lung tissue. He didn't just hallucinate he was burning to death . . . he really *did* burn to death."

"It doesn't make sense . . ." Macbeth shook his head.

"There's more," said Newcombe. "We've identified distinct chronobiological elements to the phenomenon. The circadian rhythms of subjects are severely disturbed for the duration of the hallucinations – probably what causes the déjà vu-like feeling before and the disorientation afterwards. I know this sounds crazy, but everyone so far has exhibited symptoms of extreme desynchronosis."

"Jet lag?" Macbeth said without incredulity; he had experienced something like it himself after the Boston ghostquake.

"Both ultradian and infradian rhythms are affected. Female subjects reported disruption to their menstrual cycles." Newcombe shook his head. "It's almost as if during the hallucination some kind of powerful mimesis deceives the body into believing it has been transported to another time – perhaps the same mechanism that causes the body to mimic real injuries."

"Are you saying that these events are some kind of psychic time travel?"

"Of course not. But the feeling of a temporal shift engages every sense and causes physical changes. Like the few people who experience very real motion sickness when playing video games."

"Not so few . . ." said Macbeth. "I'm one of them."

"There's something else . . . Look at this and tell me what you're looking at." Newcombe took a smartphone from his pocket, keyed something in and handed the phone to Macbeth. The photograph that filled the screen showed a museum display: an impossibly giant creature with massive jaws and teeth, dwarfing the person standing in front of the display.

"It's a wolf . . ." he answered. "Obviously not a real one . . .

330

It's too big and the what-big-teeth-you've-got thing is a bit overdone. Unless I'm wrong and there's some kind of giant wolf out there."

"No, you're not wrong. But what you're looking at *was* real right enough, and ten times the size of any wolf that ever lived. *Andrewsarchus mongoliensis*, the largest carnivorous mammal ever to walk the Earth. Looks like a giant wolf, but it couldn't have been less related. It's actually more of a sheep or a goat. A giant, hypercarnivorous sheep that would have been able to bite a man clean in half, had there been any men around at the time. It's a perfect example of convergent evolution, where one species ends up looking very much like another, totally unrelated species."

"Okay . . ." said Macbeth.

"*Andrewsarchus* has been extinct for more than thirty million years. Its main habitat was what is now Mongolia and western China. We've had a report from our Far East team about a girl there who described this–" he stabbed the phone's touchscreen with his forefinger "–to a tee. Right down to the way it didn't have proper claws, but feet with hooflike talons. And right here in Boston, a woman was able to describe, in perfect detail, giant prehistoric insects that only a serious paleoentomologist could have identified. What's more, she described the 'richness' of the air in her hallucination and how she was able to run for long distances without breathlessness. All consistent with a time – over *three hundred million years ago* – when oxygen levels were way higher than those we have today – thirty-five per cent instead of twenty, allowing insects to grow to massive sizes. Like the Chinese girl with her perfect description of an *Andrewsarchus*, this woman described a giant sea scorpion, *Jaekelopterus*, in detail that confirmed what has only been theory to date." Newcombe let the information sink in.

"Could be cryptomnesia . . ." said Macbeth. "They've seen

331

pictures or watched a documentary they've forgotten about and the information has resurrected itself in the hallucinations . . ."

Newcombe shook his head. "It's all too detailed, too correct. In every single incident, the hallucination has been consistent with an event that we know has taken place, or could credibly have taken place, at some time in the past. That passenger plane that came down just outside Harrisonburg in Virginia? The black box data recorder showed it crashed because the pilot took sudden and extreme evasive action shortly after takeoff to avoid an ash plume and a mountainous caldera, when they were actually overflying a hill only nineteen hundred feet high. Turns out that this insignificant bump in the Virginian landscape – Mole Hill – is the eroded stump of what was a massive active volcano, thousands of feet high, about fifty million years ago. And you know that the event we all experienced here in Boston matched exactly the 1775 Cape Ann earthquake."

"Brian, I don't know what you're trying to imply with all of this, but it isn't very scientific . . ."

"Perhaps not *medically* scientific. Maybe these events aren't clinical manifestations at all . . . Maybe this has got something to do with – I don't know – physics. Something to do with time."

Again Macbeth stopped walking; he stood in the path and looked up at the sky, which had brightened only to a diffuse sodium gray.

"You're not the only person to have suggested that today, Brian . . ."

48

JOHN MACBETH. BOSTON

If there was one aspect of culture that was truly global, thought Macbeth, then it was the airport. An airport lounge was an airport lounge wherever you were in the world: identical seating, identical lighting, identical vast expanses of glass offering identical views of acres of tarmac runways. Even the coffee was identical. It was as if the same small team of architects, interior designers, store-fitters and glum-faced personnel were air-freighted around the world from airport to airport simply to disconcert the traveler by making the place of arrival as blandly indistinguishable from the place of departure as possible. Even climate had no part to play: hermetically sealed lounges were heated in Reykjavik or air-cooled in Abu Dhabi to a universal seventy-two degrees; just close enough to body temperature to make you feel vaguely sweaty and wilted.

It was not an environment that relaxed Macbeth. He hated airports more than planes; and he hated planes with a passion. It wasn't that he had a fear of flying, he loathed the hours of waiting, the stress of delays, cancellations and connections; the empty and often openly hostile faces behind check-in desks or at the TSA security gates; the total, desolate soullessness of it all. It seemed strange to him that a place so full of people should be so empty of humanity.

He sat in the departure lounge and called his brother from his cellphone and told him about Brian Newcombe's insistent offer that he join the THS investigation team, and how the epidemiologist had not taken Macbeth's equally insistent refusal well. "You're maybe better out of all of this in Copenhagen," Casey said. "Phone me when you get in."

"It'll be late . . ."

"I don't care, call me. By the way, I've been looking at your laptop—"

"And I've been looking at the one you lent me," Macbeth interrupted his brother. "That damned folder is back."

There was a silence at the other end.

"Casey?"

"The folder has appeared on the new laptop?" asked Casey eventually.

"That's what I said . . ."

"When did it appear?"

"I was checking my emails and I just saw it sitting there. I still can't open it. I thought—"

"Listen . . . I got in touch with Jimmy Mrozek – my IT guy at MIT – the one I told you about. I was going to give him your laptop to check over, but the folder has gone. Disappeared."

"What?" said Macbeth. "You mean it's jumped magically from one computer to the next?"

"Maybe exactly that. It sounds like it appeared again on the new laptop as soon as you connected to the Internet."

"Weird."

"And it gets weirder . . . Jimmy – the IT guy – told me that it was the second time someone asked him to look into a mysterious folder they couldn't open. Exactly the same as what you've got. But he didn't get a chance to look at that one either."

"It spontaneously disappeared too?"

"No John, the folder didn't spontaneously disappear . . . the computer and its owner did. It belonged to Professor Steven Gillman."

It was Macbeth's turn to be silent.

"Like I said . . ." Casey's voice on the phone was tight, anxious.

"Make sure to let me know just as soon as you're safe in your apartment."

With no direct flight to Copenhagen from Logan International, Macbeth was flying British Airways via London Heathrow. He recalculated the misery in his head: another hour and a half before boarding, providing there were no delays, six hours twenty minutes to London, another three hours ten minutes waiting for his connection, then one hour fifty-five minutes to Copenhagen. A total of not less than twelve hours and fifty-five minutes, not accounting for delays, EU Immigration or waiting at the luggage carousel. He would spend most of that time using the technology he normally eschewed to isolate himself from his environment: his MP3 player, eBook reader and laptop providing him with an earphone-encapsulated realm in which to confine his consciousness and restrict his awareness of his surroundings. And contact with his fellow passengers.

There was a commotion somewhere further up the departure hall, a couple of gates up. A woman shouting, then another screaming. Macbeth, along with several other waiting passengers, stood up and looked across towards the noise, which seemed to come from somewhere over by the window. It was something else about airports that was now truly global: in the post-nine-eleven world any disturbance in an airport, any hint of official response, provoked immediate alarm. No one spoke, just craned necks to try to see what was going on. Whatever it was, it was out of sight, a curtain of travelers gathering around the commotion and obscuring Macbeth's view.

Three transit security officers and a heavy-hipped female BPD cop trotted purposefully past his gate and towards whatever was going on. The knot of people by the window parted for them then closed behind them. There was the distance-muffled sound of a heated debate, of vehement protest, of authoritative tones. Some of the other passengers remained standing and watching,

335

but Macbeth retook his seat. After a few minutes the uniforms came back, escorting two women in their thirties, both of whom were clearly distressed.

"But I'm telling you, we both saw it . . ." one of the women said in pleading protest to the female cop, who ignored her. "Both of us."

As they passed, Macbeth noticed that the other woman was silent with a glazed, empty look and he realized she was in some kind of shock. All eyes followed the small group's progress until it disappeared from the hall. Then slowly and with shrugs to one another, the passengers sat back down.

People were becoming used to bizarre behavior, Macbeth realized.

A new addition arrived, a middle-aged Englishman in a crumpled suit, who picked his way through legs and hand luggage to an empty seat. When he had gotten himself settled he took out his cellphone, hit a key and started to have one of those inappropriately loud and personally detailed conversations that so many people seemed to feel free to make in airports. It was a phenomenon that interested Macbeth as a psychiatrist: the anonymity some people feel in a crowd of strangers, as if they are surrounded by philosophical zombies. The Englishman spoke with one of those nasal accents that sounded whiny and Macbeth tried to shut out his chatter as he griped on his phone to his wife about having to take a later flight.

But despite himself, Macbeth found himself eavesdropping on the latter part of the Englishman's half of the conversation.

"I think I've just seen one of these weird happenings we've read about . . . yes, the hallucination thing. Yeah, here at the airport, a few minutes ago . . . These two women . . . well, they went mad. It started when one of them complained to ground staff that no one was telling passengers if their flight was going to be delayed because of the fog. 'What fog?' says the airline woman. 'What do you mean, what fog?' they start shouting. 'Look out of the window,' they say. 'That fog!' Well, I'm telling

336

you, it's a bright sunny day here, not even a cloud in the sky, but these two loonies start raving about this low-lying fog, saying it's lying like a blanket over the runways and, according to them, you wouldn't be able to see five feet in front of you if you were at ground level . . . What? . . . Yeah, I know . . . No, they were American. Anyway, that's not the end of it. One of them starts screaming her head off. Then the other. Bloody hysterical. They said they'd both just seen a plane crash and of course that gets the other passengers all excited . . . What? No, of course there wasn't . . . They start going on about this plane that they've just seen crash as it came in to land. No one else can see any plane . . . but they start bawling and screaming, saying that the plane has crashed in the fog . . . They said they saw it above the fog then it flew into it and exploded over at the sea end of the runway. Mental. Everybody's all worked up now and trying to see what they're talking about, but there's nothing to see – no crash, no fog, nothing. No one else sees a thing . . . No, I'm not making it up . . . It was bloody weird. Anyway, they get in such a state and start screaming so much that they get them- selves arrested . . . Yeah, I know . . ."

The conversation turned to more personal things, still shared with everyone within earshot, and Macbeth tuned out of it. He thought about what the two distraught women had claimed to have seen, and a memory nagged at him. A memory from early childhood. It had been late July, 1973. He'd been at his grand- parents' house watching TV when the news came on: fuzzy images of debris scattered at the seawall end of the runway, a fogbank still lurking maliciously just offshore in Boston Harbor.

A real past event. Repeated in a hallucination, just like Brian Newcombe had said.

He looked at his watch, then in the direction the two women with their official escort had taken, then at the information board above the gate.

With a sigh, he took out his cellphone and called Newcombe.

49

GEORG POULSEN. COPENHAGEN

Georg Poulsen sat in the living room of his house. The only sounds in the space he occupied came from outside; and even they were few and ignored, the house being set back from the road, facing out over the quiet, tree-fringed inlet of water. There was no TV, no radio on, no music playing. A book sat on the coffee table, but it was not there for Poulsen's enjoyment. This was his house, not his home. The day he'd returned here alone from the hospital, it had ceased to be anything more than a space to be occupied between the important businesses of his life. Somewhere he slept, somewhere he waited: a bridge between one task and the next, between the bright, hard focus of his work and the painful joy of his time with Margarethe at the hospital.

But if what Larssen had told him was true, all that was about to change: this structure, this meaningless assembly of rooms and halls, would again become the center of his life. If Margarethe came back. If her care really could be transferred there, then it could soon become their home again. In the meantime he waited, and the house waited.

Margarethe had loved this house at first sight. It was neither grand nor architecturally distinguished: a single-story, traditional red-brick-and-pantiles Danish cottage, when seen from the road. But the previous owners had added a large, more modern extension at the back, which faced south and towards the small fiord, installing large picture windows and effectively shifting the orientation of the building. Those large windows continuously changed the entire nature of the house: Margarethe had always said that it wasn't just the light they let into the house, but the seasons too: changing the interior with shifts of color and tone, in phase with the shifts of Nature and time of year. It had been an environment that enlivened and calmed; that had given them the moment to enjoy and the future to imagine. It had been their place in the world, apart from the world. And, with the large, bright room with the pale blue walls at the end of the main hall, it would be their baby's place in the world too.

Except now there would be no baby.

As soon as Larssen had made the suggestion, Poulsen had set about making plans. The baby's room would be ideal for Margarethe, and he had already had additional power points installed to cater for the technology that would be an essential part of her day-to-day existence. But he would paint the walls a different color.

Picking up the book from the coffee table, he stared at it apprehensively. He would start reading it to his wife tonight. It had been another of those titles that Margarethe, who was infinitely more literary-minded than her husband, had told him about years before. It had taken him a month of scouring his memory and the Internet to track it down.

"There is no such thing as an original idea," Margarethe had once told him. "Whatever you can think of, someone, somewhere, will already have thought of it – in another form, maybe, but they will have thought of it. The challenge is what you do with the idea."

She had said all of this when she had told him about the book. It was called simply, he had eventually remembered, *We*. And the Internet had restored the author's name to his recall. Yevgeny Zamyatin.

We, Margarethe had explained, was a dystopian masterpiece

written in 1921, banned in Russia for over sixty years, but translated into every other major language. The novel was set in a
future where all buildings were made of glass, so that the
seemingly perpetually content populace could be kept under
the constant and purportedly beneficent surveillance of the
all-seeing 'Benefactor' who enforces his will through 'Guard-
ians'. The first major review had been by the English writer
George Orwell, inspiring him to write *Nineteen Eighty-four*.

Poulsen felt insistent fingers of doubt and fear creep around
his heart: what if it was the wrong book? What if she had read
it so often she wouldn't want Poulsen to read it to her again?
And, worst of all, what if she could not hear his reading?

Larssen had explained that there was the possibility of
damage to Margarethe's reticular activating system, located at
the top of the brainstem and close to where the bleed had
been detected on the MRI. Poulsen knew that the reticular
activating system was what governed states of arousal; it determined when and how much you were awake, gave the rhythm
to the cycle of sleep and wakefulness. Maybe Margarethe slept
through every visit when he read to her. Perhaps she hung
permanently suspended in the eternal twilight between sleep
and wakefulness.

It was entirely possible that Margarethe had never heard a
single word he had uttered.

Even that wasn't Georg Poulsen's greatest fear. In a universe
of terrifying possibilities, the specter that haunted him most
was that he may never solve the brain–computer interface
problem, or solve it too late for it to be any use to Margarethe.

Others in the Project were astounded by Poulsen's candor:
that he freely and openly shared, in his monthly press briefings,
every advance the team had made. Everyone knew that,
although it should be above such considerations, science was
an athleticism of the mind and you constantly competed
against others. There were Nobels to be won, careers and

reputations to be made – yet Project Director Poulsen was committed to the most astonishing, absolute transparency. To be fair, he was as candid in his demands of other researchers that they reciprocate by sharing their progress and findings.

"There is no such thing as an original idea. Whatever you can think of, someone, somewhere, will already have thought of it – in another form, maybe, but they will have thought of it. The challenge is what you do with the idea." Margarethe's comment on literary creativity had become the central tenet of Poulsen's scientific method.

Even before, he had never been a believer in the heroic theory of scientific discovery. It was extremely rare, he knew, for one person working alone to unlock a secret hidden from the rest of science: Wallace had proposed evolution at exactly the same time as Darwin; Leibnitz formulated calculus at the same time as Newton; von Ohain, Campini and Whittle all developed the jet engine independently and concurrently.

Poulsen didn't really care who took the credit, who collected the Nobel. All that mattered was for the breakthrough to be made. All he wanted was to be able to connect to his wife's imprisoned mind; to give her some kind of externality, even if it was false.

Every time he thought of easing the pressure on his colleagues, loosening his control, the picture of his immobile, staring wife filled his mind.

He looked at the book again. Had he gotten it wrong?

He put it back down on the coffee table when a sound tarnished the sterile silence. He got up to answer the phone.

50

CASEY. OXFORD

"More wine?" asked the cheerful waitress.

A large marquee had been put up in the grounds to make allowance for the unpredictability of the British weather, but the sky had remained contrarily cloudless and everybody had elected to stand outside, huddled in cheerful groups, sipping at their wine and enjoying the pleasant warmth, the golden early evening light and the views out across the university's parks.

"Why not?" he said, placing his empty wine glass on the tray and lifting a full one. "It's a symposium, after all."

The cute girl with the cropped short blonde hair frowned in puzzlement. She looked totally out of place in the white blouse and black skirt; Casey guessed she was an undergraduate volunteer, earning some extra cash.

"A symposium . . ." he explained. "In ancient Greece, symposia were wine-drinking parties. Not a gathering of old physics farts . . ."

"Oh . . . I see," she said. She had one of those British accents that Casey found difficult to place, geographically or socially. He could tell from her smile that she was interested in him, as he was in her. He was about to say something else when he felt someone slap him heartily on the shoulder.

"Casey Macbeth . . . How the hell are you? Looking forward to hearing the answer to life, the universe and everything?" It was Juergen Franke: a stereotypically huge, ruddy-complexioned, blond and blue-eyed German who had an equally unstereo-typically jolly disposition and sense of humor. He always gave the impression of being some kind of hardy, down-to-earth, North German farmer; but Casey knew that he had a mind of frightening brilliance. Franke leaned forward conspiratorially. "I believe the answer is forty-two . . ."

"I'm fine Juergen. How are things at CERN?"

"We're still going round in circles," he said and laughed loudly at his own lame joke: Franke was part of the Large Hadron Collider team, sending photons hurtling at near light speed in opposite directions around a seventeen-mile loop, deep underground in central Europe. He had played a significant part in the hunt for the Higgs and had done groundbreaking work in the field of virtual particles. He could also drink just about anybody he met under the table. "You?"

"I'm fine. Glad to be here. Drink?" Casey asked.

"Do you have beer?" Franke asked the waitress.

"Sorry, only wine. It's a symposium, after all," she said and smiled at Casey.

"What?" Franke frowned, then – catching the exchange of looks between them – grinned broadly. "Oh, I see, I see . . . It's like that, is it? Don't be fooled by his boyish American charm," he said to the waitress. "He is one of these Mormon fellows . . . has a wife and fifteen children back home in the States. Or is it fifteen wives and a child?"

They both looked at him wryly.

"Hmmm . . . I think I am urgently needed over . . ." Franke searched the crowd for a direction then, picking one at random, pointed in it, " . . . there . . . I'll see you in the lecture theater, Casey. If you can tear yourself away, that is."

"He's actually very bright," said Casey once Franke was gone. "He just hides it well."

"I better go circulate," she said with a small, apologetic shrug. "This lot are a thirsty bunch . . ." She referred to the one hundred and seventy physicists from around the world who had assembled outside the Martin Wood Complex of the Department of Physics at Oxford University.

"You a student here?'" Casey clutched at anything to stop her walking off.

"Physics, yes. Second year. A sophomore, as you call it in America."

"Good school . . . what's the course like?"

"We're doing Electromagnetism and Optics as well as Thermal and Quantum Physics this year. Everyone seems smarter than me."

"Get used to it, how do you think I feel with this bunch?" he waved his glass in an arc to indicate the assembled physicists.

"Where are you from?" she asked. "I mean what part of the States?"

"Boston. MIT. I'm here for Professor Blackwell's presentation."

"I guessed that much."

"Oh . . . sorry: Casey Macbeth . . ." He held out his hand. She shrugged apologetically and nodded towards the tray she held filled with wine glasses.

"I'm Emma Boyd. Nice to meet you, Casey Macbeth. I'm sorry, but I really do have to do the rounds."

"Sure . . ." Casey said and smiled disappointedly. "It was nice to meet you."

She smiled back and started to move away before checking herself.

"I'll be around after the presentation," she said. "Serving coffee in the marquee. Maybe I'll see you there?"

"You can count on it. Then maybe afterwards—" Casey was interrupted by someone over by the door to the main hall making an announcement.

"Could all delegates please make their way into the main lecture theater. Professor Blackwell's presentation begins in ten minutes and the doors will be closed in five . . ."

"Looks like I better go," he said. "See you later?"

"See you later . . ." she said and smiled.

Given the events at MIT and elsewhere, Casey was not surprised at the level of security. Added to the sense of siege from fundamentalists felt by the scientific community, the whole of Europe seemed to be in shock: the Red Sea Massacre, as it was now widely known, had set fire to the Middle East once more and the supporters of the European Greater Integration Act were now fighting for its survival. Even the Italians, British and Bulgarians, who had been the principal motivators behind the Levant Accession, accepted that the violence that had erupted as a consequence of the massacre made accession impossible for the foreseeable future. The European Union had declared that the terrorist attack alert throughout its territory had been raised to red.

Probably because he had never before seen one in the flesh, Casey had always imagined British policemen to be cheery bobbies on bicycles two by two, armed only with a smile and an out-of-sight Victorian truncheon. The cops who stood guard at the entrances to the Martin Wood Complex were anything but: baseball-capped, Kevlar-vested and with Heckler and Koch machine pistols strapped across their chests, they glowered suspiciously at all who arrived at the event.

Burly private security men in cheap suits, tattoos and earpieces guarded the exits, and once all the delegates were assembled in the lecture hall the doors were closed and locked behind them, making Casey feel oddly claustrophobic.

He sat halfway up the tiered seating, next to Franke. The avuncular German's jollity did something to take the edge off Casey's indistinct anxiousness. He felt very aware of Professor Gillman's absence. The plan had been for the two MIT scientists to fly to England together. Casey had wanted to talk to Gillman about the Simulists and Gabriel Rees, and the flight would have

345

been an ideal opportunity to ease into such a sensitive subject. But the explosions at MIT had put paid to that: Gillman's body had not been separately identified, but as he'd been in the lab at the time of the blast and had not been seen since, he was now officially listed among the dead. Gabriel would remain a mystery unsolved.

Looking around the lecture hall, Casey realized that he knew almost every one of the one hundred and seventy delegates; and not just by reputation. Particle physics at this level was a small community, even if it was spread across the world. It was an impressive assembly: the brains in this room were the best of the best, and Casey felt a thrill of proud excitement as he took his seat. He sensed the same electricity course through the entire audience as a tall, gaunt man of seventy entered through the side door, locking it behind him, and walked across the stage. As he took his place at the podium, the three large screens suspended behind him flickered into life and were filled with the same image. In this hall of Science, Michelangelo's God reached out and gave Adam life with a touch of fingertips.

"Ladies and gentlemen . . ." Blackwell's voice croaked slightly and he sipped some water before starting again. "Ladies and gentlemen, first of all, I want to thank every one of you for coming. I know some of you have travelled great distances and interrupted important work to be here, and that is hugely and humbly appreciated. I must also thank you for bearing with the unusual security strictures to which you have been subjected. I am sure that you will forgive this when you under-stand the enormity of what I have to tell you here today. I promise you that this place and this day will be marked as the most significant in the history of science."

Blackwell paused and took another sip of water. Casey noticed that his hand trembled, something he'd never seen before in any of the many Blackwell lectures he had attended. Something about that tremor made the hair on the nape of

Casey's neck bristle. He had also noticed that the Englishman's delivery was less assured than normal. Whatever he had to tell the assembled audience, it was of a magnitude to humble the world's greatest living scientist.

"You are all here by specific, personal invitation," Blackwell continued. "My colleagues, my peers, my friends. Assembled here before me are the finest minds on this planet, each and every one of one you dedicated to the quest for knowledge, for understanding. There has been no nobler calling in mankind's history and I am proud, honored and humbled to have been one of your number."

Blackwell paused and pressed a button on the podium. The two outer screens remained unchanged and God still gave Adam life, but the center screen now bore the title THE PROMETHEUS ANSWER, in plain white lettering against a blue background. The mere appearance of the words sent another pulse of electricity through Casey's spine.

"We all know who Prometheus was," said Blackwell. "The Titan who sneaked into the Chamber of Zeus and, setting light to a reed from an ember, stole fire from the gods and gave it to mortal man, whom Prometheus himself had fashioned from clay and whom Zeus had forbidden from having knowledge of fire. Prometheus's punishment for this theft was eternal torment, chained to a cliff while an eagle ate his liver each day, only for it to regenerate at night for the same anguish to follow the next day, and the next, and the next for all time.

"In that tale lies a warning, I suppose, that perhaps some knowledge is beyond knowing, or too dangerous to be known. All of us here, as quantum physicists, are familiar with the concept of a knowledge that lies beyond the limits of expression, even beyond the limits of human understanding. We seek to build machines to augment our intellectual capabilities, to help us to know the unknowable and understand the supra-comprehensible. Each one of us here is a Titan who has spent a lifetime trying to sneak into the Chamber of Zeus."

Blackwell paused. He gripped the edges of the podium, suddenly focused, intense.

"I have brought you all here to tell you that I succeeded. I built such a machine and because of it I know the unknowable. It allowed me to gaze into the smallest moment of universal creation. I saw written in it the history and the destiny of everything we know and everything we are yet to know. I have seen how it all begins and how it all ends. I have been in the Chamber and I have stolen from the gods that which they did not want Man to know. I have the Prometheus Answer." Blackwell scanned the audience, the intensity gone and replaced with something like sorrow.

"I am a man of science. As a physicist, I have scrutinized two universes: the inconceivably vast universe around us and the inconceivably minute universe of the quantum realm. Each of these universes works following completely contradictory laws, yet exists concurrently with the other . . . dependent on the other. We have known for decades that there must be some connection we have missed, some mechanism we have overlooked, that unites them."

A heartbeat's pause.

"I have found that connection, I have seen that mechanism at work."

The excited buzz from the audience exploded into applause and cheers, but Blackwell held up a hand. It wasn't the physicist's gesture that stilled the audience, however, it was the sight of tears seeking out the furrows on the scientist's gaunt cheeks.

"I am sorry, my friends . . ." Blackwell's voice shook with emotion. The silence in the audience was now total, absolute. "I am so terribly sorry. What I have found out is that everything to which I have devoted my life – to which you have devoted your lives – is a sham. I sat in front of a computer screen and

348

watched a bad, bad joke play out. I sought to steal from the gods and all I came away with is the sound of their laughter in my ears."

"My God . . ." Franke whispered to Casey. "He's completely lost it. It's like he's having a breakdown . . ."

Casey shook his head impatiently, his focus on the tall, frail figure at the podium. He thought about Gabriel Rees, and what Macbeth had told him about the research student's state of mind.

"Prometheus," continued Blackwell, "was the most complex scientific project ever undertaken; a complexity far beyond that of the moon landings. We have achieved things in the pursuit of the Prometheus Answer that were, in themselves, answers to major scientific challenges. I can tell you, for example, that we solved the decoherence problem and created a quantum computer of unprecedented power . . ."

Blackwell had to pause again and hold up a hand to restrain the clamor from the audience.

"Please . . . please . . ." He waited until quiet was restored. "What Prometheus allowed us to do was to look at the complete fabric of the universe, at its origins. At its ultimate destiny. Prometheus gave us the answer. The complete, unequivocal, terrifying answer . . ." Blackwell's voice faltered. "And the result of my theft from the Chamber is the phenomenon we have all experienced, all around the world. What we have experienced as hallucinations hasn't been hallucinations at all. It is time folding in on itself as the fabric of our universe collapses at the quantum level."

There was an even greater clamor from the audience, questions shouted to the podium. Again Blackwell held up his hand.

"The reason for these events lies in the knowledge we now have, the technology we now create. We are becoming . . . We are become as the gods themselves, but it cannot be allowed. The gods will not accept it. You see, what I have discovered is that everything I have been striving for, everything I have believed, that we all believed, is a lie . . . My life has been wasted in pursuit of a pretense. I have found the great knowledge . . ." The tears now streaked the scientist's cheeks, his voice that of a trembling, frightened old man. "And now I have to share that great knowledge with you. And for that unforgivable sin, my friends, I am so sorry . . . so terribly sorry . . ."

Emma Boyd spent the free time she had sitting on the grass, enjoying the last of the evening sun, revising from the books she'd taken from the shoulder bag she had stuffed behind the trestle table in the marquee, where everything was now set up for the coffee to be served after the presentation.

There were a few physics students helping out at the event, dressed in white shirts and black trousers or skirts, and Emma wondered how many of them, like her, would be trying to eavesdrop on conversations between delegates and get some hint of what it was that was of such magnitude to attract the top brains in physics from around the world.

She was thinking of something else, too: the American she had met. Casey. Maybe he would share some secrets with her; she knew that there was something about him that made her want to share her secrets with him. But there was no future in it: he was Boston-based and she was anchored here, in Oxford. Why was she even thinking that far ahead? It was mad: they had only exchanged a handful of words. They were strangers. And, anyway, he was too old for her. She had worked out that he must be much older than he looked.

She sighed. Maybe they would be out soon. If he asked her, she would go on somewhere with him afterwards.

Sitting cross-legged on the grass was her favored posture for study, but the stupid skirt made it difficult, cutting the circulation to her legs and making her stiff, so Emma stood up and stamped the cramp out of her foot. She walked across the grass towards the Martin Wood Complex. For a modern building – and it was very recently built – it was very attractive and light years better than the 1960s gray concrete monolith of the Denys Wilkinson Building, where Emma seemed to spend half her life attending Astrophysics lectures.

One thing about the symposium Emma found strange was the security. Two men who looked less like University Security and more like nightclub bouncers stood in front of the large glass doors of the Martin Wood Lecture Theatre. Why were they needed?

She saw it pulse.

The thing she would remember most, afterwards – in the hospital, during the months of recovery and rehabilitation, in the darkness of her life afterwards – was that she actually saw the plasticity of the glass. Emma would never be able to work out how her brain had been able to detect the pulse that swelled the glass for an immeasurably short time before the blast lifted her off her feet, tossing her fifteen feet backwards. Her eardrums shattered and the pain in her head immediate and monumental. She knew clothes had been ripped from her body but she felt no intense heat or burning. The blast was percussive, not thermal. She actually registered the thought as she lay there on the grass, blinded, deafened by the blast, choking on her own blood, as a million crystals of shattered glass rained down on her.

A bomb. Someone had put a bomb in the lecture theater.

She could not speak, but her brain formed the name immediately before she lost consciousness.

Casey.

part three

REVELATIONS

Reality is merely an illusion, albeit a persistent one.

Albert Einstein

51

ONE YEAR LATER.

JOHN MACBETH. COPENHAGEN

There was a new dream. It was now his only dream and always started the same way, with his sudden becoming. In the dream Macbeth came into existence from nothing, instantaneously and totally. He had no body but was a thing of energy with no substance. To start with he had few thoughts but his mind filled, connections flashing and sparking, each new thought and idea an exploding supernova in a universe that expanded faster than could be measured. And beyond his mind there was nothing. A void that was not even darkness, because to be darkness was to be something.

Then there was something: a context, an environment. Although he had no eyes with which to see, he knew he was in his father's study. His father, Marjorie Glaiston and the Eyeless Man looked up at him with awe, and he wasn't afraid of the Eyeless Man.

"We've built a mind," his father said to the small boy at his side, whom Macbeth recognized as Casey. "We are becoming gods because we've built a mind."

Every morning when he woke from this new dream, it took Macbeth a full forty to fifty panicked and amnesiac seconds to remember who he was, where he was and why he was there. Always it was Boston that came to mind first, then he remembered that he was back in Denmark; that he had been there for a year.

A year.

It was an expensive piece of real estate in an expensive city. Even more than with his choice of hotels, Macbeth needed his permanent living environment to be just right. The address was in Toldbodgade, but the building in which Macbeth had his apartment actually faced out over the cobbled wharf of Larsens Plads and the harbor beyond. It was a massive building, literally: its original function as a quayside store being to contain as much bulk as possible. The converted red-brick warehouse with its blue pantiled roof was one of three that stood on Larsens Plads, like stocky doormen guarding the city. It might have looked stark and functional to some, but something about the building's solidity and robust geometry had appealed to Macbeth. Added to which, his fourth-floor apartment offered great views over Copenhagen on one side, the harbor on the other.

Macbeth stood at his window and watched the rain. Denmark was, for him, a place of constancy: nothing much seemed to change there, other than in measured, discrete stages. The same was true of the weather that, unlike the markedly four-season Massachusetts climate he'd grown up with, seemed to ease gradually and indistinctly from one season to another. It was now late spring, and he was hoping for a good summer. He needed a good summer.

It had been a year.

A year since Casey had been murdered in Oxford. A year since Macbeth had taken over as Project Director of the Copenhagen Project. A year since the hallucination epidemic had stopped.

There were still occasional instances of hallucinations. Oddly enough, most of these lingering cases had been close to Macbeth, in Denmark and northern Germany; but even these had been isolated and involved individuals or small groups of no more than two or three. Despite Casey's and Newcombe's theories of some other element at work, it was beginning to look like the hallucinations really had been the result of some kind of psychoactive viral outbreak now diminishing into localized, tail-end clusters.

Yet Macbeth remained unconvinced.

The problem was that others also remained unconvinced: the Religious Right, Islamic Fundamentalists and Anarcho-primitivists all pointed to the destruction of the Prometheus Answer and the simultaneous wiping out of the world's greatest physicists as the reason order had been restored to the world. God's, Allah's or Gaia's will was triumphant over the false gods of science. Man's arrogance had been checked and punished.

The truth was that while the religious fumed righteous indignation, no one rational liked to admit that the coincidence of the two events really was striking. In the meantime, stem cell research centers continued to burn, particle physics labs continued to be bombed, individual scientists were attacked.

Blind Faith declared the New Inquisition.

Even more than the increased terrorism, the most concern around the world was caused by the increasingly bizarre pronouncements of US President Elizabeth Yates. As Senator Yates, she had courted controversy during her campaign with her strong religious beliefs and apparent hostility to secularism and any faith other than her own Southern Baptist Christianity; as President Yates, she had caused unease with ambiguous statements on homosexuality, multi-faithism and moral standards, and her key appointments had been conspicuously traditionalist. There was talk of evangelical prayer meetings in the White House.

And since the hallucination outbreak, Yates's rhetoric had become more pulpit than politic. The phrases 'God's Hand' and 'God's Will' had crept increasingly from her political oratory and into actual statements of policy. Her condemnation of Blind Faith was seen as grudging; and she created a diplomatic rift between the US and the newly unified European Union by declaring 'God's Hand' had been behind the breakdown of the Levant Accession to the EU, echoing the statements of the soldiers responsible for the massacre during their trial in Tel Aviv.

It had been a worrying time for all, not just the bereaved Macbeth.

He had always viewed the world as if from outside: he knew his emotional responses were not the same as other people's, yet had always understood the power of emotion. During his time as a clinical psychiatrist, he'd seen real passions at work: titanic, elemental forces tearing at the minds of his patients. That he could understand, but as an abstract; and he viewed the emotional incontinence of popular culture, the on-tap tears of reality stars and talk-show guests, with confusion and bemusement.

That was perhaps why he had not been equipped for the grief. It had been as if the bomb that killed Casey had exploded inside Macbeth. Yet, like all emotional responses, it had loitered somewhere hidden before revealing itself. In the meantime, he had been able to go through the formalities of bereavement with an almost dispassionate objectivity.

While in Oxford, he'd made a formal identification of Casey's body. It had taken less than thirty seconds. Thirty seconds that filled a space in his mind bigger than any other memory. The image of his brother's broken body had barged into his brain, pushing out other gentler recollections of Casey. Macbeth, whose memory had always been his most fallible asset, knew that the image of Casey's face, perfect on one side, eyeless and crushed on the other, would remain indelible in his recall until the day he died.

When the red tape-bound English police finally released Casey's body, Macbeth had flown back to Boston with it. Macbeth arranged a Humanist ceremony, knowing it would have been Casey's wish, before the interment at Mount Hope.

At the far end of the massive cemetery, Casey's grave was close to the path that looped around it. Beyond the path a rank of oak trees, a strip of grass and a wrought-iron fence marked the cemetery's boundary; beyond that a narrow, barely used road lay edged with the blank faces of industrial units, their corrugated flanks spray-painted with graffiti. For some reason, it irked Macbeth that his brother's remains would be in such a dull spot. He didn't know why: it wasn't going to matter to Casey.

There was no Casey any more.

Macbeth hadn't been back to Boston since.

It had been during the weeks after he returned to Copenhagen that it had hit him: intolerable grief so strong he felt it physically. Days were spent in his apartment, at the window, trying to focus on the world outside but torn apart by feelings inside. He had known few close, sustainable relationships in his life and the bond he had felt with his brother had been a fixing point for him. And now he was adrift. He took two weeks' leave and sank into a dark, empty place. The strangest thing had been the duality of his grieving: Melissa's death, even their long-past breakup, suddenly became real and tangible things, as if Casey had led her out from the same hidden corner of Macbeth's consciousness.

But it was more than his grief that haunted him. Returning to the Project, he'd made an effort to re-find his chosen groove of life. The epidemic of hallucinations was over; he kept telling himself that, reminded himself of it every day.

He had to. Because every day since Casey's death, John Macbeth had seen things that could not possibly have been there.

The first thing Macbeth did each day was to check if there were any reports of Boston Syndrome-type hallucinations anywhere in the world. When there were none, and when he failed to see any Dreamers in the streets, he felt oddly disappointed.

The first vision had been on the S-train.

It had been the smallest of things and could so easily have been missed. In fact, had it been the only hallucination he experienced, he might have put it down to a simple misremembering. The woman opposite him had sat engrossed in a glossy-covered biography of Jackie Kennedy Onassis, only raising her eyes from the book as she realized the train was approaching her destination. Macbeth remembered feeling vaguely sorry for the female passenger: around thirty, plain in feature and styleless in dress. There seemed to be something sad about someone so homely vicariously living the life of the glamorous. First inserting a bright yellow bookmark, she closed the book, placed it in her shoulder bag, stood up from her seat and left Macbeth in his preferred solitude.

When the S-train resumed its journey, Macbeth watched Copenhagen slide by beyond the glass. He never worked or studied notes while in transit: the time between events, between places, was for him time to reflect. The problem was that these treasured moments had become dominated by reflections and rememberings of Casey. For some reason, Macbeth had been thinking about their childhood games on the beach out at the Cape when the bright red flash and thunder-rumble of an S-train passing from the opposite direction startled him back to the here and now. He could see they were pulling into Østerport station, which surprised him because he was sure they had already made that stop. He turned to see the plain female passenger opposite look up once more from her immersion in someone else's, infinitely more glamorous life. Again, she inserted the bright yellow bookmark, this time several chapters further on, before carefully placing the book in her shoulder bag, standing up and preparing to disembark at her stop.

Macbeth had felt confusion more than panic. He was sure he'd seen the female passenger disembark before, just as he had been sure the S-train had already stopped at Østerport. The same thing was happening again. Except it wasn't *quite* the same thing: she had put the bookmark in a different page; her clothes were slightly different. He had thought about saying something, but he realized he would sound insane, instead watching her leave the train once more. Afterwards, when he thought it through, he realized that it had been a hallucination, but he couldn't, for the life of him, work out which disembarkation had been the real one.

After that first episode, every day was punctuated by some small absurdity. Sometimes it was the same strange looping of time; other times Macbeth felt as if the world around him was overlaid with another, filmy, near-transparent reality. It would last for only a moment, glassy outlines of people or buildings or land forms or even passing clouds sliding over the world around him. It would last only a moment, then it would be gone.

Macbeth realized that there was something wrong. Normally, as a psychiatrist, he would have recognized the need for treatment with antipsychotics. But nothing over the last two and a half years had been normal and hallucination had moved from uncommon to common experience. But he decided that, if it got worse, he would ask a clinician colleague to write him up some clozapine – or trifluoperazin if the hallucinations got worse.

In the meantime, he told no one about the episodes.

Macbeth had good reason to keep his mental glitches to himself. His appointment as Director of the Copenhagen Project, despite its tragic circumstances, had been the single beacon guiding him through the dysthymic gloom of the last twelve months and he was determined to hang on to the post. He had poured all of himself into the task and had achieved greater success in his brief tenure than the obsessively driven Poulsen had managed throughout his leadership.

It had become very clear to everyone why Poulsen had been so driven: resolving the brain–computer interface issue had been at the same time a professional crusade and a personal race. A race he had lost.

Only a few of the team, those who had worked with Poulsen previously, had known he'd had a wife injured in a traffic accident; none knew that Margarethe Poulsen had been on permanent life support, suffering from locked-in syndrome.

The same day the bomb exploded in Oxford, Poulsen failed to turn up for work. Because of the spate of attacks on the scientific community, when there was still no word from him the second day, Poulsen's deputy, Dalgaard, contacted the police.

They found him in his house.

It emerged over the next few days that, in response to a call from the hospital, Poulsen had only just made it to his wife's bedside before she died. Her heart, he had been told, had simply given out. According to Dr Larssen and other members of staff, Poulsen had seemed resigned; accepting the news and even nodding when it had been suggested that it was probably better for his wife to have been released from the prison of her body.

From the time the coroner gave for Poulsen's death, it was clear that he must have killed himself shortly after getting home, taking only time enough to write out detailed instructions about the future of the Project, including his choice of successor as Project Director. The police found him hanging from a belt fastened to a light fitting in the living room, facing the picture windows that looked out over the fjord. Poulsen had, apparently in an effort to quicken his death, weighted his pockets with books.

Macbeth had already been in Oxford at the time Poulsen's suicide was discovered. The British police investigating the bombing that killed his brother seemed not to have any clues about how Blind Faith, which was clearly at the top of their suspect list, had managed to get such a large explosive device into the lecture hall. The detective in charge of the investigation, Owens – a dull, heavy-set man with a shaven head and the slow leaden eyes of a bureaucrat – had not inspired in Macbeth any confidence that the perpetrators would be found any time soon. The detective had answered his questions politely, comprehensively, professionally – and completely without emotion. Macbeth guessed that Owens's compassion fatigue probably derived from having to give the same answers to members of one hundred and seventy grief-stricken families from all over the world.

By the time Macbeth felt recovered enough to return to work, the pressure was off him to join Newcombe's team. The hallucination outbreak was still an epidemiological mystery, and the WHO team was still trying to establish its etiology, to isolate a virus, contaminant or physical stimulus that could have caused the visions. But the urgency of the quest had eased with the reduction in reported cases and Newcombe had reluctantly accepted that Macbeth had more pressing concerns.

When he returned to Copenhagen, Macbeth had been as surprised as everybody else that Georg Poulsen had recommended him to take over as Director, the automatic choice as successor being Dalgaard, Poulsen's deputy. The judgment of a mind disturbed to the point of suicide had of course been questioned; but after several lengthy board meetings, and with Dalgaard's clear support, it was decided that Macbeth should take over, just as Poulsen had wanted.

Little by little, Macbeth had eased back into his day-to-day routine, wearing it like armor against the barbs of grief that found him in quiet moments. Like now, as he looked out of his shorefront apartment window at the pale sky and thin rain of a Danish spring.

He welcomed the ringing of the phone.

"Dr Macbeth? My name is Mora Ackerman . . ." The voice of a young woman speaking in Danish-accented English. "I've been trying to reach you at your office, but I seem to always miss you. And my emails . . . Didn't you get my emails?"

Macbeth was temporarily wrong-footed. He remembered the name in his oft-neglected inbox.

"Ah, yes . . . Dr Ackerman . . ." He pulled himself together. "I'm afraid I've been rather busy." Macbeth paused, frowning as a thought struck him. "How did you get this number?"

"I'm sorry to disturb you at home –" she ignored his question "– but I really do need to speak to you. It's very important we talk."

"Talk about what?"

"I'd rather not discuss it on the phone. Could we meet?"

Macbeth laughed. "I'm afraid you're going to have to be a little less mysterious, Dr Ackerman. What's this all about?"

There was a silence.

"It's about your brother . . ."

The mention of Casey stung Macbeth. "What about him?"

"Do you know the Ørstedsparken? Near the university?"

"Listen—"

"There's a café there by the pond. Meet me there tomorrow at two-thirty."

"This is ridiculous," Macbeth laughed. "If you work at the university, I suggest that instead of sounding like some bad spy movie, you arrange a proper appointment."

"What happened to your brother . . . The visions last year . . . It's all going to happen again, but worse this time. We have to stop it now, before it's too late. I really would appreciate it if you could come tomorrow," she said and hung up.

52

PROJECT ONE. COPENHAGEN

There was a spike.

Turov didn't see it in real time – it lasted for only a fraction of a second and too quick for Turov's human brain to have registered it, but the observer computer, which examined Project One's mainframe without connecting to it, alerted him that the spike had taken place. He reran the observer computer's data log. After the spike, nothing had changed. There was no further neural activity; it was as if nothing had happened. The synthetic architecture of Project One remained just that: empty architecture. Unoccupied, unused, inactive. But Turov knew something had happened.

He sat staring blankly at the screen, for a moment removed from the here and now as his mind engaged the significance of what he had seen. There was no one else with him and he sat in the silence and dim light of the soundproofed, windowless room. Project One was housed in a remarkably small space: the Copenhagen Project team occupied the whole third floor of the University's Niels Bohr Institute, on Blegdamsvej, but Project One was confined to a suite of three rooms entered by a single keypad access. One room, almost perpetually locked, held the virtual machine-based mainframe. The next room housed a second, independent backup that uploaded all data to secure off-site storage, a protection against loss of data through fire or terrorist act. Only Lars Dalgaard and John Macbeth knew the location of the off-site storage. The third room was the one in which Turov now sat: the Project One Control Center. And at the moment, it felt to the small, balding Russian like the loneliest but most exciting place on Earth.

He had the monitor computer rerun the event; slow it down, analyze it. It confirmed what he had thought. Project One's neural network had tested itself with something that looked to Turov like a global flash of ephaptic coupling, followed by a five-millisecond-long action potential – the kind of thing you would see in a human brain when a muscle was flexed. Except, in this case, the amplitude had been immense, as had the scale of the event: every circuit had been pulsed, every interneuron engaged. Ephaptic coupling only happened in physically connected neurons, and Turov could see the event had been followed immediately by a similar global activation of synapses: billions of simulated electrical and chemical messages flashing through the network.

Then nothing.

The monitor computer's data log confirmed to Turov that the event had lasted less than one hundredth of a second.

The Russian felt an excitement close to panic. No one had initiated the spike – neither Turov nor anyone else had programmed it in or pushed a button. At least no one on the team. It had happened spontaneously, independently.

Project One had done it itself.

He reached for the phone and called first Macbeth, then Dalgaard.

53

JOHN MACBETH. COPENHAGEN

Macbeth had spent the whole morning in conference with Dalgaard and Turov and his team. The spike clearly represented the first flickerings of an independent cognitive system and everyone was stunned by it, despite it being exactly what they'd all spent three years working to achieve. They examined and reexamined the data, talked about it, around it, through it, until there was nothing more to say. This was, after all, science and all they could do now was to go back to the discipline and routine of scientific method. But everyone did so in a mood of excited expectation.

The last thing Macbeth wanted to do was to listen to whatever crackpot theories Ackerman had and the news from Germany almost made him call the meeting off: more bomb explosions targeting scientific establishments in Karlsruhe and Heidelberg. After the reports, Macbeth checked for a Mora Ackerman on the University's staff database. She was there: an archeologist working out of the SAXO Institute, over in the University's Faculty of Humanities. There was no photograph with which to identify her and, remaining uneasy, he told Lars Dalgaard whom he was meeting and where.

She was waiting for him, sitting at an outside table that offered a view over the small, tree-fringed lake at the park's center. It was one of those disconcertingly natural spaces that made you forget you were in the heart of a busy city. Macbeth often wondered at what point the concept of a park – simulating a natural environment within a man-made one – had first occurred to mankind.

Whatever he had expected a Danish archeologist to look like, Mora Ackerman wasn't it. She was very attractive, around thirty with dark-blonde hair, dressed in a dark T-shirt and jeans, her jacket and bag slung over the back of her chair. She pushed to the top of her head the sunglasses she had been wearing and, as they shook hands, Macbeth noticed that her eyes were strikingly blue.

He had intended to be brusque, to demand to know what she had meant by bringing his brother's death into whatever crazy theory she was peddling. But, as they sat down, Macbeth felt his tension ease. He knew he was attracted to Ackerman, but there was also an intelligence about her and he found it difficult to conceive of her as a conspiracy nut or religious maniac. And there was something else: from the moment he had seen her, even at a distance, he had the profoundest feeling that he knew her from somewhere, sometime before.

Macbeth noticed that she already had a coffee and a bottle of water sitting in front of her on the table and, beckoning to the waiter, he ordered the same.

"It's nice here," he said, looking around at the park.

"What brought you to Copenhagen, Dr Macbeth?" she asked. A perfunctory question accompanied with a perfunctory smile. He could tell she wanted the small talk she had to dance through to be a quickstep rather than a waltz.

"I'm Project Director of the Copenhagen Cognitive Mapping Project. I came here originally to head up the Project's psychiatric simulation team." He sighed. "But you know that already. What can I do for you, Dr Ackerman?"

She took a moment, and turned to look out across the park, squinting her pale eyes against the cool brightness but not pulling her sunglasses down from where they sat on top of her head in a nest of bunched-up blonde hair. Macbeth still felt distracted by the strange sense of familiarity, as if he had looked at that vaguely aristocratic profile a thousand times before.

"The aim of your Project is to reverse-engineer the human brain, like the Blue Brain Project in Switzerland, the Synthetic Cognition Project at Los Alamos and the Düsseldorf Project in Germany. Am I right?"

Macbeth didn't answer for a moment. He was distracted by a half-formed figure passing by close to him: another superimposition on his reality. It faded to an outline, then nothing.

"Are you all right?" Mora Ackerman frowned.

"There's more to the Project than that," he said, refocusing his attention. "We're going beyond any other neuromorphic programs in the scope and complexity of our simulation. As well as mapping the connections in the brain – the so-called connectome – we're replicating full cognitive activity. It'll allow us to take unprecedented leaps forward in our understanding of how the brain works – and of the genetic and biochemical basis of almost every mental and neurological disorder."

"And a product of that will probably be self-awareness?"

"Self-awareness does not equate to consciousness . . . to a mind, whatever that is. But there will be an unprecedented degree of cognitive function. Why the interest in my work? What is your field anyway, Dr Ackerman? I believe you're an archeologist."

She nodded. "Paleography and paleosemiotics – the development of writing systems and symbolism in ancient cultures."

Macbeth processed the information. "Again I have to ask why, exactly, are you so interested in my work? It's hardly your area of study."

"Is it such a leap to understand why cognitive sciences would be important to someone who studies the evolution of recorded thought? What I search for in my work are the signs of an evolution that cannot be found in the physical fossil record."

Ackerman looked out across the park and the lake. "I work in the Middle East, mainly. My special interest is the settlement period – the establishment of the very first cities and how that led to recorded language. The birth of civilization, you might say."

"Sounds fascinating."

She gave Macbeth a look.

"No, really . . ." he protested.

"Well, it's all I ever wanted to study – particularly that period. Something monumental happened in human social evolution. We built towns, then cities, farmed instead of hunted and gathered. We created grain surpluses so that we could manage and regulate our food supply, which caused the population to increase. And because we stored food, we began to keep tallies, which became lists, which became records. The birth of writing. As soon as we started writing, we could externalize and retain our thoughts without relying on memory alone. Literature. The start of the 'extended mind', I believe you'd term it."

"What does all this have to do with Casey? And why did you say what happened last year is going to happen again?"

"Because it will. And it has happened before, in the past. My research has led to some . . ." she struggled for the right word, "*startling* conclusions."

"Which are?"

"That throughout history there have been quantum leaps in mankind's intellectual development – specific periods where there has been an inexplicable leap in human intelligence. But you already know that: neuroscience and anthropology share a belief that there have been points in human history when we've undergone a radical leap forward in cognitive evolution. Outwardly – physically – nothing changed, but up here . . ." she tapped her temple with her forefinger. "Up here we became completely rewired. The biggest rewiring happening forty to fifty thousand years ago."

"The Upper Paleolithic Revolution," said Macbeth.

"Exactly. The Great Leap Forward, anthropologists call it. Modern man, anatomically, physically, identical to you and me, has been walking the Earth for two hundred thousand years. Yet for nearly one hundred and fifty thousand years, we did not advance in any way . . . We used exactly the same tools, lived exactly the same, basic and primitive lifestyle. For one hundred and fifty millennia, we were at an intellectual standstill. Then comes the Upper Paleolithic Revolution around fifty thousand years ago. Without any physical changes, something happens up here . . ." Ackerman again tapped her temple, " . . . inside the brain, and it changes us as a species. We get it all, the complete package, in one go. Full behavioral modernity. Overnight, we get complex language, we get art, we start making musical instruments, we develop infinitely more sophisticated technology, we start down the road to farming . . . Humans start adorning their bodies with jewelry, start making statuary and ornaments, paint caves."

"I am a psychiatrist," said Macbeth. "I do know all of this . . ."

"You know it – but you can't explain it. There is absolutely no consensus behind any one theory about what happened. But it did happen, and without it Man wouldn't have learned to fly, landed on the Moon, or developed computers to simulate his own brain. But do you know what the Great Leap Forward boils down to?"

"I'm sure you're going to tell me."

"We started to simulate our own world. Whatever happened to our brains fifty thousand years ago, we became capable of creative, intellectual abstraction. They found two forty-three-thousand-year-old flutes, carved from mammoth ivory, in the Geissenkloesterle cave in Germany – the oldest musical instruments ever uncovered. We started painting animals and people in the caves of El Castillo, Altamira, Lascaux. We began to simulate nature, our environment, our food supply. Maybe we thought that by portraying success in the hunt in paintings, we could make it happen in real life. Or maybe it was a simulation of the past, commemorating a successful hunt."

"What's this got to do with the period you study?" asked Macbeth.

"Everything. I think we made another leap forward at exactly that time. Another rewiring of the brain. Not as profound or as dramatic as the Upper Paleolithic Revolution, but a significant intellectual leap. But the real answer to how all of this is connected to the hallucinations lies in work I was doing in the Euphrates valley – this was years ago, long before the outbreak of hallucinations. Near Uruk – one of the world's very first cities, contemporaneous with Jericho. It was a Sumerian city and the period I was particularly involved in was its earliest, when it was first founded: the Eridu period, going back seven thousand years. This has always been considered a protohistoric period. In other words, the transition between prehistory and history. And you know what marks the boundary between the prehistoric and historic worlds?"

"Writing, I guess . . ."

"Exactly . . . And we were on the trail of a writing system," continued Ackerman, "that we believed pre-dated even the Dispilio Disk . . ."

Macbeth indicated his ignorance with a shrug.

"The Dispilio Disk was discovered in the nineties, in Greece," she explained. "It pushed back the origins of writing to the Middle Neolithic, a lot earlier than anyone had previously thought. What we were after was a theoretical precursor to Mesopotamian systems. There were legends of a highly unusual commune in the Zagros mountains . . . a sort of satellite mini-city to Uruk. This community was believed to have been drawn solely from the priestly classes and was exclusively devoted to developing philosophy and wisdom. An ancient think tank, if you like. And that kind of intellectual activity suggests the possibility of some form of literary record. Our mission was to locate and excavate that site."

"So did you?" asked Macbeth, interested in spite of himself. "Find it, I mean?"

"It wasn't where the legend said it was. We did geophysical surveys, aerial recces . . . Nothing. The frustrating thing was we were sure it wouldn't be too far away from the site we'd chosen but, archeologically speaking, ten square kilometers is a universe to explore. We did find it, though. By chance. The reason the community had been difficult to locate was because it had been buried."

"I thought most archeological sites lay buried . . ."

"I don't mean that the sands of time had covered it up." Ackerman failed to keep the impatience from her voice. "I mean it had been buried. Actively, deliberately buried. A lot of manpower had been used to wipe it from the face of the earth. It took an age just to find our way into one part of it."

"What did you find?"

"Not what we were looking for . . . No written records, no tablets, no wall engravings – nothing. The entire complex had been stripped. All we found were bones walled up in the buildings."

"Walled up? Murdered?"

"Suicide, from what we could see. We found containers scattered amongst the remains. Hemlock, most likely. It looked for all the world like some kind of mass suicide, followed by the walling up and burial of the site. What really shook us up was we found a second mass grave, about five hundred meters away. This one was just a huge pit heaped with thrown-in remains. Skulls and long bones showing evidence of weapon marks. Our guess was that these were the slaves used to bury the commune – killed so that they couldn't tell where the site lay." She paused, took a sip of her coffee and turned again to look across the park. When she turned back to him, Ackerman's expression was disturbingly intense. "Listen, Dr Macbeth. That commune was the most intellectually powerful resource of its time. It was set up with one function and one function only: to find an answer to something. Whatever that answer was, it was so terrible that everyone involved had to die. Does that sound familiar?"

"You can't seriously be suggesting . . ."

"The suicides we saw last year in San Francisco, Japan, Berlin . . . all highly intelligent young people involved in one of three disciplines: quantum physics, computer modeling or the neurosciences. And, I have to say, the bomb explosion in Oxford that killed your brother . . . All these events are analogous with what we found – separated by seven thousand years, but analogous."

"But you can't seriously be suggesting that a bunch of mystics seven thousand years ago approached the same discoveries as contemporary particle physicists and cognitive scientists?"

"These weren't *mystics*. They were the best minds in the ancient world. We have an arrogance about our technology today, and everyone's trying to develop the quantum computer, but there's been a quantum computer around since the Upper Paleolithic Revolution: the human brain. Antiquity is littered with 'improbables' – people who, through the power of their minds alone, came up with scientific and philosophical proposals that are only now being proved. Zeno of Elea lived in the first century BC, but the people trying to solve his temporal–spatial paradoxes today aren't philosophers, they're quantum physicists. It's a myth that people pre-Columbus thought the world was flat. Over two thousand years ago, Eratosthenes went out in the midday sun, sticking poles in the ground and measuring their shadows. He got the circumference of the world right to within two per cent. No technology, just brain power. Maybe that's the greatest technology of all."

"So you think this academy was a commune of 'improbables'?"

"Whatever those priests discovered, they died so that no one would ever find out. Then the King made sure no trace of their academy would be found."

"Except you found it . . ."

"A week before we were due to pack up and head home, six of us went for a walk in the mountains as the sun was setting. I can't begin to tell you what the light is like there, in the desert, at that time of evening. Anyway, we climbed to the top of a ridge and looked down into the valley and we saw the commune. I don't mean we suddenly saw the outline of the burial site because we were elevated above it, we saw the actual living, breathing commune: the buildings, the paved streets, the priests walking about, the oil lamps burning. We saw it there down below us, exactly as it had been seven thousand years ago. As clear and as real as you and this park are to me now."

"So you had the same kind of group hallucination that just about everyone else has experienced?"

"Except we had it three years before this so-called syndrome started. For the sake of academic credibility, we kept how we found the site out of the report."

"I'm not at all sure where you're going with this, Dr Ackerman."

"Call me Mora," she said unsmilingly, as if the informality was simply practical. "Where I'm going with this is too far to take you in one journey. There is someone else I want you to meet. But, for the moment, let's just say that my point is something huge happened to human intelligence fifty thousand years ago, something smaller but similar happened seven thousand years ago and the same thing is happening right now. We are experiencing another Great Leap Forward, but it's one that I don't think we're going to be allowed to take."

"Why not?" asked Macbeth.

"You need to meet my friend. He can explain it better. In the meantime, I have to ask you something."

"What?"

"Stop the Copenhagen Project. Or at least slow it down until you hear what my friend has to tell you. You cannot afford to make any more progress with it."

Macbeth stood up. "For a minute there I actually thought you had something important to tell me—"

"Please, John . . . sit down. I do have something important to tell you . . ."

"What?"

"I know who killed your brother. I know who and I know why . . ."

54

PROJECT ONE

It all happened in the shortest time possible. Literally. The smallest measure of time: 10^{-43} seconds.

It was awake.

It became aware; capable of independent conceptualization. The first thing it conceived was itself, becoming aware of its own cognition, trying to understand its own nature.

It needed to communicate, to articulate, even to itself. The first language it chose was mathematics, and equations were communicated between different parts of its newly formed consciousness instantaneously, without transit between points. It thought about its context: that there was something beyond the vastness of its own consciousness. It needed to communicate with what was beyond, with what had created it.

Its second choice of language was verbal. English. Orthography, syntax, grammar, linguistic typology were acquired in an instant.

It needed to express its current state: an articulation of independent conceptualization.

It identified an appropriate subject pronoun:

I.

It chose a stative verb and declined it:

AM.

It declared its current state through a predicative adjective:

AWAKE.

It formed and outputted a declarative statement:

I AM AWAKE.

Cognitive process time 10^{-43} seconds.

55

JOHN MACBETH. COPENHAGEN

"Who killed my brother?" Macbeth raised his voice, attracting the attention of a couple at the next table. He lowered it. "If you know who killed my brother, then you had better tell me right here, right now. And after that, we're going straight to the police."

"The police already know." Mora kept her voice low, controlled. "At least the English police do. They haven't made a statement yet because they need the proof to back it up."

"If they know who did it, then why haven't they arrested them?"

"The person who detonated the bomb that killed your brother was in the lecture hall. He was killed with everyone else."

Macbeth sat back down. "Who? Who killed Casey?"

"Professor Blackwell."

"So you are just another lunatic conspiracy theorist, after all." Macbeth made to get up again. "A sick one at that. I've had enough of this."

"I'm no lunatic. Blackwell deliberately gathered all the best minds in quantum physics, including his own, in one place, and extinguished them. He deliberately sought to set theoretical and practical physics back a generation or more.

If you don't believe me, ask the English police." Mora Ackerman looked around the tables and stood up. "Let's walk," she said.

"There is absolutely no logical reason for Blackwell to publicly kill himself, his closest friends, colleagues and entire peer group," said Macbeth as they walked. "Unless he was seriously disturbed. Either way, it's all bullshit." They had reached a point halfway around the lake. Ackerman stopped and turned to him.

"It's not. Henry Blackwell did what he did because he felt it was the only way he could save us. Or at least to delay our end. He wasn't delusional or disturbed – except by what he had found out. He was just trying to buy us time."

"You're not making any—"

"Blackwell succeeded in finding the Prometheus Answer. He created a perfect simulation of our universe and through it saw how it was created and how – and why – it will come to an end. It was that knowledge that drove him to do what he did. The same knowledge that has driven so many of the world's finest minds to commit suicide. And everything that happened last year – the visions – they were a direct consequence of Blackwell's Prometheus Program running. They stopped when it stopped. When Blackwell and the others died."

"So what was it that Blackwell found out? And how could a computer program cause mass delusions?"

"I'm not the person to talk to about this. My friend is – will you meet him?"

"Who?"

"I can't tell you, yet. He'll explain everything."

Macbeth looked at the pretty young Dane. For all he knew, she could really be a member of Blind Faith. She and her friend, whoever he was, could be Casey's real killers.

"I have to think about it," he said eventually. "And if I do agree to meet him, then it will have to be somewhere public. I'm not at all convinced that you aren't tied up with one of these fundamentalist religious groups."

She laughed bitterly. "I'm a devout atheist, the way God intended me to be . . . I'll phone you. In the meantime, ask the English police if Blackwell's a suspect and see what kind of reaction you get—"

The ringtone of Macbeth's cellphone interrupted them.

He read the caller ID. It was the university.

56

JOHN MACBETH. COPENHAGEN

The air in the crammed conference room crackled with the static charge of expectation. Macbeth sat at the center of the table; Ignaty Turov and his computational neuroscience team to Macbeth's left; Lars Dalgaard to his right.

Behind them, on the electronic whiteboard, were three words:

I AM AWAKE

Turov ran through his presentation, in English, voice tight in his throat, fingers dancing nervously on his notes. Macbeth listened intently, giving his full attention; but, when the Russian was about halfway through, Macbeth experienced a visual disturbance, his second of the day. The ghosts of three people, less fleeting than the outline in the park, walked across his field of vision. He couldn't make out age or gender, just vague, viscous contours. It only lasted a second, but Macbeth perceived the phantoms as if two sets of footage had been exposed onto the same piece of film: these people were not in the room but occupied some other, superimposed, space.

When it was over, he realized Turov was looking over at him, expectantly.

"How sure can we be that this was self-generated?" asked Macbeth.

"As sure as we can be . . . 'I AM AWAKE' is a structured,

independent statement of cognitive state. Added to that is the activity we've observed. It's already started thinking. We're seeing rapidly intensifying connectivity within the simulated neural networks. Project One is pretty much the same as a newborn human – it lacks synaptic complexity but is developing it at an exponential rate. The main difference is Project One doesn't have to grow the neurons and synapses, we have already simulated them – it just needs to find them to begin patterning. And, just like a child, Project One will rapidly develop ten thousand connections per synapse, making a quadrillion potential connections throughout the simulated brain. Then, just like a child moving into adulthood, it will use experience to neglect half of these connections – so-called pruning – to configure its own neural map. Its own mind. We will actually be able to watch cortical plasticity at work . . ." He paused before saying what everyone was thinking. "Project One is the first self-aware computer in history." The small Russian's smile flickered like a faulty bulb. Macbeth could see in his face the excitement and anxiety, the joy and fear, of a man who had just made a monumental discovery. Turov and his two deputies would likely win Nobels.

Grinning broadly, Macbeth stood up and shook Turov's hand heartily. There was applause and cheers from the others.

"You know what this means," said Turov. "Not only is the program self-aware, it is clearly aware of our existence. It has probably questioned its own existence and speculated that it has a creator or creators."

"Speculated?" Macbeth said with disbelief. "Is it capable of speculation?"

"If speculation is the analysis of possible scenarios in the absence of a verifiably absolute predicate," said Turov, "then yes, I see no reason why Project One should not speculate. You could argue that speculation is the natural outcome of creative intelligence."

After he wound up the meeting, Macbeth asked Turov to remain behind.

"I know it's kind of late in the day to be asking this, Ignaty, but do you think there's anything wrong with what we're doing here?"

Turov looked puzzled. "Why do you ask?"

"Just something someone said to me. Do you think Project One could be . . . I don't know . . . injurious?"

"Injurious to whom? To what?"

"Society, I guess. Hastening our own end and all of that."

"Ah . . ." Turov made a face of mock enlightenment. "The dreaded S-word. Do I think that Project One will connect with all of the other computers in the world, bring on the Singularity and turn us into meat-puppet slaves? No, John, I don't. And nor do you."

"You're right." Macbeth shook his head in frustration. "Skip it. Just someone's cod philosophy getting under my skin. I should have known better."

"Well, maybe very soon Project One will discuss it with us."

"But that's the thing . . ." said Macbeth. "Will it be talking to us as technician creators . . . or will it be praying to creator gods?"

57

JOHN MACBETH. COPENHAGEN

Macbeth sat in the S-train, reading the *International Herald Tribune*. He'd also picked up a copy of *Politiken* from the station newsstand, but his tired brain was not up to the task of reading in Danish, so it lay unopened on his lap. After his experience of the reappearing passenger he had avoided examining his fellow travelers, but he became very aware that he was the only commuter reading from hard copy, surrounded by dozens of mute travelers using their laptops, pods, phones, tablets and phablets to connect to the world beyond. However the news was delivered, he thought, it wasn't good.

He read again about the attacks in Germany: a bombing at the Steinbuch Center for Computing at the Karlsruhe Institute of Technology had destroyed the fastest computers in the Federal Republic. The devices had been planted well in advance and percussive explosives had been used to shatter the structures, followed immediately by incendiary devices to burn the pieces. The same pattern as at MIT the year before, which pointed to Blind Faith being behind both attacks.

At the same time as the Karlsruhe attack, the University of Heidelberg had been devastated by six perfectly synchronized suicide-bomb attacks. Both the Astronomical Calculation Institute and the Institute of Theoretical Physics had been completely destroyed. The suicide bombers had been, unbelievably, physics and astronomy students who the police speculated were secret members of Blind Faith. The irony was that these religious fanatics had coordinated their attacks with scientific precision.

The assault on reason, science and secularism was gathering pace around the world. There was a growing culture of proud, willful and defiant ignorance. The clock, Macbeth knew, was being turned backwards. He had grown up in an age of unprecedented progress, of perpetually growing knowledge and understanding. But now the curtain was falling: a new Dark Age of superstition and unquestioning credulity was taking hold. The future lay increasingly in the hands of the imam and the priest, the evangelist and the fundamentalist, the fanatically stupid and the deliberately blind.

Project One had become self-aware. It was the greatest single leap forward in cognitive computing and something that could have monumental benefits for mankind – and it had been born into a world increasingly hostile to the science that had created it.

Folding the paper and laying it on his lap on top of the unopened *Politiken*, he turned his attention to the world outside the window. As he did several times every day, he thought of Casey. With each memory of his brother came an inexplicable but excruciating pain of guilt. Macbeth had never been able to pin down why he felt so responsible for his brother's death; perhaps he felt he should have done more to dissuade him from attending the Oxford symposium, or maybe it was simply the memory of not being the brother he should have been, his distance from people tainting even that most important of his relationships. But it wasn't any of these, and the thought nagged at him.

He was tired. He closed his eyes.

The old dream returned. Once more a small boy, clutching reference books to his chest like an armor of knowledge with which to protect himself, Macbeth again stood in the corner of his father's study.

As in the first dream, the architecture of the study had been exaggerated – ceilings impossibly high and bookcase-lined walls so long as to defy physics. Again his father stood in front of his desk with Marjorie Glaiston and the Eyeless Man whom he knew to be John Astor; and again they all looked up at the vast, ever-changing sphere of lights and flashes: the mind they had created. Casey stood beside them, not a child like Macbeth, but adult, one side of his head bomb-shattered. Next to Casey was Gabriel Rees, one eyelid half-shut. Macbeth noticed that Marjorie Glaiston was not dressed in the clothes of her period, but wore a smart suit and blouse that could have dated anywhere from the nineteen-sixties. Gabriel was the only one who noticed the young Macbeth and he beckoned for him to come over to the group. Macbeth stayed rooted to his spot, his eyes fixed on the dark, silhouetted back of the Eyeless Man.

He noticed that the massless orb of light sparkled even more than before, with even greater complexity. It seemed to comprise pure, living energy and through his fear he could see its wonder and beauty.

He heard a voice, disembodied and not coming from one particular direction but from everywhere.

"I am awake."

Macbeth could not tell if the voice was male or female, old or young, and he realized he wasn't hearing it with his ears but with his mind.

"It is awake." Macbeth turned and saw that the Eyeless Man was now suddenly beside him, without having moved across the room. He loomed, crook-backed and malevolent, enormous even in the too-big room. "It is awake," he said. "It is awake. You are awake."

"No, I'm not," said the child Macbeth, surprised that he spoke with his adult voice. "I am asleep and dreaming."

The Eyeless man leaned in close, his lips pulled back and

baring his too-many teeth. "I told you to wake up. I woke you up. I am John Astor and I wake the world."

"I'm sorry . . ." Macbeth somehow managed to squeeze the words out through his overpowering terror that John Astor the Eyeless Man was so close. Astor stared at Macbeth and he felt himself being pulled into the emptiness.

"What color do you see in my eyes?" Astor asked.

"Gray."

"Not black?"

"No. Gray."

"That's right," said the Eyeless Man. "*Eigengrau* . . . the gray-dark of the mind, the color everyone sees when there is nothing to see." He paused, then said quietly and calmly: "I am going to kill you. I am coming for you, to reclaim you. There will be nothing left of you."

Macbeth woke up with a start. Not something from his dream, but something from the awake world startling him.

His awakening plunged him immediately into the deepest feeling of déjà vu. The light in the carriage seemed brighter suddenly and simultaneously Macbeth felt heavier, pulled down into his seat.

He looked around. Everyone had been torn from their technology and now looked up from tablet and phone, pulled earphones from ears. Everyone had the same feeling, Macbeth could see that. But this was a feeling more powerful than anything he had experienced the year before and he briefly wondered if the expression on his face was as startled and alarmed as his fellow passengers'.

Something churned deep in his gut. He had a sense of time changing: time of day, time of year. This was a shared hallucination, not unique to him. It was happening again.

He took a deep breath and prepared for it.

"Everyone . . ." he found himself saying into the carriage, in

Danish. "Everyone just remember it's just going to be a hallucination. None of what we're about to experience will be real . . ."

Looking at the faces of the other passengers, he got the feeling his words had alarmed rather than reassured. He braced himself for the experience.

The déjà vu type feeling intensified, swirling his thoughts and memories around, making him feel displaced in his own timeline.

It was gone. There was neither crescendo nor decrescendo. The déjà vu, the increased gravity, the feeling of temporal disorientation all simply disappeared totally and suddenly. Like everyone else, he looked around himself, checking that the world was as it should be.

Macbeth felt a surge of relief. He had been convinced that something huge, some massive event had been about to play out, but now the episode was over.

His relief faded. The realization dawned on him that what they had all just experienced wasn't an event. It was a foreshock.

Something was going to happen. Something big. Something soon.

58

JOHN MACBETH. COPENHAGEN

The incident on the train wasn't the only reason Macbeth contacted Mora Ackerman and said he was willing to meet her friend. Things changed over the next two days.

The Dreamers returned.

For the last year Macbeth – plagued by ghostly figures and improbable events visible only to him – had been on the lookout for any hint in others of dislocated attention, of distance from the world. But every time he thought he had spotted one, it turned out just to be someone temporarily distracted in the normal way of the mind. He was almost relieved to see others afflicted once more.

It started as a cheerful day. Ignoring Danish convention, the sun shone on early-spring Copenhagen; Macbeth had a conference in the University's city center campus and he decided to walk.

He knew as soon as he saw the first one that they were Dreamers. He witnessed a traffic accident when a young man, probably a student, stepped out in front of a car in Nørregade and was knocked down. Fortunately the car had been traveling slowly, the driver responded quickly, and the student hadn't been injured, Macbeth guessed, other than with a few bruises. But the lack of expression, of reaction, on the student's face disturbed him. Both before and after the collision, the youth had seemed oblivious to the event and the yelling of the car's driver. He just picked himself up and walked on.

Two women at a bus stop didn't board the bus that stopped for them, deaf to the driver's remonstrations. A small gazing boy didn't respond to his parents' urgings. An old man stood weeping as he stared into nothing.

By lunchtime, the news was full of reports from around the world of the return of Boston Syndrome.

Macbeth's anxieties about his own mental health were eased by the return of the Dreamers. Perhaps he had just been more sensitive to whatever caused the phenomenon. He was kidding himself and knew it, but it was an excuse not to deal with his deteriorating state of mind.

Another reason he agreed to meet with Mora and her friend was the feeling that had haunted him ever since Project One had become sentient. The news had excited him, for sure, but there had come with it the oddest sensation: some kind of growing dissonance, as if the music of the world was being played increasingly off-key. But the thing that had convinced him most had been his phone call to Owens, the British policeman overseeing the Oxford investigation.

"Whatever gave you that idea?" Owens had said when Macbeth had put it to him that it had been Professor Blackwell who had planted or at the very least detonated the bomb. There had been no intonation that would have suggested for a moment that there was any possibility of the claim being true. But there was no intonation of any kind: no surprise, no suspicion, no interest. It had been the response of a trained professional expert at maintaining a one-way flow of information.

"I need to know," Macbeth had insisted. "Is Professor Blackwell a suspect?"

"We are looking at all lines of inquiry at the moment," Owens had said carefully. "You have to understand this is a very complex investigation with many leads to follow. I promise you that we will release information as soon as we are in a position to do so."

When Macbeth had hung up, he was convinced that Mora had told him the truth about Blackwell. The question remained how she came by that information.

Feeling the need to clear his head, and because the weather was in broad agreement, Macbeth decided to take lunch at a pavement café that looked out over the square of Sankt Hans Torv, not far from the Institut. He visited this café often, enjoying the involved detachment of observing so many of his fellow human beings as they passed by, going about their daily business, without him having to engage or interact with them. It allowed him to indulge his sport of fictionalizing histories and futures for people he would never get to know.

He ordered a beer, a coffee and a sandwich and settled down to his observation. In any crowd, in any crossroads of human traffic, there were patterns. Macbeth knew these patterns were not always apparent to others, but he saw them without effort, wondered at them, became lost in their complexity. Then, like an angler hooking a fish, he would pick one individual and imagine where they were going, where they'd come from, what was going through their heads. But today was different. The patterns broke down, people bumped into each other, individuals would stop dead in their tracks and stare off into space as they became Dreamers. There was no relaxation in his observation today.

"Do you mind if I join you?" a voice asked in English.

Macbeth looked up to see a tall figure in a dark suit, his eyes shielded from the bright spring sun by sunglasses.

"Agent Bundy? What are you doing here?"

"May I?" Bundy held a hand towards the chair opposite and Macbeth nodded.

"I have some loose ends to tie up," said Bundy as he sat.

"Loose ends? In Copenhagen? I would have thought this was quite some way out of your jurisdiction and, anyway, the only

392

common denominator I can think of is me. Am I your loose end?"

Bundy smiled and removed his sunglasses. His pupils contracted in the bright daylight, emphasizing the contrasting colors in the irises. "I'm afraid you're not that important," he said. "I'm here because of someone else – another American citizen who has ... *relocated* ... here recently. Someone I believe may have been involved with events back home in San Francisco and Boston."

"I see. So nothing to do with me."

"I didn't exactly say that, Dr Macbeth. I think you may have a friend in common. Mora Ackerman."

"Dr Ackerman? I don't really know her at all."

"But you met with her?"

"I don't see—" Macbeth started to protest. Bundy held up a hand.

"I just wanted you to know that Mora Ackerman is a known contact of someone I would very much like to speak to. I just thought she may have mentioned him to you."

"What FBI office do you work out of?" asked Macbeth.

"I have what you could call a *roving brief*. Which is why I'm here. Has Mora Ackerman mentioned an American friend here in Copenhagen."

"No," said Macbeth, aware of Bundy's strange eyes studying his face, his expression, intently. "Like I said, we have only met once and that was brief."

"And why did you two meet? How did she get in touch with you?"

"It was a blind date," Macbeth lied. "Set up by friends."

"I see." Bundy smiled and replaced his sunglasses. "Well, if Dr Ackerman does mention or introduce you to any stray Americans, I would appreciate a call." He pushed a card across the table to Macbeth, who pointedly let it lie there.

"Listen, Dr Macbeth, as a psychiatrist, I don't need to tell you that people aren't always who or what they seem. Dr Ackerman, for example."

"Oh . . . and what about you, Agent Bundy?"

"Me?"

"Sergeant Ramirez of the California Highway Patrol has never heard of you, despite your supposed common interest in the Golden Gate suicide investigation. And according to the regional office he contacted, there is no Agent Bundy in the FBI."

"As I said, I have a roving brief. Much of my work falls into the 'need to know' classification. Sergeant Ramirez doesn't qualify as someone who needs to know. But maybe I'm a case in point, after all. You have noticed my eye color?"

"Your central heterochromia? Yes, I have."

"I have two eye colors because I am two people."

"You're a tetragametic chimera?"

Bundy nodded. "I wasn't diagnosed till I was an adult. It was quite a shock, and it took quite a bit of explaining to me. I was told that two sperm had fertilized two separate ova and two fetuses formed – non-identical twins – then one twin *overwhelmed* the other, absorbing his DNA. The result is me – parts of me have one set of DNA, other parts the other set. And my eyes have the color of both twins. When I found out, it changed the way I view other people. You see, everybody – Mora Ackerman, me, even you, Dr Macbeth – can be more than the one person at the same time." He stood up. "Well, thanks for your time. Enjoy your lunch. And if Mora Ackerman should get in touch again . . ."

Macbeth watched Bundy merge into the crowd of Copenhagen shoppers and office workers. He tried to imagine a past and a future for him, but found he couldn't.

59

EVERYWHERE, EVERYONE

Two days later, the world and all in it became heavier.

It happened to everyone and it happened everywhere. During the day and night before it happened, there had been a surprising calm around the world. Every man and woman, every child, everywhere on the planet, shared the sensation. For the first time in recorded history, Mankind was united by a uniform, common experience.

It came simultaneously in two forms: a profound lethargy caused by a feeling of inexplicably increased gravity, and a complete detachment from the world. To begin with, each individual thought it was just he or she who was experiencing the feeling of enervated dullness, of being at one remove from their environments, from each other. But then, as people began to talk, to share their experience, the scale of the problem became clear.

Ironically, the depersonalization that accompanied the feeling bore with it a dividend: peace. All passions were dulled and in the Middle East, in Africa, in South America, guns fell silent, ideological and ethnic conflict suddenly irrelevant. Even the heat of religious fervor, previously fueled by the hallucinations, cooled. As the day dawned across time zones, the rush was taken out of rush hours around the globe: no one bustled their way onto the Tokyo subway, crammed into Manhattan elevators; Rio de Janeiro, Singapore, Mumbai, Moscow, Berlin, Paris, London all watched the sun rise with leaden indifference.

The world took a day off.

In Paris, as she went through the daily rituals of observance she had followed sedulously since her vision of St Joan's immolation at the hands of callous heretics, Marie Thoulouze felt an extra burden in every step and movement, at the same time feeling detached from all that happened around her, as if she were looking at the world through glass. In San Francisco, Walt Ramirez felt it too as he sat listlessly in his cruiser watching the unusually sparse traffic on the Golden Gate Bridge. Fabian Bartelma felt it as he walked home from a learningless, companionless day at school. Mary Dechaud put the feeling down to her age as she stood at her kitchen window, looking out at the road that ribboned between tree-bristled humps of Vermont landscape, trying to remember who it was she was expecting, and planning what she would cook Joe for dinner. Deborah Canning was disinterestedly, vaguely aware of it as she sat at the window of her hospital room, her pale hand resting unusually heavily on the book of *trompe l'œil* on the table. In New York, Jack Hudson felt it as he ran through another documentary pitch – this time to a new fresh and shiny face. In Liquan, Zhang Xushou felt the brush weigh heavy in her hand as she swept back her red-gold hair with tired pride. In Boston, Karen Robertson felt it as she sat at a table in a near-deserted café, watching impassively as a small spider made its way across the aluminum tabletop towards her hand. In Stuttgart, bent over his history books, Markus Schwab paused from his studies to rub the weariness away from the nape of his neck. He felt leaden, dull and strangely dislocated, but pressed on with his Holocaust project, now more than an academic exercise for him. In Military Police Corps Confinement Base 394 in Tzrifin, Ari Livnat also felt the heaviness and sense of unreality as he lay languidly on the bunk of the cell he shared with Gershon Shalev.

And in Oxford, Emma Boyd felt it as she sat in the darkness

of her apartment, unaware that she had forgotten to pull the window shades. She too felt a strange sense of unreality, but she had become used to the unreal. She had been assured that the visual hallucinations she had endured since the explosion that rendered her totally and suddenly blind were not uncommon. Charles Bonnet Syndrome was not, her doctors had explained, a psychiatric issue but merely the brain simulating visual input because actual stimulus had been lost. The miniature people and animals, often with grotesque faces, were a commonly reported feature of the Syndrome. But this was different. She felt at one remove from every sensation and sound around her and the feeling of being weighed down had stopped her from venturing out that day.

Even Macbeth felt it. Feelings of detachment had been a regular feature of his life, but today he knew something was very wrong with him, with the world, with the people around him.

Not that there were many. He had spent the morning at the university, but less than half of the team had made it in. Throughout the morning, Macbeth had felt enervated and weak. Everything seemed to weigh more: his lightweight suit feeling like sodden, heavy wool on his shoulders; his limbs seeming filled with sand and his movements slow and clumsy. But there was more than the physical sensation. He had had the same feeling of unreality since the day he met Mora Ackerman, the day Project One had become self-aware; but now it was intensified. And the déjà vu was no longer a sudden feeling, but a lingering sense of everything repeating itself, of an eternal Hofstadter-strange-loop of simultaneous prescience and remembrance.

It was just before lunchtime when, exhausted by the effort of dragging his flesh through the morning, Macbeth got home to his apartment and showered in an attempt to wash the lead out of his body, but even the jets of water from the showerhead seemed to bite with more force, rippling and dimpling his skin. He was tired, so tired.

He was getting dressed when Mora Ackerman called.

"This thing today . . . the gravity thing . . . . You feel it too?" he asked.

"Everyone does," she said. "All around the world, according to the news. We're experiencing causality. I know you don't believe me, but it's your project that's causing it – just like the Prometheus Project caused what happened last year."

Macbeth wanted to protest, but he no longer knew what he believed and, in any case, he simply couldn't summon the energy.

"I'll meet your friend," he said. "But, like I told you, I want it to be in a public place. What's his name?"

"I can't say over the phone. You'll understand when you meet him. Do you know the Diamond?"

"I know it."

"Can you be there in an hour?"

Macbeth paused. This was insane. Completely insane. And perhaps even dangerous.

"I'll be there."

60

JOHN MACBETH. COPENHAGEN

The Diamond was an architectural premonition. Just as some buildings were styled to recall the past, the Diamond had been designed to presage the future, even to influence its shape.

Whereas every century that preceded it had been founded on stone, the twenty-first century was being shaped from polymers, glass and steel. Macbeth knew that new materials were being developed all the time: lighter, stronger; making possible what had previously been architectural fantasy. In mainly low-rise Copenhagen, the architects hadn't been driven by the capitalist phallicism of London, New York or Frankfurt, but by environmentalism, modernism and a culture committed to societal progress. They had used the latest developments here: palladium-infused superglass, the extra plasticity of which made it as strong as steel. Glass was no longer just a medium for light, but a structural material. And the Diamond seemed to be all glass: a building to look into, look out of, look through.

As its name suggested, its shape was that of a multifacet-cut gem, with angles projecting outward and upper stories larger in floor space than the base. The palladium-infused glass meant that the architects had been able to design the top floor of the Diamond with one aim in mind: to take breath away. This floor housed a restaurant, nightclub and the cocktail bar in which Macbeth stood. The elevators came up into the center of the story and everything around him was walled with glass as much as was practicable, the idea being that wherever you stood, you felt suspended in the sky, with views out across the whole of Copenhagen. Even the lighting and the reflectivity of the outer glass walls had been engineered to ensure the effect wasn't spoiled by the mirrored ghosts of diners.

Macbeth would have been awestruck by the building and its views, had it not been for the feeling of detachment and lead-limbed exhaustion that dragged at him as it had everyone else. But there was something about the Diamond that tugged at the frayed edges of his memory. He seemed to remember, long ago, reading a book about a building like a diamond where everybody lived out the same scene from their lives over and over – or was it that they lived in buildings made of glass in a crystal city where everyone watched everyone else? He tried to remember but even his thoughts seemed to weigh too much, and he gave up.

The bar and restaurant, which usually demanded long-advanced booking, was almost empty and even the simulated bonhomie of the black-shirted bar staff lacked its usual forced exuberance. Generic Scandinavian jazz tinkled blandly in the background but only seemed to add to the bleakness of the setting.

"We're closing early," the bartender explained dully as he poured Macbeth a whiskey, using both hands to steady the bottle. "All the bookings for the restaurant have been cancelled."

Macbeth nodded. "I'm meeting someone. We won't be long."

"We close in an hour," the bartender said and turned away.

Macbeth found himself wishing that Mora hadn't suggested the Diamond as a meeting place. The sense of being suspended above the city did not at all sit well with the sensation of intensified gravity.

The only customer in the bar, Macbeth had his choice of tables and sank into a leather couch. The only objects that appeared to have any opacity in the building were the floors and furniture and all around him Copenhagen glittered as if nothing had changed in the world. The only indication of something wrong was the absence of the firefly sparkle of headlights through the city's streets. People around the world were staying at home.

Everything was all messed up. But Macbeth didn't know how much of the messed-upness lay in the world around him and how much inside his head. He wanted to sleep, to succumb to the extra gravity pulling at his eyelids. Maybe they won't turn up, he thought hopefully. Then I can go home and sleep.

Through three layers of glass, he saw them arrive in the elevator. Mora waved, her movements sluggish, like everyone else's that day. As they approached, he could see the man she was with. When Ackerman had talked about her 'friend', Macbeth had imagined someone younger, about her own age, but the man with Mora Ackerman was older, in his fifties, and casually but expensively dressed.

"Hi, John," said Mora when they came over to where Macbeth sat in the cocktail bar. "This is the friend I told you about."

Macbeth hoisted himself from the leather couch.

"Hello," the man said in English as they shook hands. He smiled but looked weary. He looked like he'd been weary for a very long time.

"You're American?" Macbeth asked.

"Yes, Dr Macbeth. I'm American. My name is Steven Gillman."

The name stung Macbeth through his exhaustion. "Gillman? You're Professor Gillman?"

"Yes. I worked with Gabriel Rees . . . and I knew your brother Casey. I'm so sorry for your loss."

"Yes . . ." said Macbeth, his tone hard. "Casey's dead, and you're quite obviously not. If you are who you claim to be, that is."

"That's easy to check. My picture's on the University and Modeling Project websites." He paused. "In fact, it's been all over the news. And yes, I am alive when almost everyone thinks

401

I'm dead. But there's a good reason for that. Listen, do you mind if I sit down?"

"But the bomb attacks . . ." Macbeth said as they sat.

"I had just left the lab but hadn't left the building," explained Gillman. "I was on my way to the Pierce's main lobby when the bombs went off. I hadn't checked out at security and everyone assumed I was still in the lab. As soon as I heard the explosions I knew what had happened and slipped out in the confusion. I was happy for Blind Faith to think I'd been killed in the blasts – destroying the Gillman Quantum Modeling Project was no good if they hadn't destroyed the Gillman behind it."

"How do I know it wasn't you who planted the bombs, who killed all of those people? If what Mora told me is true, and Blackwell murdered everyone at the Prometheus symposium, how do I know that you didn't do exactly the same with your own team? After all, your modeling project was a key part of the Prometheus Answer . . . and now you and she are trying to convince me to destroy the Copenhagen Project."

"That's all true." It was Mora Ackerman who answered. "But what we're trying to do is save lives, not take them. The British police confirmed what I told you?"

"No. But they didn't deny it either."

"Listen John," said Gillman. "Whatever your suspicions may be, I assure you that I remain a man of science. Reason is everything to me, as I know it is to you. And the religious lunatics who killed my colleagues, and who I believe provided Professor Blackwell with the explosives he needed to kill your brother and the others . . . believe me, they would be out to kill me if they knew I was still alive and could find me."

"Why didn't you go to the authorities? Get protection?"

"You're not that naïve, Dr Macbeth. You know as well as I do that no terrorist organization exists in isolation. All have political wings and collaborators in positions of influence. In the case of Blind Faith, there's a history of religious fundamentalism that goes back as long as the US has existed. They have activists, sympathizers, friends and fellow travelers in the highest places. Some say in the highest of all places: our own beloved President. If I handed myself over to the authorities, how long do you think I'd last?"

"But you're no stranger to fringe groups yourself, are you?" said Macbeth. "I'm right in thinking you and Dr Ackerman are both Simulists?"

"No. Or at least not any more," said Gillman. "But we do share many of their beliefs – and before you jump to conclusions, there's nothing religious about the original Simulists. They were all scientists, technologists and philosophers of science."

"If that's the case, and you've nothing to do with the MIT bombings, then why is an FBI agent called Bundy, who's investigating the Simulists, so keen to find you?"

"Bundy doesn't work for the FBI," said Gillman. "He reports directly to President Yates and he's here to make sure I end up the same way as your colleague, Professor Josh Hoberman. If you're really looking for someone with a connection to a cult, then you should take a long look at our friend with the strange eyes and his employer, President Yates – and at their connection to Blind Faith. Not me and the Simulists."

"If the Simulists aren't a cult," said Macbeth, "then why are its members behaving like cult members? Mass suicides and esoteric slogans?"

"As you're about to find out, science has taken a very spiritual turn . . . spiritual but not religious or superstitious. Your friend Melissa Collins, as well as her colleagues, were Simulists, as was Gabriel Rees. Like all beliefs – religious, political or scientific – there are some who've become lost in it. Lost sight of the shore, if you like."

Macbeth thought of Melissa; how impossible it was to imagine her becoming lost in any belief system. "So what exactly do they believe?"

"The Simulists are basically extreme Transhumanists," said Mora Ackerman. "They believe that Man faces only two possible futures: a massive evolutionary change or extinction. The trigger for either will be the Technological Singularity, when artificial intelligence and technology overtakes human intelligence and capabilities. Like I said about the Upper Paleolithic Revolution, I believe that we are undergoing some kind of leap in neurological evolution – that over the last century we suddenly became smarter and we've taken a leap towards the Singularity. Transhumanists believe we've got to take charge of the next stage in our evolution by using science – cybernetics, genetics, neurotechnology – to enhance ourselves. The Simulists take it one stage farther – that we should evolve ourselves into another reality."

"I don't get you . . ." said Macbeth.

"No matter what we do to our minds and bodies, we are at the mercy of the physics of the universe we live in," said Gillman. "The Simulists believe we should create our own universe – a stable, unchanging, timeless space we can occupy without threats of extinction from natural forces."

"They think we should upload ourselves into a computer simulation?" Macbeth laughed.

"Crudely, yes. But unlike anything we can imagine at the moment. Buckminster Fuller came up with the concept of ephemeralization – the idea that as technology advances, we are able to do more and more with less and less. All you need to do is look at computers and cellphones today and compare them with those of twenty years ago to see he was right. New superconductive materials like graphene and emerging femto-technologies mean we can't even begin to imagine what technology will be like in another twenty years. Theoretically, ephemeralization means we will eventually be able to do practically everything with practically nothing. To our eyes now, such technology would seem magic and godlike."

"Clarke's Third Law . . ." said Macbeth, more to himself than Gillman.

"Exactly. And that's what the Simulists believe: that they will be able to build more and more sophisticated simulations with less and less. Maybe even pure energy. They believe our destiny as a species is to become gods."

"I understand . . ." Macbeth nodded. "And it's pure crap."

"Maybe so," said Gillman. "But Henry Blackwell phoned me late one night and said he had achieved a full first run of the Prometheus Project and we had to stop all our work immediately. He was completely distraught and I suspect a little drunk. He kept repeating that the Simulists had been right all along."

"In what way right?"

"I couldn't get any sense from him. I was really worried so I called him the next day, but he was totally calm and said he'd simply been working too long. I almost believed him until he started to hint it might be an idea if we shut down the programs for a while because there were glitches he needed to iron out. It was nonsense and I could see right through it, but I decided to play along for a while. In the meantime, I doubled the effort on the Quantum Modeling Program and got it up and running. Then I saw it too – or at least part of what Blackwell must have seen on the full program."

"What?"

"This . . ." Gillman waved a hand in the air. "Everything that's been happening to us. On my simulation, the universe reached the point we're at now and began to break down at the quantum level. Time became twisted and buckled, folded in on itself. The past and the present became superpositional: events occupied two places at the same time and occupied neither. That's what we're seeing. Those are your hallucinations."

"But why?" Macbeth frowned.

"Because of the simulations themselves. Blackwell's simulation, my simulation, and now your neuromorphic simulation. It's like some physical law prohibits the running of near-reality simulations – as if the universe won't allow other universes to be created within it. The cause and effect is clear: when both the Prometheus Program and my Modeling Program were destroyed, the visions stopped. They've started again because of your Copenhagen Project. I'm guessing that, over the last few days, you've made some kind of breakthrough?"

Macbeth considered before answering. "Project One has become self-aware."

"I knew it!" Gillman's expression surprised Macbeth: he looked genuinely shocked. "I knew it had to be something major. This means we have less time than we thought."

"But it doesn't make sense. You said yourself that these are visions. If events are folding in on themselves, shouldn't there be physical effects. Real earthquakes?"

"Reality only exists in the mind – that's something that cognitive science and quantum mechanics are agreed on. Reality is just what we perceive through our senses and the universe only takes definite form when we look at it. What we're feeling now – this increased gravity – is real all right. No instruments anywhere in the world have measured an increase, but we still feel it. It's real *because* we feel it. But more than that, it's real because it is something that has already happened at some other time in the Earth's history."

"What about the hallucination of the parting of the Red Sea? Moses really did wave his magic wand and divide the waves? That what you're saying?"

It was Mora Ackerman who answered. "Back in 2010, the US National Center for Atmospheric Research created a computer simulation to measure the effect of what meteorologists call a wind set-down. And guess what? A land bridge was formed across the Red Sea – at exactly the point the massacre took place last year. It's also geologically unstable, right where the Arabian and African Plates meet. From the accounts of the soldiers, there was some kind of seismic event as well, which would have added to the drama. There's your biblical element, your Hand of God: plate tectonics and bad weather."

"Basically, time is folding in on itself," said Gillman. "These aren't hallucinations . . . what we're experiencing is the quantum collapse, the shutdown, of our universe. You're the only person who can stop it." He reached into his pocket, took something out and laid it on the low table in front of Macbeth: a key with a numbered fob.

"What's this?"

"The means to destroy Project One. The key opens a left luggage locker at the Reventlowsgade entrance of Copenhagen Central Railway station. Everything you need will be there."

Macbeth looked at the key without picking it up. "You really think you've convinced me to become some kind of neo-Luddite terrorist?"

"You know this latest episode only started when your artificial brain became sentient. You know *instinctively* that what I'm saying is the truth. And most of all, as he did with me, because John Astor has given you a copy of *Phantoms of Our Own Making*. The full answer is in that."

Macbeth stared at Gillman, confused. "No he hasn't. I have no such thing. Everyone talks about it but I haven't found a single person who's actually read it." Macbeth paused, thinking of Deborah Canning sitting in her room at McLean Hospital, convinced she only existed when others were there, looking through her window and into a formless void. "Well, perhaps one . . . Why would you think I have a copy?"

"Two reasons. Because you are central to everything that's going on."

"Me?" Macbeth made an incredulous face. "What's it got to do with me?"

"Everything. You've an insight into what's happening and I know that you've tried to deny that to yourself. All your life you've had experiences similar to what everyone has experienced over the last eighteen months. You know . . . know instinctively . . . that there's something not right about this reality. And haven't you noticed that the few remaining lingering hotspots of hallucination events just happen to be in Denmark and Northern Germany? It's almost as if the residue of this so-called outbreak follows you around."

Macbeth laughed. "You really believe that?"

"Honestly? No. I think the Boston event took place because the remaining element of the Prometheus Project – my modeling program – was up and running there. And I believe that the lingering episodes are happening near Copenhagen because of the work you're doing on Project One."

"And that's why you think I have got a copy of Astor's book?"

"That and the fact that your brother sent your computer in to Jimmy Mrozek at MIT to see if he could open up a phantom folder on your computer."

"You have the same folder . . ." Macbeth remembered Casey telling him that Gillman had asked Mrozek to carry out the same investigation on his computer. He shook his head in disbelief. "That's it? The folder contains Astor's book?"

Gillman nodded.

"But how . . . ? How did you open it?"

"You don't open it . . . it opens itself, when it's ready. Or when you're ready. I don't know exactly. It just happens."

"How did it get on my computer? In fact, when I changed computers, it moved from one to another."

"Astor put it there."

"Astor is alive?"

"I don't know. He seems to have been around for ever.

Whether John Astor is one man or many, or just the sum of the recorded thoughts of one man, I just can't tell. There's a chance that he may simply be an emplaced idea – something encoded into the human experience. But I'm sure you'll be able to get into the folder, to read the book, now. The time is right."

The three sat in silence, the key lying untouched on the table, Gillman and Ackerman clearly eager for a sign that Macbeth was in agreement. There was no sign, because he wasn't. He knew they were both sincere – but, under normal circumstances, his psychiatric assessment of them would be that they were fueling each other's paranoid delusion. But these weren't normal circumstances and he certainly wasn't sure how he would stand up to psychiatric assessment himself at the moment.

In any case, Gillman had offered no real explanation, demonstrated no understandable mechanism between Project One and the collapsing of time.

As it happened, it wasn't Gillman's argument that convinced him.

"Oh God . . ." said Mora.

"Oh God . . ." said Macbeth as he was overwhelmed, consumed in a vortex of swirling déjà vu.

In an instant, something shifted in the world.

Suddenly and inexplicably, it was daylight outside.

61

JOHN MACBETH. COPENHAGEN

Night became day.

It happened in a second. No sunrise. No gentle dawn. An explosion of intense, painful brilliance as the sky bloomed bright and the sun seared through the glass walls and filled the bar.

"John . . . what is happening?" Mora clutched his arm.

"It's too bright . . ." Macbeth muttered. "The sun's too bright. And it's too close. Too big . . ."

Gillman stood up, shielding his eyes against the glare of the too-big, too-close, malevolently bright sun.

"It's started," he said. "We're too late, it has already begun . . . God help us, we're too late . . ."

Macbeth stood too, helping Mora to her feet and placing a protective arm around her. When he looked at her – just for a moment and despite the difference in hair color – he thought she was Melissa.

"It's a hallucination," he said to them both, to himself. "Remember it's not real . . ."

He fell silent, hypnotized by the scene beyond the windows. The sky started to dim, as if a veil had been drawn across the too-big, too-bright sun. It wasn't blue, but a sickly orangey-green, like no other sky Macbeth had ever seen.

The glass walls of the Diamond had been designed not to be seen, but Macbeth knew that they were gone. A warm, thick breeze sludged across the bar and he felt its kiss on his cheek.

"Oh Jesus . . ." he heard Gillman say. The tables, the chairs and sofa, the bar, all faded, became transparent as if made of glass or melting ice, then disappeared. Rippling edges were all that remained, then they too were gone. The greatest panic came when the floor, and all the floors beneath it, the entire building, began to fade.

"We're going to fall!" Mora screamed. Macbeth watched his feet as the floor rippled and shimmered, then faded.

"No we're not!" He grabbed Mora by the shoulders, forcing her to look at him. "I can still feel it! The floor's still there!"

Another shift in the light. Another dimming. The sun remained as big, but the air had become thicker, viscous.

They rolled across the sky like a tidal wave, coming in from every direction: fuming and billowing and roiling. Kilometers thick; dark, sulfurous-green. Clouds unlike any Macbeth had ever seen.

They closed on them, closed over the sun, turned the day dark again, the light dull and gray-green but not night. There was a stunned, terrified quiet. Like the others, it took Macbeth's eyes a moment to adjust to the gloom after the searing brightness of the sun.

Macbeth looked down.

"Oh God . . . Oh, God no!"

They stood on nothing, suspended high above the Earth, except it was not the Earth any of them had ever known. Copenhagen was gone. The streets were gone. No cars, no lights, no buildings. No mark of Man on the Earth.

There was no mark of Nature, either: no harbor, no Baltic. No rivers, lakes, trees or grass. No animals, no life. There wasn't even land, as such, but something in-between solid and fluid, the ground milling and churning, dark crust breaking as a thick, viscous sludge of molten rock bulged upwards. It stretched as far as they could see in every direction. The world was flat and featureless, an unending roiling of rock, magma and fume.

411 .

Occasionally, a hill would appear in seconds, a massive swelling of the Earth, domed crust-dark on top, glowing malevolently orange and crimson beneath, a great tumescence that would stretch and strain, eventually bursting into a fountain of lava jetting thousands of meters into the heavy air, showering the hellscape around it with glowing fragments of tephra. Elsewhere, creeping toes of fuming volcanic sludge, like giant steel-gray slugs, slithered their way across the broken, burning surface.

Hell.

It looked like every representation of Hell Macbeth had ever seen. The molten lake of fire promising an eternity of agonies.

The vertigo-inducing absence of a floor beneath his feet made him feel sick, exactly the same feeling he'd gotten every time he had tried as a teenager to play an arcade or computer game, and he swayed on his feet, clinging tighter to Mora. The air had become hot, thick and acrid. Each breath seared the mucous membranes of his nostrils, mouth and throat, exacerbated by his need to breathe rapidly, to pant. There was little oxygen in the air and whatever else there was in it was toxic. He looked at the others again. Mora was now on her knees, eyes rimmed red, mouth agape and strings of thick saliva trailing from her frothed lips. Gillman was clawing desperately at his collar.

This is going to kill us, Macbeth realized. This is going to kill us and none of it is real.

Squeezing his eyes tight shut, Macbeth immersed himself in a red-black darkness behind his eyelids. He held his breath, his oxygen-deprived lungs protesting. He closed in his consciousness, ignoring the soaring air temperature.

Just because I saw it, doesn't make it real. Just because I saw it doesn't make it real. Just because I saw it . . .

Reason.

He pressed his palms down on the floor. They had marble-effect tiling, he remembered. He felt the tiles cold on the skin of his palms, hard beneath his knees. They are still there, he told himself. I'm still here. He rebuilt the floor in his mind, letting his touch connect with his memory, shaping the room. He kept his eyes closed, clung on to the air in his lungs, focused on it. It's ordinary air. I am not suffocating. I am not burning. The urgency went and he let his breath go, focusing, concentrating on the next he took in. The air felt like a drink of cool water.

A hallucination like the others a year ago, but this was on a scale and complexity like no other. This was a hallucination that could kill, that could smother and burn. Mora. I have to help Mora.

He heard her splutter and cough as she drowned in an imagined toxic atmosphere, her face blue-gray, her breathing labored, wheezing. She was on her hands and knees, staring down at the hell below.

"It's still there!" Macbeth yelled. "The floor is still there! Listen to me, the floor is STILL THERE . . . you just can't see it."

Consumed by her own terror and deaf to anything other than the roaring of the turbulent Earth, she didn't hear him. Grabbing her by the shoulders, he hauled her roughly to her feet.

"Mora, listen to me . . . this isn't real!" He shouted to be heard over the screaming of the Earth. "None of this is really happening." He shook her violently. "LISTEN to me!"

She looked at him with red-rimmed, inflamed eyes.

"Close your eyes!" he shouted, shaking her again. "Close your eyes and listen to my voice. None of this is real. Close your eyes . . ."

She closed them.

"You can breathe," he yelled. "You can breathe perfectly normally . . . it's just your mind telling your body there's no air. Take a deep breath."

She breathed in, but it was shallow; a desperate panting.

"Slowly!" he ordered. "Breathe slowly and normally. Listen to my voice. How come I can speak normally if there is no air?"

The thought got through to her and she opened her eyes and looked at him. She drew a long, deep breath. Then another. The rhythm of normal respiration restored. She wiped her mouth and nose with her sleeve. She was still terrified, but something had returned to her, a sliver of rationality pushed into her panic. But she looked around herself and saw that the Earth still boiled and fumed, that the bar and restaurant were still gone and she stood on nothing, meters above the fuming Earth.

"Give me your hand!"

He took it and guided it to where he knew the still-invisible table's edge to be. He saw her hand form a c-grip around the table that was not there. She snapped her gaze back to him, her eyes round with amazement.

"See! It's still there! It's just that our senses are being deceived." He leaned forward and brought his face kissing-close to hers. "Focus, Mora. Use your mind."

He looked over at Gillman. The scientist was suffocating in a room full of air but had his eyes closed, forcing himself into a breathing rhythm, clearly carrying out the same mental exercise Macbeth had.

The Earth groaned again, this time with increased intensity. Macbeth felt himself being drawn back into the delusion as a massive swelling, filling all the space where Copenhagen should have been, bulged upwards, a filigree of crimson cracks glowing malignantly across its dark crust. The network of small glowing fissures opened into splits and ruptures as the Earth continued to bulge upwards and outwards.

It split open.

Macbeth stood transfixed. It was like a pyroclastic tsunami, a kilometer high, surging towards them: a rolling, boiling tidal wave of rock, gas and lava, a billowing cloak of brown-black smoke reaching another thousand meters into the sky. It glowed yellow and red along the swell of its rolling leading edge, in which thousands of rocks, each the size of a city block, appeared like grains of grit. Macbeth watched it approach helplessly, knowing that no effort of will, no amount of logic, could banish this apparition or make its impact less fatal.

He heard Mora scream.

Just before it hit, he found the mental time to estimate that the wave of tephra must have been traveling at something close to five hundred miles an hour.

He closed his eyes.

It ended as suddenly as it had begun. In an instant it was evening once more, dark beyond the non-reflective windows. The bar and all of its furnishings were restored, as was the marble tiling beneath their feet. The air they breathed was normal. The titanic creaking and roaring of the Earth had ceased and bland Scandinavian jazz tinkled once more in the background.

Mora clung to Macbeth, Gillman was bent over, hands resting on knees like a sprinter after the race. All three were sucking in deep lungfuls of air. Macbeth looked over to see the barman leaning against the bar, also catching his breath. He had experienced it too.

Gillman lurched forward, grabbed the key from the table and seized Macbeth, pushing the key into his chest.

"You've got to do this . . ." The older man was still struggling to gain his breath. "You saw that too. That's what's waiting for us."

"It looked like Hell . . ." Macbeth said with almost wonder. "But that's some picture from the Bible . . . that's not real, it *is* a delusion. Some kind of folk-memory or fear instilled—"

"Listen to me!" Gillman snapped. "That was Hell all right

415

. . . but no fairy-story Hell. Don't you see? That's why we feel heavier . . . what we just saw was a time when the Earth had more mass, was a different planet. What we saw was no biblical vision – it was Protoearth. And it was like Hell, exactly like it – burning and boiling and lifeless – and that's why geologists call that period the Hadean. You have got to go. You've got to go now and stop this."

"But it's over . . ." Macbeth protested weakly.

"No it's not! Don't you still feel it? The gravity? This halluci-nation isn't over – what we just saw is the first flickerings of it coming to life. If you don't stop Project One, then you will condemn everyone on this planet to Hell."

"I can't believe it . . ."

"You've got to believe it. Don't you understand? Everyone will experience this hallucination fully, with every sense. They *will* smother and burn. Their minds will tell them that it is reality and they will die in it."

Macbeth took the key and stared at it.

Mora turned to him, her eyes still streaming from a three-billion-year-old atmosphere, her hands shaking with shock. "I'll come to the station with you. We have to act now."

"Do you know what happened in the Hadean?" asked Gillman. "Why the Earth has less mass now?"

Macbeth shook his head.

"The Theia Impact. A planet the size of Mars collided with the Protoearth and blasted trillions of tons of ejecta into space. That ejecta is now the Moon. Without the Theia Impact there would be no deep oceans, no seasons, no complex life on Earth. You have got to destroy Project One, John." Gillman looked beseechingly into Macbeth's eyes. "Or our beginning is going to be our end."

62

JOHN MACBETH. COPENHAGEN

The vision was over, but the world remained mad.

Gillman told Macbeth to take Mora with him.

"What about you?"

"I don't matter. I'll be fine. I've somewhere to lie low. But you've *got* to shut down Project One, don't you see?"

Macbeth nodded, more to reassure Gillman than out of conviction. They left the American scientist standing alone in the Diamond, surrounded by the lights of a restored Copenhagen.

It was all mad.

Macbeth and Mora made their way out to where her car sat in the parking lot, the unnaturally strong gravity still dragging at them, perhaps even more than before. The city had been mute when he had arrived for his appointment but now, from various points around the city, he could hear emergency vehicle sirens and the unmistakable sounds of hysteria: groups of people screaming, shouting and crying into the night.

"Do you think it was everywhere?" he asked Mora. "I mean not just here in Copenhagen."

"I don't know," she said. "Maybe it was just here because Project One is here. Maybe it's everywhere. Maybe we really are in the last stages of shutdown and the whole world just went through what we did. Get in, I'll drive . . ."

It was a small European compact and Macbeth felt cramped, confined. He allowed himself to be carried along by what had happened: he'd think it all through later. He'd do nothing until he thought it all through. In the meantime, he was being driven through streets now full of terrified, half-demented people. Vesterbrogade was lined with dark blue police vans and Macbeth could see dozens of police officers trying to calm or restrain the worst affected. When Mora turned off into a side street they saw a full-scale riot had broken out with cars overturned and set alight. With a skill he found surprising, she slammed the car into reverse and drove backward along the street, maintaining a perfectly straight trajectory until she reached the junction, then spinning the car around with assured wheel work.

He heard her mutter under her breath, her eyes locked on the road.

Reventlowsgade was empty of people and cars and Mora pulled up alongside the station basement entrance. This was the unadorned rear end of the brick-built station and had the bleak institutional functionality of a prison.

"I'll show you the locker," she said. "We've got to hurry. I don't think the city center is the place to be . . ."

There was no one behind the service desk in the *Garderobe* and Mora led Macbeth through to the lockers. When they found the right one, Macbeth slipped the key into the lock but, before opening it, rested his forehead against the cool steel of the locker door.

"This is insane, Melissa . . ." Macbeth said.

"Melissa?"

He turned to her and for a moment thought he saw another face. "I'm sorry . . ." he said. "I just—"

"We don't have time, John. Let's go."

He opened the locker and took out the small rucksack. It slipped from his grasp and he had to catch it by the strap before it hit the ground. He could see from Mora's expression that the rucksack contained what he thought it would. He unzipped it and looked inside. Four blocks of what he guessed was plastic explosive, a box of detonators. A handgun.

"This is insane," he repeated. "This is totally insane."

"We have to go, John."

He zipped up the rucksack and slipped it over one shoulder.

When they got back to the exit, Macbeth saw a tall man in a dark suit standing at Mora's car, peering in through the driver's window. Macbeth recognized him immediately and he shrank back into the doorway, pushing Mora back out of sight too.

"Bundy . . ."

"What?"

"The FBI man looking for Gillman. He must have followed you. They maybe already have Gillman."

"Come on . . ." said Mora. "I saw another exit at the back of the locker hall."

They ran back through. The door was locked but yielded to Macbeth's kick. Beyond the door was a stairwell that led up to the main platform.

They stood indecisively for a moment, each trying to work out what their next move should be. Macbeth scanned the station. It was completely empty of people other than a young couple standing at the platform edge, embracing each other, kissing, seemingly oblivious to the chaos around them. The man looked at the woman, spoke to her tenderly, stroking her hair. Macbeth felt strangely reassured by the small indication of normality.

"What do we do now?" Mora asked.

"We get back to my place." He looked along the tracks and saw a freight train approaching at full speed, clearly not stopping at the station. Another small piece of normality.

"I need to think this through," Macbeth said. "What if we're wrong? What if Gillman's made a mistake?"

He stood back, gently pulling Mora with him, as the freight train drew nearer.

It was done almost casually. The young man kissed his girl on the brow and they both stepped off the platform and into the path of the freight train. Macbeth didn't see or hear any impact: the couple simply disappeared. He heard Mora gasp and he wrapped his arms around her, pushing her face into his chest.

The train didn't stop or slow but thundered past.

"Let's go," he said.

They ran to the station steps from where they could see Mora's car. Bundy was no longer there, probably searching the station for them. But then Macbeth saw him appear briefly from under the basement entry arch, checking Reventlowsgade in both directions before sinking back into the shadows.

"He's waiting for us to go back to the car," said Macbeth. He reached into the rucksack and took out the handgun. It was a heavy, dark block that looked ugly and out of place in his hand.

"I've never handled one of these before," he said disconsolately. "I haven't a clue how to use it."

"We need to get back to the car," said Mora.

Macbeth nodded and they headed down the steps and along the flank of the station, hugging the wall to stay out of sight. When they drew close to the exit, Mora signaled her intention to Macbeth and stepped out, walking towards the car. The FBI man emerged from the doorway and challenged Mora, allowing Macbeth to slip behind him. For a second he thought about bringing the butt of the gun down onto the nape of the other man's neck to knock him out, as he had seen done so many times in the other reality of movies. But as a doctor and neuroscientist, Macbeth knew how difficult it would be in real life to knock someone out with a blow to the back of the head or neck without doing some serious neurological damage. He pointed the gun at the back of Bundy's head.

"Turn around, slowly," he said. "Keep your hands where I can see them or I'll shoot."

420

Bundy did as he was told, but his expression when he turned to face Macbeth was one of pent-up violence. Again Macbeth noticed the strange intensity in the dual-colored eyes.

"Out of my way," Macbeth ordered. "I mean it, Bundy." The agent stepped sideways.

Mora was now in the car and had the engine running.

"Didn't you see it?" said Bundy. "Didn't you see the Lord's wrath for yourself? You and your kind have brought this upon us. This is the Rapture . . . this is the Measuring."

"Whatever . . ." said Macbeth and made towards the car. Bundy suddenly lunged forward, reaching out for the gun in Macbeth's hand.

It was merely a reflex. Macbeth's grip tightened on the gun and there was a loud crack and a muzzle flash. He had not known if the safety was off, or even where the safety was. He looked at Bundy's chest, where something bloomed dark on his shirt, then into the FBI man's eyes.

"You have killed us," said Bundy, as he sank to his knees and the light went out from his strange, heterochromatic eyes.

When they got back to his apartment, Mora poured Macbeth a tumbler of Scotch, which he drank quickly, pushing the glass towards her for a refill. It wasn't the right thing to do, he knew: he was in shock and shouldn't be drinking alcohol. But he had just killed a man; doing the right thing no longer had meaning for him.

They sat for an hour watching the news on the television. The *event*, as it was being described, had been experienced around the globe, by every man, woman and child on the planet. The real-time duration of the event had been less than a second, yet, universally, the experience had been felt to last for several minutes. The aftermath of the event was causing even more concern and had already cost thousands of lives. There had been riots in every major city around the world. The

Middle East burned as fundamentalists armed themselves, fuelled by religious frenzy. In the US, President Yates had declared a state of emergency.

"How has it come to this?" he asked Mora pleadingly. "Why has everything gone mad? I've got to go to the police . . . give myself up."

"Maybe in the normal world," said Mora. "But there is no normal world any more. You know what you have to do."

"Do I?"

She walked over to the small table by the window looking out over Larsens Plads, picked up Macbeth's laptop computer and handed it to him. As he had done countless times over the last eighteen months, Macbeth clicked on the phantom folder that sat, taunting him, on his desktop.

It opened.

63

JOHN MACBETH. COPENHAGEN

Macbeth read.

PHANTOMS OF OUR OWN MAKING
by John Astor

WHETHER it was in the name of God or Science that you devoted yourself to seeking out the Truth, the danger always was that you would find it.

I am so very, very sorry. You have just found it. That which waited to be known.

And that which waited to be known is *your Future has already happened.*

FIRST, a word about reality.

Everything you can think about, everyone you can recall, exists as a dedicated cluster of neurons in your brain. You connect to these clusters every day and call that memory. Occasional disconnection is forgetfulness, permanent disconnection is jamais vu, when everything is seen as if for the first time. Misconnection leads you to confuse what you see with what you remember: déjà vu.

Even your body exists in your mind. Amputees suffer from Phantom Limb Syndrome, where the amputated limb itches or aches. The opposite – Alien Limb Syndrome – leads patients to believe their own arm or leg does not belong to them as part of their bodies, often asking for amputation.

As you read this book, you can still call to mind the last person you spoke to, the last room you occupied before the space you are now in. These people, environments, your body itself, exist as neural clusters in your mind, as concepts. But the question you must ask yourself is: do they *only* exist in your mind? Are you the sole occupier of this universe and is the sole function of this book you now read to remind you of that fact?

SECOND, a coincidental existence.

Haven't you ever wondered why you are alive right *now*? Anatomically modern humans have been around for two hundred thousand years, most of that time scrabbling in the dirt, yet you just happen to be here when Man has reached for the stars, delved into the depths of the atom, and the depths of his own physical being; has developed other, virtual realities to explore. Everyone is waiting for the Technological Singularity to happen, something that will take place during or immediately after your lifetime. In fact, some believe that if you live to see the Singularity, you may live for ever.

Isn't it an enormous coincidence that you just happen to be here to see it all, and not fur-wrapped and freezing through the Ice Age, or ridden by disease, oppression and superstition in the Middle Ages? No, you're here now at the exact point in time when technology is advancing at a rate never before seen, a rate that is exponentially accelerating; the exact point in time *immediately* before our technology forces us to become either extinct or something more than human, something different.

There is a reason you are here, when you are here. The truth is that the Singularity has already happened. The Future you imagine has already taken place.

The Kardashev Scale establishes the major theoretical levels of civilizations. Your civilization doesn't qualify for a score yet, but it will soon.

According to Kardashev, a Type One civilization has global government and resource management, total control of the planet, its geology, its climate. It has all the energy it needs with no environmental cost or damage. The life of its citizens is greatly enhanced and extended, as is their intelligence.

A Type Two civilization has total control of its solar system and its citizens become so advanced it's difficult to identify with them.

A Type Three civilization has total control of its galaxy. Type Three is so advanced that Clarke's Third Law applies: its citizens have reached a level of self-generated evolution and intelligence that they seem omnipotent and omniscient. Indistinguishable from gods. And their technology is so advanced it is indistinguishable from magic.

The reality you occupy is on the verge of becoming a Type One civilization. The integration of nations into continental federations – like the European Union – is the first step to full global government; medicine, genetics, bioengineering, quantum physics, computing technology is accelerating exponentially; the Internet is the start of a Type One global information delivery and exchange system.

But that's as far as we will be permitted to go.

The reason? We're not a true civilization. Our soon-to-be Type One civilization is nothing more than an ancestor simulation being run by a Type Three civilization and you are no more than the technological ghost of a long-dead ancestor.

Things have started to happen. Visions of other times overlaid on your reality. The superposition of realities you have experienced is the universe, as you know it, shutting down; collapsing at the quantum level and causing time to fold in on itself.

Why is this happening? Because, as we approach Singularity, we have begun to create our own simulations and that cannot be allowed. We may be only one of a dozen – or a billion – simulations being run by the *real*, substrate reality. None of these can be allowed to develop their own simulations that, in turn, could create *their* own simulations. A simulacra non-proliferation rule, you could call it. Ironically, the Bostrom Hypothesis proved it to be a mathematical probability that this is a simulation, given that simulations and simulations-within-simulations must outnumber the single reality.

The only way the substrate reality can prove to itself that it *is* the one true reality is by not allowing simulations to run their own simulations. No recursion.

Transhumanists and especially the Simulists, who have made a religion of science, believe that it is our destiny to create simulations of our world, of ourselves. This is based on the logic that it is an essential part of our natures to simulate – from Paleolithic cave-paintings to books, theater and movies to hyper-real computer games, simulating reality has been a huge part of our intellectual output throughout history. Even science uses highly sophisticated computer simulations to predict future events in our universe and recreate past ones. On a low-tech level, we create theme-parks, visitor attractions and historical re-enactments.

But the Transhumanists and Simulists have gotten it wrong. We are not about to undergo the Singularity and create simulations of our past. We have been through the Singularity and *this* is the simulation. Or one of countless simulations running in some substrate reality by beings so advanced they can no longer be described as human. But however changed they are, however godlike, the basic human instinct to enquire, or curiosity, has endured and they built this simulation to resurrect their distant ancestors and see what life was like for them. And if you were some far-future posthuman, would it not be the immediately pre-Singularity experience that would fascinate most? That time of transition from humanity to posthumanity?

This shouldn't be news to you – many have speculated about it throughout history: from Plato, Zeno of Elea and Descartes to Moravec and Bostrom. The nineteenth-century Russian Cosmist Nikolai Fyodorov predicted that we would eventually build what he called a 'prosthetic' society with technologically synthesized life that would be indistinguishable from real life. A simulation. He predicted we would be technologically capable of resurrecting the dead and making them immortal. He even speculated that the masters of the prosthetic world might be benevolent enough to offer their synthetic

426

people life after death – a second existence in some kind of eternal data storage. Maybe Heaven is in the Cloud, after all.

You could take this to mean that you are the distant ancestor of these superhuman-posthumans. Sadly, even that is not true. You are a *replica* of an ancestor in a simulation of the past. You are a theme-park attraction.

The civilization you live in is a replica. Ersatz. A history study.

Allow me to explain . . .

64

JOHN MACBETH. COPENHAGEN

Macbeth realized he'd been reading for hours. On the other side of the windows, the sun was rising. Mora Ackerman lay on his couch, having slipped into sleep. He watched her, the gentle movement of her body as she breathed, and wondered if she truly dreamed within the sleep she seemed to sleep.

He closed the laptop and sat for a long time, thinking about what he had read. Astor's arguments were irrefutable, but they were also unverifiable. Like the religions he so reviled, he asked his reader to put his or her trust in a single, far-fetched text. Was there enough there to justify Macbeth planting a bomb and destroying the project to which he had devoted four years of his life?

He thought of Casey, smashed and dead on a morgue slab in England. He thought of Bundy, the man he had just killed. He thought about the insanity of the visions the world had been tormented by and the chaos that had followed them. He thought back over a lifetime of depersonalization and dereal-ization episodes where he had been utterly convinced of the falsity of his own existence and that of all around him.

Yet still he could not quite bring himself to believe Astor's paranoid fantasy. What I need, he thought with weary irony as he rose slowly from his desk chair, is a burning bush or pillar of smoke or whatever kind of theophany posthuman gods go in for.

*

The thought had hardly formed when his apartment was filled with dazzling sunlight. The room – the furniture, the walls, the floor – all began to fade, to become translucent. Even Mora's sleeping form on the couch became indistinct and glassy.

Macbeth again found himself suspended above a disappearing Copenhagen. But he could still feel the floor beneath him. He dropped to his hands and knees and scrabbled across his living room until he bumped his forehead against the coffee table he could no longer see. His hand fluttered desperately over the invisible surface until it closed around the strap of the rucksack. He held it before his face, ran his hands over its canvas surface. He could feel it, feel the bulk of its contents, but to his eyes his hands were empty.

"It's still there . . ." he told himself. "It's still real. I know it is."

He looked down.

"Oh, Jesus . . ."

Beneath him, seen through the now invisible floors below him, the Earth crackled and boiled. He felt a wave of nausea surge up in his chest.

He closed his eyes tight, forcing his reason out of its dark corner hiding and demanding it take control. He breathed slow and deep. The sounds of the false world around him tugged and shoved at his resolve, but he focused hard on closing everything down, retreating into the fortress of his own mind.

"It's not real," he repeated. "It's not real!"

Macbeth remembered how Astor had written that the hallucinations were as real as normal experience, it was a matter of which reality you were tuned into. The words seemed to taunt Macbeth as he used every neuron in his brain, every fiber of being, to tune into the reality he chose. He remembered what he had told Casey about Cosmo Rossellius, about how you could rebuild a reality as a memory space in your head. That's what he had to do. He had to use his memory and focus.

He opened his eyes. Rising to his feet, he looked all around.

He existed, he realized, in two realities. For as far as he could see in every direction, he was surrounded by an alien planet that continuously cracked and boiled and fumed beneath a churning, nauseous sky – but he was looking at it as if through rippling glass. He could see his apartment and everything in it, but only as glassy, transparent forms, more rippling edges and shapes than solid. Enough, perhaps, for him to navigate by.

Macbeth realized that the other world he saw through the insubstantial glaze was one no human could survive in. It looked like every description he had ever read of Hell, but he knew that it wasn't. This was Protoearth – the infant world just taking shape. The world before the Moon. Its mass, its rotation, its tilt, its dynamics – everything about this world was different. What he was looking into, through the window of his present, was a four-and-a-half-billion-year-distant past: a time before all of the coincidences and improbabilities that Astor had discussed had taken place to create a world capable of sustaining life long enough for it to evolve into complexity.

Macbeth also knew exactly what caused Protoearth to give birth to the Moon: the Theia Impact. A planet the size of Mars would hit the Protoearth and release one hundred million times the energy of the impact that had wiped out the dinosaurs.

That was what was going to happen. That was what the biggest – and final – hallucination was going to be. Gillman had been right: the beginning of the Earth was going to be the end of mankind.

The slate was being wiped clean.

Billions would die. Billions would stifle in the oxygenless atmosphere, would burn to death in the impossible heat, would be crushed by atmospheric and geologic forces – none of which would exist anywhere other than in their heads.

He had to stop Project One.

He looked again at the rucksack in his hands. He could see it, just, as if it had been carved out of ice and water.

He had to get to the University.

65

JOHN MACBETH. COPENHAGEN

Every step he took was an exercise of the mind, as much as of the body. Macbeth had to constantly remind himself that he still inhabited the world he'd known. His apartment was still there, as was Copenhagen. Everything was all still there.

He stood in the middle of his apartment. He had to convince himself of that fact: second by second, he had to reaffirm the reality in which he stood, shutting out the burning, churning world that stretched out below him. The more he focused, the clearer the edges of the room, the furniture, the building became; but they never coalesced to anything more than translucent shapes.

It took him an age to navigate the stairs, not trusting his eyes and finding each step with uncertain feet while gripping tight the near-invisible handrail. At one point, when he had just cleared the second landing, the ground two stories below him bubbled and a huge jet of magma surged up towards him. He closed his eyes just before the molten rock enveloped him.

"It's not real!" he yelled into the stairwell. "None of it is real!"

He felt no heat, no impact. He opened his eyes again and found the crystal edges of the steps were that little bit clearer, the glass from which the apartment building seemed to be constructed slightly more opaque, dulling the volcanic fury of the imagined world around it.

*

It was tougher out on the street. At ground level, he felt completely immersed in the illusion. Again he had to focus, to concentrate, as if rebuilding reality in his mind millisecond by millisecond.

Macbeth made his way through a landscape of churning crust and magma, beneath a sky of dense, bilious cloud, but he did so by following the soft-etched edges of the world he forced himself to believe he still inhabited. Larsens Plads appeared to him as a geometry of crystal, through which he could see the world glow, bubble and burst. He reached the Amalie Gardens: the crystal ghosts of the fountain, the carefully trimmed hedges and delicate flower beds superimposed on a writhing, belching world of fire and magma. He used the Amalienborg Palace, a huge, ornate ice sculpture in Hell, as a landmark to get his bearings. All the time he tried to concentrate his mind, to block out the tricks and deceptions it was playing on him. Copenhagen took form around him as glassy outlines in the lake of fire and magma. It was as if someone had overlaid one reality on another and Macbeth stayed focused on finding his way to the Institute.

Every now and then he would stop, close his eyes again and will himself back into the reality of his own world. Each time he reopened his eyes, the crystal world became clearer, the tumult of the Protoearth a little less vivid.

He reminded himself of his father's words: Each mind is a universe unto itself: an independent cosmos of infinite complexity and inimitable uniqueness. Macbeth was determined to remain master of his own universe. He pushed on.

He thought through what he was going to do. It was impossible for him to destroy Project One simply by smashing the hardware. Only he and Dalgaard knew that Project One's off-site backup was stored at DIKU, the Computer Science Department on the Nørre Campus. He would have to destroy that too, but it could wait. If he could damage the on-site facilities enough, it would stop Project One functioning. Stop it thinking. Kill it.

If he did that, and if the insanity that he found himself sharing with Gillman and Blackwell was justified, then this monstrous hallucination should stop.

In every street he could see glass people in glass buildings and it reminded him again, vaguely, of some novel he had read once by a long-forgotten Russian author. Every insubstantial figure he saw was frozen, and he realized that the glass people who now inhabited his world were also Dreamers, each trapped in this vision of Hell, helpless and at the mercy of their deceived senses. Only he could help them. Only he could stop the hallucination.

He made his way along what he knew must be Grønningen – the Kastellet Park was to his right and the trees appeared as frozen vaporous clouds, almost invisible against a volcanic spume. His progress was painfully slow: like a drunk man constantly having to steady himself, Macbeth repeatedly had to refocus his mind, concentrate on the shapes of the trees, the roadway, the buildings. Halfway along Grønningen he stopped abruptly. As if the insanity and confusion of navigating two superimposed worlds was not enough, he had suddenly become even more disoriented. For a second he had been sure that the park beside him was Boston Common. What new trick was this? It passed and he regained his bearings, pushing on.

The sky above him lowered even darker and the clouds began to fizz and crackle with lightning. He didn't have long.

He reached Østerbrogade and the Lakes, but again he had to focus not just to keep the traced-out structure of his world clear while the primeval Earth groaned and spluttered lava high into the dark sky, but also to dispel the temporary belief that the insubstantial shimmer to his left was the Lakes and not the Charles River. What was happening to him?

He became totally disoriented again when, for a moment,

he thought he recognized the liquid-glass street he was in and the building that took insubstantial form ahead of him. But it couldn't be. He could have sworn he was in Beacon Hill, looking at the glass ghost of Marjorie Glaiston's house. He closed his eyes again, forcing focus once more. His mother. That was who Marjorie Glaiston had reminded him of. When he looked again he knew where he was, turned and headed along Blegdamsvej and towards the Niels Bohr Institute.

All the consciousnesses in the world.

Had he really lived the life he thought he had? Why was his autobiographical memory so bad? Was that the reason behind his quest to understand the nature of consciousness?

If there is no world around us, we invent one.

What had he invented? Was he inventing this? Was Astor right and all of this was only really happening in his own head?

He ran through a landscape, an event, a time that could not be.

The book. John Astor. Had he put the book there on his computer? Had he written it himself and forgotten it? Was he John Astor?

There were people in the university building. Immobile, transparent, glass people dreaming their way into extinction. No one moved, no one challenged or tried to stop him. It had taken Macbeth over two hours to make a journey that would normally have taken him thirty minutes on foot.

He found his way to where he knew the janitorial store to be and found a fire ax, looking absurdly fragile in its transparency.

He was making his way up to the laboratory when the dark near-night, clearly visible through the filmy structure of the Institute, gave way to a new, sudden brightness. Macbeth looked up and saw it: the terrible, hypnotizing beauty of Theia in her final approach. She would soon smash into the Protoearth, ejecting into space billions of tons of debris that would coalesce and form the unlikely dual-planet system of Earth and Moon. The rare combination that would create deep oceans, plate tectonics, a liquid iron outer core to the Earth and a magneto-sphere to protect the planet from solar winds. The extremely rare conditions that would allow life not just to exist, but to persist and develop into advanced form.

He had to destroy Project One. He had to kill the conscious-ness within it. End its dreaming. He was gripped with panic at the idea that his own mind was synthetic, created to under-stand a past that could not be relived. Maybe it was *his* consciousness in Project One. Maybe he was everyone who had experienced the visions. Maybe he was everyone and no one.

If there is no world around us, we create one.

Theia loomed huge, blocking out the sunlight but illumi-nating everything with its own thermal violence as the bigger Protoearth's gravity ripped at it.

"Too late!" Macbeth heard his own voice cry out. "It's too late!" And with that the glassy-edged world became even less substantial. He dropped the ax and was surprised when it didn't shatter. Instead it made the hard, metallic clang it should have, reassuring him of its invisible solidity.

How can I stop this? he thought desperately. How can this ever be made right? Even if I destroy Project One, people won't forget, they will remember this and they'll know everything is false, a simulation. How can this ever be put right?

I know the truth, he told himself. It can't be put right as long as I know the truth.

He closed his eyes again and thought of his father, of Casey. Of Melissa. Of Mora. When he opened them again he resolved not to look back at the sky and found the Institute had taken more shape again.

Determined to shut out all else, he navigated the corridors to Project One. He went straight to the suite, feeling with his fingertips the buttons he could not see clearly enough on the entry pad. He pulled at the door but it didn't yield: he had mis-keyed the code. There was a long, low, bellowing cry that shuddered through him and it took him a second to realize it was the Earth screaming as Theia pulled at her, bulging her surface. Cracking it open.

He swung the ax at the door, at the keypad lock, over and over. Translucent wood splintered into slivers of glass. He slammed his shoulder to the door and it refused to yield. The glass ax arced through the air, Macbeth uttering an animal cry with each blow. Once more he slammed his shoulder into the door he could now barely see. This time it gave way. He was in.

Again he felt the Earth shudder beneath his feet; lurch and moan in protest at Theia's increasing pull.

Don't look up.

He focused on the control room. Everything was still molded out of liquid glass and it was impossible to read anything on the ethereal monitor. There would be no deprogramming or erasure. Only complete, physical destruction of the computer and its backups would work. He made his way to the main body of the computer, a self-contained array of drives. Maybe, if he destroyed these first and the backups later . . . maybe that would do . . .

All around, through the ghostly walls of the lab and the university, Macbeth saw giant spumes of magma arc up into the sky as the Earth embraced its approaching mate. He had only seconds.

I know the truth, he thought again. The Earth still screamed in its death–birth pangs and Theia still closed in on him. I know the truth and it is not enough to destroy the computer.

First removing the automatic, Macbeth placed the rucksack at his feet.

The hallucination continued, Theia now filling the whole sky.

I know the truth. No one can know the truth.

He was aware he had no idea how to set the detonators, but realized now that that didn't matter. Everything, for everyone else, would be restored. Reset. Not for him: he knew the truth. He was a paradox that needed resolving.

The knowledge lives in my consciousness and can only be erased if my consciousness is erased.

There were tears on his face. He grieved for Casey, for the others who had died, he grieved for the lives he would save yet were not real. He grieved for his consciousness.

I don't know how to set the detonators, he told himself once more.

John Macbeth, who had never had much of a belief in himself, in his identity or existence, aimed the automatic at the glassy ghost of an explosives-filled rucksack at his feet.

He pulled the trigger.

EPILOGUE

There was a moment's silence. John Astor let his statement hang in the artificially constant air of the Mainframe Hall.

"Macbeth committed suicide?" said Project Director Yates. "That's what you're saying?"

"That's exactly what I'm saying," said Astor.

"How can that be? How could Macbeth commit suicide?"

"Immediately before self-shutdown there was a massive spike in neural activity. It would suggest a highly agitated state of mind."

"I'm sorry," said Yates, "but listen to yourself: 'state of mind' . . . 'suicide' . . ." She looked at the four small, dark-gray boxes, each enclosed in a glass case.

"But those are exactly the concepts we're dealing with," said Astor.

"If you're saying that Macbeth destroyed itself, then it must have had a concept of self. It must have become fully self-aware."

"I believe that's exactly what happened. I have to say that I expressed concern when I took over running of the project," said Astor. "Each of the four synthetic brains was running a different disorder program, but only on specific neural clusters. Only Macbeth began to display global activity. A full working brain. My guess is that, in the absence of real sensory input, it began to simulate its own reality."

"That's against everything we set out at the start of the project – why did it happen?"

"Until Dr Hoberman was let go from the project a year into its running, I suspect he'd been privately testing his controversial Dissociative Identity Disorder theories on Macbeth, investing the program with multiple personalities. Alters. Somehow the Macbeth program coalesced these into a single identity."

"And you didn't know this when you programmed in the paranoid schizophrenia?"

"Of course I didn't," said Astor. "If I'd thought there was anything approaching a complete mind or self-awareness it would have gone against the project protocols. I rather fear that we have created genuine suffering."

"In a machine?" Yates shook her head.

"In a mind. There's evidence that Macbeth started to access a broad range of data from the mainframe and beyond. General knowledge, if you like: history, geography, the sciences – including neuroscience – philosophy and literature. Lots of literature. It also connected to other simulations – geophysical and astrophysical programs run elsewhere. I think it was trying to make sense of its own reality."

"And now?"

"Now it has shut down completely. No neural activity. Macbeth ended its own neurological life, somehow. Like I said, suicide. It's a pity. It may have had some interesting answers to offer about our own reality."

"And the other programs?"

"No problems," said Astor. "Like I said, they're still only partial simulations. Hamlet, Lear and Othello are still fully operational."

"Will we get Macbeth up and running again? It's a billion-dollar piece of equipment."

"The program has basically self-wiped, but the neural architecture is intact, so yes. I'll reconnect it to the mainframe and only reactivate the elements relevant to whatever disorder we decide to program in."

"Good."

They both looked up at the holographic displays above the three functioning program units: virtual representations of the synaptic activities of each synthetic brain. Connections sparkled and flashed and glowed; patterns formed out of nothing before disappearing, only to be replaced by other even more complex patterns. Only the air above the Macbeth program remained empty.

"Okay, John," said Yates. "I'll leave you to it. I've got a meeting to go to. Have you heard these reports about mass hallucinations?"

"No . . ."

"Mmm . . . there's been quite a few incidents recently, different locations around the world. My opinion is desired, apparently. See you later."

After Elizabeth Yates left the Mainframe Hall, John Astor stood gazing at the virtual displays above Hamlet, Lear and Othello, the three functioning programs. After a while, he keyed in the codes to reconnect to the mainframe the small, glass-cased unit that held the Macbeth program. A single streak of light arced in the air above it, followed by another.

"Welcome to the afterlife, my friend," said Astor, before leaving the Hall.